Dear Christine ...
I did ...
you
... ... through

A Hole in the Heavens

the summer
without
this
xx dyan

Dyan Elliott

(socially distant)

Bagwyn Books

Tempe, Arizona
2017

Published by Bagwyn Books, an imprint of the Arizona Center for Medieval and Renaissance Studies (ACMRS), Tempe, Arizona.

Table of Contents

Acknowledgments

Many people encouraged and abetted me in this endeavor. My first debt of gratitude is to the National Humanities Center for its wonderful staff, ebullient fellows, and atmosphere of incomparable serenity. I will never forget and will always be especially thankful for the friendship and support of Paula Blank and Drew Cayton, whose recent deaths have shocked and saddened their many friends. I would also like to thank the rest of my ur-audience—Fred Anderson, Anthony Bale, Cynthia Brokaw, and Patricia Ingham—cheering me on amid wine and pizza. Soon I began to ply my wares more widely, imposing upon a pliant, but keenly intelligent, circle of family and friends. I am grateful to the late Leonard Cohen for years of friendship, inspiration, and encouragement, and will never cease to mourn him. Dori Elliott, Helga Elliott, Mary Favret, Susan Gubar, Wendy Harris, Ruth Karras, Lee MacDougall, Barbara Newman, and Jerry Singerman were generous with their time and their collective insights alike. But special thanks are due to Donald Gray and Paul Strohm for their incisive critiques and crucial, though sometimes painful, strategies for revision. (E.g., "Every time you find yourself explaining something about the Middle Ages, cross it out.") And I am, of course, happily beholden to Bob Bjork and Roy Rukkila of Bagwyn Press for their generous support. I would also like to thank Anastasia Davies, my manuscript editor, for her quick eye and astute comments.

Finally, I want to acknowledge the unflagging enthusiasm of those on the home front. Dydo, Roo, and especially Maggie, literally devoured my manuscript, not only once but at least several times, which I recognize to be the highest of canine compliments. I am especially grateful to my husband, Rick Valicenti, who never tired of cheerfully goading me to write the "Great American Novel." (He even bought me a special desk for this purpose.) I recognize that no one in her right mind would think a novel about the Middle Ages, written by a Canadian, would ever fit this bill. Even so, there would be no *Hole in the Heavens* without Rick, and there would be a big hole in my heaven without his loving support. Although he is no great lover of fiction, this book belongs to him.

For Rick Valicenti

Prologue

Paris, 1397

Anthony was awakened by a noise. It prompted him to get of bed, throw on a robe, light a taper, and move through a series of rooms. The sound of voices was coming from the refectory. He stood at the back, watching in fascination. It was Baldwin, standing in the middle of a circle of young clerics, his shadow elongated by the light of the lantern. He was engaged in a quodlibet. The question he was disputing was:

> If Satan were to appear in the form of Christ, would the person who worshipped him be damned for idolatry or excused for insurmountable error?

The dimly lit scene reminded Anthony of other gatherings long ago: tonsured heads leaning forward in excitement, familiar faces made strange by the half-light, the ritual of a nighttime meeting. Only it wasn't disputations in the old days, it was stories. Frightful stories. For the first time in years, Simon bubbled to the surface of Anthony's consciousness, eyes alight with malice. Anthony shuddered, trying to tamp down the unwelcome memory. The image of Simon departed, leaving a sense of dread in its wake. That was when Anthony first sensed that all hell was about to break loose.

Chapter 1: *Literati et Idiotae*

St. Gregory's Mass

Rose had waited all her life to meet a holy man. The moment that she saw the Franciscan, she knew. Something deep inside of her moved in recognition. He recognized her as well. She could tell by the way the slow smile lit up his face in stages, one feature after another: white teeth against red lips, nostrils flaring ever so slightly, somber fire in nighttime eyes. *Thou art beautiful, O my love, sweet and comely as Jerusalem, terrible as any army.* Yet his message to Rose was one of peace. *Let your heart be at rest. God's first commandment was to be fruitful and multiply. It was God who inspired you to love Philip.*

Rose wanted to believe him. But she had always been told that it was only holy virgins who would follow the Lamb. The others, the daughters of Eve, were subject to their husbands, and doomed to bring forth children in suffering and pain. Death was the midwife. Women bore children in the valley of death. Tears started to form in Rose's eyes as she thought about her sister. Five days of pain, prayers, and bleeding. The parade of towels going into the room white and coming out red. Rose pledged her virginity to the Lord the day her sister died. She was seven years old.

The Franciscan leaned closer. His breath on her face was sweet. *You are Rose; the Rose of Sharon; the beloved of the Lord. And you shall receive your due.*

Something rigid and painful inside of Rose was beginning to dissolve. It was her commitment to virginity. Rose had promised her virginity to Christ because she believed that virginity was stronger than death. The Virgin Mary went straight to heaven without burial, and the bodies of the holy virgins never corrupted. *Wasn't this true?*

She asked the question, but the friar never answered. Or, if he did, he answered with another question. *Is this what virginity means to you? Eternal life?*

No one else could hear these words. They resonated inside her head. Rose nodded. *Thank God, he understood.*

If so, I can give you what you wish. Then the friar said aloud: "Are you ready to receive the Lord's body, my child?"

And she suddenly was. The guilt over her impending marriage and even fear of death was dissipating, leaving behind a warm glow. Rising to her feet, she accepted his hand and he drew her into the little Magdalene chapel. There were several others present, but the Mass was all for her. It felt like her first communion. Or rather, she was like a bride at her nuptial Mass. No, that wasn't quite right either. She was the bride being led to her marriage bed, and the consummation was at hand. When she received the Host, her entire body was trembling. She heard the familiar words: *bibite ex hoc omnes hic est enim sanguis meus*, but once again she wasn't hearing the voice with her ears. It was inside her head. She opened her eyes and looked up. The friar was standing directly in front of her, offering her the chalice. It had never happened before, yet for some reason Rose wasn't surprised. She closed her eyes and drank. The liquid was warm and thick — not at all like wine. It was blood; the chalice was filled with blood. But she felt no revulsion. She remembered the Franciscan's sermon about St. Gregory's miraculous Mass. Rose was experiencing a miracle! The blood was a sign that God understood and condoned her choice.

Rose kept her eyes shut. She could feel the liquid moving through her veins — a crimson stain starting on the inside and spreading outward. Licked by the tongues of a million small flames, her body was filled with light. She was reminded of Philip's caress, only whatever she was feeling now didn't tease or tempt, it overpowered. The beating of her heart became louder and more insistent. When her pleasure mounted until it almost felt like pain, Rose opened her eyes in alarm. The Franciscan was watching her. His gentle smile gave her all the reassurance she needed. Rose's body began to stiffen with expectation, holding itself as tight as a spring about to be released. Weak with yearning, she waited.

And then it began: in her mind's eye, she saw her heart pulsing, a ruby blossom ready to be plucked. The Rose of Sharon. The Franciscan's hand approached. She watched as it slid inside, entering the cavity of her breast. As if succoring a small bird, the slender fingers encircled her heart and began caressing the lobes. Rose was being strummed by a master troubadour; the melody was bliss. Her body started to shudder. But just when it was on the verge of buckling under the weight of her pleasure, the hand began to retreat, taking with it her beating heart. Rose was untroubled, wondering in a detached manner if she could survive without a heart. But it didn't matter. Her past life paled in comparison to what she was now being offered. What had come before didn't seem like a life after all, only a dream about life. She might have been sleeping; she might have been dead. All previous experience was a kind of death. Real life was beginning at last.

The hand was returning, bearing something red. She couldn't make it out at first. Its vivid hue drained the color from everything else, and her eyes were dazzled. Then she saw that it was another heart — the friar's own heart. A beautiful rose-colored heart just for Rose. While the hand was implanting the new heart in Rose's breast, she tried to pray. *Oh God, make it end. Oh please, never stop. Holy, holy, holy, Lord God of hosts. Make me holy. I am ready.*

Something monstrous was overshadowing Rose: monstrous in its beauty, beautiful in its monstrosity, exquisite in its intensity. She surrendered herself. When it departed, she felt empty, depleted. At the same time, she was exhilarated by what was stirring in her breast: the stirring of new life. Rose had been reborn.

The regeneration of Rose was not the only marvel that took place in the church that day. Three other members of the Faithful were present at Mass. They were not offered the chalice. Nor were they aware of the special distinction that Rose had received, absorbed by a miracle all their own. The Hosts that Brother Jacques had consecrated were turning from stale bread into moist, glistening flesh. Not daring to consume them, the three Faithful stood immobilized, weeping with joy. Touched by St. Gregory! That most holy of pontiffs had interceded with God so they too could experience the miracle of his Mass.

The Franciscan was the vehicle for this threefold marvel, yet his behavior was a model of humility and discretion. He made no determination about the meaning of what had occurred, nor did he express surprise.

"My beloved friends, let us rejoice by all means, but in a seemly manner. This is a matter for the bishop." He took the three Hosts from their awe-struck recipients, placed them in a glass container, and set the vessel at the center of the altar. Thinking together as one body, the Faithful wordlessly took turns watching over what they were certain was the Real Presence of Christ: that most hallowed of relics. The Hosts continued to ooze blood throughout the night.

The Priest and his Concubine

At the very moment that Brother Jacques was elevating the Hosts in consecration, a man on the other side of the church wall made an audible sigh. The man's name was Hervey Rousseau, the curate for St.-Jacques-de-la-Boucherie. He was sitting in the presbytery. It was an irregularly shaped dwelling that not only shared a wall with the church, but even had a secret door for the priest. A manuscript lay open on his lap, but he was not really reading. Instead, he was imagining an alternative life; the kind of life he might have led had he remained at the university. Hervey had completed his Bachelor's degree, and was just beginning that all-important commentary on Lombard's *Sentences*. But that was over two decades ago. The endeavor was interrupted, and he would never become a master. His hopes of entering the Dominican order were likewise dashed. All that remained of that dream was an unbound manuscript containing a life of the Dominican saint, Peter Martyr — the manuscript that he was holding, but not reading. It was a relic of a life unlived.

Yet if Hervey had pursued this alternative life, it could not have included Felice. The priest gazed at the young woman. Although she had looked up when the priest sighed, she was now bending over her book of hours, face veiled by hair. Auburn tints gleamed against the green shawl wrapped around her shoulders. It was an old shawl that had once belonged to Hervey's mother, and it had been mended in several places. Hervey smiled. Long ago there had been a woman, a scandal, and, in due time, a squalling infant. Hervey took the child: raised her, praised her, chastised her, and loved her. She was his *pearl of great price*. And the price was more than an aborted academic career; it also seemed to entail one unfortunate benefice after the next. First there was the stint at the

Hôtel Dieu. Most of the inmates were literally sick to death, but they still had the energy to boo his sermons. Hervey couldn't blame them — he had yet to divest himself of over-theologized jargon. The only lodgings available were in Rue Glatigny — an infamous neighborhood infested with sewage, vermin, and prostitutes. The rats got into everything, leaving behind droppings the size of almonds. Poor Felice had such delicate skin that between the lice and the fleas, she would scratch herself raw. Disillusioned and disgusted, Hervey found a position in Reims, where he served as vicar in a large parish church. But the incumbent was both indolent and tight-fisted, and they barely scraped by. Meanwhile, Felice was growing: she wanted to become apprenticed to a craft. *There is nothing to be ashamed of in honest work,* she would argue. But he wouldn't have it. Nor would he allow her to take in sewing. *You will never make a good marriage if you are doing the work of a drab.*

Their luck changed when Hervey received the benefice of St.-Jacques-de-la-Boucherie. The church was in the presentement of the monks St.-Martin-de-Champs, and the abbot happened to be godfather to Hervey's father. Yet while the fortunes of Hervey and Felice improved, there was one thing that never changed: the scandal that followed them wherever they went. In Reims, Hervey was regarded as a priest who had not only rescinded on his vow of chastity, but also was sufficiently shameless as to raise the fruit of his depravity in the open. By the time they returned to Paris, Felice had become quite a beauty; his new parishioners assumed that the young woman was Father Hervey's concubine. So as lovely as she was, Felice had no suitors. As a clerical bastard, she was not good enough to marry; as a concubine, she was as good as married. Even so, Hervey had not abandoned hope. In Reims, there had been several young men who showed interest in Felice. One was the eldest son of a well-to-do mercantile family. Any other woman would have been eager to secure him as a future spouse. But Felice never paid him much heed. The boy had a stammer, it was true. But Felice was so kind-hearted that a disability would just as likely advance as hinder his suit. Hervey could never be sure about Felice. He suspected that she had yet to see a man that she could love.

Hervey was staring into the fire. On quiet nights such as these he had gotten into the habit of looking for a salamander — a beast that was said to live in flames. His vigil was interrupted by Felice, who had given up trying to read in the half-light and put her book to one side.

"There were no eggs in market again."

Hervey shook his head without looking up. "A bad sign. Animals know."

"What? What is there to know?"

"Latin please."

"*Ne quid est cognoscere?* Or should I say, *Ne quid cognoscent?*"

The priest laughed, delighted by her aptitude. Either version would do. Yet, when pressed, he had to confess that the specifics of avian knowledge eluded him. Even so, he had grown up in the country and did know this: when birds went off their feed or stopped laying eggs, there was something wrong. It had happened just before King Charles lost his mind. He was riding with his army through the forest of Le Mans when, without warning, he was overtaken by a violent rage. He slew four of his knights, while his brother, Louis of Orléans, barely escaped with his life. The birds had known ahead of time.

Hervey poked the fire. Tiny explosions of sparks raced up the chimney, looking as if they were alive. Maybe this is what the bestiarist mistook for a living animal. Maybe there was no salamander.

There was a knock on the door. It was hours after sundown, and they were startled. The priest approached the door with caution.

"Who is there?" It was one of those starless nights when the setting sun took everything with it, except the dark. So Hervey spoke in a loud voice.

"Father, it's Anna." The voice was tearful. "My daughter has taken a bad turn. I beg you to come."

Hervey didn't bother to inquire which of the dozen or so parishioners named Anna was standing outside. Felice handed him the stole; he kissed it, and put it around his neck. Then he reached for the viaticum and the bottle of holy chrism. In a second, Hervey was out the door, following the light of the woman's torch. Felice was left alone, wondering whether the chickens could have known of the daughter's illness. She thought not.

It was Anna Kent, the baker's widow, and the sick girl was Rose — her only remaining child. When Rose returned from her weekly prayer meeting that evening, her eyes were gleaming. She talked on and on about the new preacher, hardly touching her dinner. Her mother went to bed first, but was awakened by what she thought was the sound of voices speaking softly. She assumed it was Rose with her young man, Philip, and smiled to herself. She wouldn't dream of interrupting the lovers' tryst. Then Anna heard a gurgling noise, like someone swallowing the wrong way and choking. She rushed into the other room to find Rose alone, collapsed in a faint — her eyes open and unseeing.

Father Hervey looked at the girl with concern. Anna had shaken Rose, thrown water on her face, assailed her with pungent odors and pinches — all to no avail. Rose could not be awoken from her swoon. The priest prayed over her unconscious form and applied the holy oil to her forehead. It was impossible to give her the Host while she was unconscious, despite her mother's entreaties. Hervey spoke optimistically about Rose's imminent recovery. Yet when he looked down at Rose, he felt doubtful. Her face was beginning to take on a waxy, unreal quality — as if she were wearing a mask. The priest felt chilled, and looked away.

"Anna, you must get a doctor."

The widow looked down, ashamed. There was no money for a doctor: she still owed from her husband's sickness. Tears streamed down her face. Hervey understood. He reached into his own pocket, and felt around until he discovered the silver *sol* he kept for emergencies such as this.

When Hervey returned with the doctor, nothing had changed.

A week later, Rose still hadn't come around. Anna somehow managed to pour enough honey-laced milk into her mouth to keep her alive. She would change her daughter's position, and ensure that her linen was fresh. But Rose never moved. Felice had been friendly with Rose and never forgot her. She would come by with flowers or fresh lavender for the sick room practically every day. Anna was encouraged by the fact that Felice would sit with Rose, speaking cheerfully as if she expected Rose to answer.

One day when Anna was gone, Felice dropped the façade of conversation. She sat at the bedside looking at her friend. *Where are you, Rose? Where have you gone? Come back so I can braid your hair the way you like; come back to dance on the parish green; come back and marry your Philip. Come back and live!*

One of Rose's hands was lying outside the blanket, with its palm facing downward. It looked blue with cold, the veins so prominent that they could have been traced on the outside of her skin. Felice leaned forward to tuck her friend's hand under the blanket, but jerked back. *What was that?* It felt like something was moving — something under the skin, running through Rose like a subterranean river. Felice stretched out her hand a second time. Once again she felt the tremor. Her hand ached ever so slightly after she removed it, like from a subcutaneous bruise. It was as if something were inside Rose, sending out a warning signal to anyone attempting to disturb her. *Something protective, perhaps, like a living charm? No, that's impossible. I mustn't be fanciful.* Felice was about to touch her friend again, but suddenly changed her mind, dropping her hand into her lap. It wasn't right to disturb Rose; she was afraid to disturb Rose; could Rose be disturbed? Felice experienced a stab of fear.

She returned to an empty presbytery, but this was no surprise. Most of Hervey's week had been taken up with matters revolving around the Miraculous Bleeding Hosts. Felice grimaced: she tended to take a dim view of Eucharistic miracles, regarding them as repellant and useless in equal parts.

"Why wouldn't God choose to do something more useful, like turn our well water into wine?" she had asked.

A slight spasm of annoyance disturbed Hervey's usually serene features.

"Affirming the faith is always useful," he said. They had been having the same argument since Felice's first communion.

Whatever their differences over the utility of the marvel, both Felice and Hervey experienced a parallel dismay over the disruption it caused. Every possible official body in Paris felt compelled to weigh in on the status of the Miraculous Bleeding Hosts. The bishop sent his *officialis*, the Franciscans and Dominicans each sent a pair of senior monks, even the king made his presence felt when a sergeant from the provost appeared. But representatives of officialdom were nothing compared to the pious traffic that the miracle occasioned. Priests from all over the diocese had already begun assigning penitential pilgrimages. People with every manner of illness arrived in droves, bearing votive candles. Of course, it was too early for a firm determination, but everyone (excepting perhaps Felice) seemed to believe that the miracle was authentic.

By the time Hervey returned, Felice had immersed herself in a book. When he asked after Rose, Felice just nodded without looking up. It was only when Hervey cleared his throat and announced, "And this is my Felice," that she became aware that there was another person in the room. She quickly got to her feet, apologizing. Standing next to her father was a cleric whom her father introduced as his former classmate, Anthony. Felice had heard her father speak of Anthony so often that she had, quite naturally, formed her own mental picture of her father's friend. It didn't at all correspond with the heavy-set stranger who stood in front of her. His deep-set eyes had a brooding quality and his nose was prominent. He made an interesting foil for her father, who was stately and conspicuously handsome. Even so, the years had been kinder to Anthony. While Hervey's hair had mutated into a steely grey, Anthony's remained untouched. There were no wrinkles on his brow. He didn't appear just a few years younger than Hervey, but at least a decade.

Anthony was also studying Felice. His eyebrows met in a furrow as if she presented a problem of sorts. Then his expression resolved itself into a smile. Felice, who prided herself on being a connoisseur of smiles, felt certain that he was a good man. Perhaps it was this nebulous charisma of goodness that made Anthony seem so familiar. She felt certain that she had seen him before.

"Hello Felice. We have met before," he said, as if reading her thoughts. "You were only a babe, however." Then Anthony turned to Hervey: "*Bene, Hervius. Beatum factum fecisque puella formosa est.*" (Well done Hervey. You have performed a good deed and the girl is beautiful.)

Hervey and Felice burst out laughing simultaneously at his compliment.

"I am sure Felice is flattered. But I should have warned you, Anthony. Felice is fully Latinate. I saw to that myself."

Anthony was embarrassed: how clerical of him to equate *femina* with *idiota*! Felice accepted his apology with good humor. Then the three sat down together, sipping wine from earthenware cups, while the two men caught up. At first they talked about people: who got what parish; who became a mendicant; who was caught with his cassock up, as it were. It was only after these conversational milestones were passed that they got around to the reason behind Anthony's visit to St.-Jacques, which was, of course, the Miraculous Bleeding Hosts. He had been sent by the Chancellor of the University to assess the situation. His preliminary judgment was neutral.

"I see no evidence of fraud: the Hosts are still bleeding. And the Franciscan seems to be behaving himself, which is all to the good." The bells for Nones began to peal, and Anthony arose. "As canon of the cathedral, Our Lady requires a daily Mass from me — whether there is anyone to hear it or not."

Hervey would not let Anthony leave until he had accepted an invitation for dinner on Friday.

"Felice's cooking is almost as good as her Latin," Hervey said with a smile.

Dinner with Simon Magus

Rose remained in a comatose state with her eyes open. And this is how Brother Jacques found her some twenty days after she had fallen ill. During this interval, Anna had hardly stirred from her daughter's bedside. But the friar's visit coincided with one of the rare occasions when her mother was obliged to leave Rose. Felice was away, and Anna could find no one else to sit with her.

"It's the bakers' guild, my love. I have to see about our money," Anna said, speaking as if her daughter could hear her. Anna fussed over Rose, adjusting her cover. "If I don't go, I might lose my widow's pension." She said a little prayer over her daughter, made the sign of the cross, and left for the guild hall. When Anna returned, Rose was sitting up in her bed and sipping water. The Franciscan was there at her side, speaking to her in hushed tones. He looked up and smiled. "She was only sleeping; I woke her up."

Felice and Hervey were among the first to see Rose and to congratulate the happy mother on her daughter's recovery. Rose, still weak and painfully thin, was propped up against pillows, staring at nothing in particular — pale as the covers on her bed. She never spoke. But Anna, with words enough for both of them, praised Brother Jacques to the heavens.

"It may be his greatest miracle, but not his first. The man is a saint. The pope should hear about this!"

Many in the parish seemed to concur. As news of Rose's cure spread, both the kind and the curious came to visit, bringing gifts of fruit, cakes, and spiced wine. But such comings and goings were nothing compared to the disruption visited on the Franciscan priory. The Miraculous Bleeding Hosts had attracted a crowd, which assembled at the porter's lodge in hopes of catching a glimpse of Brother Jacques. The number of the simply curious was now supplemented by those desperate for a cure. It was a wrenching sight: mothers with sick babies, wives with crippled husbands, the aged with palsied limbs, others who had never seen or had long since lost their sight. The miracle seekers were disturbing the orderly life of the community, and the Friars Minor, impatient with this pious invasion, were wondering when their brother from the south would finish his business and depart.

When Father Anthony arrived for his appointed dinner with Felice and Hervey a couple of days later, the parish was still abuzz over Rose's remarkable recovery. They had just finished what even the self-critical Felice was prepared to grant a very good meal. Since it was Friday they had, as a matter of course, served fish. But the red mullet had been simmered with lentils and sage. A custard tart sweetened with honey and spiced with cinnamon followed. They had remained seated around the table, sipping their mead. The topic of conversation was, understandably, whether Rose's cure constituted a miracle. Anthony's assessment was guarded. An official miracle required witnesses.

"Besides, miracles performed by someone still alive are not as weighty as those performed after death," said Anthony.

Felice nodded in comprehension. "I see what you mean. A living wonder-worker might receive his powers from Satan, like with Simon Magus," she responded.

Anthony exchanged a furtive look with Hervey before he answered. "Exactly. The only safe saints are dead saints. Posthumous miracles prove that the deceased is in God's presence."

The conversation of true and false sanctity continued into the evening, but Felice seemed riveted by the figure of Simon Magus and kept bringing the conversation back to him. It turned out that Anthony had made quite of study of Simon in his youth, and was knowledgeable of details not just from biblical sources, but also from texts both erudite and obscure.

"Simon was a genius at self-presentation. Among the Jews he was the messianic Son of God; in Samaria he was the Father; elsewhere, he was the Holy Spirit. And the people were taken in. The senate and people of Rome accepted him as a deity and even erected a statue in his honor," said Anthony.

What especially captured Felice's imagination was Simon's relationship with a female companion named Helen. Simon claimed that, in his capacity as creator of the universe, his very first thought had manifested itself as a female principle — that very Helen — created to do his bidding. It was Helen who made the angelic hosts which dwelt in the lower regions of the air. Unfortunately, the angels proved to be jealous ingrates, rebelling against Helen and creating the earth as her prison.

"Shut up in a female body, she was reincarnated many times — most notably as Helen of Troy. But when Simon finally descended from the heavens to rescue Helen, she was inhabiting the body of a prostitute from Tyre," said Anthony.

"So who exactly was Helen?" asked Felice.

"Well, probably just a prostitute. But Simon presented her as much more of a 'what' than a 'who.' He cast her in the role of platonic demiurge — the agent who acts on behalf of the actual creative force."

Anthony and Felice were so intent on their conversation that they hadn't noticed Hervey's peculiar restlessness. He stared into his empty cup, tapped his foot, then got up and walked across the room, pretending to examine the non-descript tapestry of St. Jacques. All at once he broke out with, "These apocryphal accounts are utter nonsense! I urge you to find a more appropriate subject."

Felice was surprised at her father's uncharacteristic outburst. She looked disappointed — so disappointed that Hervey, ostensibly mollified, said, "Pray continue." And continue they did. Anthony gave a detailed account of Simon's rapid rise to fame, attracting a wide following from all walks of life.

"Yet he sounds like such a charlatan. How can you possibly account for his success?" Felice asked.

"As far as I can tell, he had two things going for him," Anthony said. "First, he was a genius at appropriating the religious doctrine of other groups. The story of Helen is perhaps the most fanciful instance."

"And the second thing?" Felice prompted.

"Oh that's simple. He could back up his claims with magical effects."

Anthony went on to describe Simon's many marvels: how statues smiled and walked about, images of dogs barked, brazen serpents slithered. Not only was Simon an adept at unlocking doors, but his mere glance could melt iron. And his gift for shape shifting was unparalleled. Some accounts even credited him with the power to raise the dead.

"At the very least, he was a fabulous magician," Anthony concluded. "Naturally, he assumed that the apostles were magicians as well. When Simon saw them administering the Holy Spirit through the laying on of hands, he offered money to learn what he believed to be just another trick. Peter cursed him for his impiety."

"So what happened to Simon?" asked Felice.

"Well I suppose you could say that Peter did him in. Simon was demonstrating how he could fly before Nero and his household. Everyone in Rome had turned out. But Peter's prayers stopped Simon in mid-air, and he came crashing to the ground in the middle of the forum. The crowd turned and stoned Simon to death."

"How did they know that Peter wasn't the magician?" asked Felice.

Hervey, who knew that many of Felice's reflections on religion were open to misinterpretation, had to stop himself from interrupting. But Anthony just laughed.

"Good question. Perhaps they would have opted for whichever magician won. And there were some who claimed victory for Simon. One heretical tradition alleges that the first pope was really Simon Magus, not Simon Peter."

"Well, now we have two popes: perhaps one is descended from Simon Peter and the other from Simon Magus," observed Felice wryly.

This led to a vigorous discussion of the papal schism. There were rival popes in Rome and Avignon. After the death of Clement VII, the king had begged the cardinals of Avignon to postpone the election of a new pope, but they wouldn't listen. Instead, each one swore that, if elected, he would abdicate. When Benedict XIII ascended the papal throne, however, it soon became clear that he had no intention of stepping down, in spite of the vow. The university had proposed the *via cessionis,* urging both popes to resign. But then the king censured this position and forbade any further debate on the matter.

"It's sad," Anthony sighed. "The university's solution might have worked."

"Surely the king's intervention is indicative of an unsettled mind," said Hervey. The three of them were quiet for a moment, reflecting on the melancholy situation of their ailing monarch with his sudden metamorphosis from Charles the Beloved to Charles the Mad. Felice broke their silence with another of her unsettling observations.

"It seems the whole debacle was France's fault. Why ever did the monarchy insist on the popes coming to Avignon in the first place?" asked Felice.

With Anthony present, Hervey felt uncomfortable listening to his daughter's potentially treasonous line of reasoning. She seemed to have momentarily forgotten that France continued to support the Avignon papacy. In fact, Anthony was not in the least dismayed by Felice's frankness, but found it refreshing.

Anthony had come on foot, and had plenty of time to reflect on the way home. Although genuinely pleased to reencounter Hervey after all these years, Anthony had anticipated the dinner with mounting trepidation, dreading an evening mired down by Hervey's reminiscences and regrets. At least this is how Anthony explained his reluctance to himself. The dinner had been thoroughly enjoyable, however—delightful, in fact. His old friend had lost none of his mental acuity, while Felice seemed every bit as sharp. The only area for possible regret was the discussion about Simon Magus. Hervey was clearly put out. But wasn't it Felice who introduced the subject? Anthony couldn't be sure. Responsible or not, Felice seemed intent on Simon, and was difficult to deter. Was she always that willful? In other women, such single-mindedness might have been an unattractive quality. Yet this woman was different. As beautiful as she might be, she reasoned and talked like a man. But Felice shouldn't bear all the responsibility for the direction of the conversation. Anthony knew that he was to blame as well. Once the subject of Simon had been introduced, Anthony could not help himself. He had never lost interest in the dark magician.

The Forbidden Quodlibet

Dah; Dah; Dah. A persistent knocking on the door: not terribly loud, just a steady pulse. Anthony didn't want to wake up because he knew who was on the other side of the door. Simon had returned. He was out there! After all these years, he had finally tracked Anthony down. And Simon was angry that he had been banished, shut out. So here he was—indignant and hungry; hungry to live; hungry for life. The knock got louder. *Dah; Dah; Dah.* Resourceful Simon, clever Simon—smiling, beguiling, and terrifying—knocking on the door.

The knocking became more insistent, and Anthony was suddenly awake. His dream about Simon was routed and temporarily forgotten.

If it is a student, I will speak to the Chancellor and have him expelled! But Anthony's day had broken ironically. When he pulled some clothes on and opened the door, it turned out to be a student summoning him to the Chancellor.

"Can he wait?"

"I think not," the pimply youth stammered apologetically. Anthony nodded, walked over to the basin, and splashed some water on his face. He drew the door shut behind him and walked alongside the youth, neither of them speaking.

Chancellor John Gerson had assumed his office at the early age of thirty-two — almost ridiculously precocious in view of his inauspicious origins, and he knew it. He was the son of an artisan who made cartwheels. Anthony remembered Gerson as a student — taciturn, sullen, with no apparent friends, but unusually adept. It was not long before he made a name for himself as a scholar to be reckoned with. Still, there were those who claimed that the most impressive aspect of Gerson's work was its sheer volume.

Although they had communicated by messenger, Anthony had not actually seen Gerson since his elevation to the chancellorship. The two years in office had taken their toll. Gerson's hair had already begun to grey and, though never profuse with smiles, he seemed to have now all but banished them from his lexicon of expressions. But Gerson wasn't alone. A young cleric was standing to one side of Gerson's writing table, eyes downcast. It was Baldwin. *Of course it was!* Thank God the boy had the good grace to look abashed.

Anthony bowed in front of Gerson, who remained seated, his face rigid.

"Master Anthony, as resident master of the college it is only right for you to know that one of your charges has gone too far."

Gerson went on to describe the circumstances surrounding Baldwin's transgressive disputation at length, unaware that there was no need. But for Anthony to acknowledge that he had been a witness to the event would only make matters worse.

"The question of Satan masquerading as Christ was condemned by university statute over forty years ago. No one is permitted to debate this point. Baldwin must be expelled," Gerson said.

Anthony resisted, arguing that Baldwin was a good student with an excellent record who had all but finished his degree. As it happened, Anthony was less concerned by the fact of Baldwin's disobedience than the form it took.

"Over the past decade, the university has witnessed a heightened preoccupation with demons and the extent of their powers. I believe that the current fascination with the forbidden question is a symptom of sorts. Baldwin is not alone. He is representative of a certain curiosity that is on the rise," Anthony said.

"Well, you know what I think of curiosity," responded Gerson, sourly.

Of course Anthony knew. Everyone knew what Gerson thought about curiosity: it was an issue he returned to repeatedly in his innumerable tracts on curriculum. "*There is nothing new under the sun.* Never were there truer words. Students should be reading men like Bonaventure, not running after novelty," or words to this effect. Anthony prayed that Gerson wouldn't bring up Bonaventure again.

"Why waste God-given talent on something as preposterous as Satan appearing as Christ? We should be reading our great forbears — like Bonaventure," Gerson said.

Anthony suppressed his smile. Any sign of levity would send Baldwin back to his ancestral home in Brittany. Besides, he didn't want to alienate the Chancellor. Gerson was the head of the most important theological faculty in all of Christendom; Anthony might need Gerson's help. Help for what? It was impossible to know. But just the thought of Baldwin's evening quodlibet filled Anthony with nameless dread. Anthony had always scoffed at the many prophets of doom who were springing up all over Christendom. Yet here he was with a powerful sense of foreboding that something was about to happen. Something bad. Why were they quibbling about student foibles when there was danger in the air?

"Let's look at the larger picture," Anthony began cautiously. "Our Lord did warn us against the many false Christs who would be appearing in His name, and history has revealed many. Simon Magus claimed to be Christ. And in the lives of the desert fathers . . ."

"Yes, yes. And antichrist is just around the corner. But I stopped attending your theology classes years ago, master," Gerson snapped.

This sounded like a rather uncharitable reflection on the change in their respective positions, but Anthony wasn't offended. In fact, the chancellorship didn't look very appealing from where he sat. Gerson clearly hadn't received an official residence on his accession to office. Why else would he be conducting business out of a squalid room in the cathedral cloister? The floor was filthy. The mortar between the stones was moldy. And it was so wretchedly cold. There was a fireplace, but Gerson didn't seem to be using it. Was this a symptom of his ascetic humility, or did he have no servants to call on?

Meanwhile, Gerson seemed to have fallen into some kind of a reverie, staring at his stylus as if he had never seen one before. Anthony stirred restlessly in his seat.

"Chancellor?"

Gerson started. He had clearly lost the thread of the conversation, and peevishly asked Anthony to repeat himself.

"The point I was making is that we seem to be entering a time when it is especially difficult to distinguish between good and evil. There is a great need for what the fathers called spiritual discernment — the ability to distinguish between the divine and diabolical inspiration," Anthony said.

When Gerson bristled, Anthony realized too late that he had reflexively presumed to offer a definition for a theological term, and this was a false step. He was thinking how he could smooth the Chancellor's ruffled feathers when Gerson spoke up.

"Coincidentally, I happen to be writing a treatise on spiritual discernment." This was said with just the right degree of hauteur to indicate that he was, indeed, offended.

A door suddenly swung open in Anthony's mind and he was on his feet with excitement, oblivious to Gerson's tone. There had been a string of Parisian masters who had written on precisely this matter over the past fifty years. And now Gerson was among them.

"Don't you see that a Satanic Christ epitomizes the problem? Baldwin's disputation turns on the failure of spiritual discernment!" Anthony's voice was raised by a sense of urgency, prompting Gerson to look up with an expression of surprise, peppered with distaste. He seemed on the verge of speaking when his expression changed. The look of irritation faded and Gerson's face gradually assumed a more contemplative aspect. Anthony knew that he had made his point.

Gerson sighed before he looked up and met Anthony's gaze.

"Alright, Master, though I would prefer that we discipline the young fool." This was the first time he actually looked at Baldwin, who was standing as still as a statue. "But I agree that he is not alone in these prurient interests. I want you to investigate. You must keep a list of anyone interested in this or related topics. Faculty as well. Then we should meet again and discuss the situation."

Anthony was relieved that the conversation had been resolved this way and that there was no punishment in store for Baldwin.

"Thank you for understanding."

The Chancellor had already begun poking around on the table in front of him, piled with papers and fragments of parchment, behaving as if Anthony had already left. At Anthony's last remark, Gerson looked up and scowled. "But I don't understand. Do you?"

The question was clearly rhetorical, so Anthony withdrew with Baldwin in tow.

The next day, Baldwin was still fuming. He was sitting in the cloister of Robert of Sorbon's college, home to the late-night disputation. It was a windy day in March, and he sat huddled under his cloak. *Why the fuss over a simple disputation? Scholars speculate. That's what we do! The more bizarre the subject, the better. Scripture says we must prove the spirits, determining whether they come from God or Satan. The Satanic Christ isn't just some noisome hypothetical; he appeared to St. Martin — one of the few possessed of the gift of discernment. But it is a rare gift. We need alternative means for determining good from evil. Heaven knows that Christendom would benefit! There are two people claiming to be pope: what if one of them were the antichrist?*

The threat of rain hung in the air like a shroud. For a moment, the cloister seemed unfamiliar to Baldwin. Its slender columns, designed to keep the world at bay, were more like prison bars, locking everyone in. His eyes lighted on a carved capital depicting the death of Judas. The hanged man's face was etched in despair with bulging eyes and lolling tongue, thirty pieces of silver scattered at his feet. The twelfth apostle who thought he was serving God but was actually serving the devil! An oblique facet of the capital continued the Judas story. The doomed apostle's soul, a tiny wizened doll in swaddling clothes, was being carried away by a triumphant demon.

For the first time ever, Baldwin felt trapped in his vocation. Yet he hadn't been forced into the church like so many other younger sons. He had embraced the opportunity. The world of learning would more than compensate for the celibate's lonely bed, or so he had once thought. But now it seemed as if the world of learning was never on offer, just a parochial plot governed by the university. Stray ever so slightly and the heavy arm of the church came down, even in a refectory in the middle of the night!

Rupert's Commission

On the other side of the Petit Pont the vocational aspirations of a young Dominican named Rupert had also sunk to its unhappy nadir. Considering the order's mandate for preaching, Rupert realized that the Dominicans were a strange choice for him. He had a marked stammer and would never make an even passable preacher. It was the love of learning that had attracted Rupert to the Dominicans. This was the order of Albert the Great and his still greater student, Thomas Aquinas. Thomas had even taught at the University of Paris. But Rupert had been working on his Master's degree in theology for two years, and it seemed like an eternity. The deeper arcana accessible to his learned forbears seemed consistently denied to Rupert. Yet, the intellectual demands placed upon him were simultaneously taxing and stultifying. The curriculum had been determined for centuries: every candidate for a degree in theology had to write a commentary on Peter Lombard's *Four Books of Sentences*.

The format was carved in stone. There was a series of questions that must be answered in a certain order. He was still on book one and currently tackling the scintillating matter of "Whether the Son is sent only once or often." Rupert wished for his own sake that the answer was "only once" so he could be done with it. But wouldn't you know? "The Son is said to be sent in two ways: that in one way He is sent once, and in another way often; and in one way in order to be a man, and in another way in order to be with man."

Rupert was twenty-eight years old, but it already seemed as if he were gazing down a long corridor toward the end of his life — a straight line, with no twists, turns or surprises. Time had never passed so slowly. It didn't help that the scriptorium where he was sitting was incredibly gloomy — high vaulted, cold, and drafty. There were frescoes on the wall that had long ago succumbed to the damp. On the right there were two figures — one standing, one kneeling. The face of the standing figure was destroyed, but the crossed halo remained, designating Christ. The kneeling figure was anyone's guess, however: Mary Magdalene in front of the risen Lord? The newly resurrected Lazarus? A healed leper saying thank you?

Meanwhile one of Rupert's fellow students sat in the corner laughing to himself. Rupert wondered whether his snickering confrere had found the infamous book of fabliaux. It was rumored that such a book did exist somewhere in the library. A truly scurrilous story might lift his spirits. Rupert fondly remembered the party where he once heard a jongleur recite *The Knight Who Conjured Voices*. It was all about an impoverished knight to whom some sympathetic fairies gave the ability of making a woman's secret parts speak. And his unlikely gift made his fortune.

Rupert looked aimlessly around the room, wishing it were time for the midday meal — knowing that it was at least an hour away. Then his eyes fastened on the life-sized crucifix that hung at the front of the room. It was just such a crucifix that spoke to Francis of Assisi in the little church of San Damiano, calling him to his vocation. It was too bad that this one couldn't speak; otherwise he might have asked Him whether He had been sent only once or often and settle the question once and for all. Uh-oh. Was he being blasphemous? Probably. Rupert mentally said "Lord Jesus, have mercy upon me" by way of apology. The crucified Christ didn't seem to care one way or the other, continuing to grace the room with His blank, but tranquil, gaze.

At that moment, Prior Giles entered the study hall. Generally Rupert resented figures of authority: he told himself it was from an innate defiance, when in fact it was from a fearful tendency to cringe before judgment of any sort. But the prior was different than other officials, wearing his power lightly. He could glide behind the various scholars, looking at what they were reading or writing, but somehow managing to do so in a warm and collaborative manner. He touched Rupert's shoulder lightly before moving on to his colleague, the snickering monk. There was the sound of a codex closing quickly, but not quickly enough apparently: the monk soon retreated from the room, blushing with shame. So there really was such a book!

Giles' peaceful gliding was momentarily interrupted when the pudgy subprior, Brother Marcus, entered and spoke to the prior in a low voice. Marcus seemed agitated, but all Rupert overheard were the words *Franciscan, miracle,* and *faithful.*

"Perhaps, we should be grateful," said Giles. "They are supposed to be our pastoral responsibility, but we haven't been very attentive."

"But they seem to want to confess all the time! Especially the women." For some reason, everyone in the scriptorium seemed to have heard this last statement and looked up. Giles cleared his throat, made a slight sideways gesture with his head, and the senior monks exited.

Later that day, Rupert received the summons from Prior Giles with dread. What could he possibly have done now? He searched his mind, but couldn't think of anything particularly out of the ordinary for which he could blame himself. It is true that he had spent much of the afternoon trying to discover the whereabouts of the naughty manuscript, but with no results. If anyone had seen him clambering up and down the ladders, checking the most unreachable shelves, how would that person know that he wasn't looking for something erudite by a church father? But now Prior Giles was asking for him. He doubted that it could bode well.

When he arrived in the prior's office, Brother Marcus was there as well, which struck Rupert as a bad sign. Perhaps Marcus had seen him in the library, gleaned his purpose, and, in the spirit of fraternal correction, denounced him to the prior. Rupert bowed and stood before them, hands concealed in the sleeves of his habit, and waited. Yet there were no reproaches or even stern looks. Just an invitation to sit down, followed by an awkward pause. Finally the prior bestirred himself.

"And how is the commentary on *The Sentences* going, Brother Rupert?"

This was not a particularly original question, or one that Rupert wanted to answer, but it was far preferable to what he had feared.

"It g-g-goes, prior, sometimes more s-s-slowly than I would like."

"Nevertheless, you will finish." Giles nodded with a warm optimism. "I look forward to the pleasure of calling you 'Master'."

Rupert literally blushed with delight, thanking the prior for anticipating the day. Again silence reigned — only broken by a preternaturally loud rook outside. The prior soon got down to business. He wanted to know if Rupert knew anything about the Faithful — the order's lay affiliates. There seemed to have been a mysterious Franciscan who had undertaken their spiritual direction. This was unusual: each order tended to look out for its own. The prior had been told that Rupert's sister was in some way affiliated with the Faithful, and wondered whether Rupert had any particular insights into the group.

Rupert looked startled. "Prior, I have no knowledge of th-th-them. A-A-Alicia just attends their meetings. She has taken no vows. I h-h-haven't seen her in months — almost a year. My studies. . ." Rupert broke off rather lamely.

"Even so," said Prior Giles in a soft voice, "you may be able to help us."

For a moment, Rupert was afraid he was being asked to take over the meetings from this Brother Jacques, and his pulse sped up with alarm. But the prior reassured him on that score. He only wanted Rupert to act as the order's eyes, as it were: to meet this friar; see how he conducts himself; watch him. The Faithful met on Thursdays before Vespers. But Giles recommended that Rupert first meet with his sister to hear her account of Brother Jacques.

At this point, the subprior cleared his throat and excused himself, having pressing business in town. He gave the prior a significant look. "It is a problem with that donor I mentioned to you."

Prior Giles nodded. "Brother Marcus is always so solicitous on behalf of the community. He handles most of our business, you know," he said to Rupert. "Go, brother. And thank you for all your efforts on our behalf."

Feme Fole

The only "donor" that Subprior Marcus was scheduled to see was a prostitute named Margot de la Barre. Prostitutes were known as common women — *common because we belong to no one man,* Margot would often reflect. *But most of us share a common past as well. It always begins with a man. Mine was so handsome, as most rogues are. He talked about love like a poet. We were to marry as soon as he found a job. There was no work in Beaune de Gastinois, or none that he wasn't too good for. Once we left, he found it easier to let me do the work. I couldn't say no. I was alone and far from home, and he would have left me. At first, it was just his friends. But soon it was just about anyone who would pay. And so it was: two ribauds, wandering all over France, living off what I made. Did he ever love me? Not much. The moment I got pregnant, he was gone.*

That was forty-three years ago, but many of these years were not spent in what might be described as active duty. Prostitution was a competitive profession which forced most practitioners into retirement by forty at the latest. So it was with Margot, who now made her money renting out cubicles on the upper floor of a rather derelict house on Rue Glatigny — that venerable center of vice in the heart of the Île de la Cité. Most of her customers had disappeared over time. But a few still remained. Marcus had been a client for years — even before he had professed as a monk. He still visited once a month — more from habit and conviviality than from lust. Margot remembered when he was still a novice, and a slender one at that, with a riot of brown hair. Now he was decidedly plump, and the circle of his graying tonsure had expanded like the ring from a stone dropped in a pond. *Soon, he'll no longer need to shave his head,* Margot thought. He had once had a handsome face, but now it was considerably rounder and with multiple chins. His eyes, which had retreated behind creases of flesh, were the only things about Marcus that seemed smaller. Even the mole on the side of his nose had swollen considerably. *But I can't be too critical; look at me!* Marcus was still enthusiastic and jolly. His throaty laugh sounded just as often, though now sometimes ending in a worrisome, spluttering cough. He was easily winded. Sometimes she wondered if her old friend was dying. But she was careful not to betray this thought. Instead, she began with her usual bawdy overtures.

"Come here, Master Upright" (this said with her hand over his penis which was not, in fact, erect). "You friars have it good. All you have to do is preach; mutter the Mass in Latin — if that really is Latin: who's to know? There's always food on your table. You probably have a fat penitent to warm your bed."

He chuckled appreciatively. "None of them can touch you." Margot was always touched by his valiant efforts at flattery: she was just going on sixty. Her once ample curves had been whittled away by the years, leaving behind the contours of a scarecrow.

He reached for her as testimony to his words, but it was a false move. When he rolled over, he inadvertently passed wind: "*Insidia corporis veteris,*" he muttered. But, alert to the problem, Margot had struck her elbow against the wall to make a diversionary noise while he recomposed himself. What passed as discretion on the one side of the partition was an unwelcome interruption on the other. Her neighbors, who had been going at it with gusto and had clearly reached a critical point, responded with a volley of thumping. The friar and the prostitute looked at each other and burst out laughing. But the passing mention of a penitent gave Margot pause.

"Confession. I haven't been to confession since I was a young girl," she said in wistful voice.

"It's just as well, you know. You can't confess your evil way of life unless you are resolved to give it up. Otherwise you would be misusing the sacrament, and your sullied soul would reap yet another mortal sin." Marcus had responded automatically, without any malice of forethought. But his words stung like salt on a wound. *Sullied soul be damned*, she thought. The conversation had taken a bad turn. Suddenly, Margot was aware of the way his chins wobbled — that his eyes looked hard, and his mouth mean.

"Do you think my life so evil?" she asked.

This time he deliberated, not over the answer, but the delivery — belatedly aware that this was a delicate issue. "My dear, you know my feelings for you. Yet I can't lie. If you were to die without turning away from your wicked ways, you would undoubtedly go to hell." Margot gasped, but Marcus had his eye trained on an academic distinction, and was unstoppable.

"Prostitution is a necessary evil. As the blessed Thomas Aquinas says, prostitutes are like sewers: if you removed them, the excrement would overtake the city."

Margot was indignant. "What a filthy mind! Did this Thomas even know any women?"

"He was a friar; ergo he lived in a city; ergo he couldn't avoid encountering women. In fact, there's a tale about Thomas and a prostitute."

Marcus smiled at Margot, raising his eyebrows, waiting for some encouragement. Margot tried to look game, yet she was doubtful that this story would reflect well on her profession. She was right about that. Marcus proceeded to tell her about the infamous incident, which occurred when the Dominican Order was still in its infancy. Thomas wanted to join, but the family, ancient and proud, insisted that Thomas become one of the Benedictines of Monte Cassino. He resisted. So his brothers imprisoned him in the family castle for several months and even sent in a prostitute to break his resolve altogether. When she attempted to arouse him, he slapped her face and burst into tears. Margot was on the verge of launching a defense for the prostitute, who was, after all, only doing her job. But Marcus had reached the climax of his story: how Thomas's holy resistance occasioned a miracle. Two angels descended to gird Thomas in a holy belt, and he was never tempted again.

Margot didn't know what to make of this marvel. She wondered if it represented a kind of castration, but it seemed crude to ask explicit questions about a saint's genitalia.

"No wonder he didn't like prostitutes," she eventually responded.

"Well, at least he acknowledges that you are performing a public service."

"More than a service," she replied. "Sometimes I feel like we were taking away the sins of the world, just like Christ."

His hand went over her mouth. "The devil take your evil tongue," he shot back. "Only a crazy woman would talk that way," said Marcus.

"But I *am* a crazy woman," said Margot. Crazy woman — *feme fole* in French — was a common euphemism for prostitute. Margot pretended to relish the pun in order to conceal her hurt. Then she fell silent, and the friar was sorry. They were probably the two oldest lovers in Paris — much too old to fight.

He gave her an affectionate hug, saying, "Bring me some of that vinegar you call wine." Margot obeyed. It was part of the bill anyway — sex and a measure of wine.

Usually the entire engagement took about an hour. In fact, there wasn't much sex between them anymore. They just lay on the bed partially undressed and cuddled. They still had a good half of his visit in front of them, usually the best part. Now was the moment when they traded stories about their pasts, or at least their so-called pasts. Margot made up half of her stories, and assumed that Marcus did the same. But there was an unspoken rule that they were not to ask if the stories were true. It was her turn, and she had a good one.

"When I was a young woman, before I came to Paris, I spent some time in Flanders. I met a woman there called Concubina.

"That basically means 'slut' in Latin," he smirked. "Not much of a nickname."

"Don't interrupt! Anyways, her lover left her for another woman, so I became her roommate."

"You see? And now she's living with another slut." Marcus was enjoying himself.

"Shush!" *That was a rather nasty crack*, Margot thought, before continuing.

"One day her former beau wanted to admire his you-know-what, like men often do. He reached into his britches, but couldn't find it. He checked and checked again, but his body felt entirely smooth all the way down. No bumps or bulges. It had totally disappeared!"

Marcus shifted uncomfortably.

"Then he remembered Concubina's parting words: *You will have no luck in love when I am gone.* She must have stolen it! Concubina denied everything at first, but, when he threatened to call the authorities, she confessed. She took him to an old gnarled tree, and told him to climb up. So up he went to the top branch, only to discover a nest brimming with penises, moving all on their own! They were nosing around for the grains of corn scattered about."

"Oh, really!" Marcus said. He was incredulous, yet psychically smarting on behalf of his sex.

"Yes, really!" said Margot adamantly. She resumed her narrative: "Concubina shouted up that he should take one. So he naturally chose the biggest. 'You can't have that one,' she snarled. 'It belongs to the parish priest!'"

Marcus laughed. "Naturally the priest's is the largest; anyone could have told you that. Celibacy stores up our manhood: we become more virile by leaps and bounds. That's why we are all so magnificently endowed," he smirked, slapping her on the thigh. "But how did you come to know about this?"

Her answer was ready: "Because once Concubina had to go away for a week. I was asked to feed the little fellows."

"Oh that's rich — a dick-herdess. Were they difficult to tend?"

"Not if you knew how to handle them." They both laughed.

A door slammed. A woman had entered the upper room and was calling Margot's name.

"In a minute, *cherie*," Margot answered.

The two aged lovers raced to get their clothes back on.

"I'm sorry," mouthed Margot.

"I have to get back to the priory for dinner anyway," said Marcus in a hushed, but peevish voice. He put on the white alb and the black scapular — representative of virginity and self-mortification, he once told her. And then with a quick kiss on each cheek, he was gone.

Chapter 2: Heretics

Brother Martin

Everyone was going to the devil. Or so it had seemed to Anthony for some time. Students and masters alike were writing about the bodies of demons, demonic prophecy, pacts with Satan, alchemists conjuring demons, demons appearing as confessors, and popes demonically inspired to expound heretical doctrine. It was as if they were all taking dictation from the same source. The talk with Gerson had, strangely enough, come as a relief, because it allowed Anthony to articulate some of his apprehension. It was good to face this problem head on. Anthony's immediate task was to ascertain how widespread these interests were, but was unsure how to proceed. He couldn't go around saying: *Greetings. Do you ever have the urge to examine the apparent convergence of the divine and the satanic?* Since such questions were forbidden by university statute, who would own up anyway? Totally at a loss, Anthony decided to ask his old friend, Brother Martin, for his opinion. Martin had been one of his theology professors long ago: he was sharp, inventive, and one of the few Dominicans that Anthony could stomach.

The two of them were sitting in a corner of the scriptorium — the same room in which the disgruntled Rupert had sat in mute protest against the Lombard. It was just before Vespers, however, and there was no one there to be disturbed by their conversation. Martin's advice was direct and pragmatic.

"Your friend Baldwin had the right idea. Why not just stage some kind of public disputation and see who shows up?"

"Then we would probably all end up in prison," Anthony objected.

Martin just chuckled. "Oh, ecclesiastical prisons aren't so bad. Take it from one who knows."

It turned out that the old friar wasn't joking. Martin related his stint as an ecclesiastical felon to his younger colleague like it was yesterday. He had just taken his life vows when he was assigned as scribe to the papal curia of Benedict XII in Avignon. Before his elevation to pope, Benedict had been Jacques Fournier, bishop of Pamiers who had conducted a prolonged inquisition against the heretical Cathars between 1294 and 1324. The inquisition was centered on the town of Montaillou — a village in the Pyrenees that bordered on Spain. Every citizen above the age of twelve was arrested.

"When I first learned about Fournier's inquisition, I was amazed. The Cathars had been wiped out over a century before when the pope called a crusade against them. How could there be any left?" Martin was intrigued and determined to get his hands on the inquisition register.

"It was foolhardy, perhaps, but not impossible. Fournier had been so proud of his work that he had a copy made that accompanied him to Avignon. He was obsessed by his register. I often saw him perched on some parapet of the papal palace reading it."

When the personal secretary of his holiness fell ill, Martin saw his opportunity and volunteered as a replacement. He managed to smuggle the manuscript out of the pope's private office on his last day working there, but could not devise a plan for returning it. Predictably, the pope soon missed his favorite tome, and had everyone's room searched. When it was discovered under Martin's mattress, he was thrown into prison for a few weeks.

"I think everyone knew that I didn't really mean to steal it. They just put me in the prison to shake me up. Afterward, I was put on endless lavatory duty. My hands still smell like a latrine." He held them up, laughing. Then he cocked his head to one side, remembering.

"Actually, my jailor was a really nice chap. We used to play chess."

Anthony whistled in amazement. The old man was full of surprises. If Martin was a member of Benedict's curia, he must be in his seventies now. That was incredible: he looked fifty at most.

"Was the register really worth all that bother?" asked Anthony.

Martin was silent for a few moments, considering his answer. "It all depends on what you mean. If I had been looking for something to test my faith, it would certainly have been 'worth the bother.' But sometimes I wish I had never set eyes on it."

Anthony was intrigued. He had always regarded Martin as the paradigm of stability and common sense — not someone who could be easily undone by anything he read. But the old Dominican went on to explain.

"As you know, the Cathars were dualists. They believed the material world was created by Satan, and therefore irretrievably evil. It had never occurred to me that there were people with an entirely different worldview who still identified themselves as Christians — claimed to be the only true Christians, in fact."

"What about the account of creation in Genesis? I thought they accepted it," Anthony said.

"In a sense. But the devil is in the details, one might say. The general contours were the same, but their interpretation was radically different."

And so it was. According to their reckoning, Satan, God's second in command, led his angelic followers in a revolt. The Lord was so angry that He smashed a hole in the floor of the heavens with His staff and threw the miscreants out. The rebellious angels fell through the hole in droves for many years, until God eventually rose from His throne and stopped the hole up with His foot. Satan, proud and remorseless, went on to create the material world in imitation of the spiritual homeland. He forced his fellow angels into bodies — the very "tunics of flesh" in which God was said to have clothed Adam and Eve after they ate the forbidden fruit. The witnesses in Fournier's register referred to these bodies as "tunics of forgetfulness" because they worked like a drug, causing the angels to forget their true nature and spiritual home alike.

Martin sighed. "Tunics of forgetfulness! The image haunted me because, on some deep level, I felt it might be true. The body has such a dulling effect on the spirit."

The old monk paused, allowing a moment for his words sink in. He always did this in the classroom when he wanted to emphasize an important point. The scriptorium seemed very still, almost as if it were holding his breath for him to continue.

"Satan compelled the captive angels to copulate, generating new bodies: new prisons of flesh. The moment that someone's spirit was released through death, it was reincarnated — forced back into yet another prison. And so the exile from the spiritual homeland was perpetuated."

Anthony felt flummoxed, shaking his head in bewilderment. "A religion is supposed to provide comfort and support. Why would anyone align himself with a religion in which Satan was the ruler of the world?"

Martin gave a weary smile, but didn't answer — suddenly transported back to a time when it seemed as if Satan were the ruler of the world. He had just left the papal court and was back in Paris when the plague struck. Everywhere, people were dying; the air was filled with lamentations borne on the stench of putrefaction. Martin looked on helplessly as his entire family died: both parents, his two sisters, even their little dog, Scholastica. He couldn't blame the people who ran away — even the ones who abandoned family members to save their own wretched skins. Paris was so crowded back then; everyone said it was safer in the countryside, and Martin's priory was in shambles. Both the prior and the subprior had died, and the cellarer was filling in. No one would have objected if he tried to leave. So Martin packed the few things of value that had been overlooked by marauders in his parents' house, and set off on his own. The plague was said to have come from the south; perhaps if he journeyed north, he could escape it. He headed for the enceinte of the Right Bank, protecting his nose with the sleeve of his habit against the stench of death. A number of the houses he passed had crudely carved crosses on the door, with the supplication *Lord, have mercy on us*. But the houses were empty. There was no mercy, only devastation and lamentation. He had almost reached the Porte de St.-Louis when he was overtaken by a horse drawn cart, moving much too slowly. Martin soon saw why. It contained five passengers in all: a young couple and their three children. The entire family was dead. Their necks were covered with boils, and their fingers were black as if dipped in paint. The little ones were all under five years of age. They had clearly been trying to flee the city when death overtook them. Martin realized that it was impossible to hide from death. So he stayed in Paris, working in the community's infirmary. It was no stretch to believe that Satan was the absolute sovereign and Death his implacable viceroy. No compassionate God of love could have been responsible for this reign of horror — only an evil deity who thrived on pain and death.

Anthony watched his friend with concern. For a moment, the old Dominican almost looked his age. He soon rallied, however.

"Apart from providing explanations for the existence of evil and suffering, I would have to agree with you. Cathar doctrine is not very appealing."

Nevertheless, Martin privately wondered whether early Christianity had been any more palatable. Christ constantly said that His kingdom was not of this world. He required His followers to hate their parents, siblings, spouses, children — even their own lives — in order to be accepted as His disciples. If taken literally, Christ could Himself be described as a dualist. What Martin said out loud was more temperate, however.

"Remember that Christ's followers lived a poor itinerant life themselves, much like the Perfect, which is what the Cathars called their priesthood. Both groups had their eyes trained on heaven, not earth. Both were prepared to die for their religion."

"The church still has martyrs! What about your order's Peter Martyr?" responded Anthony.

Peter Martyr. He was the reason that Martin had wished to enter the Dominicans in the first place. But Peter, brave as he may have been, did not defy a coercive tribunal; as an inquisitor he was a part of a coercive tribunal. All Martin said aloud, however, was:

"Peter was ambushed in the pursuit of his office. So he did not choose a martyr's death, though one prays he was prepared."

"But you had known about the Cathars for years. Why did the register make such a difference?" Anthony asked.

"My dear Anthony, I'm afraid you are being rather obtuse. It all fits so perfectly with your present concerns." The old friar was wearing the maddening expression that he habitually wore when resisting student entreaties for help with some impossible question he had posed. He always insisted that they get there on their own. But Anthony was feeling rather slow-witted that day, and Martin, though disappointed that Anthony didn't want to play, relented.

"All right then. For the first time ever I considered Cathar claims seriously: that Jehovah, the creator God, could be Satan; that the Old Testament is simply a chronicle of the evil god's activities. That would mean that the church has been leading Christendom in devil-worship for centuries."

And suddenly the significance of what Martin was telling him became apparent. "In other words, from a Cathar perspective, the orthodox church mistook Satan and Christ. So our religion embodies the forbidden question."

Martin was pleased. "That's it! And after I read Fournier's register, I couldn't stop wondering: supposing we *have* mistaken Satan for Christ. Are we damned?"

Anthony had always regarded the Cathar faith as a kind of lunacy — not a belief system with any rigor or logic. And yet, people were still preoccupied with the possibility of worshipping Satan in error. Even though the Cathars were vanquished, their challenge continued. A key component was still missing, however.

"You said that the Cathars believed themselves to be the true Christians. But what about Christ?"

"He was sent to earth to show the way back to the celestial homeland," Martin responded.

"So they believed the same as we do: that Christ assumed flesh for our salvation," Anthony said.

Martin responded by rapping his knuckles sharply on the desk and shaking his head. "You are listening, but not hearing me." This infuriating adage was one of Martin's favorite pedagogic distinctions. "If the Cathars believed that matter was evil, it follows that Christ never assumed a body. He was pure spirit without any taint of flesh."

Anthony reflected for a moment before asking, "Wouldn't such contempt for the body cheapen human life, authorizing the most violent and brutal behavior?"

"But it didn't. The Perfect were strictly forbidden to interrupt any creature's cycle of incarnations by taking a life — especially a human life. They would never have called a crusade against us," said Martin.

"What about the incarnate Christ?" asked Anthony.

"Most Cathars denied that such a being existed," Martin replied. Then his expression darkened. "But I have read that some Cathars maintained there was a carnal Christ, born in Bethlehem and crucified in Jerusalem, and that this Christ was the embodiment of evil."

The First Vision

The rendezvous between the prostitute and her clerical lover had been interrupted by Marion: a member of the Dominican Faithful, now returning home from the meeting at St.-Jacques. Although Marion knew that Margot rented rooms to prostitutes, she had never known her to entertain clients herself. So it was with surprise that Marion saw a stout Dominican hustling out of Margot's cubicle. He looked at Marion with concentrated contempt, and then hurried down the stairs.

Marion was not a prostitute herself, but had only narrowly escaped becoming one. Her father had been a cloth merchant. When he died, Marion was left alone with abundant debts and the expectation that restitution be made for her father's alleged usury. The priest refused to bury her father in consecrated soil if the full amount wasn't paid. There was nothing left for a dowry. Marion tried to find work. Over eighty guilds in Paris accepted women, but she lacked the connections and cash necessary to become apprenticed in any of them. Eventually a man came to the rescue: an English squire named Richard, with whom she lived happily for about a year until he was called back to England by his lord. When Margot first encountered Marion, she was a shivering waif trying to eke out a living by selling flowers on the docks by the Seine, always on the look-out for Richard. Margot gave her a room and found her work as a seamstress. She had been living at Margot's for more than a year when she met Hainselin at the Thursday meetings. Very soon, they had fallen in love.

While at her needlework, Marion would prattle endlessly about her future with Hainselin: what she would wear for their wedding, whom she should invite, what they would eat, where they should live, even how many children they would have. She wanted to be married in June, right around the midsummer feast of John the Baptist before it was too hot. It was the time of year that Marion thought most beautiful, when all the world would be laid out in floral finery in sympathy with her own good fortune. The one time that Margot asked about Richard, Marion only bent her head over her needlework, never answering. She was thinking about a cherished keepsake — a strange little piece of moss that she kept in her coffer; the last thing she looked at before going to bed. Margot didn't bring Richard's name up again. Instead she listened, and nodded. She even smiled. But nothing Marion could say or do managed to remove Margot's sense of alarm. It wasn't just that Hainselin was a man and, hence, not to be trusted. It was that he shouldn't be trusted with Marion. She was one of those delicate women who could not endure the kind of mistreatment that Margot had accepted in her own life without question. Richard had been right for Marion: he understood how to care for something of great fragility without damaging it. But when Richard disappeared, Marion went to pieces and it fell to Margot to put her back together. It could never happen again — not because Margot would be unwilling to help a second time; rather because Marion would never be able to endure it. There must be no second time. And so Margot would sit patiently while Marion dreamed her future with Hainselin out loud — hoping against hope that there was no hole in Marion's vision of heaven or, if there were, that God, in His mercy, would cradle Marion in His heart so she wouldn't fall through.

Marion was especially talkative that night, but this time her conversation was divided between two men: Hainselin and Brother Jacques. Margot listened in her indulgent manner, asking the occasional question, more to reassure Marion that she was listening than from genuine curiosity. Then all at once, Margot felt the stabbing pain behind her eyes. She realized that one of her spells was coming upon her. Pleading fatigue, she retreated into her room and sat stoically in her chair, waiting for the veil of darkness to descend. Margot had come to fear these blackouts. They had started when she was around twelve years old, but she had never grown used to them. Once again she could feel the shadow world drawing her in, its somber veil blocking out sight and sound.

When at last it lifted, Margot found herself walking in the fields below Montmartre. It was lovely and peaceful and, for a precious moment, she felt happy. She broke off a small branch from a bush of wild rosemary and inhaled its spiced sweetness. In the distance a herd of sheep was grazing, filling the air with soft bleats of contentment. The sheep were white and black piebalds. At the edge of the flock stood a shepherd, dressed in work clothes browned by dirt. He nodded politely, touching his hood to acknowledge her presence, and Margot smiled back. Her eyes followed the flight of two dragonflies clamped together in love, their dazzling wings whirring with tints of blue and green. The crickets were chirping with spirit and a meadow dove was cooing softly behind her when, without warning, the world fell silent. The sound was shut out so quickly and completely that the effect was as startling as a loud noise. She looked over her shoulder: the flock of sheep was much closer than before, as if transported by magic. Two baby lambs stood at the edge of the flock. Margot had a sudden longing to sink her hands into their wool and pet them. Dropping to one knee, she plucked some grass and held it at arm's length. The lambs approached on wobbly new legs, stretching their pink lips forward in anticipation. But when they got close she noticed, in horror, that they had no eyes. Their eyes had been stitched shut so there was only wool fleece where the eyes should have been. By now, the entire flock surrounded Margot. None of them had eyes.

The Palimpsest

Hervey seemed to have misplaced his book of offices. He rarely consulted it and couldn't remember the last time he had seen it. But now some elder son was being knighted, and he wanted his sword blessed. There was a ritual for this, and Hervey had better find it.

He discovered the book in the presbytery, of all places. It could only have migrated there with the help of Felice. Was she really so desperate for Latin texts that she would resort to something as dull as church *ordines*? When Hervey opened the volume to the appropriate place, he started with surprise. The page was entirely covered with mysterious marginalia in thin spidery letters. The ink was as ephemeral as cobwebs, looking as if it could be smudged by a mere glance. Hervey was certain that these markings hadn't been there before.

Fascinated, he sat down at the table, trying to decipher the tiny letters. It was hard to make out, but the writer invoked the first person so often that it seemed to be a journal of sorts. He was gingerly turning a page when Felice appeared beside him. Her expression was sheepish.

"It turns out that your life of Peter Martyr was written on top of another text that had been scraped off. That's my transcription of the hidden text."

So the life of Peter was a palimpsest! Hervey knew that manuscript so well that it seemed impossible. He went over to the cabinet and removed a box, from which he lifted the manuscript with reverence. It had never been much to look at. There were no illustrations, or even colored letters at the beginning of chapters. It was written in a cramped cursive, and highly abbreviated with many a dot and squiggle. The abbreviations made the text much harder to read — especially considering the indifferent quality of the handwriting. He held a folio up to the window and squinted, his eyes traveling up and down its length. At first he could see nothing. Then he noticed a letter that was distorted as if it had been written on an uneven surface, causing the scribe's quill to dip into a small groove. When he ran his fingernails gently above the line of writing, he could feel scratches and indentations: he even began to perceive some very fine lines. Still, he couldn't make out any of the letters. Then it occurred to him that the original text might be written perpendicular to the one which later had been superimposed. This would mean that the original text ran horizontally along the parchment rather than vertically. Hervey turned the manuscript sideways and squinted in concentration. He could discern letters that, though effaced and written over, had never been entirely obliterated.

So the mysterious scribblings in the volume of *ordines* represented Felice's efforts at a transcription. The most heavily afflicted pages complemented specific rituals that she deemed inconsequential.

"War is a sin, so you can't bless a sword. And you yourself have told me that there are practically no virgins in the parish, so there are none to consecrate," she said.

Hervey suppressed a smile. Whatever Felice might have discovered, she had no right to efface church property.

"We have to buy some parchment," he said. "That means I'll have to dip into the money I've been putting aside for your dowry. When do you think you might marry?" Even though this was a real question for Hervey, when spoken out loud it sounded ridiculous. They both started to laugh.

Good to his word, Hervey very soon did acquire four quite large pieces of parchment — enough for a quire of eight when folded. They were not particularly fine specimens: two of them were quite discolored, as if they had been improperly tanned. The parchment had been assailed by warble flies, which had once laid their eggs in the hides of the poor beasts. The hatching larvae left substantial holes behind. The outer sides of the hide had been inadequately scraped, leaving a bumpy, rather hairy, finish. Nevertheless Felice was thrilled to have her own parchment. Hervey also produced an instrument for symmetrically pricking along the sides and a rule for drawing lines between the dots. These implements were topped off by a bottle of iron gall ink and a small horn for use as an inkwell. After preparing the parchment with care, Felice set about copying her efforts from the book of rituals. Hervey watched as Felice, no longer constrained by narrow margins, wrote in her characteristically fair and confident hand.

The text wasn't very long, but the transcription took several hours because it was three-tier. The top line repeated the letters as she discerned them on the page, including the abbreviations. Immediately underneath was a version in which the abbreviations were expanded into words. Felice had underlined the letters so that there would be no confusion over what she saw on the page and what she thought it signified. The bottom register provided a translation of the Latin text into the vernacular. This wasn't strictly necessary because the Latin was so simple. But the very sparseness of the text rendered it cryptic in spots: a translation allowed Hervey to both see, and challenge, her interpretation. Felice's expansions were purposefully on the conservative side: any ambiguous abbreviation was left as she found it.

The two of them leaned over the first folio together, careful not to get too close before the ink was dry. Hervey had been correct in his surmise. It was a terse, rudimentary journal written in an elementary schoolboy Latin. The account began abruptly, suggesting that they did not possess the journal in its entirety. It was dated according to the regnant year of some ruler, following the Roman system. Without knowing where it was written, it was impossible to know who the ruler was, or what year it was written — let alone by whom. All they knew for certain was that the journal must have predated the anonymous life of Peter Martyr.

Its first two entries were:

> ãñ xix aδ vii íδ. apʒ
> δesᵗo op vᵒ ÷ pft

> an*num* xix a.δ. vii íδ. aprílis
> δes*ero* op v*olo* *esse* pft

> *Year 19; 7ᵗʰ day before the Ides of April [April 7]. I left the
> OP. I want to be pft.*

> ãñ xix aδ xvii ƙaſ. mai
> Is. δesᵗít ofm man3 cû mᵉ ãíc' car'm'

> an*num* xix a.δ. xvii ƙaſ. mai
> Is. δes*erit* ofm man*et* *cum* m*e* *amicus* car*íssimus* m*eus*

> *Year 19; 17ᵗʰ day before the Kalends of May [April 15]. Is.
> left the OFM. He is staying with me. [He is] my dearest
> friend.*

Felice knew that *OP* stood for *Ordo Praedictorum;* Order of Preachers — the Dominicans, even as *OFM* represented *Ordo Fratrum Minorum;*
Order of the Little Brothers — the Franciscans. But if these expansions
were correct, it would mean that both the annalist and his friend were
not only deserters from the mendicant orders, but also collaborated in
their defection. It seemed odd to Felice, so the abbreviations were left as
she found them.

There were a number of entries detailing the mundane events in the
life of the author and his friend, Is., with whom he seemed to share lodgings. Then suddenly, a threat emerged — apparently coming from outside
the community.

> ãñ xíx aδ ív íδ. maí
> R. veᵗ cū exʳcíto

> annum xíx a.δ. ív íδ. maí
> R. venít cum exercíto

> *Year 19; 4ᵗʰ day before Ides of May [May 12]. R. came with*
> *an army.*

> ãñ xíx aδ víí kaſ. íun
> R. exívᵗ fř síſ př

> annum xíx a.δ. víí kaſ. íun.
> R. exívít símíſis pater

> *Year 19; 7ᵗʰ day before Kalends of June [May 26]. R. left.*
> *[He is] a brother like his father.*

The identity of *R* was a mystery, as were his comings and goings. Felice
was also aware that the expansion of *fr* as "brother" did not make much
sense.

The following two entries were even more opaque.

> ãñ xíx aδ ví íδ. íun
> ℳ. aegᵃ cmo eg3 mᵒít'

> annum xíx a.δ. ví íδ. íun
> ℳ. aegra cmo eget morítur

Year 19: 6ᵗʰ day before the Ides of June [June 8] M. is sick.
She needs the cmo. She is dying.

ãñ xíx aδ v íδ. íun
ℳ. ÷ mᵒtua pᵗ eδm

annum xíx a.δ. v íδ. íun.
ℳ. est mortua post eδm

Year 19; 5ᵗʰ day before the Ides of June [June 9]. M. is dead
after edm.

It occurred to Felice that *cmo* might represent some kind of medicine for M., but she was by no means certain. Neither Felice nor Hervey could make any headway with *edm*, however.

There were only a handful of entries for that fall — mostly to do with domestic matters like fuel and food. Then came a particularly enigmatic segment.

ãñ xx aδ ív íδ. ían
eᵒ Ís.q: š pftⁱ fiβʳ e c'ne
gᵒ gauδeã' crδˢ cãtãt

annum xx a.δ. ív íδ. ían.
ego Ís.que sunt pftí fibrí e carne ergo gauδeamus
crδs cantant

Year 20; 4ᵗʰ day before the Ides of January [January 10].
Is. and I are pfti. Free from the flesh. Therefore let us
rejoice. Crds are singing.

Hervey was careful to check this part of the transcription. Felice had always been sympathetic to the theologian Origen, who taught that that all sentient beings began as spirit, devolved into matter, but would eventually rise again as spirit. *Free from the flesh. Therefore let us rejoice*, put Hervey in mind of this doctrine.

"To be honest, I was surprised by these words myself. Still, I can't think of what else they might mean."

"Could it be 'free from *carmine*;' free from song? Maybe the *crd*s were terrible singers."

Felice didn't dignify this quip with a response.

"What could they possibly be celebrating?" Hervey continued, "The journal certainly hasn't been very festive so far." He frowned, considering the possibilities.

"Freedom from the flesh, one can only assume. But seriously, I think the verb has to be *gaudeamus*. What other verb beginning with *g* would fit? Can you think of one?" asked Felice.

Hervey could not. Nor could he shed any insight on the variations of *pft*. He felt rather useless. Felice had done all the hard work, and he had little to contribute.

The next fifteen entries or so were more of the same: lots of *pft*s, a few *cm*s, but still no possible clue as to what they meant. But then there was an entry that indicated a religious context for wherever the community encamped.

> ãñ xx aδ non. feƀ
> pᵉegⁱ ferūt pčs aδ pftˢ

> an**num** xx a.δ. non. feƀ.
> pe**regrini** feru**n**t pcs aδ pft**s**

Year 20; the Nones of February [February 5]. Pilgrims are carrying pcs to the pfts.

The presence of pilgrims suggested the place in question was a recognized shrine. But neither Hervey nor Felice could fathom what they might carrying. At first, Felice had expanded *pcs* as *pecunias*: money for making an offering. Hervey acknowledged this as a possibility, while noting that *pecunia* as a plural was rather arcane and an unlikely choice for such an unsophisticated author. Then Felice came up with the theory that the pilgrims were carrying *pisces*: fish.

"Pilgrimage is a penitential condition, after all. The pilgrim is theoretically fasting, so he shouldn't consume meat, but he is allowed fish," she reasoned.

"Wouldn't the fish rot?" objected Hervey.

"Not if they were salted," responded Felice.

Yet for all their ingenuity, Felice had to admit that her readings were tenuous at best. But she was not daunted.

"What if *ferunt* were translated as bearing rather than carrying? The pilgrims might be bearing *peccatas*, sins," Felice posited.

"But Felice, *peccatum* is neuter; so the plural ending is *peccata*. There is no such form as *peccatas!*" said Hervey, reflecting that Felice's eagerness was wreaking havoc with her grammar. "I also think that the whole concept of bearing, or carrying, sins to someone is rather bizarre," he continued.

They returned to the transcription. It would seem that later in the same year, the fortunes of the community began to decline — the pervasive sense of gloom quickening into full-scale disaster. The turning point was the following entry.

ãñ xx aδ v ƙaſ. íun
cᵗδˢ exũt ĩ nocte cũ fts ex ꓘ. ínqⁱ š occíδí
Ꞗ. ꓘᵗnδ & Ste' sꓔɦ. patíemʳ

an̲n̲u̲m̲ xx a.δ. v ƙaſ. íun.
cr̲δ̲s̲ ex̲í̲v̲e̲r̲u̲n̲t̲ ín̲ nocte cu̲m̲ fts ex ꓘ. ínqu̲í̲ su̲n̲t̲
occíδí Ꞗ. ꓘr̲n̲δ e̲t̲ Ste. . .u̲s̲ sꓔɦ. patíemu̲r̲

Year 20; 5ᵗʰ day before Kalends of June [May 28]. Crd[s].
left in the night with fts from A. inqu̲í̲ were killed. G.
Arnd. and Ste...us STh. We shall suffer.

The mysterious *crd*s again appeared — only this time they were not singing; they were slaying. Hervey, moreover, had a theory about who was being slain and, possibly, why.

"*Inq̇* could be expanded as *inquisitores*. The name of one of the inquisitors began with *G.*; the other one, *Ste*, was probably Stephen, hailing from a town named for Saint *Th*-something," he said.

Whoever the victims may have been, they seemed to have had powerful friends because the writer's community was soon attacked, presumably in retaliation. The ensuing entries were consistent with a state of siege, interspersed with accounts of dwindling provisions, austerities that resulted in hunger and thirst, and a general sense of dread. The last two passages that Felice had transcribed were poignant, despite their general obscurity.

ãñ xxi aδ non. mar
pftⁱ vocãt nos oʳaʳᵉ & δᵉ ꝑⱭƩ mɤte ſacʳme

annum xxi a.δ. non. mar.
pfti vocant nos orare et δicere ꝑⱭƩ multe ſacrime

*Year 20; Nones of March [March 7]. Pfti call us to pray
and to say PN. Many tears.*

ãñ xxi aδ xvii ƙaſ. apr
miſˢ cõgʳgavʳnt pftˢ cõbussʳnt cc

annum xxi a.δ. xvii ƙaſ. apr.
milites congregaverunt pfts combusserunt cc

*Year 21; 17ᵗʰ day before the Kalends of April [March 16].
The soldiers gathered the pfts. They burned 200.*

Father and daughter looked at one another in silence. Hervey eventually
cleared his throat and spoke.

"My dear, I believe we are reading a journal that belonged to a member of a heretical group — one that resisted the inquisitors with violence. And this brought about the community's demise."

This came as a surprise to Felice. She had always assumed that the murder of Peter Martyr was the exception. Now she learned that there were other instances in which the laity rose up against and even killed the inquisitors. She would have been interested in learning more about such incidents, but Hervey, who understood the church's reluctance to publicize such incidents, didn't want to prolong this discussion. Felice had a disconcerting way of looking awry at church policy.

"Well, that's as far as I have gotten," said Felice. "There isn't much more."

They were both startled by the sound of bells. It was beginning to get dark, and Hervey had to prepare for Vespers. Before leaving, he urged Felice to get rid of the evidence of her malfeasance, pointing to the book of *ordines*. Fortunately, it was disposed of very easily. Felice had been using her own concoction for ink, consisting primarily of charcoal and water. The letters were soon dispelled — though the affected folios would forever suffer from a somber affliction.

Montségur

Within a couple of days, Felice had finished the transcription. The rest of the entries provided details about the siege and the eventual denouement. By now, it seemed almost certain that the journal was written by a member of some heretical sect or other. But Hervey's knowledge of heretical doctrine was limited. Perhaps Anthony could help.

"So this is what was lurking under your precious manuscript all these years! Who would have thought?" said Anthony, his eyes sparkling with delight at the discovery. He agreed that it was clearly the journal of a heretic, probably a Cathar.

"Of course, the author could be a Waldensian. But the Waldensians hewed much closer to orthodoxy: they never presented a doctrinal threat parallel to Cathar dualism. That's why they are still around. The Cathars were more actively persecuted," said Anthony.

Even so, it was impossible to be sure without some kind of purchase on the mysterious abbreviations. Anthony immediately thought of Martin — a bibliophilic theological polymath who, it turns out, was especially apprised of the nuances of Cathar doctrine. He hadn't had a chance to visit the old Dominican since their discussion about the purloined Fournier register. So it was a rather strange coincidence that their next meeting should also involve a manuscript in distress, and very possibly of Cathar provenance. Anthony had checked Felice's transcription, which struck him as very sound. But he brought along both the transcription and the manuscript just in case.

When Anthony arrived, Martin was dictating to not one, but two scribes. Such was the nature of his mind that he could work upon two unrelated treatises simultaneously. It was said that Aquinas had that capacity, but Anthony had certainly never encountered it in anyone else, apart from Martin.

The old friar didn't mind being disturbed, however; in fact, he welcomed the break. He dismissed his scribes in a friendly enough way, but complained to Anthony that the prior must imagine him in his dotage. "One scribe can't spell and the other can't write! Did he really think I wouldn't notice?"

Martin spent less than five minutes with the transcription before he solved the mystery. The author was, as Felice had suspected, a defector from the Dominican Order who went to join the Cathars. Martin thought it possible that he was initially part of the inquisitorial entourage in the area. At first he was simply one of the believers or *credentes* in the sect (which explained the abbreviated variations of *crd*s), but eventually he became one of the Perfect (hence the repetition of versions of *pft*). The heretical community was in all likelihood the one established at the foot of the fortress of Montségur — located in the Northern Pyrenees on a truly daunting peak of about 5000 feet high. It had long been a Cathar stronghold: after the crusade, it became their chief headquarters and a place of pilgrimage. Dying believers were often carried there on horseback. The inquisitors referred to it as the "Synagogue of Satan."

"The place was flanked by three valleys, and could only be scaled on one side. So it was called *Mons securus;* the Safe Mountain. An ironical misnomer to be sure," Martin said with a sigh.

"What happened to them?" asked Anthony.

"One night a number of Cathar sympathizers slipped out of Montségur and combined forces with some *faudits* from Avignonet, which is where the inquisitors were staying." Martin pointed to abbreviations *fts* and *A.* in the transcription as he spoke. "They murdered the inquisitors while they slept. I believe there were seven victims. The leaders of the inquisitorial party were the Dominican, William (*Guillelmus*) Arnald, and the Franciscan, Stephen de St.-Thibéry — whose names are abbreviated here." Martin indicated the appropriate letters. "These names place the identification beyond doubt."

"*Faudits.* So the perpetrators from Avignonet had all been disinherited for heresy?" Anthony asked.

"More probably for their ancestors' heresy. Remember, the heretic wasn't just personally disinherited for his own error: all his heirs were likewise punished."

The sins of the fathers shall be visited upon the sons, Anthony thought to himself. One could certainly empathize with the outrage of the disinherited. In fact, it was difficult to imagine a strategy better engineered to inspire disaffection in heretical offspring — even those not initially inclined toward heresy. Very shortsighted on behalf of the church. No wonder the laity came to associate the inquisitors with greed.

According to Martin, it was the murder of the inquisitors that precipitated the siege, which lasted nine months in all. Eventually the besieging army managed to scale the rocks by night, and the fort was forced to surrender. There was a brief truce before the heretics who refused to recant were executed. Two hundred Perfect were burned in a single pit surrounded by palisades — hence the numerals *CC* in the journal.

"The presence of so many Perfect, incidentally, explains the pilgrims bearing fish. So your remarkable female scribe had it exactly right. The Perfect don't eat meat or any fruits of copulation, including eggs or dairy products. But they could eat fish because they were spontaneously generated without sex," said Martin.

Anthony wasn't sure that this was zoologically sound, but there didn't seem much purpose in disputing the point. "What about the abbreviations associated with some sick woman, M?"

"These would be references to the Cathar rituals: *cm* means *consolamentum*. It is a ritual laying on of hands administered by the Perfect that ends the cycle of incarnations, allowing the soul to return to the celestial homeland. Believers receive the *consolamentum* on their deathbed, after which they are expected to undergo a fast or *endura* — until they die. Here it is abbreviated in the accusative as *edm*."

Martin went on to explain that when the *consolamentum* is administered earlier, it serves as ordination to the priest caste. It renders the recipient complete or perfect — hence the name, Perfect. When a Perfect died, the succession of mortal lives likewise came to an end and the soul was liberated. But the path to perfection was arduous: an aspiring Perfect could only receive the *consolamentum* after a period of prolonged chastity, a lengthy series of fasts, and every other conceivable austerity. This high level of abstinence must be maintained throughout the Perfect's lifetime.

"And *PN*?"

"... is Pater Noster," said Martin. "The Perfect would lead the believers in the recital of the Lord's Prayer — the cornerstone of their prayer meetings."

"The same Lord's Prayer that we use?" asked Anthony.

"The very same."

Martin believed that the dates corresponded with the reign of Count Raymond VII of Toulouse, whose name was abbreviated as *R*. His overlord, Louis IX, had forced Raymond to take an oath to capture Montségur, but his efforts were half-hearted at best. The journal compares Raymond with his father, Raymond VI, who was believed to have heretical sympathies. Both father and son were hence designated as fautors. The abbreviation the author used was *fr*, which Felice had understandably expanded as *brother*. Martin wasn't convinced that the younger Raymond had heretical leanings.

"But the father was clearly sympathetic, if not an actual believer. He repented before his death, but the church refused to lift the sentence of excommunication. His son protested and insisted on an inquest. Over a hundred religious were willing to swear that Raymond VI had died repentant, but the pope wouldn't relent. So the elder Raymond's body remains unburied to this day, rotting in the house of Hospitalers of Toulouse."

This grotesque story led to a series of digressions into Raymond VI's efforts to stave off the crusaders from the North and his vilification at the hands of church chroniclers. To Anthony, it sounded as if the extent of the count's guilt was his desire to defend his vassals from persecution. Eventually they returned to the manuscript and the question of the younger Raymond's involvement in heresy.

"Even if he were entirely orthodox, I suppose Raymond wouldn't have taken any more kindly to inquisitorial interference than his father. Some blame him for the attack at Avignonet. It happened at one of his houses, although Raymond was apparently not present at the time."

By now they had reached the end of the manuscript, which proved to be abrupt and elliptical in equal parts.

> Is. vivit ñ m'rit' sp^r vivit cefo
> ī puteû te^rês
> Is. vivit non moritur semper vivit cefo
> in puteum terrens

What followed was illegible — just a jumble of indecipherable figures which Felice had copied as they appeared on the page.

And then finally:

> viδ3 me

There were no longer any dates; the handwriting had deteriorated drastically. But most of the writing was still legible. Martin read the transcribed words out loud.

"'Is. is alive. He didn't die. He lives forever. / I am hiding in the well, terrified.'" He skipped over the unintelligible characters to the very last words. "'He sees me.'"

Martin looked up at Anthony. "The writer avoided the fate of the other Perfect, but he may have met an equally tragic end. He is clearly frightened of someone named *Is*."

"But *Is*. is the abbreviation for his friend — the one who was perfected at the same time," said Anthony.

"Maybe it is someone else. *Is*. could stand for a lot of different names."

The two men stared at the last few lines in silence. Eventually Martin shook his head.

"Without more information, I doubt we will ever solve these riddles."

Chapter 3: Doubt

The Second Vision

The vision began beautifully. Margot was in the most splendid church, with rich stained glass — all in blues and reds — depicting scenes from the life of the Virgin. There was a labyrinth carved into the floor of the church like the one she had once seen at the cathedral of Chartres. One of her clients had driven her there long ago, and she still remembered it with awe. In the vision, Margot could smell the incense and hear the sound of a Mass being sung in the background. She wandered into a side chapel, empty except for a crucifix with some candles burning in front of it. The larger than life crucifix looked the same as the one in the church of San Damiano, which had once spoken to St. Francis.

At the foot of the cross were depictions of the saints who were present at the Crucifixion: Mary, the Blessed Virgin; Christ's favorite disciple, John; the holy harlot, Mary Magdalene; and the Roman soldier, Longinus. They were dwarfed by the giant figure of Christ. Above its head was a smaller image of Christ anticipating His future ascension, attended by admiring angels. At the very top was the hand of God reaching out of the heavens. The crucified Christ was wearing a simple loincloth. He did not seem nailed, but superimposed on the cross as if floating. The blood from His wounds welled up like roses. Francis of Assisi had experienced great pain from his stigmata. But this Christ was not in pain. His beautiful deep-set eyes were open; His bearded face was serious, but serene. Brown hair gracefully framed His face; a large crossed nimbus adorned His head.

Margot was reassured by the presence of Mary Magdalene, dressed in the brightest red — the color of love. If Mary could be forgiven for her sins, perhaps Margot could as well. So she knelt before the crucifix and prayed — asking forgiveness for her squalid existence, begging Christ to come into her life. The hand of God moved, as if in acknowledgement of her petition. All at once the figures were in motion, talking to one another in hushed tones, their eyes focused on Margot. The heads of all the angels swiveled around, shifting their gaze from the small figure of the ascending Christ. Last of all, the great image on the crucifix stirred. It fixed its eyes on her and smiled, and then proceeded to step down from the cross, descending by an invisible staircase. Margot was elated. This was all she had ever wanted. Here was her true bridegroom, the consummate lover whose blood would wash away her sins. Her body swayed, agitated by a heightened degree of hope.

But as the Christ figure grew nearer, Margot's feelings changed. His great unblinking eyes bore down on her; massive arms outstretched for a crushing embrace. Her elation turned to terror. Blood from the crown of thorns ran down His face; blood oozed from His wounds; blood streamed from the gaping hole in His side. Margot tried but was unable to scream. Still the bloody Christ advanced. He had almost reached her when she finally managed to wake herself up.

Felice and Baldwin

There was no rest for Felice until she had learned everything conceivable about the Cathars. She exhausted her father with questions he couldn't answer, for which she felt guilty. Not only had he been forced to abandon the university because of her, but now here she was reminding him about his educational deficiencies. It pained her to pain him, yet she couldn't hide her frustration. The church of St.-Jacques had a number of books, but most of these were collections of ritual or prayer books — an ad hoc assortment that did not warrant the name library.

So Hervey was determined to get his hands on some books. To be sure, the requisite books concerned heresy, which was rather unnerving because of his daughter's proclivity for alternative viewpoints. Heresy was the ultimate alternative. Hervey was confident that, at root, Felice was a faithful daughter of the church. Still, every time she came up against a received truth, she couldn't help but test it. Some people were custodians of tradition; others were challengers. And, as with most natural challengers, her intellectual gifts were considerable; of this Hervey was in no doubt. He only regretted that such an astute mind should be hobbled by circumstance. If Felice were a nun she would at least have access to a library of sorts. But then there was the taint of illegitimacy. Even if Hervey had the money for a convent dowry, Felice would still be barred from any community venerable enough to possess a decent library. Although Hervey never spoke to Felice about these painful matters, he had little doubt that she was aware of the impediments associated with bastardy. Felice was always two steps ahead of everybody else.

Felice's desire for books overrode any possible trepidation that Hervey might have about their heterodox content. He would exert what pressure he could on Anthony. Fortunately, Anthony understood perfectly. Empathizing with Felice's curiosity over the Cathar journal, Anthony agreed to smuggle (that was the only word to describe it) some works on the Cathars from the cathedral library for her perusal.

On this lovely day in April, it was Anthony whom Felice awaited. Hervey had been called away on parish work: a tanner's wife had delivered prematurely, the child was weak, and an emergency baptism seemed in order. So Felice was left alone with her spinning, barely able to contain herself for excitement. Eventually she abandoned the task altogether in favor of what had become an almost obsessive pastime: examining the secret journal and puzzling over its final entries. But by the time she heard the bells ringing for Nones, her excitement was gradually subsiding into disappointment. Anthony wasn't coming.

And this is how Baldwin first beheld Felice: at a battered wooden table in the presbytery, bent over a manuscript. The door was ajar and he could see her in profile through the doorway. Afternoon sunlight spilled through, illuminating her right cheek and igniting the red tones in her hair. The subdued homespun of her clothing cast the brilliance of her tresses into relief. Her right hand, which was holding a stylus, threw an impossibly long shadow, replete with fingers of unlikely length but elegant taper. Felice's concentration had rendered her so still that he could see her breast rise and fall with every breath. Baldwin was enthralled: he couldn't remember having ever seen a woman reading before — at least not with such intensity and confidence. She didn't need to form the words with her lips, like a child mouthing unfamiliar food. And he had never seen a woman whom he thought so beautiful.

Without warning, Felice looked up.

"But you're not Master Anthony," were the first words that came to her. Baldwin, blushed, disconcerted to have been discovered watching her. Yet, he couldn't help but laugh.

"And you, most certainly, are not Father Hervey."

Felice regarded the friendly looking intruder with interest. Baldwin was standing in the open doorway with the sun behind him, lit by the same rays that illuminated Felice. She had to shield her eyes from above to see him properly. For all his somber clerical garb, he looked glorious — his golden hair curling in every direction, creating a halo effect. He reminded her of the smiling angel of Reims. There was a short silence, then they both laughed. Felice stood up and the two of them introduced themselves, bowing slightly as they exchanged names. Baldwin explained that Anthony had been detained, and had entrusted him with the delivery of the books, instructing that the package be placed directly into the hands of Father Hervey.

"I hope you don't mind waiting. I am expecting him shortly." Felice didn't think there was any point in explaining that the books were really for her. Since Baldwin made no demurral, Felice went on to suggest that they sit outside. The weather was finally warm enough so that Felice only needed a light shawl.

Baldwin was unaccustomed to female company and, at first, the conversation was rather halting. Felice, however, was used to cajoling and encouraging even the most truculent of parishioners. Eventually her gentle, but persistent, inquiries brought Baldwin out of his shell. In no time he was describing the evening of the fateful disputation.

"It's censorship, plain and simple. In fact, I am not even supposed to discuss the matter!" he complained. He privately thought that this was just as well: no woman would be able to follow his learned perambulations.

Felice may have intuited Baldwin's tacit misogyny, for she was prompted to say: "Oh, but I imagine it would be safe to discuss it with me. I am, after all, a woman: deformed at birth, indiscreet by nature, and shockingly simple-minded. I probably won't be able to follow whatever it is you have to tell me and, if I do, am destined to forget it."

Baldwin glanced at her in surprise, not knowing what to think. It is true that Aristotle referred to the female as a deformed male (and Thomas Aquinas concurred, though he added that it was a fortunate error). But was this woman really aware of the learned tradition that deprecated her gender? Even if she were aware, it was strange that she seemed complicit with its determinations. Then he observed the hint of a smile around the corners of her mouth. *I am a fool: she was being ironic.* Female ironist, or not, any doubts that Baldwin had about Felice's aptitude were vanquished and he embraced this opportunity to air thoughts on a subject that had become very near to his heart.

Felice, for her part, was captivated. "So, if someone were to worship Satan instead of Christ, what would it ultimately mean? Could that person achieve salvation?"

Delighted by her question, Baldwin meticulously laid the evidence before her, reflexively framing it in terms of the pros and cons of a disputation. He told her about the great Abelard and the ethic of pure intention: that a person was innocent, provided that he was following the dictates of conscience. Practically all authorities agreed that conscience was morally binding, and yet, they also recognized that conscience was fallible.

"Thus an erroneous conscience was still morally binding. So a person could, in good faith, make the mistake of worshipping Satan," Baldwin wound up.

Caught up in his disputational mode, Baldwin's eyes were fixed on some invisible opponent at an indeterminate point in the distance. But his monologue tapered off when he glanced over at Felice, who now seemed totally abstracted. Was she listening at all, he wondered?

In fact, Felice had been listening very intently. She was struck by that fact that conscience was, in a certain sense, divine: it retained its moral imperative even if it contradicted church teaching. This concept resonated with Felice. It meant that a heretic was not just the putrid limb of clerical metaphor, but also a person of conscience. A merciful God would have to be forgiving of a heretic's conscientious errors. But what if errors weren't in good conscience? What if they were vicious and cruel? *What if the persecution of heretics was just such an error?* Felice would later recognize this moment as a monumental turning point in her thoughts.

Although initially disconcerted, Baldwin welcomed Felice's temporary abstraction since it gave him the opportunity to stare unabashedly at this most fascinating of women. He never knew women could think this way. In fact, he had never bothered to think about whether women could think. But now he found himself desperately wanting to know what she thought — particularly what she thought of him.

At length she spoke. "The Cathars *do* believe that we are worshiping Satan instead of God. What if they are right, and *we* are the heretics? According to the tribunal of conscience, would we still be saved?"

This simple question achieved something that Master Anthony had often thought impossible: it succeeded in unnerving Baldwin. Despite his inclination for risky inquiry, Baldwin had never been able to see this far outside the paradigm of orthodoxy. His university education, for all its rigor, helped to ensure that he would not. So the very idea that orthodoxy might be heresy — which meant its enforcers might be the real heretics, not the people they persecuted — had hitherto been unthinkable. Felice's question had the effect of humanizing the faceless heretic, even as it stripped orthodox enforcers of their humanity. For the first time ever, Baldwin realized that, while he had thought at length about heresy, he had never thought about heretics. They had always been like fixed stars in some ideological firmament: obstinate and unmovable in their error. He had never considered them as malleable, vulnerable individuals afflicted by the burden of conscience as were the members of the true church. Of course he knew, at least theoretically, that an individual who was orthodox could drift into heresy and vice versa. Still, on the deepest level, he had imagined heretics born with their perversity. He reasoned that nobody would actively seek a deformity; who, then, would deliberately choose heresy?

It was at this juncture that Hervey returned. Baldwin introduced himself, handed over the books, and left. Hervey found Baldwin's farewell to his daughter overly solicitous, but Felice seemed too preoccupied to notice. For the moment she forgot all about the books. She felt as if she were seeing the church for the first time with a dark clarity. What if the Cathars were right, and the Christian community was worshiping a Satanic Christ? If this were the case, then the so-called Christians would be guilty of murdering the true followers of Christ — the Cathars. One might object that the church wasn't to blame: that the pseudo-Christ had lured its members away from the path of righteousness. But was this really the case? One of the things that Christ was most adamant about was that you should never take a human life. Both the church and the Cathars acknowledged this to be the case. But the so-called Christians killed anyways — perhaps to their damnation, while the Cathars died as martyrs.

Impending Crisis?

Anthony found the Chancellor exactly where he had left him: poking around in the pieces of parchment that were arranged in discrete piles on his desk.

He looked up with a frown, "Are you here to tell me the end of the world is nigh?"

"Frankly, Chancellor, I came here confident that you would tell me."

Gerson laughed. Apart from Gerson's penchant for caustic word-play, already in evidence when he was a student, this was the first time that Anthony had detected anything resembling a sense of humor in the Chancellor. He had never seen Gerson laugh. And for Gerson's part, it was the first time in a long time that he had laughed. It felt good. Gerson leaned back and smiled.

Anthony took this as encouragement and proceeded to report what he had learned about academic trends. As he suspected, the interest in the pseudo-Christ turned out to be considerable. A number of scholars, students and masters alike, had taken the problem to what would be the next logical level by asking whether one can win merit from a heart-felt worship of the pseudo-Christ. When Gerson attempted to dismiss such pursuits as the curiosity of the young and impetuous, Anthony deftly refuted this assumption.

"Your predecessor, Peter d'Ailly, disputed the question of whether an illiterate who is instructed in heresy by his bishop can win merit by adhering to that heresy, and resolved that he could," Anthony pointed out. This was something of a blow to Gerson, who had immense respect for Peter. He was a scholar of substance who had long since left the levities of youth behind.

Anthony watched the Chancellor, trying to gage the effect of his words. He knew from experience that Gerson was stubborn. He could not be led or drawn; he did things according to his own internal processes. Anthony was more than ever convinced that the question of mistaking Satan for Christ was not merely academic: it was symptomatic of a more general crisis afflicting Christendom. But he had to choose his words carefully.

"Chancellor, I have come to believe that Christendom is currently being tested, and it all comes down to questions of discernment."

Apart from a skeptical lift of his brow, Gerson made no answer.

"On the most apparent level, there is the papal schism. I have had parishioners seek my advice over who is the real pope, fearful of inadvertently committing a mortal sin by venerating the wrong one," said Anthony.

The Chancellor shifted uncomfortably. He preferred to see the schism in terms of the fallibility of God's servants; that a bunch of bumbling cardinals had made a terrible mistake. To his mind, it hardly qualified as a pitched battle between good and evil.

Anthony continued, "The pope is the vicar of Christ; debating who is the real pope is very much akin to debating who is the real Christ. It is conceivable that one of the alleged popes knows that his claim is fraudulent, which would place him in league with the devil. The same issues are raised by the war with England. Two men claim to be the rightful heir to the French throne. Since the king is God's anointed on earth, the question of whose claims to kingship are legitimate is akin to asking who truly represents God."

Gerson winced. The war with England was always there: the pestilence that sapped the strength of France. The Truce of Leulinghen may have been renewed, but everyone knew that the peace was fragile and war could break out at any time. Meanwhile, Anthony had risen to his feet and was beginning to pace back and forth unconsciously. Gerson's eyes followed him, reminded of his student days. Anthony used to pace like that at decisive points in the lecture.

In fact, Anthony had reached such a juncture: he wasn't sure just how much he should reveal to the Chancellor. There was no doubt in Anthony's mind that the series of convergences in his own life spoke to the matter at hand. The evidence wasn't empirical; it was diffuse, anecdotal, and personal. Even so, he believed God was revealing something important. Sharing his personal insights with the ever-querulous Gerson, however, was not a pleasant prospect. Even so, it was Gerson who had called upon Anthony to look into the matter of the Miraculous Bleeding Hosts. It was Gerson who summoned Anthony when he was on the verge of expelling Baldwin. And now the two of them were involved in a collaboration regarding spiritual discernment. Surely this too was God's will.

Anthony decided to trust Gerson. He first told him about the marvels associated with Brother Jacques, and how the parish of St.-Jacques was becoming a veritable matrix for issues of discernment. Then he went on to relate the conversation with Martin, dwelling particularly on the Cathar contention that the Christian God was really Satan. He kept quiet about the remarkable Cathar journal, however. Gerson would certainly be interested and want to see it, if only for its peculiar history. Yet Anthony was hesitant. He told himself that the journal didn't really speak to questions of discernment, apart from providing a testimonial to the Cathar faith. Besides, Anthony needed first to obtain the permission of its owners. And Anthony was also silent about Baldwin's current line of research.

Gerson found Rose's case the most compelling part of Anthony's narrative — especially because it revolved around the same man whose Mass resulted in the Miraculous Bleeding Hosts. To his mind, miracles got to the heart of the matter. Christ had warned that there would be many false Christs who would show *great signs and wonders*, deceiving many. The fact that the friar claimed merely to have awoken the girl from sleep may, on the surface, seem humble.

"But when Christ raised the daughter of Jairus from the dead, He also said that she was only sleeping. So the friar's remark could harbor considerable hubris," observed Gerson.

There was a marked change in the Chancellor's tone. Initially he had been cantankerous and resistant. In the discussion of miracles, however, Gerson was not only much less contentious, but even keenly interested. Encouraged by the more collegial attitude, Anthony took his leave. He was almost out the door when Gerson asked:

"And how is Master Baldwin? I am correct in assuming that he has become a master by now?"

Anthony nodded.

"Is he behaving himself?"

"He is doing his best. But his current work fits the pattern I have been describing."

Of course Gerson wasn't satisfied with this parting enigma and required Anthony to sit down again and explain. Anthony sighed, bracing himself for the reemergence of Gerson's prickly double.

"Baldwin had selected an entirely unobjectionable topic to treat as a disputed question after he finished his commentary — the soul. His initial focus was the mind-body relation in rapture, including instances when a holy person actually levitates," said Anthony.

"That makes perfect sense: the miraculous revelation of body and soul as a psychosomatic unit," responded Gerson, nodding.

"Unfortunately, his research turned up numerous instances of individuals who were elevated by the devil. Now Baldwin is working on divine versus diabolical rapture," said Anthony, bracing himself for Gerson's response.

But Gerson did not explode: he only made a derisive sound of exasperation. "I refuse to consider that evidence of anything except of the young man's perversity."

Anthony, who was extremely fond of Baldwin, was nevertheless in partial agreement with this indictment. He fretted on the way back to his room, concerned that he may have gotten his young friend into still more trouble. Anthony would have been relieved to know that the Chancellor was no longer thinking about Baldwin at all, however; he was thinking about Brother Jacques, wondering if his miracles could be true. A deep longing arose in Gerson's breast: how he longed to meet a truly holy man!

Sleep eluded Anthony for the longest time that night. His conversation with the Chancellor kept running through his mind — especially the portions concerning Brother Jacques. What did the friar mean when he said that Rose had only been sleeping? It is possible that the friar was, himself, something of a naïf, and meant it literally. Yet it seemed more likely that he was tacitly comparing himself to Christ. But, was that so bad? Weren't they all supposed to imitate Christ? Supposing Jacques knew that he had been the vehicle for a miracle. How would that feel? How was he supposed to behave? Was he supposed to remain quiet? Maybe not. If a miracle were sent to demonstrate God's power and glory, thereby reaffirming the faith, to keep silent would defeat the purpose. It would be the equivalent to hiding God's light under a barrel. And yet, Christ's miracles were generally accompanied by the dictum: *Go and tell no one.* Perhaps this level of discretion would be a truer form of imitation.

It was difficult not to be skeptical: there were so many fakes. In his own village there had been the case of Donna Barbara — an old woman who allegedly lived in an ecstatic trance. She was sustained entirely by God's love, existing without sustenance or even a need to void herself. There was a constant procession of people at the door of her little cottage — all with a request, a wish, a prayer; all bearing their discreet offerings. They would file past the bed where Donna Barbara lay, oblivious, in her state of grace, an otherworldly smile fixed upon her face. But then there was the day that Anthony was taken there to pray for the soul of his father. Over-awed in the presence of such great holiness, he had dropped the coin that was intended as an offering, and it rolled under the bed. Before anyone could stop him, he dove to retrieve it, disturbing a concealed tray of food and upsetting a chamber pot. A malodorous exposure, indeed. Ever since then, Anthony had just naturally assumed that most, if not all, miracles were faked.

Anthony dreamed about Gerson that night — only it wasn't Gerson, the careworn Chancellor. It was a much younger Gerson. He looked exactly the way Anthony remembered him in class, only there was a difference: he looked happy. He was seated among a circle of students, laughing. It was the first time that Anthony had ever seen him with any companions. Then Anthony realized this wasn't just any group of students; it was Anthony's old friends, the storytellers. There they were, seated around the fire, drinking wine from the single earthenware flask that was being passed around: Hervey, Gerson, Baldwin, and a youth with red hair whom Anthony recognized but whose name eluded him. It was Gerson's turn to speak. Somehow Anthony knew he was going to tell a story about Simon. But he mustn't! The others knew as well. Anthony could see the fear in their eyes. They knew that if Gerson even said the name that something horrible would happen. They wanted to warn Gerson; to stop him! But they couldn't speak. None of them was capable of saying anything. Gerson was just beginning his story when Anthony awoke.

Chapter 4: The Faithful

Siblings

The Faithful sat in the corner of the nave of St.-Jacques-de-la-Boucherie waiting for Brother Jacques. Alicia glanced sideways: there was Marion talking to Hainselin. She looked more like a fake damsel from a romance than a penitent, one of the fair-seeming ones who turns out to be a demon. Yet Hainselin, like all those foolish knights before him, seemed entirely taken in. Once Alicia had thought herself in love with Hainselin. He was doing some work for her father — something to do with the roof. Was it leaking? She couldn't remember. But she found herself making excuses to go outside and talk to him. He was so sweet and gallant, always making a slight bow when she approached — even when he was on the ladder! Just the sight of him used to make her heart pound. Had he ever found her attractive? Not that it mattered. They couldn't have been a match. Father would never have consented to someone with such limited prospects.

Alicia recognized that this particular door was closed to her. She had chosen the celestial bridegroom over any temporal husband. She'd begged her parents to let her enter a religious order, like Rupert, but they refused. They were convinced that she would grow bored with her "virginal nonsense" and make a "good" marriage — meaning the kind that would advance the family. How typically selfish! The communal life of a monastery is what Alicia longed for. It would have provided structure for her life: to be chanting the opus dei with her sisters, her days punctuated by the ringing of the canonical hours. Living at home with her parents, she was left too much to her own devices: her only responsibilities were to pray, meditate, and cultivate a deeper relationship with God. But it was no use. Her spiritual life was as flat and colorless as her material life — tedious, disappointing, lonely.

Just when Alicia imagined things couldn't get worse, they did. Her aggravated disaffection was evolving into an acute crisis of faith. That homily about St. Gregory's Mass was so strangely timed: could Brother Jacques somehow have known about her doubts? Had he guessed that, in her heart, Alicia was not much different than the woman who mocked the mystery of the altar? Alicia was afraid of going to hell, but she just couldn't help herself. The very idea of eating Christ's real body made every mental impiety run riot. If Christ were really in the sacrament, He must have been as big as a mountain! Then it was impossible not to wonder what happened to the Host *after* it had been ingested. Digestion and defecation were hardly the stuff of divinity. Was she the only person afflicted by such skepticism? As far as she knew, yes. She had heard about all these female mystics who seemed to revel in consuming Christ: they were said to receive the Host from Christ Himself, drink from the wound in His side. One German widow even claimed to have received Christ's foreskin in her mouth during Mass, for heaven's sake! Alicia was divided between envy and disgust. Why didn't God distinguish her? She was a virgin, after all. Many of these women were matrons. That he should prefer women who were defiled over those who were still intact went against everything she had ever read. At the same time, the spiritual consolations that these women received seemed so unspiritual.

Alicia looked over at Hainselin again: *I hate Marion. I hope the red plague strikes her. Perhaps some pockmarks would teach her humility!*

But then Brother Jacques was suddenly in their midst, interrupting these bitter thoughts.

"I have come to speak to you of love. A rich prince seeks your hand. He lives in NearFar — a remote land, to be sure, but one that sometimes seems so close that you can feel its enchanting breezes on your face. This prince has looked everywhere for a virginal bride, as pure as the soul that resides in each of you. At last, he has found you. Enraptured by your beauty, he has commissioned a picture to be painted of your soul the way it really is — naked, gleaming, exquisite. But this is not how your soul appears at present. Instead, it is dressed in the plain clothes of a traveler. Its garments are muddied with the dirt of sin, wrinkled by ennui, torn by doubt. Your soul has travelled a great distance to reach the prince, traversing mountains, forests, thickets of thorns. When it finally arrives at

NearFar, your soul feels weary and unlovely. But do not be dismayed. The prince has sent his servants to watch for you. They have prepared a bath, scented with the most delicate fragrances — with frankincense, lavender, rose water. The sorrows disappear as the delicious waters wash over you. The servants dry and anoint you with perfume. And then the Virgin Mary arrives to help your soul dress so it will look splendid and voluptuous for her son — just as a bride should look for her groom. Finally, your soul is being led to the marriage chamber..."

Alicia closed her eyes, his words filling her senses. Brother Jacques was speaking to her. She knew he was. He had sensed all her sorrow and disappointment. He recognized the shame she experienced over her doubts; that it was this shame that had kept her from confession. She was afraid of revealing just how imperfect she was in the love of God. Without confession, she hadn't dared receive communion, afraid she would *drink to her own damnation*. These fears had vanished. For the first time in weeks, Alicia made a full confession, disclosing all her misgivings and even her blasphemous thoughts. She laid bare her spiritual vanity — the desire to be singled out by God. When Brother Jacques absolved her, she believed herself to be shedding the sullied rags of doubt that had been smothering the beauty of her soul. Now she did indeed feel ready, scented and lovely to behold — ready to partake of Christ's feast. She was the bride who was about to give herself to the celestial bridegroom from NearFar.

It was during communion that it finally happened. At the point when Christ enjoined his disciples to drink his blood, Brother Jacques approached Alicia with the chalice. All at once she was filled with a great thirst, which she knew could only be sated by this. She drank deeply. The liquid was delicious — so fragrant and sweet. She looked up in gratitude toward the figure of Christ, suspended from the cross in such pathos, the eyes shut in pain and exhaustion. *Christ died for me. He died for me. Now He has come for me.* The great eyes opened and looked down on her with a gaze as lucid as it was penetrating. But Alicia was unafraid; indeed she was prepared. The eyes were lit by a flame that expressed longing and desire — a flame which, in turn, enflamed Alicia. She felt the stirring of a delicious warmth: a sensation beginning in her upper thighs, a slow circular motion as gentle as a lingering caress, and yet powerful. Gradually the feeling spread — inching its way into Alicia's deepest recesses. Her entire lower body began to throb with desire. What had begun as a warm glow developed into an intense heat, not derived or generated by anything else, but a living source in its own right. Lightning incarnate. At first this energy remained coiled, in all its vigor, at the base of her spine. But then it began to unwind itself, creeping slowly up her back, vertebra by vertebra, like a serpent emerging from a long sleep. Alicia caught her breath. There was a density building in the very core of her being. An angelic hand seemed to be caressing her heart, massaging its lobes, encouraging it to open like flower. Little flames flickered up and down her spine, creating an achingly sweet pressure at the base of her skull. An explosion of bright blue light, and her body was bathed in delectable flame. Her eyes never left the crucifix.

Alicia moaned softly. Her discontent was vanquished; her prayers answered.

After Rupert's interview with the prior, he walked back to his cell, deep in thought. A Franciscan with a vocation to preach to the Dominican Faithful. Well, why not? Of course, one had to be careful. It was possible that the man was really a lecher, or at least had a weakness for women, who decided it was more discreet to indulge this weakness outside his own order. The Thursday meetings would be an excellent hunting ground for a cynical predator. There were always more women than men. He thought of his sister, Alicia, wondering how she was doing in her quest for God. He would visit his family's home in the morning and have a talk with her. Peter Lombard would have to wait.

Rupert's parents weren't expecting him. They were so happy to see him, and made such a fuss, that he felt guilty for not coming more often. He accepted a cup of mulled wine, with the pungent fragrance of cloves, and sat with them for a while, exchanging news.

"And how goes the great commentary," said his father, raising his eyebrows as he always did when referring to Rupert's intellectual endeavors. Rupert interpreted this, correctly as it happens, as tacit sarcasm. Since he was the eldest son, his father had expected him to take over his business. Thank heavens that his brother had no scholarly ambitions. All he needed was some training in the notarial skills for keeping accounts. He was at school now.

"It g-g-goes," said Rupert, giving what had come to be his stock answer while staring into his cup. It was unusual for Rupert to stammer within the intimacy of his family circle: the fact that he did on this occasion was a measure of his distress. Then followed the inevitable question, which always made Rupert cringe.

"When do you expect to be done?" — this time spoken by his mother. Her curiosity was rewarded by a reproachful look; he had thought that, at least from her, he could expect some mercy.

"It's difficult to say. I am in a tricky sp-sp-spot right now." Husband and wife exchanged glances. His answers were always so evasive. It's not as if they were scholars who could follow the intricacies of his commentary. But they weren't idiots either. They had been properly catechized, and certainly knew the seven sacraments. He might try to include them a little.

"Where is Alicia?" said Rupert, abruptly changing the subject.

"At church. We are expecting her any time now," her mother answered. Five minutes passed in rather desultory conversation. Then the front door opened, and they could hear the rustle of a servant helping to remove someone's outer garments.

"That's probably Alicia now."

Rupert seldom sought his sister out. In fact, he never did. There was no point. She had always struck him as someone who was beyond help, wallowing in self-pity. A sense of discontent had been permanently etched on her face, as if she never received what she considered to be her due: her mouth was often pulled down at the corners as if she had just swallowed vinegar. He hadn't seen Alicia for some months, an omission he felt rather guilty about. After all, friars weren't cloistered like other monks: he could easily have stayed in better touch with his sister.

So when Rupert finally saw Alicia, he was entirely unprepared for the change. She was radiant. Catching sight of Rupert, she immediately came over and kissed his hand. Rupert stared at her in disbelief. For the first time ever he thought she was beautiful; what he did not realize was that, beautiful or not, for the first time ever he was seeing her happy.

Rupert wanted to be alone with Alicia before raising the subject of Brother Jacques and the prayer meetings. It was too difficult to have a private conversation with his parents hanging on his every word. So he suggested a walk. Alicia was happy to oblige, even though she had just arrived home. Husband and wife smiled at one another. They had always hoped that their two eldest children would become closer. Maybe they were finally witnessing a possible benefit from a shared religious inclination.

Far from abating, Rupert's amazement over his sister's demeanor only grew. Her radiance was reflective of an overall change in her disposition. Strolling with her was pleasant; conversing with her easy. Thirty minutes went by before Rupert remembered why he had come.

"Alicia, I understand that your prayer group now has found a leader — a Franciscan, I believe." An awkward beginning, but his sister didn't seem to notice. Instead she turned, her eyes shining with joy.

"Brother Jacques. Yes, we are blessed. He was born to spread the word of the Lord. He gives the most wonderful sermons and homilies I have ever heard."

Rupert smiled with condescension. He didn't wonder. The Franciscans had a simple way of putting things because they themselves were simple. It was their inferior training. But this could be an advantage when it came to speaking to the laity. Franciscans tended to be especially popular with women. Rupert couldn't help but articulate some of these sentiments — the fine fruits of rivalry between the orders, steeped in clerical misogyny — though he spoke without any particular malice. His remarks were simple placeholders reifying the superiority of Dominicans over Franciscans, clergy over laity, men over women. At one time, Alicia would have bitterly resented the implicit aspersion on her sex. But now she just smiled.

"You may be right about the Franciscan appeal to women. I really believe Brother Jacques understands us in an unusual way. I have never felt so," she paused, searching for the right words, "appreciated before."

"Meaning?"

"Meaning that he seems to understand our desire to act, to accomplish, to participate. He so admires Catherine Benincasa. She was always active on God's behalf and so fearless. I feel proud that she was a Dominican, don't you?" Alicia didn't wait for Rupert's reply, instead telling him about a wonderful German prophetess named Hildegard.

"She claimed that the reason God spoke to her was because men had failed in God's work. So God necessarily turned to the weaker sex. Brother Jacques thinks we are again entering such times, and that women must step forward," she concluded.

This comment alarmed Rupert. "God created women subordinate to men. And the Apostle said that he would not suffer a woman to preach. Does the friar contest these things?"

"Of course not!" laughed Alicia. "Even so, there is a special dignity to the female sex."

She would have stopped there, but Rupert urged her to continue.

"It was through Mary that the redeemer was born, sanctifying the female body, especially those parts that we never think of as sacred," said Alicia. The last part of this remark was uttered quietly, her head lowered in modesty. At least she has the good grace to look embarrassed, Rupert thought. Any argument advancing the blessedness of women's genitalia was not only dangerous, but also disgusting. Such pandering to women concerned Rupert more than he let on. He simply changed the direction of the conversation, asking what she knew about Brother Jacques. But Alicia had little information on that score. All she knew for certain was that he was from a Franciscan house somewhere in Languedoc, and that he was sent north on business for his priory. And then a frown appeared on her brow, momentarily obscuring the sense of quiet contentment she projected.

"Rupert, were you sent by your house to gather information about Brother Jacques?"

Rupert blushed in spite of himself; he felt stupid to have been so obvious. She was now looking at him with clear concern.

He was caught. It was best to own up. "In a way, yes. You see, it is the prior's responsibility to oversee the religious instruction of its lay affiliates," Rupert said.

Alicia gave a little laugh. "We were all under the impression that the prior and the rest of you would like nothing better than if we all disappeared and spared you the bother."

Anything he said to contradict this judicious assumption would be an outright lie. So he got directly to the point.

"I would like to meet Brother Jacques. Do you think I would be welcome at your meeting?"

Alicia's face lit up. "Of course! Come as soon as you can. Come this Thursday!" she said. When Rupert nodded his agreement, Alicia laughed again and clapped her hands. He didn't remember her laughing in the past, but the sound was sweet. It reminded him of the trill of little bells rung during Mass. "I think the group will be amazed that we merit not just one, but two friars at our meeting. So much wisdom; such learning!"

Rupert looked at Alicia quickly. She was not being facetious; she actually meant it.

"I hope you will address the group and share your love of God with us," she added fervently.

We'll see about that, thought Rupert, giving a non-committal smile.

They arranged to meet on Thursday afternoon and walk over to St.-Jacques together. Then Rupert began to say his goodbyes outside their parents' door.

"It is wonderful to see you," Alicia said with genuine feeling. He took her hand. It suddenly struck him that she had lost a considerable amount of weight since he had last seen her. Even the hand seemed thinner, more fragile, the veins more pronounced. But before this impression was fully formed, she had slipped through the doorway and was gone.

Mary of Egypt

Rupert only sketched the general contours of his conversation with Alicia to the prior. He did mention that Brother Jacques encouraged women in their involvement with the church, but that was all. The young Dominican wanted to observe his Franciscan confrere first hand before he said any more. The prior was pleased about the projected appointment for the next meeting. He smiled genially, and nodded, but all this friendly affect was a prelude to something disconcerting.

"Brother Marcus has volunteered to attend tomorrow's meeting with you." Rupert tried to adjust his features to look accommodating, if not pleased. He had never really liked Marcus. There were stories that he frequented prostitutes. That wouldn't be surprising: Marcus certainly had the face of a satyr. But Rupert rebuked himself, recognizing that this uncharitable supposition was based on mere rumor.

"Of course," Rupert murmured, bowing in compliance.

And so the next day Alicia was met by not one, but two Dominican brethren. Rather than being in any way disturbed, as Rupert feared she might be, she laughed with pleasure and kissed the hands of each. Rupert was, again, struck by Alicia's transformed disposition. She was a woman who, only last year, couldn't endure surprises. The road was too busy to accommodate three abreast. When Alicia and Marcus fell into step together, Rupert walked a little behind, where he could only hear snatches of the conversation. It consisted mostly of Alicia enthusing over Brother Jacques. Rupert was afraid that this would only make Marcus, a staunch Dominican partisan, more inclined to find fault with their Franciscan confrere. The prospect of the meeting was becoming progressively onerous.

The group had permission to meet in the church of St.-Jacques, so long as they remained discreetly in the west end. They entered the nave and Alicia immediately led them toward the group. Usually there were somewhere between fifteen and twenty laypeople. This time, however, there were an additional dozen on the fringes of the meeting, hoping to catch a glimpse of the new miracle worker. It was easy to distinguish the core group from the curious, however, by virtue of their characteristically drab, penitential clothes. Demographically, it was much as Rupert had expected: the majority—about two thirds—were women. Although the group ranged in age from about seventeen to fifty or so, he thought that a large proportion of the group was probably under thirty-five. At the front of the gathering stood a man of medium height dressed in the brown habit of a Franciscan. His face was in no way unusual—his features were regular; his hair was dark brown, and he wore a short beard. Although wearing the customary tonsure, Rupert could tell that he still had a full head of hair without a trace of white. On first impression, Jacques looked remarkably young—perhaps under thirty. But what impressed Rupert most profoundly was how familiar the man looked. Surely Rupert had seen him before, or someone very much like him, but he couldn't quite fasten on when or whom.

Meanwhile, Brother Jacques had noticed them and came forward at once. When he smiled, the presence of tiny wrinkles at the corners of his eyes was the one feature that placed him over thirty. But not by much. Jacques welcomed them warmly.

"My dear brothers, I have long hoped to be acquainted with the Dominican priory. I am truly gratified by your presence. Honored." Jacques concluded with a low bow. From anyone else, this effusion might have sounded formulaic, perhaps even overdone. But Brother Jacques spoke with such simplicity that it was hard to doubt his sincerity.

The parishioners of St.-Jacques were accustomed to standing for the divine offices as there were no pews or chairs in the church. There were a limited number of crude stools in a cupboard near the porch, however.

When all were settled as comfortably as possible on their precarious tripods, Brother Jacques began to speak. Or rather he began to pray, invoking Christ, who descended into humble flesh for the redemption of humanity. He thanked the Lord for the restoration of Rose.

"She has awakened from a long sleep and returned to health in order to pursue her work for God. It was not yet her time to leave us," Jacques said. He turned and smiled at a young woman at his side of about eighteen years of age. She was gazing at Jacques with utter devotion, seemingly oblivious to all else. The group murmured among themselves with both satisfaction and concern. Rose was with them again, but her emaciated form was alarming.

Jacques went on to thank the Almighty for the visit of their Dominican brethren, who took after their founder, Dominic.

"He was the *Domini canis*: the hound of God. Dominic was there to ensure that no splinter of foul doctrine or error would ever stain the beauty of our bridal souls. Let us listen to them, like the children that we are, as they bring us the wisdom of the Father."

All eyes were now turned to the Dominicans, and Rupert felt his face grow warm. There was the, quite natural, expectation that they should say something. Rupert's blank look was but a screen for considerable anxiety. Fortunately, Marcus was armed for just such an event with a homily.

"Beloved children. God is wonderful in His mercy. Here we are brought together in prayer, united in humility by our founder, St. Dominic." Then remembering himself, he added: "and our meeting is doubly enriched by the presence of Brother Jacques, who comes from the order of St. Francis — that noble warrior of God who took to him Lady Poverty as his bride." It was then that Rupert suddenly realized of whom the friar reminded him: St. Francis — the man whom many believed to be the most Christ-like to ever walk the earth. The frescoes from the life of St. Francis in the basilica at Assisi were still fresh in Rupert's mind. But the resemblance was more than physical: Brother Jacques was possessed of the same sense of peaceful self-containment that was imprinted on the features of the saint. By the time Rupert returned from his reverie, Marcus had already launched into his homily.

"Dear friends: last Sabbath, the Kalends of April, was the feast of a very special lover of God: Saint Mary of Egypt. But she wasn't always God's lover. Mary began her life as a lover of men — a prostitute who sold her body, the temple of the Holy Spirit, for money. A harlot to the very bone, she would wear transparent gowns encrusted with pearls, diamonds attached to her breasts, rubies in her navel." Such embellishments certainly weren't present in the *Golden Legend,* Rupert thought. He was beginning to wonder how appropriate this homily was. Marcus had succeeded in capturing his audience's attention, however.

"Mary's lewdness knew no bounds. She actually made a pilgrimage to the Holy Land in search of more customers. As Mary would later confess: 'Whose tongue can tell, whose ears can take in all that took place on the boat during that voyage! And to all this I frequently forced those miserable youths even against their own will. There is no mentionable or unmentionable depravity of which I was not their teacher.'"

Marcus went on to relate how Mary was miraculously barred from entering the church of the Holy Sepulchre alongside the other pilgrims. Recognizing that this was owing to her evil life, she was for the first time sorry, repenting her misspent youth. Mary went to the desert and did penance for forty-seven years.

"Her beautiful breasts, fondled and covered with lewd kisses by many, were withered with fasting. Her skin, once soft, fragrant, and gleaming with the sheen of rich ointments, had hardened and blackened in the sun. But when the holy man, Zosimas, discovered her and heard her story, he recognized her for the person of great holiness whom the angel of God had told him to seek out," said Marcus.

Now for the moralization, thought Rupert.

"The example of Mary shows the immense compassion of our Lord — how great depravity can resolve itself in great sanctity. God's grace knows no limits, whereby, as Christ Himself promised, the last can and shall be first. Now in the name of the Father, the Son. . ."

If the rumors about Marcus' personal acquaintance with prostitutes were true, his homily was not without irony, thought Rupert. Still, in view of Alicia's representations of Jacques' pro-woman stance, Marcus could hardly have chosen a topic better suited for ingratiating himself. And indeed, the Franciscan was extremely appreciative. After everyone had crossed themselves and said their Amens, Marcus received the most fervent thanks from Jacques. And then, almost as if it were rehearsed, Jacques picked up the strains of Marcus' homily.

"Let Mary be a model for us all. She turned away from the filth of her profession. But, she is also exemplary for her initial participation in that profession." Jacques waited long enough for people to register surprise, before going on to explain that—however evil the prostitute's life might be, however abject and cut off from the rest of society—they could all learn from her love. "When it comes to God, we are all, as it were, prostitutes wallowing in our lascivious desires, given to lustful excesses beyond measure. But God, loving us in spite of ourselves, comes to us with full hands, wishing to be our only client, urging us to sell ourselves, body and soul, to Him. And then He will come to us, and we will embrace Him, covering Him in kisses, anointing Him in fragrant oils, and giving ourselves totally. We can feel His breath on our skin, touching us in the most secret places, igniting us with desire."

Rupert glanced over at Alicia. Her face was lifted up as if she were gazing at the stars; her expression ecstatic. When Jacques described God's persona of lover, a shudder of pleasure ran through her entire body.

"But this should not surprise us," continued Jacques. "God has always favored the prostitute—the abject person who knows how to give of her love without measure. It was to Mary Magdalene that the risen Lord first appeared. Hence her title 'Apostle to the Apostles.'" Jacques' smile was brilliant, his voice as soft as down, caressing the entire audience. "So prostitute yourself to the Lord; let Him fill you up with the seed of His Word."

Soon after the meeting broke up. Rupert was due back at the monastery, but thought that he should escort his sister to their parents' house. Alicia had something to discuss with Jacques, however, and said she would make her own way home. Assuming that his sister wished to make her confession, Rupert discreetly withdrew. He was conflicted about what he had heard and seen today. As a rule of thumb, clerics who cultivated female disciples were not to be trusted. Women were so needy; it was such a cheap way for a cleric to assert himself. You could recognize a true man of piety by the distance maintained from women. Only heretics actively cultivated female followers. Even so, Rupert felt drawn to Jacques in spite of himself.

As the two Dominicans departed, Rupert glanced behind. Alicia and the emaciated woman named Rose were standing on either side of Brother Jacques with faces so full of love and admiration that they could easily have been the prototypes for the statues of saints surrounding the Savior. Alicia smiled at Rupert, and then accompanied Jacques and Rose into the chapel dedicated to the Magdalene.

It was only the three of them at Mass. Alicia stole a look at Rose, who smiled back. This is how they liked it best: just the two women, with Brother Jacques officiating. It meant not only that they would have Brother Jacques to themselves, but that they would also receive the chalice. Their love of the Lord seemed to increase with every draught.

Alicia had continued in what she believed to be a state of grace, praying that God would keep her there forever. Maybe He would. A recent conversation with Brother Jacques suggested that such a thing was possible.

"St. Paul promised that sin shall have no dominion over us; that we are not under the law, but under grace," Jacques said.

"But father, is it really possible to attain a sinless state while in the body?" she asked.

"The soul annihilated in God becomes one with God, and is thus beyond sin," Jacques said.

Alicia sighed, closing her eyes for a moment as she imagined what it would be like to dissolve into the Lord. The freedom from temporal cares, the exquisite abandon, the intimacy!

"How can I achieve that state of closeness, father?"

The Franciscan smiled and leaned toward her — so close that she could feel his breath upon her face. "You have been chosen, my dear child. This I know. The Lord has touched you and intends to keep you close, and keep you pure. Remember how Paul said that *all things are pure to the pure*."

Alicia kept all these words, pondering them in her heart.

Fallen Women

On her way home Marion thought about the two Marys: the Magadalene and the courtesan of Egypt. Both were fallen women saved by the grace of God. Priests usually painted prostitutes in lurid colors with exaggerated vices — seductive, lascivious, insatiable. Just like their mother, Eve, only more so! But it wasn't true. Prostitutes weren't any different from other people. A job was a job. There were good prostitutes and bad prostitutes, just like there were good bakers and bad bakers. But whatever her profession may be, Marion knew Margot to be the kindest and most loving person in all of Christendom. Brother Jacques' comparison between the prostitute's love and the love of God flooded Marion's heart with hope. Margot's love was just as Brother Jacques had described: full and unstinting. Could Margot's love for others somehow win her entrance into heaven? Why shouldn't the love that her friend bestowed on the people who needed her help win credit with God? Hadn't Christ said that what one does for the least of His children was really done for Him? Over the years, Margot must have cheered and comforted a veritable army of clients. Many of them were society's outcasts — like lepers that no one would touch; the least of God's children. Margot often despaired of salvation, growing ever more despondent with age. Marion wanted to reassure Margot. But what if Margot was no mere prostitute performing the devil's work, but an ardent lover performing God's work? She rehearsed as much of Brother Jacques' message of hope as she could recall.

But these considerations were soon crowded out by a thought that had been uppermost in Marion's mind throughout much of the meeting: where was Hainselin? His master's demands seemed to have been especially onerous of late. She had only seen him once this week. But maybe Hainselin would come to Margot's place tonight. The thought hastened Marion's footsteps.

As she drew nearer to home, she passed by a Dominican friar and was reminded of Brother Marcus, and his presence at the meeting. Marion frowned. The homily he gave today was unnerving. He might have been the one to introduce the story of Mary of Egypt, but all his comments suggested that he judged her very harshly and saw prostitution, and the prostitute herself, as unmitigated evils. This was such a cruel judgment, especially coming from someone whom Margot described as her oldest and most loyal client. Had he seen Marion among the Faithful? She rather hoped he hadn't. Brother Jacques claimed that God was forgiving, compassionate, and ready to accept people at whatever point in their lives they reached out. The Franciscan was extending the possibility of redemption and change even to women like Margot. But somehow the presence of Brother Marcus gave Marion pause. The clergy were supposed to be set apart and superior, having arrived at a holiness of life to which the rest of the world just aspired. Yet Marcus was a monk who frequented prostitutes, and was hypocrite enough to condemn them. As a religious, he had privileged access to God, but nevertheless had chosen to move away from God. So a person's religious quest was not the steady ascent that Marion wished for her friend, or herself for that matter. Underneath the habit of religion there could be a base sinner. Things were never as they seemed.

As disturbing as Brother Marcus' presence may have been for Marion, it was nothing compared to the dismay he felt when he saw her among the Faithful. For Marcus judged the world of prostitution even more harshly than Marion could possibly have imagined. To him, the prostitute was the repository of the world's sinfulness, nay more: the sins festered and grew putrid inside of her, much like the wasted seed she took into her body. Thus she became a veritable incubator of the sins to which she had been exposed. For this reason, God had sealed her womb. It was a medical fact that the filth of a prostitute's uterus rendered it sufficiently slippery that she was incapable of conceiving. This was just as well: a prostitute's child would inevitably be prone to evil. The prostitute constituted social detritus that was only acceptable in one environment, the brothel, where she was free to perform her evil, but necessary, function. While he could imagine a monk, like himself, going to a prostitute from time to time without losing his aura of sanctity, he could not extend this type of boundary crossing to a prostitute. Not only did she fornicate in her own right, but also she made her living by ensnaring the souls of others — even men of God, like himself. She was doubly sinful. For any chance at salvation, a woman like Margot would have to embrace the kind of monumental penance undertaken by Mary of Egypt.

What was a whore doing at a meeting of the Dominican Faithful? Not only was her presence an abomination that should be anathematized, but also it could present a distinct threat to himself. Was it possible that she had recognized him as one of Margot's clients? Supposing she did; would she tell anybody?

It was a scholarly rendezvous — perfectly innocent, Felice told herself. She nevertheless checked her face in a little hand mirror before she left the presbytery, one of the few luxury items their household afforded. Then there was the fact that she omitted to tell her father where she was going. These things were unusual enough, but Felice also had an unfamiliar feeling. It was probably only her imagination, but her heart really did seem to be missing the occasional beat. Was such a thing possible?

Felice had thought it was a figure of speech. She crossed over to the Île de la Cité in a state of abstraction, oblivious to the world around her. When a cortege of pilgrims, bound for Compostella, attempted to pass her on the narrow street, she automatically gave way without even registering the presence of the little procession. A butcher and his customer stopped their haggling long enough to give Felice a bold but appreciative look — something that ordinarily she would have found annoying. But she never saw them. All Felice could think about was her appointment or, more precisely, the person whom she was appointed to meet.

When Felice arrived at the great cathedral, Baldwin was already there, sitting in a chapel near the transept that was dominated by a stained glass window depicting scenes from the life of the Virgin. Although pretending to read a small book, he was in a condition that was, perhaps, even less conducive to concentration than was Felice. After greeting one another, the young couple sat side by side on the little bench — happy, nervous, and momentarily without words. Then Baldwin bestirred himself, and proceeded to relate the particulars of a scholastic question that he had discovered in his college library about divine deception.

"There is any number of cases in which God deliberately deceives. He caused some evil angels to impart false information to his prophets: they predicted Ahab's victory in battle when the king was, in fact, killed. And then there's the dream of the Magi in which an angel of the Lord urges them to deceive Herod by returning home through another route."

When Felice objected that the use of angelic intermediaries clouded the issue, Baldwin countered with Christ's appearance before two of His disciples on the road to Emmaus. *Their eyes were held shut, that they should not know Him* — to Baldwin's mind a clear-cut instance of deception. Felice still wasn't convinced.

"It could be only the human part of Christ that was doing the deceiving, not the divine Christ part," Felice objected. "But I have a better example. What about the Eucharist? The consecrated bread and wine are supposed to be the real presence of Christ. And yet they maintain the form of bread and wine. Isn't that deception?" she asked, her head cocked to one side.

"Oh, that's good! You were meant for this line of work!" said Baldwin with admiration.

Felice, who had never been comfortable receiving compliments, pretended not to hear, instead asking for Baldwin's *determinatio.*

Baldwin's answer was prompt. "I think it's clear that God does deceive. The emphasis on intermediaries is really beside the point. He could clearly do without them. To argue otherwise would be to place limits on God's power and question His omnipotence."

Felice nodded, as if in concession. But her brow was knitted together in thought, and she was looking down at the paving stones in momentary abstraction. When she looked at Baldwin directly, her eyes flashed defiantly.

"But what if I were to argue that these instances of deception were the work of another force — an evil force?" her voice had dropped in volume.

Baldwin tried to hold her gaze, but it was like looking into the sun. "I assume you are thinking about the Cathars," he said softly.

Felice nodded. "Don't you see that the existence of two gods would make one good God possible? Such a God would never stoop to deception or cruelty. He would be a God of love, with a church overflowing with love." Since she had first begun to learn about Cathar doctrine, the rejection of the Old Testament was never far from her thoughts. Jehovah, the creator of this world, had not only identified Himself as a *jealous God,* but had shown repeatedly that He was as violent as He was vindictive. A true *bridegroom of blood.*

It was impossible for Baldwin to agree with her. As a member of the clergy, he understood the church's need for force. They were only doing God's work. Christ and the apostles had lived in simpler times. Even so, he couldn't help but be impressed by her arguments. Felice was so intellectually resourceful by nature; so impervious to risks.

"If you could attend university, what a pair of comrades in arms we would be!" said Baldwin.

"Oh, if only I were a man!" said Felice fervently.

"Still, I think I prefer things as they are now." Baldwin's voice had sunk almost to a whisper. Felice could feel his breath close to her face. When he leaned his head against her temple, she reached up and put her fingers on the side of his face. She intended to push him away, but instead found herself drawing him closer — longing to draw him closer still. So she settled for merely exploring his jawline lightly with her fingers. Something in the core of her being was stirring, a force that she never had imagined was there. Whatever it was made her pulse race, her breathing unsteady, and her face flush. When she closed her eyes there was a delicious explosion of colors. *Is this passion? Could I be in love?*

An Accident

When Hainselin had first seen Marion, he thought her the loveliest creature he had ever beheld. She was tall and slender with elegant, long limbs — willowy without being too thin. Her brow was unusually broad, almost a hand's span, crowned by a delicate widow's peak. Its V-shape gave the curious impression that she was wearing a wimple, suggesting an innate modesty. Her blonde hair was thick and long, reaching just between her shoulder blades, and always smelling of cinnamon. Her clothing accentuated the color of her eyes. He had never met a woman with grey eyes before, but hers were as grey as the limestone he carved. Marion was not like the other women he knew: she was a woman of quality. She had spent several years in a monastic school, where she had learned to read a little and could even write her own name. They had been together for almost a year, and he was still mesmerized by even her most simple gestures — removing her boots, smoothing her skirt, combing her hair. Each moment they spent together confirmed him in his love. Hainselin knew that she was not a virgin. She had lived with another man before Hainselin had even known her. Marion never attempted to conceal this fact, as other women might. But her past didn't matter to him. Brother Jacques had impressed Hainselin with the possibility of new beginnings. And heaven knows that Marion deserved such a chance. She would receive it in a life with him. He instinctively knew that Marion would make the most loving and faithful wife possible. Hainselin was so sure of his feelings that he told Marion he intended to marry her after having known her for only a month. She had wept with joy.

It would be a long time before they could marry. Marion made very little with her sewing and embroidery. And Hainselin was just a journeyman in the stonemason's guild. The system was rigged against men like Hainselin — men without family or connections. There was a fixed number of masters, and these positions were hereditary. Martin Heberde, the man with whom he had apprenticed, didn't have a son. But his widow would be allowed to assume his place and continue his workshop. So Hainselin was a long way from affording a home to which he could bring Marion. He continued to board with the Heberdes in a beautiful stone house called the Hôtel Grifon — named for the mythological beast carved over the front door. It was located in St.-Germain — the wealthy parish to the west of St.-Jacques. The neighborhood around the Hôtel Grifon was the very opposite of Rue Glatigny.

And so Hainselin worked very hard, accepting extra hours whenever possible. He usually managed to arrange his week so that he could take off an hour or so on Thursday afternoons for the meetings of the Faithful. But this past Thursday, his master was shorthanded on the townhouse they had been working on. The owner, an affluent banker, wanted all the renovations in place before his marriage — which was just a couple of weeks off. It had been an unlucky project from the beginning. First, the stone was late in arriving and, when it did come, it was flawed and a considerable amount had to be sent back. Then the March weather had been against them for the crenellation of the roofline. To top it off, yesterday one of the workers had fallen off the scaffolding. He wasn't badly hurt, but he wouldn't be climbing any scaffolds for at least a fortnight, hence the master's present need. Hainselin didn't mind. Heights never bothered him, and he could use the money.

But the string of bad luck associated with this project continued. Sometime late in the afternoon, just around when Brother Marcus was beginning his homily, Hainselin's chisel slipped. It could have been much worse: he might have lost a finger or two. Still it was an ugly wound across the back of his left hand that bled like the devil. Master Heberde was very concerned. He bound Hainselin's hand tightly in a clean cloth, put him in the wagon, and drove him back to the house to get the wound properly dressed. His wife, Joan, was away at market, but his daughter, Agnesot, was there.

"Oh goodness, what a mess!" she exclaimed when she saw Hainselin's hand.

Her father looked at them both a little apologetically.

"I'm afraid I have to get back. Take good care of him, Aggie." And to Hainselin: "I will see you tonight, my boy. I hope it doesn't sting too much."

Sadly, it did. When Agnesot began to clean the wound with vinegar, Hainselin only remained seated with difficulty. But after the initial flash of pain subsided, he was able to keep his hand on the table, relatively still, while she attempted to remove the bits of dirt and lint that were caught in the wound. Hainselin had never really paid attention to Agnesot before. Occasionally he had been invited downstairs for Sunday dinner, but the daughter of the house had always remained in the background, hustling the servants, checking on the food. Hainselin focused on Agnesot now to keep his mind off the pain. She was one of those big-boned women who looked clumsy but, in fact, moved quietly and efficiently and whose touch was remarkably gentle. Agnesot did not wear her hair loose like many unmarried women, but had it bound up like a matron. It was as if she had already given up on the possibility of marriage. He felt sorry for her. She was probably in her late twenties or even thirty — at least five years older than he was — but that was hardly old. It is true that she was rather plain. Yet she was by no means ugly — it's that she just didn't seem to care, or perhaps know how, to present herself in a way pleasing to men. Her mother, no beauty herself, hadn't been much help. In any event, Hainselin was profoundly grateful that Agnesot was there and that she proved to be such a competent nurse.

Brotherly Love

The plan had been for Rupert to report back to Prior Giles after his attendance at the meeting of the Faithful. But the spring was a busy time for the prior. First there was the work associated with the provincial chapter. And then there were some new appointments to be made at the priory's school that were time-consuming. So Rupert was rather hazy as to the question of whether he was required to attend the Thursday assemblies on a weekly basis or whether he was supposed to alternate with the subprior. Discretion determined that he should attend regardless, just to be on the safe side. In point of fact, he did not mind. The last meeting had turned out to be more interesting than he had supposed possible (assisted by Marcus' wildly inappropriate homily, of course). Rupert also felt that his presence was a support to his sister.

He arrived at the church a little bit early. Alicia was already there, speaking with animation to Brother Jacques and the gaunt woman named Rose. Alicia turned when she saw her brother, her face illuminated with another of her beatific smiles. All three walked over toward Rupert — Jacques in the middle with the two women on either side.

"Well met!" said Jacques with conviction. "You disappeared so quickly after the last meeting that I thought you must have seen the devil."

"What does he look like, brother?" asked Alicia in a mock-innocent voice.

The Franciscan and his two companions began to laugh, and Rupert joined in. Yet, he felt clumsy and dim witted. Jacques had the kind of quick mind and lively imagination that made for a good preacher, which, of course, he was. And the liveliness of his personality seemed contagious: Alicia had developed a sense of humor.

"Laughter is an excellent way to begin a friendship, don't you think?" asked Jacques. Rupert politely agreed, but with some private reservations. The church tended to disapprove of laughter. He wasn't exactly sure why. Is it because Christ had never laughed?

"I know that laughter is often frowned upon," continued Jacques, almost as if he discerned Rupert's train of thought, "which, come to think of it, is funny in itself—the idea of frowning on laughter." The Franciscan gave a warm smile, and Rupert found himself smiling back.

But then Jacques became serious. He had a favor to ask: would Rupert mind remaining after the meeting to hear confessions?

"Yes of course," Rupert said with alacrity—attempting more confidence than he felt. "The Dominicans really should assume more responsibility for their Faithful."

"But in the end of all, what does your order or my order matter? Aren't we all doing God's work?" Jacques raised his eyebrows quizzically before continuing. "Our holy founders never met in the flesh. Yet I have seen paintings in which they are embracing in heaven, which I well believe to be the case. But here on earth, their followers disgrace themselves by squabbling."

Before Rupert could respond, the last of the Faithful had arrived and taken their seats, and it was time to start. It looked like Brother Marcus was not coming, for which Rupert was grateful.

The meeting followed the same basic format as last time: a homily and then prayer with intercessions. Jacques was every bit as eloquent as Rupert remembered. As the meeting broke up, several of the Faithful lingered, doubtless wishing to confess. The two friars positioned themselves at opposite sides of the church.

As the numerical odds ordained, all three prospective penitents turned out to be women. Indeed, one was an exceptionally beautiful woman — her appearance enhanced by the harsh penitential garb. Rupert cringed, mentally willing her to keep her distance. As a confessor, Rupert was especially flummoxed by sexual sins. Once a voluptuous young woman confessed the sin of masturbation. Rupert was required to follow up, with questions: *When? Where? Were these thoughts involuntary, or did you solicit them?* When it was time for Rupert to mete out penance, his stammer had become so pronounced that the penitent had to ask him to repeat himself several times. He afterward walked around with an erection for the entire week.

As luck would have it, however, Rupert's sole penitent was one of the older women, who was exceptionally plain. The only sin that she confessed was gluttony. Although the sacrosanct seal of confession protected a penitent's privacy, sacerdotal discretion was hardly required in this case: the poor woman was obese.

Rupert's penitent had just risen from her knees, with difficulty, and had begun to waddle away when he felt the light pressure on his arm. It was the Franciscan, who wanted to express his gratitude. What Rupert had done for him was friendly and collegial, and Jacques hadn't found Paris very welcoming thus far. The last of the Faithful had left and the two men were now standing alone in front of the choir. This was Rupert's second time in this church, and he still couldn't get over how irregular it was. He absently scanned the erratic bays of the nave wall while thinking about how to say what he must. His conversation with Alicia had convinced him that a mild warning, or perhaps even a gentle rebuke, was in order regarding the Franciscan's over-zealous promotion of the female sex. The emphasis on women's special spiritual merits seemed misguided, and could do more harm than good. Rupert was still groping for the right words when Brother Jacques made an unexpected observation.

"Brother Rupert: I hope you won't take what I have to say amiss, but I have noticed how you seem to shun women; even look down on them. Perhaps, in this respect at least, you were not well-served by your education, which has made you so acutely aware of their inferiority." Rupert was not only taken by surprise, but he could feel the blush rising right up through his tonsure. Jacques continued as if he didn't notice.

"If I am correct, I can only say that I pray the Lord will dissolve this *hardness of heart*. Women are God's creatures and, I believe, possessed of more potential for true piety than men. Women, unencumbered by learning, move more quickly in the race for God."

Rupert was surprised to find himself preempted in this way. It took him a moment or so to compose himself before answering. "You m-m-mistake me, brother. If I seem to shun w-w-women, it is because excessive familiarity with them is dangerous. The church fathers support me in this. If you remove the motive of l-l-lust from the equation, a male companion is in every way to be preferred over female company," said Rupert. Jacques' unexpected overture had the effect of rendering Rupert much more direct than he might otherwise have been.

Jacques' initial response was a laugh of incredulity. "Good heavens! Do you really accept this?" he cried.

Rupert was stunned into silence while Jacques continued.

"The church fathers were fighting a war to secure a celibate clergy. Our Lord never avoided women — quite the contrary."

"Of course. B-b-b-ut our Lord wasn't married," protested Rupert.

"Do we know that for a fact? He was a Jew and all the Jewish patriarchs and teachers were married. They adhered to God's mandate from Genesis to *be fruitful and multiply*," Jacques responded.

"But M-M-M-Mary and Joseph. . ." began Rupert.

Again Jacques interrupted: ". . . probably went on to have children after Christ was born. That is what the earliest fathers of the church assumed," said Jacques.

"But celibacy is the higher path precisely because it places us above nature," Rupert said stolidly.

"And why would we want to be above nature anyway?" Jacques asked with quiet amusement. "Isn't God the author of nature?"

But then Jacques became more serious and went on to concede that clerical celibacy was hallowed by tradition. "But vows of celibacy don't justify the church's ongoing disparagement of women," he concluded.

Rupert was at a loss for words. Did clerical celibacy really foster the belittlement of women, or was it his mistrust of women that had drawn him to the priesthood in the first place? Then before Rupert knew it, he found himself confiding in Jacques, trusting him with secrets that he had never shared with anyone — not even his confessor. He had never told anyone that he had once been in love — painfully, hopelessly, in love. She was the daughter of the parish priest; otherwise, she was perfect in every way. But his parents would never have let him marry a clerical bastard.

And the woman didn't seem to care for him anyway. It was only when he was certain of her indifference that he decided to join the Dominicans.

"I still think of her sometimes." It was a painful admission. Jacques nodded in silent commiseration, before Rupert continued, head bowed: "If I seem to shun women, it is because I continue to d-d-desire them. That's why I can't endure hearing their confessions." He was almost sobbing at this point.

Brother Jacques placed his hand gently upon Rupert's head: his scalp began to tingle, almost as if the hand was the source of a secret energy.

"I have yet to celebrate communion today. Will you come and assist?" said Jacques in a warm, compelling manner. Rupert nodded. They entered the Magdalene chapel, and proceeded to say Mass together. There was no one else in attendance, just the two of them, and it was a wonderful experience: intimate, fraternal, and yet solemn. When it came to the consecration of the wine, Rupert perceived that Jacques had poured a little too much in the chalice. This meant that Rupert should probably drink more deeply when the chalice was offered to him. He wasn't afraid of becoming inebriated: usually wine didn't affect him much. Yet this time, the moment the cup touched his lips, Rupert felt intoxicated, and this condition opened a floodgate of feelings. He experienced an outpouring of love of unprecedented intensity for Brother Jacques. Here finally was a man in whom he could confide; a man of such holiness and compassion, to whom he could reveal anything with impunity. *A man I could love; even venerate.* Rupert felt a strange stirring in his heart as if a new life were unfolding within him, a whole new order of existence emerging. *A man deserving of worship.* His eyes closed. The feeling of joy was so powerful that his body was shaking.

After the benediction was said and the two men were about to leave the church, Jacques put his hands on Rupert's shoulders and looked directly into his eyes.

"My brother, I will pray to God that from this time forward you will be troubled neither by women nor their confessions."

And, indeed, Rupert never was. Nor did he ever again stammer.

Brother Jacques bumped into Hervey as he was leaving the church.

"Vespers, is it?" said Brother Jacques.

"Yes, but sometimes I wonder why I bother. Nobody comes!"

"Ah, but the Lord is always watching!" Hervey thought there was a trace of irony in the Franciscan's voice. Yet when he looked at him directly, he could detect no irreverence, so Hervey just nodded in agreement. The friar's hand was already on the Porch Door when he looked over his shoulder and asked, "And how is your beautiful and learned daughter?"

"Very well, thank you," said Hervey, reflexively. It was only after Jacques had left that Hervey had a chance to puzzle over his question. Hervey had only met Jacques a couple of times, and Felice hadn't been with him. How did the Franciscan even know that he had a daughter, let alone that she was beautiful and learned? Of course, people talk, and Hervey knew that Felice was bound to be a particular subject of speculation around the parish. Yet the question still struck him as odd.

On leaving the church, the Franciscan's smile faded quickly. He made his way along La Rue St.-Denis toward the bridge, scanning the faces of the people who were passing as if he were looking for someone. There was a chill in the air, and Jacques was walking briskly. When he reached the portal at the bridge's entrance, he collided with a man who was carrying a bushel of oats. The man, who was knocked to the ground, swore aloud: "The devil take you! Watch where you are. . . ." But when the friar turned to look at the speaker, the rebuke froze on his lips and he found himself apologizing instead.

Brother Jacques proceeded over the bridge to the Île de la Cité, moving swiftly past the moneychangers and the jongleurs singing for coin — still searching the faces of passersby, still looking. In the cathedral square, he was detained by the confused cacophony of three rival confraternities, all attempting to process on behalf of their respective patrons over the same route simultaneously. Each was loudly challenging the right of the others. Jacques pushed his way through the crowd, moving purposefully, but scrutinizing faces along the way. It was only when he reached the Hôtel Dieu that he seemed to have at last found what he was looking for: a little beggar boy with a crippled leg, sitting peaceably beside his mother. Jacques nodded to himself before turning away.

Chapter 5: Demimonde

Margot and Marion

"Please Margot, come to a meeting. If you heard Brother Jacques speak, you would be filled with such hope!"

Marion and Margot were sitting in chairs facing a window that opened up to the Rue Glatigny. Marion had removed her shoe and was massaging her heel. Margot was peeling and quartering onions. There was a pitcher of wine between them. Crude voices and cruder smells filtered in from the street. There was a loud game of dice being played directly beneath by several particularly foul-mouthed men.

Ever since Margot's conversation with Brother Marcus, the time that he had treated her possible damnation as a near certainty, she had become progressively despondent. Even if she were to repent today, her salvation would hardly be secure considering all the sins she had amassed over the years.

"Marion, what's the point? You have to repent to achieve salvation, which would mean changing my way of life altogether. Or do you think I belong with the *Filles-Dieu*?" said Margot.

"Maybe," replied Marion. In the dark days after Richard's disappearance Marion herself had thoughts of entering one of these convents for reformed prostitutes, and even made inquiries, but there was no room.

Margot clicked her tongue in disgust. From what she'd heard, many of the so-called nuns simply substituted black veils for their original saffron, and continued to meet their clients. But her young friend was speaking in earnest, and Margot didn't want to sound cynical. All she said was, "I am too old to change. This is the only world I know."

"But you don't even sleep with customers much anymore," Marion said with some discomfort, not quite sure how to reference Margot's advancing age. "I mean, you are much more choosey now," she wound up, rather awkwardly.

Margot laughed. There was no mistaking Marion's allusion.

"What you say is true. I'm really too old to attract anyone who has the use of his eyes. But I am still renting rooms, which means that I continue to make money through sin."

"Brother Jacques spoke of Mary of Egypt as a great lover of God — not just because she rejected prostitution, but also because she gave of herself without measure when she was a prostitute. The same is true of Mary Magdalene herself." Judging from the look of incredulity on Margot's face, Marion was afraid she might have misunderstood the friar's message.

"Well I doubt that this Brother Jacques has cleared his message with the Chancellor," Margot responded. She remembered the words of Gerson's sermon as if it were yesterday. *Since a prostitute lives in a perpetual state of mortal sin, she is under a permanent sentence of excommunication and, hence, barred from communion.* He did grant them the right to make donations to the church, however. That was Margot's experience of the church: push away with the right hand, take money with the left.

"What did Hainselin think of the homily?" Margot asked.

Marion's face fell. "Hainselin wasn't there. His master called him to work at the last moment, and he had an accident." Marion was concerned about more than Hainselin's physical state. Apparently he couldn't go back to work for at least a few weeks. Was his job in jeopardy?

"Bring him over here. We will get some wine into him and cheer him up," Margot said, and was rewarded by one of Marion's wondrous smiles. But the smile was soon replaced by a worried half-frown.

"Hainselin wasn't there, but guess who was?" Marion tried to sound playful, but she would have made a dreadful actress.

"The king? The pope? Come, my dear. How can I possibly guess?" Margot was not in the mood for games.

"Your *bel ami,* Brother Marcus," Marion said, still striving, however unsuccessfully, for a teasing note.

Margot was almost as surprised as if it had been the pope. She didn't know why exactly. The group was, after all, Dominican. And Marcus was subprior of the Dominican priory. Yet, despite their off-color humor regarding his vocation, Margot was not accustomed to thinking about Marcus in this capacity. In fact, she experienced something comparable to Marcus' response when he saw Marion among the Faithful, though clearly with less justification and none of the judgment. Where should a friar be, if not at church? It was his presence at the house of a prostitute that was the true anomaly. Margot was certainly aware of this fact. Still, she experienced the same pained feeling that she always felt when the real life of a client forced itself upon her. How many times had she seen various *ribauds* in the streets with their wives, or out for a family excursion on one of the barges that cruised the Seine? At present, Margot was having a version of this response, only the incumbent feeling of loneliness was more intense. She had a profound sense of how different she was from the rest of the world. It was a strange realization that her life was only central to herself and a few familiars. To her clients, however, she was peripheral — perpetually on the margins. And their real lives were, in turn, marginal to her. It didn't matter that the commodity in which she traded was intimacy; it was an intimacy that rarely brought about true union, except in the most carnal sense. And if this intimacy was disclosed in other venues, it became an instrument of division. Hence these different realities with their radically different orientations and sets of priorities — distinct worlds, really — were better off separate. The alternative was dangerous for everyone.

Lost in this uncomfortable reverie, Margot did not hear Marion's question until it was repeated a second time in tender, beseeching tones.

"Would it bother you too much if Brother Marcus saw you? He's only been to the meeting once. He may never come again." Although Marion regretted having introduced Brother Marcus into the conversation, she had to prepare her friend for the possibility of an encounter, if she were to attend. Then a more cheerful idea occurred to her:

"Perhaps Brother Marcus would be pleased if you came to the meeting. He is, after all, a priest who is genuinely fond of you. Shouldn't he seek your conversion?"

Before Margot could answer, her daughter came through the door, living proof against the contention that prostitutes could not have children. Though a mature woman of forty, Joan still lived with her mother, helping her with the rooms. She was strictly a business associate, however. Margot had seen to it that her daughter never became a prostitute herself. Joan bent over her mother from behind her chair, and casually planted a kiss on her cheek before greeting Marion. The two friends readjusted their seats to face Joan, who had drawn up a chair for herself.

"Whom do you suppose I saw?" she asked, grinning. Without waiting for an answer, she trumpeted, "The Dane!"

"The Dane? Who is that?" asked Marion.

"Only another crazy woman like mother," answered Joan. "Her real name is Marion, the same as yours. But everyone calls her the Dane because of her blonde hair. She's really from Flanders."

The Dane was, apparently, up to her old tricks. She tried to sell Joan a potion that was guaranteed to make her look twenty-five again. Joan wouldn't think of buying it, however, not confident in the Dane's skills.

"I might end up as wrinkled as an old apple — just like mother!" Margot furrowed her brow, pursed her lips, and shook her head in feigned anger. Joan reached over, smiling, and squeezed her arm affectionately.

"I'm amazed that she has never been arrested," continued Joan.

"She's pretty sharp — always two steps ahead of the law. I think she left Flanders just before she was charged with sorcery," said Margot, laughing.

Marion was listening attentively. "What kind of potions does she make?" she asked quietly.

"Oh, she says she can do just about anything," was Margot's answer. "But her specialty is love. The Dane claims to be the mistress of everything from love potions to making unwanted pregnancies disappear."

"That just about sums up modern love," said Joan rolling her eyes expressively and grinning. "Still, she would be a good person to know, even if only half of her claims were true."

Apostates

Anthony had provided Felice with two codices. The first was a weighty tome combining a number of works on heresy. The two that addressed the Cathar heresy were both florilegia of excerpts. One was produced by orthodox authorities for the use of inquisitors; the other was comprised from texts which had once circulated among the Cathars. The second codex was a diminutive volume, no bigger than Felice's hand. It contained a series of Cathar rituals, all written in the same bold hand.

It was dense reading that took over a week. But Felice was happy to have a more nuanced understanding of the faith. She looked outside. The sky had cleared, leaving behind one of those anomalous spring days when the atmosphere felt sharp and crisp, yet soft and balmy at the same time. Felice had always found walking conducive to thinking, and was on her feet and out the door before realizing that she was still in her slippers. The streets would be awash in muck and sewage. When she went back to change into her clump shoes, she also grabbed a light cloak.

Paris was its noisy, noisome self. Full of traps for the unwary, a city not ideal for someone contemplating religious truths. And yet there was Felice, thinking about omniscience. *Some Cathars claim that Satan was a creation of the one all-knowing God, against whom he rebelled; others believe that there are two opposing Gods of equal power and Satan is the evil one. Surely the second view is more reasonable. If an omniscient God had known ahead of time that His angelic creation would sin, wouldn't that be the same as willing them to err?*

Felice was passing under the portal of the Grand Pont, musing over the irony that the members of so beleaguered and persecuted a sect would allow themselves the luxury of a schism, when a man grabbed her elbow. "Mind, miss," he said, steering her away from the pile of indeterminate waste, whether animal or human was unclear. Felice wrinkled her nose in distaste. *At least they all agree that the material world is disgusting!*

The bridge was lined with booths of moneychangers. One entrepreneurial spirit had brought his two trained monkeys dressed in what, for all intents and purposes, looked like the royal livery with the fleur-de-lis. They danced and caroused on hind legs as slender as bent wicker. *If the Cathars are right about the transmigration of souls, I might have known these monkeys in an earlier incarnation!* At this point, one of the little beasts, perhaps attracted by the brightness of her hair, lunged toward Felice, but the trainer yanked it back by its chain.

Felice had now crossed over to the Île de la Cité, and was passing by the Rue Marmousets. She glanced at a razed area, in front of which stood a small statue. A butcher shop had stood there, famous throughout Paris for its paté and pasties. Mad King Charles had been an especial devoté. But it turned out that the proprietor had an arrangement with the murderous barber next door, who provided the meat of freshly slain customers. The scheme was exposed by a dog, which kept a pathetic vigil outside the shop where its master had disappeared. The two men were burned at the stake, and a statue was raised to the dog. *And the church says that dogs don't have souls!*

Felice found herself standing directly before the central portal of Notre Dame Cathedral, over which there was a tympanum depicting the Last Judgment. In the lintel above the door, two heralding angels were literally raising the dead. Kings, queens, bishops, bearded patriarchs, knights in their mail, and noble matrons with their headdresses, were all rising from the grave. They were lifting the lids of their tombs, and struggling to get out of their shrouds in anticipation of judgment. At the top of the frame was Christ — not Christ the Good Shepherd, however, but Christ the Judge, stripped of all empathy and compassion. The Virgin Mary and John the Evangelist knelt on either side, interceding for the human race. Yet despite their best efforts, at least half of the people appeared to be damned. On Christ's left, enchained souls were being dragged away by demons. The person at the front of the line was being thrown head first into a gaping hell mouth. *And this is the first thing that people see when they walk into church! A religion of fear. Why would a God of love create us only to damn us? Why let us die and rot, only to resurrect us? Why do we need bodies in the afterlife anyway?* Felice looked down to where three blind men were sitting beside the portal. They had heard her footsteps and began to chant: "Prayers for alms!" She felt in her pocket, but hadn't brought any money. *The Cathars believed that everyone would eventually be released from the body and be free to return to the celestial homeland. Wouldn't a God of love want everyone to be saved?*

Felice proceeded toward the Petit Pont, which led to the Left Bank. She could feel the vibration of the mill wheels turning underneath the bridge. A man was carrying a tray of meat pasties, which put her in mind of the depraved barber-butcher team. She had always hated the smell of meat, and turned quickly away, almost colliding with a very pregnant woman. Both women apologized at the same time. They were about the same age. *If I were to marry, that could be me,* a thought which made Felice shudder involuntarily.

Felice was now walking past the manuscript stalls and, for the first time ever, did not pause to browse. She was beginning to understand. *The material world blocks out the spiritual one, just like the body eclipses our true angelic selves. And we worship the evil creator god, who's responsible for this calamity. That's what the prophet Jeremiah meant when he spoke of mankind serving a strange God in a strange land.*

It might seem like a gloomy doctrine to some. But it spoke to Felice's sense of boundaries and displacement unlike anything she had ever

heard or read. She had always felt that there was an obstruction that separated humanity from a true apprehension of reality — a veil of enigma,
as it were. *When you look for it, you see it everywhere: the way the literal gets
in the way of the symbolic, words stop short of true meaning, and the beauty
of creation conceals something, even as it points to something else just out of
reach. It is like the palimpsest: the life of an inquisitor concealing the journal of a Cathar Perfect. Perhaps my entire life is a palimpsest of sorts. Outwardly, I appear to be a priest's concubine, while inwardly I am still a virgin,
living blamelessly with my father. Outwardly, I am an orthodox Christian;
inwardly, I may be becoming a Cathar!*

Felice wondered if she would ever have the courage to turn herself
inside out.

On the other side of the Seine, Baldwin was also preoccupied with problems pertaining to the body. He was in a permanent state of arousal
thinking about Felice. Her impact was inversely proportionate to his
exposure to women, which was slight. Baldwin had been sent away to
learn his letters at a monastic school when he was seven, arriving at the
university when he was barely fourteen. So his was a world of boys and
men. He had lived with them, fought with them, thought with them. But
it was women that he dreamed about, and those dreams generally ended
with soiled sheets, a sense of defeat, and, later, the sound of his confessor's booming voice asking: "How many times?" As he grew older, Baldwin gradually achieved a degree of mastery over his body. But he remembered a time when he would avert his eyes even before the more comely
figures of the Madonna.

Baldwin had never been intimate with a woman, despite a heightened level of youthful desire and ample opportunity. One could hardly
move around the close of Notre Dame or go anywhere in the Latin Quarter without tripping over a prostitute. Yet even in his adolescent years,
when his natural instincts were the most impervious to his chaste vocation, he had always found the concept of love for sale repugnant. Now
he was ordained to the priesthood, and formally bound by vows of chastity. His studies served to reinforce his vows. It was not just that he had
become so busy with the Lombard: in truth, the more he studied, the

more aware he became of woman's natural frailty. Yet this entire corpus of learning was undermined the moment that Baldwin met Felice.

Anthony could not but notice the difference in his usually buoyant friend. At first he assumed it was a case of career jitters. He remembered how he had himself been torn between different options when he was at Baldwin's stage: whether he should remain in Paris, teach, pursue a doctorate, get a benefice, and all the rest of it. But when his young friend's mood persisted for a couple of weeks, Anthony decided it was time for a frank conversation. The day was glorious, and Anthony suggested a walk along the Seine. Initially, Baldwin demurred, pleading intense entanglement in some academic issue, but then he changed his mind. Whatever Baldwin's problems, the openness of his disposition was still intact. So it wasn't long before Anthony was apprised of his quandary.

"It's a relief to tell someone," Baldwin admitted. "There is so much I don't know about her. And I can't help but wondering: is she really Hervey's daughter? They don't look at all alike."

The two men were seated on a bench by the river. Anthony had found a stout stick and was meticulously removing its bark with a small knife. It would make an admirable cane for Martin. But he put his knife to one side to give his full attention to Baldwin's question.

"The answer to your question is a real *Sic et Non*. It's a sad story. Felice's mother was one of Hervey's penitents. She got pregnant and claimed that Hervey was the father. She was lying, of course," said Anthony.

"What did Hervey do?" Baldwin asked.

"At first he protested his innocence. But no one believed him. His handsome looks finally turned around and bit him in the ass, as it were. He was ultimately expelled. And then the mother gave birth and promptly disappeared, abandoning the infant. So Hervey took pity on the child, and brought her up as his own," said Anthony.

Baldwin was surprised and delighted. "Not only is Hervey's story a marvel, but it comes as a great relief. Do you know, I was afraid you were going to tell me that Felice was really his concubine?"

Anthony was watching the progress of a small boat loaded with sacks of something or other progressing down the river. It was riding low and looked dangerously close to capsizing. He wasn't surprised by Baldwin's surmise about Hervey and Felice: it was what most people thought. That is why it took so long for such a worthy man to get a decent benefice, and all because Hervey accepted responsibility for a child that wasn't his. It was a deed right out of the *vitae patrum*. In fact, there was an Egyptian hermit, St. Marcarius, who was also falsely accused of getting a woman pregnant. Marcarius never bothered to defend himself. Instead, he started working to support his new wife, forwarding all his money to her. Yet when the woman went into labor, she couldn't give birth until she confessed the truth. So in the end, Marcarius wasn't responsible for the child's upbringing after all. Hervey did him one better.

"I wonder if Hervey's a saint," said Baldwin.

Anthony was struck by the concurrence of their thoughts. "I do know him for an extremely good man. And one of the surprising features of sanctity is that it is hardly ever where you would expect to find it," replied Anthony.

"It would be refreshing to see it in the papacy," said Baldwin.

Anthony laughed, but then his tone changed. "I hope nothing untoward happened when you met with Felice. She is a woman of virtue and should be treated as one," he said.

Baldwin reddened slightly. "Of course not. I only met with her the once — and in a church, no less." He sighed. "To be frank, I've begged her to meet me again, but she won't."

"That's to her credit. Try and put her out of your head. She is off limits to you," said Anthony.

Baldwin knew that Anthony was right. But all attempts to loosen Felice's hold on his imagination had been entirely unsuccessful. Baldwin had never met anyone like her before — so lovely to look at, so intelligent, so capricious and funny. She was a complete revelation to him.

"I know Felice is off limits. But technically speaking, she is still single," said Baldwin, still awash with relief that she was not Hervey's mistress.

"Baldwin," said Anthony in a voice that was stern but not entirely devoid of compassion. "You are now ordained. A priest is not a journeyman whose work can be put to one side. There is no possible future for you and Felice."

"Perhaps not a lawful one in the eyes of the church," stammered Baldwin. "But you said yourself that there were probably many people who thought that Felice was Hervey's concubine."

"There are prelates in both Reims and Paris who know the truth, however. Otherwise he would never have received St.-Jacques."

"Jacques of Vitry's sermons are full of exempla concerning priests' concubines," Baldwin responded in a sullen voice.

"Be that as it may, it would be extremely difficult for a parish priest to live openly with a concubine in Paris," said Anthony.

"Is there any place where it would be easier?" asked Baldwin.

Anthony shot him a glance.

"I am just curious. Where could a priest and his concubine have a good life?" Baldwin persisted.

"Iceland," Anthony responded firmly.

"Iceland may be a bit far," Baldwin said with a smile. "But what about a small parish in the countryside." For a brief moment, he saw it all: the quaint stone church with its wooden roof; a small house with an apple tree in the front yard and a garden to one side. He could hear the laughter in the adjoining field and see the bright glint of Felice's hair as she chased two beautiful redheaded children.

"I know that ordination is supposed to be indelible. . ." began Baldwin, but Anthony interrupted him.

"It is not just ordination. It's life that is indelible. That is the hardest part of getting older — being aware of all the things that will never be; all the things that *you* will never be."

Poor Baldwin looked so wretched. Anthony felt it was high time to move away from this volatile topic. He knew that there was a certain wisdom to airing desires; otherwise a person might explode, just like wine fermenting without a vent. But too much air could result in a conflagration. So Anthony turned the conversation to Baldwin's theological dilemmas — less explosive, from a certain perspective, but equally dangerous. Baldwin perked up, and gave him an animated account of his latest readings and cogitations.

"Well Baldwin, you never do things by halves," said Anthony. "Let me make sure that I have this right: you wonder why a good God permits evil, whether God causes sin, and whether an individual, misled by an erroneous conscience, can win merit through heresy? Is there anything else?"

"That's it for now," said Baldwin, laughing in spite of himself. "Unless you want to tack on whether clerical celibacy can be mandated by the church since St. Paul declared it a gift of the Holy Spirit."

The two friends eventually parted: Baldwin figuratively to bury himself in his books, Anthony literally to bury one of his parishioners.

The Dane

Marion had no difficulty locating the woman known as the Dane. Every-one seemed to know her. She had once worked in one of the houses in the Glatigny nearby Margot's place. But that ended when the Dane got into a heated argument with the abbess of her brothel: it took three *rib-auds* to pull her away from her less robust opponent. After this episode, the Dane decided it would be better (and safer) if she removed to the right bank. Now she was a regular fixture in the tavern near the bridge on Rue Champ-Flory. Marion had never been there before. All she knew was that it was yet another quarter given over to prostitution. It wasn't very far from St.-Jacques-de-la-Boucherie, however. So Marion made her way to the tavern early Thursday afternoon, confident that she would still have time to get to the meeting of the Faithful. It was Holy Thursday: Easter was exceptionally late that year. Marion, who never frequented taverns, felt guilty for doing so on a solemn feast day for purposes that were distinctly unholy.

She had no trouble recognizing the Dane, who was very blonde indeed. She looked like the kind of woman who might avail herself of Dame Trot's recipes for hair dyes. At first, Marion merely stood by and watched. The Dane was sitting at a table, holding forth to several other women who were all coiffured in unusual hues. Marion wasn't used to such loud company: every utterance seemed to be accompanied by guf-fawing and table-thumping. But eventually she got up the courage to go over to the table, hovering until the Dane became aware of her presence and turned. The other women took note of Marion — young, nervous, and clearly not a prostitute — and discreetly melted away. The Dane invited Marion to sit down, looking at her quizzically but not unkindly.

"I am terribly sorry to bother you," stammered Marion. "I heard about you at my friend Margot's."

"Who's that?"

"Margot de la Barre. In the Glatigny."

"Ah ha!" cried the Dane cheerfully, once she understood whom Mar-ion meant. "Whatever she has told you about me, I can do her one bet-ter — I promise you. There's enough dirt to bury us both."

Marion, who tended to be very literal, was concerned that she had given offense. "Oh no," she said. "Margot didn't say anything bad about you. In fact, it was her daughter, Joan, who brought your name up."

"Joan! Now there's a fine one for you. A great business woman, to be sure, but with a face like a raisin. I was trying to sell her some ointment that could have given her back ten, maybe fifteen years! But she wasn't interested. She's always looked like an old shoe."

The Dane recreationally took to examining her own shoes, which were not in very good shape, as it happened. There was something dark stuck to the sole as if she had trod in something squishy that had since hardened. Marion looked away. Then she remembered herself and asked the Dane the question she had doubtless been waiting for: could Marion buy her a drink?

"Of course," said the Dane with conviction, "if you will join me," she added with a politesse seldom called for among her acquaintance. And so Marion asked the attendant for some wine. He returned with two tumblers and an earthenware pitcher, which he plunked on the table abruptly, causing some wine to slosh over the top. The Dane grabbed the back of his apron: he turned, she pointed, and he wiped up the spill with a filthy rag. The two women raised their cups and drank to one another's health.

"But you haven't introduced yourself, sweetheart," said the Dane, as she wiped her mouth on her sleeve.

"Oh excuse me! My name is Marion."

"So is mine!" boomed the Dane, as if this were a truly remarkable concurrence.

Marion blinked nervously. There was a silence: awkward for Marion, amusing for the Dane.

"So what brings you to Rue Champ-Flory?" the Dane said eventually. "Certainly not the flowers!" She chortled over her pun. Marion tried to smile appreciatively. She was not used to drinking wine this early, and her face already felt hot.

"It's about my fiancé, Hainselin."

"I figured. Men are trouble — women's main trouble, if you ask me. Hard to live with them, impossible to live without them. Who else would pay us just for lying on our backs?"

She forgot momentarily that Marion was not a prostitute. "Take my man, John de Savoy. He calls himself that, but I doubt he has ever been there. To Savoy I mean. I think he just likes people to think that he has travelled. Do you want to know what I think?" She leaned over conspiratorially toward Marion. "I think that he really just crawled out of the Seine, and hasn't had a proper bath since!" The Dane gave Marion a gleeful wink.

Now that the weather was getting warmer, this comment was especially evocative. Marion wrinkled her nose at the stench rising from the river. The conversation was not going the way she planned, but she tried her best to look at ease.

"Whenever he has a cup or two, he starts singing. The devil take him, he has a terrible voice. Give him three or four cups, and he is off whoring!"

Marion saw a fleeting opportunity to intervene, and took it.

"Do you mean he is unfaithful to you?"

"Good lord, yes!"

"But doesn't it bother you?"

"Not as much as his singing!" bawled the Dane, slapping her thigh,

"Well, it bothers me," said Marion with a sigh.

"Why should you care where John lets down his britches?"

"Not John. I mean Hainselin," said Marion.

"Who the devil is Hainselin?" No one had ever accused the Dane of being a good listener.

"Hainselin is my fiancé. Well, not formally, perhaps. I mean we are not actually betrothed. But he says he will marry me."

"Then you are a damn fool! Who the hell wants to be married?" said the Dane.

"I do!" cried Marion pathetically. Tears were beginning to form in her eyes, turning her irises a darker grey. This managed to get the Dane's attention.

"There now, sweetheart, don't go crying. There, there."

"I thought you might be able to help," Marion said. Her eyes were now brimming with tears, which began to spill over her face. The Dane was grateful that the tavern was dingy. Otherwise, people might get the idea that she was blackmailing Marion or playing the bawd.

"Hush, hush," said the Dane in tones she hoped were comforting. "I feel for you, sweetheart. Really. We all went through it when we were young. You'll get over it. Honest. And wine will be just as sweet as it was before."

"Please help me," implored Marion.

"But I'm not understanding you. How could I help?" said the Dane.

"They told me that you could make love potions. If Hainselin stops loving me, I will die," sobbed Marion.

Now Marion had the Dane's complete attention.

"Did Margot send you here?" she asked gruffly.

"No. She doesn't know I am here. And I hope you won't tell her. But I heard Joan say that you could do all sorts of things," said Marion.

"Well, she's a liar!" Marion looked so miserable that the Dane was immediately sorry she had said that. The Dane did know a number of spells and potions. She pitied Marion and wanted to help, but didn't want to get involved. Then she hit on the answer: she would tell her about menstrual blood. It was a simple solution, requiring no special potions, no magic words. It was something Marion could do herself. The Dane lowered her voice, and after looking around the darkened room, asked Marion if she could keep a secret. Marion nodded, and the Dane proceeded to explain.

"You don't need a lot," she cautioned. "Just enough to put a drop or two in the wine. Then the two of you should drink it together. That will help deepen his love."

Marion was aghast. She couldn't imagine anything more disgusting — and dangerous. Menstrual blood was worse than poison: a menstruating woman could ruin a mirror by just looking into it. How could she possibly give this corrupt substance to her beloved Hainselin to drink, let alone drink some herself? She sat brooding while the Dane helped herself to another tumbler of wine. Then Marion realized that the Dane had provided all the help she was prepared to give. Was she expected to offer the Dane money? Marion had a few coins in her pocket. The Dane, however, shook her head vehemently. As far as she concerned, taking money would only make whatever offense she may have committed that much worse.

"I don't want anything. It's women's lore and it's the property of all women. Mind, you never heard any of this from me," said the Dane.

Marion reassured her that she hadn't, not entirely certain that this was the correct response. The Dane looked amused. Marion was on the verge of leaving when a distressing thought crossed her mind.

"What if it doesn't work?"

"If it doesn't work, don't come back to me! Margot knows as much as I do. More, probably. Ask her."

The Third Vision

It was nighttime. Margot was on the top of a cliff surrounded by high walls. But despite the height of the walls, she could still feel the wind blowing on her face. The air smelled foul: filled with the smell of charred meat that had an unusually acrid quality. Ashes were floating everywhere: they made her eyes water, and burned the back of her throat. Somewhere nearby she could hear the sound of many people weeping; weeping as if their hearts were broken. She walked through narrow, cobbled lanes looking for help — someone who could tell her where she was and what was happening. Margot stopped suddenly in front of a well. There was someone hiding in there. She walked toward it, frightened, but wanting to know who was concealed there. But a voice in her head told her, *Move on. He is not the one you have come for.*

There was a small unadorned building ahead. Margot thought it might be a chapel, but if it were, it was an unusual one: no sculpture on the exterior, no stained glass. The inside was the same: the walls were whitewashed without any adornment. There was no cross, no holy images. A forlorn lamp was burning on a ledge jutting out of the wall where the altar should have been. The place had a morose atmosphere that made Margot anxious to be gone. She was just moving toward the door when the same voice said, *Look!* And there, in front of the lamp, was a triptych joined together by hinges. Christ was depicted on the central panel, flanked by two kneeling female saints. Margot couldn't be sure which saints they were supposed to represent. Blue was the usual color for the Virgin; red for the Magdalene. Both of these figures, however, were clothed in plain black and white. The women were exquisitely beautiful, with the long attenuated limbs of a Byzantine icon. Both were turned toward Christ in adoration. Christ wore a simple robe of brown homespun, and was crowned, not with thorns but gold. He was standing in the *orans* posture, both hands raised palms upwards in supplication. Underneath His feet was the inscription.

Ƈuʳ āïʳm

Margot stared at the letters. Of course, she couldn't read them. But she studied them carefully, recognizing that they must be important. When she looked up again, it felt as if the eyes of Christ were trained on her. She had heard about such pictures. They were somehow painted to give the impression that the eyes were following you. Even so, the figure's gaze made her uncomfortable. Its eyes were augmented by circles of gold, but they reminded Margot of rings of fire. She turned to leave but looked back when she reached the door. The impression was even stronger; the eyes seem to have moved in their painted sockets. She fled.

Once Margot had returned to her senses, she thought long and hard about this vision. At length she became convinced that, taken in conjunction with the other visions, it could only mean that God was calling her — encouraging her to turn away from her evil life. First He appeared as the Good Shepherd. She clearly was one of the blinded sheep who was rejecting salvation. The second vision in which Christ descended from the cross and walked toward her very literally demonstrated Christ's desire to reach her; to touch her. This new vision seemed to corroborate the others. Margot was figuratively wandering in a desolate world — dark and filled with the stench of her sin. The burning of meat indicated the carnal nature of her sin. She walked into what should have been a church, but it was empty, without an altar — probably signifying her continued absence from church and her withdrawal from the blessed sacraments. Even so, Christ, mercifully, was still watching her. And the fact that there were two female saints on either side was a reminder of Christ's special ministry to women. Christ had healed the woman with flux — a woman in a permanent menstrual state who was unclean — unclean like Margot. He had taken Mary Magdalene to His heart, forgiving all her sins because *she hath loved much.* The fact that Margot was resistant — even frightened — in these visions signified the extent to which she was hardened in her sinful ways; that she continued to turn her back on Christ.

And so Margot resolved to do what Marion had requested of her, and finally attend one of the meetings of the Faithful. It was possible that this Brother Jacques, whom everyone spoke about in accolades, would be capable of understanding the kind of life she had led. His comments on the prostitute saint were encouraging in this regard. Maybe she could even confess to him. What a relief that would be. Perhaps these visions, as painful as they may be, were a blessing from God, calling Margot back to Him.

There were still a couple of elements in the vision that she found confusing. She did not understand the significance of the person in the well. Was that something biblical? Christ met the Samaritan woman at the well. But why was Margot told to pass by it in the dream? The other thing was the baffling letters in her vision, which she still remembered. Margot traced their contours as best she could with a piece of charred wood on the back of a door. It seemed strange for someone who could not read to receive a vision with letters. Clearly, she needed to enlist some help in order to decipher them. Marcus hadn't been by for weeks, probably because it was Lent. But she would ask him when the opportunity presented itself.

Chapter 6: Brother Jacques

The Report

It was several weeks after their first meeting that Prior Giles finally had the leisure to ask Rupert and Marcus for their impressions of the mysterious Franciscan. Out of deference to his seniority, Rupert waited for the subprior to speak. Marcus cleared his throat with due ostentation. He admitted that when he attended the first meeting, his expectations were low. The Franciscan brethren too often manifested an aura of superiority, as if they had a special purchase on God's grace. Francis was a good and simple man to be sure, but Marcus didn't accept that he was more Christ-like than any other of God's chosen. The Dominicans' own Catherine Benincasa had also received that special grace of the stigmata. Of course, the Franciscans did their best to deny these claims, purposefully obstructing the glory that God visited on this fragile woman.

"I admit to an occasional prejudice toward our Franciscan Brethren," Marcus said.

Both the prior and Rupert struggled to conceal their smiles: everyone knew Marcus loathed the Friars Minor. Oblivious to their mirth, Marcus wound up: "Yet my predisposition proved to be a bad counselor in this case. Brother Jacques is, in my opinion, a good man — a man of God. Were he a Dominican, I am certain he would be a credit to our order."

The prior now turned to Rupert.

"And what about you, my son. Are you in agreement with Brother Marcus?"

Rupert thought about his last meeting with Brother Jacques. It was strange: although they had disagreed about matters as fundamental as clerical celibacy and women's place in the church, all his qualms had nevertheless been resolved in favor of the charismatic Franciscan. He could thus answer the prior's question with conviction.

"My respect and love for Brother Jacques has grown with every meeting. He possesses eloquence without condescension, learning without pride, and, I believe, compassion for sinners without reserve. We are lucky that he has the time to concern himself with our Faithful."

The prior unconsciously rubbed his hands together as he did when he was pleased. He was hoping to establish a permanent Dominican presence at the meetings. But since Rupert and Marcus both had such high opinions of Brother Jacques, neither would object to attending. The subprior had so many demands on his time that the prior suspected the responsibility would more often fall to Brother Rupert, no doubt. It would constitute a good break from the Lombard, however.

"How is the commentary going, Brother Rupert?"

"It goes, prior," replied Rupert, mentally cringing.

The prior smiled with satisfaction, rising to signify that the meeting was over.

While sincere in their comments concerning Brother Jacques, both Marcus and Rupert were holding something back. Marcus' private thoughts were not particularly edifying. He was pleased with what Jacques had said about Mary of Egypt — that God had a due appreciation for sinners. It indicated that Jacques was broad-minded; a man of experience. For friars were not like ordinary monks: they lived in the world and sallied forth to do battle in the city every day. The Franciscan understood that absolute chastity was an ideal to which they all should aspire, but that only a few could achieve. A person couldn't consistently remain at such perilous ascetic heights: there wasn't enough air! Each individual had to descend from the mountain and deal with the flesh, as it were — even if he were a monk. Marcus' periodic lapses from chastity were relatively few and far between, but necessary. He was, after all, a man. He knew that many of his brethren turned to one another for sexual solace. If the claims of grass drying under the feet of a sodomite were true, then every cloister would be a wasteland. But however convenient sodomy undoubtedly was, it just wasn't for him. His weakness was for women. He'd never felt apologetic for it, however. The kind of casual sex he enjoyed with a prostitute was hardly more culpable than a nocturnal emission — an act of impurity that didn't even engage the will. Marcus had never bothered to confess these so-called demonic illusions in the days when he was a frequent sufferer. Visiting Margot provided the same kind of necessary release: he never confessed this indulgence either. Doubtless, Brother Jacques would understand Marcus' past relations with prostitutes — perhaps even condone them.

Brother Rupert's thoughts were diametrically opposed to those of his confrere. Far from seeing Jacques as a man of the world, he saw him as a man of great simplicity, integrity, and sanctity. Jacques had been able to look into Rupert's heart and see the ongoing struggle he endured over contact with female penitents. Jacques observed Rupert's suffering; he empathized; and he healed him. With a single touch, he had taken away all of Rupert's undesired desire; and with it went much of his anxiety, leaving Rupert with a sense of contentment that he had never before experienced. The peace that had descended upon him was not limited to this newfound control over his sex drive, but seemed to affect other personal characteristics that had hitherto seemed intractable, leading Rupert to the brink of despair. The stammer, the bane of all social interactions, had disappeared. Rupert thought that Jacques must have done something similar for his sister, Alicia, who continued to glow with happiness.

Jacques had demonstrated that he, like God, was a *seer of heart and reins*. Rupert had experienced a miracle at Jacques' hands, and thought that the Franciscan might well be a saint. But Rupert hadn't shared this conviction with anyone. He might have told the prior had Brother Marcus not been present. Prior Giles was a genuine man of God who would have understood. Still, he was glad he hadn't spoken. He wanted to keep these precious thoughts to himself for the time being. They filled him with a warmth and confidence that seemed to bring him closer to God. For the first time ever, Rupert perceived God at work in his life, and he was deeply grateful.

Rose

It was hours before Vespers and no one else was in the church. Hervey was in the vestry fiddling with the thurible. Its chains were so twisted that when the deacon went to bless the offerings at Mass, the entire bowl tipped over scattering charcoal and incense all over the choir. Hervey, who was distinctly unhandy, was only making matters worse, and had actually managed to yank one of the chains free from the bowl entirely.

Then he heard movement in the nave and stuck his head out of the vestry. It was Rose's fiancé.

"Welcome Philip!" Hervey called out. "How are things at the forge?"

The young man nodded, "Pretty much the same, father."

Hervey was walking toward Philip when it suddenly occurred to him that he should take advantage of the timeliness of Philip's visit. He signaled Philip to wait while he ran back to the vestry, returning with the offending vessel. Philip examined the thurible with solemn care, as if he were handling a fragile relic. Then he offered to attach new chains for no charge — an offer that Hervey gratefully accepted.

"Well now that you have helped me, how can I help you? My guess is that you have come to confess." This was something of a standing joke between the two of them. Philip was conventionally pious: once a year during Easter week was enough confession for him, and Easter was only last week.

"What, do you take me for — one of the Faithful, father?"

"No Philip, I refuse to flatter you!" Both men laughed over this. "But what can I do for you, my son? You are probably not here to talk about the Faithful."

"In fact, father, I am in a way."

Hervey looked at him thoughtfully. "Go on."

The first thing that Philip wanted to know was how the Faithful came to be in the church. This question didn't surprise Hervey. He had learned over the years that parishioners were very territorial about their church, and Philip was no exception in this regard. After all, they paid their tithes, and celebrated many of their joys and sorrows in the church. It was only natural that they should have proprietary feelings about the building. The answer to Philip's query was easy enough. Several of the Faithful approached him and asked for the use of the church. They pointed out that a substantial number of the Faithful were from St.-Jacques — more than half, in fact. The Dominicans weren't very helpful either in providing them with a meeting place or ministering to their spiritual needs. So Hervey took the matter up with the churchwardens, who agreed that the Faithful could use the church. A number of clerics took turns leading the group in prayer, hearing confessions, saying Mass. Hervey had stepped in whenever he could. But it was difficult to make time for them.

"It seemed a godsend when Brother Jacques showed up," Hervey wound up.

"What do you know about the man," said Philip in a cautious tone, looking down at the floor.

"Admittedly, not much; only that he comes from the south and is a fine preacher," Hervey said.

"Do most friars spend so much time with women?" Philip asked, bluntly.

This question did not surprise Hervey. It wasn't likely that a strapping lad like Philip would be jealous of the Franciscan in any usual way: most laymen regarded clerics as men in skirts. But Hervey had often seen instances of a woman's excessive piety arousing resentment in her husband or lover, and this resentment was frequently leveled against any cleric who ministered to her. It wasn't just a question of her time in church representing time taken away from home. Rather, the husband had some inchoate recognition that the confessor or spiritual director was enjoying a special kind of intimacy with his wife — a spiritual intimacy. It was only the very rare husband who was prepared to cultivate this kind of relationship with his wife. But even though he didn't want it himself, he wasn't prepared to let other men enjoy it.

"It is true that not every friar is so attentive to women. But it is lucky for the Faithful that this one is. More than half of the Faithful are women, after all," said Hervey.

"Some say Brother Jacques is a miracle worker," said Philip, this time looking directly at Hervey, as if watching for his reaction.

Hervey was careful to remain impassive. It was a subject that needed to be approached with caution.

"I know there are some people who think so. I wasn't there, so can't judge. But I will say this: if his prayers helped to bring back your Rose, we are all very grateful; and you must be especially so."

"Please pray for Rose, father. Pray for us both," Philip said. Then he turned around and left, carrying the thurible with a care that was touching.

A Miracle

Nobody knew quite how it happened. Apparently the boy slipped. It wasn't surprising. He was a little boy — crippled in one leg, and thus chronically off balance. Everyone knew who the child was. He was a common enough sight around the Hôtel Dieu, where he often sat with his mother, the two of them begging. A number of people saw him fall, but were forced to stand by helplessly while he foundered. A boat loaded with a freight of flour was passing. By the time the crew pulled him from the Seine, he was dead. His little body, blue from the cold of water and the greater chill of death, lay on the road in all its pathos. A light powdering of flour lent his face a ghostly quality.

The Hôtel Dieu was almost in the Chancellor's back yard. So it was natural that Gerson, returning from a deeply unsatisfactory meeting with the bishop, should come upon the scene. He was walking with his usual haste, when he heard the general commotion, above which he could discern the sharp cries of a woman. A number of the people in the crowd recognized the Chancellor, and made way for him. They looked at him expectantly. Gerson felt that he should do something: say a prayer, provide some words of comfort, but was very much at a loss. He looked at the diminutive cadaver — a familiar figure made strange by death. Sickened by his own sense of impotence, Gerson mechanically made the sign of the cross over the boy and covered the body with his mantle. He tried to speak kindly to the mother and gave her some money for the boy's funeral. But the woman was beside herself, and stared at the coins as if she didn't know what they were. He was on the verge of leaving to seek help from the hospital when the sea of faces parted and a Franciscan stepped forward. Gerson had never laid eyes on the man before, but he somehow knew that this must be Brother Jacques — the man whom everyone was talking about. Without glancing at Gerson, the friar knelt down in front of the child in prayer. Then he leaned over the boy and said something in a soft voice. It was an intimate moment in a public place, and the wondering bystanders were sensitive to this fact. Everyone seemed to be holding their breath. The Franciscan straightened up and said a single word aloud: "Awaken!" The silence continued. Nothing was happening, but there was a tension in the air. Gerson felt something. He shuddered as a current ran through him; a palpable force. Then it started. The mantle seemed to move ever so slightly, so slightly that Gerson thought it must be his imagination. But after a moment or two it was manifest — an ever so subtle rhythmic movement, like breathing. Then a distinct stirring: the mantle surged upward, and slid off the little face. The boy was sitting up. The woman, mad with joy, threw her arms around her son — crying and laughing at the same time.

Gerson was transfixed, staring at the mother and child in wonder. By the time he bethought himself and started to look around, the Franciscan had disappeared. After ensuring that both mother and child were taken care of by attendants at the hospital, Gerson retrieved his mantle and began to walk back to his office. Still in shock, his progress was slow. Upon opening the door, Gerson flung himself into his chair, clutching the mantle. He remained stationary a long time, considering what he had just witnessed: a moment of healing that was powerful enough to turn back time, to defy death. And the Franciscan was the conduit of this mighty force. If Gerson had only reached out and touched the Franciscan, he too might have been transformed. But even standing there as an observer, Gerson thought he had felt something. It seemed to him that everything had changed now that God had made His presence known in Paris. Of course, Gerson was well aware that God never truly absented Himself, but on this day He seemed to have drawn nearer than ever before in Gerson's lifetime. It was the Franciscan who elicited His holy proximity.

Gerson was startled by a knock on the door. It was Master Anthony and his young protégé. Gerson had forgotten about the appointment; indeed, he looked so taken aback that Anthony wondered if Gerson even remembered what they were meeting about. This was the first time Anthony had ever seen his former student rattled.

"Chancellor, is this a bad time? Would you like us to come back later?"

"No, no. It's fine," said Gerson. He stood up and went over to the pitcher standing on a chest under the window, still carrying his cloak. He set it aside to pour himself some water, but picked it up again when he returned to his chair, draping it across his lap. The two priests stood in the middle of the room; Baldwin was looking at his desk for clues as to what the Chancellor, that youthful prodigy, was working on now. But Anthony looked at Gerson with evident concern.

"Please, masters. Please be seated." After a rather awkward silence Gerson went on to say, "I have had a bit of a shock." Both men looked at him with such concern that Gerson could feel the beginnings of tears forming in his eyes. He took a sip of water, trying to compose himself.

"Chancellor, can I do anything for you?" said Anthony.

Gerson shook his head, but then seemed to reconsider.

"Masters, I want to tell you about something I witnessed that is very strange and wonderful. I'm sorry to impose, but I really don't have anyone else to tell." At this moment, all of Gerson's guardedness and prickly defenses seemed to have vanished, and he smiled in a sad, self-effacing way. Then he recounted from start to finish what he had witnessed in front of the Hôtel Dieu.

"I have seen dead people often — too often. It's a vocational hazard. So there is no doubt in my mind that the boy was dead. And everyone else knew it as well. But then the Franciscan came..." He broke off for a moment. "It was a miracle. It must have been."

Anthony and Baldwin sat there in silence. Was this really Gerson, the famous skeptic who scorned the proliferation of saints and wonder-workers?

"How salubrious it would be to have a saint in our midst in these troubled times!" Gerson paused, and then continued in a soft voice as if thinking out loud. "But such initiatives require evidence. It's never too soon to begin collecting documentation for possible canonization. I will see to that."

Gerson began rehearsing the upward momentum of the Franciscan's miraculous repertoire: the Miraculous Hosts, the young woman, and now the boy. There was a marked progression from Jacques as a passive vessel of grace, consecrating the Hosts, to active miracle worker; from restoring health to restoring life itself. The last miracle had been performed in the open for all of Paris to see. These witnesses must be tracked down.

Gerson's eyes were shining with excitement, his visitors forgotten. He remembered them now, however.

"Master Anthony, what do you know about the Franciscan's life?" Gerson spoke in an eager, almost urgent, tone.

"Very little. He is from a house near Toulouse and hasn't been in Paris for long."

"We need to know more. Much more." Gerson was now thoughtful, as if weighing options. He looked up. "I am on good terms with a several of the Franciscans at the priory, and will make some discreet inquiries. But masters, I need your help as well. Those weekly meetings of the Dominican laity: I want you both to begin attending."

Anthony and Baldwin agreed, promising to report back to Gerson the following week.

The three men never alluded to the subject for which they were gathered. That the conversation took the direction it did was clear indication that the problem of spiritual discernment was no longer strictly academic. It was only natural that Anthony and Baldwin were more skeptical about the Franciscan's claims to sanctity: they hadn't been there and hadn't seen what Gerson saw. Still, they were both intrigued. The three priests parted with greater amiability and warmth than any of them would have expected.

Although Gerson rose when his guests were leaving, he never let go of the cloak. When Anthony turned to close the door, Gerson had already resumed his seat and was gently stroking its fabric.

Recognitions

Marion worked on Margot, constantly talking up the merits of Brother Jacques — his eloquence, his compassion, his general aura of goodness — until she succeeded in overcoming Margot's natural resistance. Eventually, Margot agreed to attend one of the Thursday meetings. With feelings that were a conglomerate of hope and curiosity, Margot was anxious to meet the much vaunted Brother Jacques. Perhaps Marion was right and this was someone who was capable of getting beyond the veneer of Margot's occupation to perceive her as she saw herself — as a simple soul caught up in sin, but struggling for change; as someone who wanted to find God in her life. Margot even considered staying behind for confession — probably not this time, but eventually. It was true that most, but not all, of her rooms were rented to people intending to use them for expressly sinful purposes. But was that really the same as sinning herself? If only she could negotiate with God; make Him understand that she would quit renting rooms as soon as it was feasible. There were too many beggars in Paris. It couldn't be His intention that Margot become a beggar as well. She suspected, however, that God didn't negotiate; she remembered the days when she wouldn't either.

For the first time in a long time, Margot thought about her appearance. Once, she had done her best to skirt the sumptuary laws and ape the costumes of the gentry — albeit it through cheaper materials and gaudier colors. And she still wore what was left of this faded finery for economy's sake. But for Thursday she would borrow Joan's black linen gown and wear a clean apron and even a wimple, just like a widow or a nun. She didn't want Marion to be ashamed of their relationship. She found herself hoping that Brother Marcus would not be there. If he was, however, there was a chance that he wouldn't recognize her in this modest attire.

Marion had been held up by a female client who insisted on altering the length of her *cotte* to give it more of a train. This was the second time, but Marion was so meek and kind-hearted that she never would agree to charge extra. So the two women were among the last to take their seats alongside the Faithful. Hainselin was there for the first time since his injury and was seated in front of them beside a rather dowdy woman. Margot, who noticed him right away, was surprised when he didn't greet Marion. Perhaps he hadn't seen her. But shouldn't he be anxiously on watch for his beloved? Margot had been to this church before with Marion. So the only other people she recognized in the congregation were the rector of the church and his pretty concubine, who were just arriving.

Hervey and Felice were the last to join the group. Despite their proprietary position with regard to the church itself, they were still outsiders of sorts. After it had been determined that Jacques would be a consistent presence at the meetings, Hervey had shown the friar around the church. But that was the only significant amount of time Hervey had ever spent with the Franciscan, and that was before Rose's recovery. After the conversation with Philip, however, Hervey decided that he would like to have a look at Rose and her wonder-working benefactor himself. He couldn't imagine what he was looking for. So he insisted that Felice accompany him; he needed her sharp eyes and sharper wits. When Felice at first demurred, he reminded her about the manuscripts — intonating that she owed him a favor. She gave in with good grace.

The group had continued to grow with the news of the recent miracle. Some people came from genuine piety. Rose's mother Anna, for example, had begun to attend in the spirit of thanksgiving. But at least half of the newcomers were comprised of the simply curious, hopeful that there might be a new marvel in store. There was a tension in the air as if the group was collectively holding its breath in anticipation. Where one might expect the gentle murmur of conversation, there was only silence. Then all attention was focused on the east end of the nave. Five people were solemnly making their way down the aisle. In the lead were

two young women, clothed in the distinctive black and white habit of the
Dominicans, walking side by side, and bearing candles. Then came the
Franciscan with his large sad eyes, and beautiful smile. The little procession was brought up by two Dominicans — one corpulent and middle
aged; the other young and strong. Hervey had the impression that the
five of them had issued out of the sacristy, but thought he must be mistaken — that this area was off limits to women. The procession stopped
in front of the gathering and Brother Jacques seated himself in a high-
backed chair on a slightly raised platform, his Dominican colleagues on
either side. The women extinguished their candles and sat on stools at
the foot of the platform.

"Isn't that Rose?" Hervey whispered. Felice nodded, and Hervey's
heart sank. Poor Philip. Rose was dressed in the Dominican habit, which
meant that she had taken vows.

This was not the only recognition that took place: Marion immediately attracted the unfavorable notice of Marcus while he was still processing down the aisle. *What is that prostitute doing here? And who is that
ancient baggage that she has brought along with her? Probably her mother
or some widowed aunt, hoping that her presence would somehow make
Marion seem more respectable. Well it won't work!* When Marcus realized
that the older woman was Margot, his face went white with rage. He
wouldn't keep quiet any more. He would tell Jacques what Marion was;
what Margot was! Women like this didn't even belong in a church, let
alone among a Dominican congregation.

Margot experienced an even greater shock, entirely unrelated to
encountering Marcus. She was stunned by the realization that the Franciscan, Brother Jacques, was the figure that had been appearing in her
visions. However unbelievable, it was nevertheless unmistakable. The
same face; the same eyes — large, dark, and probing. She searched her
mind in an effort to explain this concurrence, trying to think of any possible circumstance where she might have encountered him earlier. But
she couldn't. Nothing like this had ever happened to her before. It was
as if the phantoms from her spirit world had escaped, and come to stalk
her. Filled with a sense of dread, Margot remained anxious throughout
the meeting, hearing little of what was said. She saw Marcus, but barely
registered his presence.

From his position to the right of Brother Jacques, Rupert also experienced a recognition of a more mundane order. He saw Felice. There she

was, as large as life, standing beside her father. She was very much as he remembered her from Reims — her hair gleaming like embers against her dark mantle, emphasizing the clarity of her pale skin. Yet somehow she was no longer as lovely as she once had seemed. Of course, Felice's diminished beauty had more to do with his own perception than any external factor. He knew this was the work of the Lord.

After the intercessions, Brother Jacques stood before the group with a look of exultation on his face.

"My dear brethren, I have two joyful announcements to make. First, let us rejoice on behalf of our beloved sisters, Rose and Alicia, who have taken their vows as Third Order Dominicans. Aren't they lovely in their habits?" He indicated the women seated before him. The two women looked rather bashful, but at the same time pleased by the attention.

"The rule of life for the Third Order carries with it a presumption of chastity for the unmarried. They have chosen marriage with the heavenly bridegroom. May God help them with this pious resolve," he smiled at the two women indulgently.

"But for the rest of you, I want you to remember that St. Paul referred to chastity as a gift of the spirit, not recommended for all. It would be a sad day if everyone did abstain sexually. Who then would populate God's glorious creation? Chastity goes against nature. The normative mandate is the one the Lord gave to our first parents: be fruitful and multiply. Reproduction is very much God's work and will be rewarded by Him, even as the virgin state is rewarded. And that is why I am elated to announce the forthcoming marriage between Hainselin Planiete and Agnesot Heberde."

There was a murmur of surprise among the core group. They were, for the most part, aware of Hainselin's relationship with Marion. But the sound was not enough to mask Marion's single and involuntary cry of pain.

"Thus, my dear friends, we have two of our numbers entering upon a more ascetic existence; and two embarking on the task for which we were created. Let us rejoice for them all and pray that they encounter success along their respective paths."

Jacques then began to intone the psalm *Venite exultemus* — a psalm of thanksgiving, praising God for the creation of the earth.

Brother Marcus left as soon as the meeting concluded. Any encounter with Margot would be extremely unseemly, he thought. Rupert whispered something to Jacques, and both men made their way toward the congregation. The two women followed at a discreet distance. Knowing what was due to the incumbent of the church, Jacques first greeted Father Hervey with graceful deference. Before Hervey could even begin to present Felice, Jacques had made a polite bow and said: "It is a great pleasure to see you again, my dear."

"I believe you are mistaken, friar. We have never met." Felice was not flustered, as one might expect. Her voice was clear and unwavering.

The Franciscan seemed on the verge of responding when he seemed to change his mind. Instead he just smiled:

"I apologize. But here is someone that I am confident you will recognize." Jacques drew Rupert forward.

"Look father! It's Rupert!" Felice had been entirely oblivious to Rupert's passion. His reappearance only brought back pleasant memories. Hervey smiled his recognition.

"Rupert, my boy! I had heard you were a scholar now! How is that commentary on the Lombard going?"

"It goes, father." This time, however, Rupert pronounced his stock answer with more amusement than resignation. Then Hervey began to ask solicitously after his family.

"We have all moved to Paris, now, and are quite well, I am happy to say. My brother is learning the family business. But my sister, Alicia, is right here. Perhaps you didn't recognize her." One of the women who had processed in front of Brother Jacques came forward, wearing a radiant smile.

"I see that there is another, less secular, family business afoot," Hervey joked, indicating her Dominican habit.

"As you heard, I have only just taken my vows," said Alicia, flushed with pleasure. And I made them into my dear brother's hands!" She looked up at Rupert with love. "Rose made her vows at the same time," added Alicia. She looked behind her, but didn't see Rose.

While chatting with Rupert and Alicia, Hervey couldn't help but be struck by how much more content the two siblings seemed than the way he remembered them. Alicia had been a plain, sullen girl who always seemed angry at the world. And Rupert had been painfully shy, afflicted by the most terrible stammer that always got worse when Felice was around, poor man. Yet now Alicia was all smiles, and Rupert's stammer had entirely disappeared. That just goes to show what a difference discovering your true vocation can make, Hervey reflected. He felt exceedingly happy for them both.

It was at this point that Anthony and Baldwin approached. The two clerics had been seated near the front of the congregation, so their presence was a surprise to both Hervey and Felice — a delightful one. Baldwin had agreed to attend the meeting with an alacrity that Anthony interpreted as proportionate to his desire of encountering Felice again. In point of fact, Anthony wasn't opposed to such therapy. Part of being a priest was learning both to coexist with and resist beautiful women. The new arrivals were introduced to Rupert and Alicia, and the six of them happily conversed for a while. Hervey looked around for Rose, hoping to have a word with her, but she was nowhere to be seen. She must have left. This rather surprised him since her mother, Anna, was only now effusively taking her leave of Brother Jacques.

Meanwhile, Margot was doing her best to steer her friend out of the church as expeditiously as possible. Marion, who had gone very pale, was insensible from shock and barely ambulatory. They were almost at the door when a hand came down on Margot's shoulder. She turned to discover Brother Jacques. He looked from Margot to Marion.

"My dear, won't you introduce me to your friend?"

Marion stared at Jacques with a look of total incomprehension on her face, so Margot was forced to introduce herself.

"Very glad to make your acquaintance, mother," he said — in familiar, yet respectful, tones. "But must you go? I was sure you had come here to confess."

He looked pointedly at Margot, gazing deeply into her eyes. It was only then that she realized, with shock, that the sense of recognition that she had experienced worked both ways: he recognized her as well.

One of the chaplains was saying Vespers that evening, so Hervey was at liberty. He insisted that Anthony and Baldwin come back to the presbytery for some wine and comfortable chat. The two priests consented with pleasure. Soon they were seated — each with a tumbler of wine and a plate of Felice's truly superior oat cakes in their midst.

Anthony explained that he had been initially asked to attend the meeting by Gerson, but within hours Gerson's initiative was seconded by the bishop who sent a message asking the Chancellor to send someone.

"And who can blame him? Any self-respecting bishop who had a little known Franciscan performing miracles in his diocese would naturally be concerned," said Anthony.

The others agreed. The revival of the boy was a very flamboyant occurrence with many witnesses. As a result, all the religious authorities, Gerson included, were carefully observing how Brother Jacques conducted himself: whether there were any irregularities — anything that might betray a less than orthodox profile. Hervey took this opportunity to bring up the vexed question of women in the sacristy, much to Felice's chagrin.

"Father, I assure you that both Rose and Alicia were waiting for the clerics *outside* the sacristy. So your bastion of clerical privilege remains unpolluted," she said with not a little heat.

There was a brief silence.

"Well, how usual is it for women to process with candles in front of priests? Isn't that position reserved for acolytes or other clerics in minor orders?" asked Baldwin.

"In a formal service, certainly," responded Anthony. "But this struck me as more of a liturgical improvisation. I don't think any rules were broken."

"It seemed hubristic, processing down the aisle in that way," persisted Baldwin.

Anthony disagreed. "I was struck by the effectiveness of the symbolism: it was an economical way of announcing that all three priests, both the Franciscan and the two Dominicans, were now presiding over the meetings."

"And the women?" asked Felice.

"Well they were certainly being singled out. But surely this was a special occasion: they had just taken their vows," responded Anthony.

And yet, although distinguished, the women did not receive the praise one might have expected for their vows of chastity. There was no mention of chastity as the higher path; nothing about the virgins following the Lamb. In fact, Brother Jacques went in quite the opposite direction, stressing the importance of procreation. It struck the four of them as very odd.

"It was as if Jovinian had won the chastity wars," said Hervey.

"In all probability, the Franciscan's emphasis was strategic and pragmatic. The majority of his audience was comprised of married members of the laity, after all, not consecrated virgins," said Anthony.

"Yet Brother Jacques bends the rules. There's no doubt about that," reflected Felice. "But so did Christ. And so do His saints. I suppose the crucial question is whether our Franciscan should be considered among them."

A lively discussion ensued about the potential merits of the Franciscan's case. But it was all hypothetical. The Franciscan was as enigmatic as he was charismatic. None of them shared Gerson's conviction as yet.

Hervey did not take part in this conversation. He was thinking about Rose. So she'd taken vows. Rose wouldn't be the first woman to choose the celestial bridegroom over a terrestrial one. Perhaps her choice was even less surprising after a near-death experience. But why wouldn't she have told Philip first? Of course, she might be inspired by the example of the virgin martyrs. They all despised their former suitors. St. Agnes called her fiancé a bundle of sin and a morsel of death. But still.

It was getting late and the two visitors began taking their leave.

"I know that Chancellor Gerson will want me to continue my surveillance, but I am sure he wouldn't mind if I delegated you," Anthony said, his hand on the door. Hervey shook his head:

"Oh no! I think that for the parish priest to be over-present would look, at best, rather officious and, at worst, highly suspicious."

"Then you might see me sooner than you would expect."

Baldwin, ever curious about questions of discernment, assured Hervey that he too would be in attendance. Hervey looked at Baldwin narrowly: he couldn't help but notice the manner in which Baldwin's eyes lingered on Felice, especially whenever he thought she wasn't looking. That was understandable, even forgivable, as long as he continued only to look. But to be fair, Baldwin was not without encouragement: Hervey could see how Felice lit up when Baldwin was in the room. Of course, it was impossible for Felice not to be attracted to anyone as buoyant and mischievous as Baldwin — so like Felice herself, in fact. Hervey only hoped that no serious, and impossible, partiality would sneak up on her unawares.

The four of them agreed to reconvene in the next few weeks. On the way out the door, Baldwin managed to get close enough to Felice to give her hand a gentle squeeze.

Betrayal

Margot led Marion home from the meeting carefully as if she were an invalid. She helped her into a chair. Even with eyes swollen from crying, Marion was beautiful. The tears had succeeded in making her eyes look like dark glass. By contrast, her skin was pale like the Flemish wool that was famous the world over for its delicacy. Her lovely neck, now bent downward in sorrow, curved like the neck of a whippet. She trembled like one as well. Eventually, Margot got Marion to lie down on her bed and close her eyes. It was impossible to tell if she was really asleep.

By the time that Margot had arisen the next morning, Marion was gone. Margot went about her work, fretting all the time, but not knowing where Marion was or what she herself should do. It was not until late that afternoon that Margot heard the door bang in the outer room. A woman was screaming. Was it one of the *fillettes*? You could hear scuffling in the adjacent cubicles where the various couples were scrambling for their clothes in fear and confusion. Maybe it was a raid. That was Margot's constant fear: she had heard that the sergeants of the Châtelet were cracking down on illicit prostitution. Margot's house was not licensed as a brothel: she could be fined and, possibly, imprisoned if discovered. Then Marion came through the door and Margot realized with surprise that Marion, usually so quiet and demure, was the source of the commotion. For the next half hour Margot divided her time between trying to quiet Marion and reassure her clients. Eventually Marion became calmer. Margot handed her a cup of wine and tried to get her to drink. The first cogent thing that Marion said was:

"It didn't work!"

"What didn't, darling?"

"The spell."

Margot had no idea what she was talking about until Marion explained about her visit to the Dane: how, even before she had heard about the engagement, she was afraid that Hainselin might stray; how, following the Dane's advice, she had saved her menstrual blood and put it in the wine that she had shared with Hainselin.

"Marion, you must be crazy to take chances like that! You could be burned at the stake!"

"I don't care, now that I know it's true. I went to see him, and heard it from his own lips. The marriage is in June. I can't bear it."

Margot shook her head in disgust and cursed under her breath. "I knew it. Just another cheating coward!"

Marion didn't bother to defend him. She just hung her beautiful head and wept.

"Marion, don't cry. You're worth fifty of him."

But Marion just shook her head slowly from side to side, moaning in despair.

"What shall I do? What shall I do?" was all she would say.

"I'll tell you what to do. Go to the beguinage: there are some good women there and they can find you work. And wait for Richard." Margot was at a loss for what else to say.

There was a long silence, punctuated only by sobs.

"Richard is dead," Marion said in a low moan.

This is what Margot had privately come to believe. Richard had been besotted by Marion, but it had been more than a year since she had heard from him. Only death could account for his defection. Still Margot asked: "But how can you know? Have you had news?"

"No. But I had a dream," Marion said. Margot waited in apprehension; this was a medium she understood.

Marion closed her eyes. "It was foggy. I was in a forest with tall trees. Too tall to be real. Then I heard music. The mist parted and I saw a host of people dancing in a circle. There were many knights and noble ladies. One of them stepped out of the ring and turned toward me. It was Richard. He offered me his hand, inviting me into the ring. But then the shape of a terrible wound began to appear on his forehead, all bloody and edged with grey — as if his brains were leaking out." Marion said these last words sobbing so hard that her body shook.

Margot had heard about those dances of the dead. She shuddered and wanted to cross herself. But she wanted to reassure her friend.

"Marion, it was only a dream." Yet Margot privately prayed that if Richard really was present among those accursed dancers, that he may someday find rest.

"He's in hell because of me," Marion whispered.

"I don't believe that," said Margot. "God is a God of love. He would never punish someone for loving truly, as Richard loved you."

Marion stopped crying, her face contorted with anguish.

"But we weren't married! Our love was a mortal sin. And now I have sinned with Hainselin. God has punished me by taking them both away." She began sobbing again.

Margot shook her head vigorously.

"No! The only mortal sins are sins against love."

"Then Hainselin is a sinner because I know he loves me, not Agnesot. But she has a dowry and I am poor. And he will inherit the shop when her father dies."

In a gentle but firm voice Margot said: "You must forget him, my dear. Hainselin was not like Richard. He did not love you in the same way. He lied to you about marriage. And now he has treated you as if you were a *feme fole* — that he could use and then throw away."

Marion's sobs became hysterical laughter.

"I would rather be Hainselin's *feme fole* than anyone else's honorable wife. He's driven me mad!" Marion was becoming more and more agitated, and Margot felt helpless. She managed to get her to drink a little wine and applied a damp cloth to her forehead. But Marion wouldn't lie down, and she never stopped weeping. All at once she sprang up from her chair and grabbed Margot's arm.

"Help me, Margot. The Dane said that you could. In God's name, help me."

The Seers

Brother Jacques was *a seer of hearts and reins*, of this Rupert was convinced. What he sensed in others were the very secrets they kept most carefully guarded. When Rupert had unburdened himself concerning his former love for Felice, he had made a pivotal leap of faith toward Jacques. But now he realized that he was only divulging what Jacques already knew. The friar seemed to know everything! Yet, he was an exemplar of patience; his address was invariably kind and gentle. Rupert never felt pushed or coerced.

And Jacques took such an interest in Rupert. At first it made him feel special; and now, he knew that he was special. Rupert was among the chosen: one of the four elect. They all felt the same way about Jacques;

he knew without asking. Brother Jacques could see into their hearts as well. How did Rupert know this? He wasn't sure; he just knew. It was as if there was a common well of information from which they all drank. They knew without being told that Philip, the man to whom Rose had been betrothed, hadn't accepted her conversion; refused to give up. They knew that Philip had raised the hue and cry, prompting the priest Hervey to attend the last meeting of the Faithful. They also knew that the incident involving the drowned boy would attract the attention of the authorities: that Chancellor Gerson, who had witnessed the event, would send someone over to check up discreetly — hence the presence of the two priests standing with Hervey and Felice.

And Brother Jacques' elect also knew that there was another seer in the vicinity — someone who was aware of Jacques and even shared some of his abilities — the moment they saw the old woman among the Faithful. Alicia recognized what she was first; then the others knew. The woman was one of the weak; she put no trust in her powers. But had she been stronger, it wouldn't have mattered. Brother Marcus was acquainted with her; she would do nothing to interrupt the progress of the Lord's work.

Meanwhile Margot, as preoccupied as she was with Marion's increasing misery, was incapable of dispelling the alarm she experienced upon seeing Brother Jacques. The visions played repeatedly, over and over in her mind. The meaning of the first one was becoming clearer: the shepherd was not simply the Good Shepherd, he was Brother Jacques. The brown work clothes were but a thinly disguised version of the Franciscan habit. The black and white sheep were the Dominican Faithful. When she first had the vision, the revelation of their blindness was terrifying. At a distance, however, she was inclined to favor a benign interpretation: sheep needed their shepherd — blind sheep even more so. The other two revelations seemed to corroborate the friar's pastoral role. For a priest to appear as Christ was not really surprising. As a girl, she had often been told that the priest stood *in loco Christi* — the closest one could come to encountering Christ on earth. The women represented in the icons of her last dream were wearing the habits of the Dominican Third Order. Their adoration of Brother Jacques was doubtless in recognition of the Christ-like aspect of the priest.

But her visions were also reminders of the awesome and fearful aspect of the divine. The same parish priest from her childhood had been fond of a certain biblical passage: *it is a dreadful thing to fall into the hands of a living God.* Margot had never quite understood what it meant, but it continued to haunt her. Now this scriptural truth had been dramatically manifested in her visions. She had been frightened of the visionary Christ. But wouldn't this response be appropriate in the context of the Last Judgment, when Christ returned to judge the quick and the dead? Brother Jacques' appearance as Christ might also augur his future role as Margot's confessor.

But many things remained opaque — particularly in the last vision. Why was there desolation and weeping? What was that terrible smell? Who was concealed in the well? What did the letters mean? And why did her recognition of Brother Jacques only serve to heighten her dread?

A Dinner Party

Prior Giles himself had invited Jacques for dinner at the Dominican priory. He felt it was the least he could do. This Franciscan had, after all, been doggedly pursuing work among the Faithful that was really the responsibility of the Dominicans. And he had, by all accounts, been doing an impressive job. Both Marcus and Rupert, brethren whom Giles correctly intuited were inclined to agree about very little, jointly sang the praises of Brother Jacques. And now it was rumored that this same Jacques was something of a wonder-worker. Giles hoped that the invitation wouldn't be interpreted as an instance of prurient interest in the wake of his alleged miracles, though admittedly there was some of that. Nevertheless, the prior felt that such an invitation was not only warranted, but should have been extended earlier.

Giles decided to make an ecumenical night of it, inviting the Cistercian abbot as well. John Gerson, the university's young Chancellor, was also included on the guest list. This was yet another invitation that Giles had been intending for some time. It was said that Gerson was rather reserved and could sometimes be quite difficult. Even so, Giles always did what he could to ensure smooth relations between the order and university officials. It made life so much easier. The table was rounded off with several brothers from the priory. It seemed only natural that Rupert and Marcus should be among the guests. Giles also thought it would be fitting to include Brother Martin. He had earned that right, both by virtue of his venerable age and the fact that he was probably the most learned of the priory's brethren. Giles would seat the old friar beside Chancellor Gerson in the event that either developed a penchant for scholarly disputation while still at table. Martin's mind was as keen as ever.

Martin, for his part, was only too glad to be asked, welcoming a break from routine. The members of the community had already taken their places when the prior's guests filed in, heading toward the elevated table at the east end of the refectory. The prior had recently been criticized by some guest for having too ascetic a board, so Martin eyed the various platters positioned on the table with interest. There were two different kinds of fish prepared in special sauces, and he also saw a bowl of what appeared to be fresh water eels. Spiced lentils and plenty of bread — wheat bread; not rye. One sip of wine was all that was needed to ascertain its superior quality. So the prior had clearly stepped up to the occasion. Martin saw with satisfaction that he was seated next to the young Chancellor, and anticipated some interesting conversation.

The blessing was barely over when Martin launched into a detailed account of the mysterious palimpsest and the challenges it presented. At first, Gerson seemed taken aback by this unexpected onslaught of ardent verbiage from a relative stranger. But when he came to understand the source of Martin's excitement, he couldn't help but be intrigued.

"Yet it seems doubtful that a manuscript could have survived Montségur with all the pillaging and burning that took place," said Gerson.

"Your skepticism would be justified under normal circumstances. But our author was hiding in a well during the disastrous denouement. Of course that makes for a wretched script. There are parts that neither I nor Master Anthony can decipher. But I refuse to give up. I still have a few tricks up my sleeve," the old friar said with satisfaction.

"Master Anthony? Who might that be?" asked Gerson. "I know several masters by that name."

"The only middle-aged theologian I know who still looks like a schoolboy!" Such a description was unmistakable, and Gerson smiled.

"That is quite a coincidence," Gerson remarked. "At present, Master Anthony and I are collaborating on an interesting problem."

Brother Martin's response was prompt. "And I think I know which one: the implications of mistaking Satan for Christ. Am I correct?" He looked to Gerson, who, though surprised, conceded this was so.

Martin continued: "The palimpsest may actually speak to questions of discernment. But don't tell Anthony yet. I want to surprise him."

Brother Jacques was seated between the Chancellor and Prior Giles. Yet despite this signal place of honor, nobody seemed to be talking to him. Gerson, who wanted nothing more than to engage him in conversation, tried to angle himself in such a way that he could speak to the Franciscan without turning his back on the old Dominican. But the Chancellor's hopes of drawing Brother Jacques into the conversation were dashed when a serious faux pas, occurring just down-table, wafted their way like a fetid wind. Everyone's attention became focused on the Cistercian abbot seated to the left of Giles, who was introducing an extremely awkward subject. Initially sniffing ascetic disapproval at the opulence of the prior's table, the abbot had finally relaxed into second helpings of just about everything, washed down with a liberal amount of wine. Now he was saying in a very clear voice to no one in particular:

"I understand that there is a miracle worker afoot in Paris. Apparently some cleric or other claims to have brought a boy back to life." Whether the abbot didn't notice, didn't understand, or perhaps even resented the prior's efforts to shush him, is unclear. He continued:

"St. Bernard once attempted something of the sort. When a young boy on the borders of Burgundy died, his family immediately sent for our saintly abbot. Bernard knelt in front of the boy for some time, deep in prayer. Eventually, he was prompted by God to prostrate himself on the boy's body. So when Bernard stood up, the onlookers waited for the boy to arise as well — confident they were privy to a miracle in the making." He paused for dramatic effect: "Nothing happened! The boy remained dead."

The embarrassment arising from the abbot's gaffe was deepened by the story's apparent pointlessness: why report a miracle if no miracle occurred? Most of the guests were probably as flummoxed as Bernard's disappointed onlookers. The tacit consensus was that the old abbot clearly had too much wine. But there was a considerable range of responses to his behavior. Prior Giles was still desperately attempting to silence the abbot without publicly humiliating him. Martin, who had seen many pillars of the church come to grief in Avignon through overindulgence, chuckled softly to himself. But Gerson, who had always felt a special devotion to St. Bernard, was chagrined, and wondered why every Cistercian felt free to bandy Bernard's name about as if they owned him.

The abbot, oblivious to his audience's reaction, continued relentlessly. "My point is that God's ways are never transparent. If it is possible for a miracle to be withheld from a true saint, it is just as possible for someone who is not a saint, perhaps even someone of suspect character, to effect a miracle."

There was a terrible silence. All eyes unconsciously turned to Brother Jacques, who had been listening attentively with admirable composure. Prior Giles cleared his throat and turned to his Franciscan guest.

"My dear son, I am certain that the abbot does not understand your role in these recent events." He smiled at the abbot and patted his hand in a reassuring manner before he resumed. "I promise you that his comments were in no way intended to cast aspersions on your character."

All the color had drained from the Cistercian's face, who only now realized his blunder. "No certainly not! My apologies, brother, if I have offended you," he spluttered.

Brother Jacques leaned forward so he could look directly at the mortified monk. His smile was amused and friendly.

"There is certainly no offense taken, abbot. In fact, I take heart that there are still some people in Paris who don't know about the incident and so aren't inclined to follow me around pointing." Everyone laughed in relief and gratitude. His easy humor had saved the evening.

Gerson never achieved the richly anticipated conversation with the Franciscan at table. Nevertheless, he had seen enough to be impressed. Extremely impressed. When Anthony and Baldwin had reported back to Gerson about the Thursday meeting at St.-Jacques, their assessment of Brother Jacques had been riddled with ambivalence. They placed considerable emphasis on doctrinal points, dwelling on the Franciscan's failure to recognize sufficiently the superiority of the celibate state. Gerson shared none of their equivocation. The friar's demeanor bespoke unfeigned modesty and humility. It was too soon to speak to the question of holiness of life, but Gerson construed what he had witnessed tonight as a favorable indication.

A gentle pressure on the arm interrupted Gerson's thoughts. It was Jacques.

"Chancellor. May I have the pleasure of walking with you?"

Gerson was both euphoric and unnerved to be addressed by a man over whom hung the presumption of sanctity.

"Friar, I would be delighted, but it is out of your way."

Brother Jacques knew that of course. But it didn't matter. Apparently he had been every bit as anxious to talk with Gerson as Gerson was with him. Imagine that! And Gerson was not alone in being unnerved. Jacques apparently stood in awe of the Chancellor for his wisdom and learning. The Franciscan confessed he wasn't a learned man himself. He was not at home in the university; nor did he think that men with extensive university training had much time for him. But he had read some of Gerson's sermons and found them deeply moving. There was one in particular that Jacques had read several times: it was written on the feast of St. Bernard, and followed the saint's progress in transcending worldly trials. Throughout, Gerson addressed the audience in the voice of Bernard: so deep, yet so accessible. The Franciscan was thrilled at the opportunity to meet the man who knew Bernard so well; who could recognize and describe his saintly trials with such precision and empathy. It was the next best thing to being with Bernard himself.

The night was fine and the moon was full: it was only natural that the two men would stop in the square to admire the cathedral by moonlight. Then, like old friends who could anticipate the whims of one another, they sat down on a grassy knoll to talk. This was done without any premeditation or prior agreement. They both apprehended a shared desire. And how they talked! Their conversation ranged over just about everything: the schism, the war, the role of the university in this time of crisis, the strained relationship between the mendicant orders and how they could be improved — everything. But parts of their conversation were much more personal. Brother Jacques shared the sense of alienation and loneliness that he felt since arriving in Paris. He missed the nave of the cathedral of St. Sernin with its exquisite rhythm in stone; the astringent wine of the region; food cooked in olive oil rather than butter; the familiar sound of the *langue d'oc* over the harsh twang of the northern *langue d'oïl*. But most of all, he missed his beloved brethren in the priory. It was only among them that he felt understood and embraced for who he was. And then it was the Chancellor's turn. Gerson found himself revealing the loneliness he had endured. It had begun when he was but a youth entering university. He was more serious than the other boys, more studious. And he was from a more humble background. He didn't know how to play and jest like the rest of them, and he was mocked. His isolation was augmented by the assumption of an office that he had only accepted with ambivalence.

Their conversation was so all encompassing and wide-ranging that afterward Gerson couldn't begin to enumerate all the things they had talked about. It was not until the clock in the Conciergerie struck three that they got to their feet, once again impelled by wordless consensus.

"I was there, you know. When the boy drowned. I was speaking with the poor bereaved mother." Gerson blurted this out before he knew it. But that wasn't surprising: the incident had remained uppermost in his mind. In addition to scouring Paris for witnesses, scribe in tow, Gerson had returned more than once to interview the mother and her son. The doctors whom Gerson had brought to examine the boy found an erratic pulse and a level of damage to the lungs consistent with someone who had been drowned. But they were optimistic that there was room for improvement. In short, Gerson's conviction that what he had witnessed was a genuine miracle was stronger than ever.

"Were you indeed there? I wasn't aware of much — apart from the boy," said Jacques.

There was a profound silence — one that Gerson could have filled with many questions, but didn't dare. There was so much Gerson wanted to know. But it would be unconscionable to pry into a person's relationship with the Lord; the most personal thing there was. Even so, Gerson found himself asking.

"What was it like?"

A simple question that was a stand-in for so many others. How did it feel to have God's healing power coursing through you? Did Jacques see anything? Hear anything? A surge of energy, perhaps? The touch of a ministering angel? Was this the first time? What was it like when Jacques prayed? Did he hear voices? The rush of wings? Did he see images? Or lights? Did he ask specific favors of the Lord or merely give himself over in prayer, basking in the sweet sun of justice and divine grace? *What was it like*?

The Franciscan shook his head and smiled. "My friend, I can't tell you with words. And even if I could, you wouldn't be able to make sense of it."

It was said in such a way that Gerson didn't feel rebuffed or humiliated. He understood that he couldn't understand.

Before the two clerics separated, they embraced, exchanging the customary fraternal kiss on either cheek. When Gerson first felt the touch of the Franciscan's lips, he was powerfully moved. There was something underneath the kiss: a life-generating current that Gerson sensed was capable of filling him up, of completing him — if only he could abandon himself to its power; if only he would allow it in. A phrase from the Canticles played over and over in Gerson's mind: *Let him kiss me with the kisses of his mouth, for thy love is better than wine.* The Franciscan looked at Gerson with an expression of lucidity and comprehension, as if he knew what Gerson was thinking. Then he took Gerson's hand. For a moment the Franciscan's features were illuminated as if he were leaning over a powerful lamp. There was a transfer of energy — a charge so intense that Gerson lost consciousness for a moment, though still remaining on his feet. He was filled with a surge of elation. It only lasted for a moment, but it was a moment outside of time: an eternal moment. And, when it departed, bliss. Gerson was grateful. So grateful. For Jacques had given him a taste, just a taste, of what it was like.

The effect of his meeting with the Franciscan continued into Gerson's dreams. Gerson saw himself dressed in a Franciscan habit, standing in a high mountain pass. Close by, there was another man kneeling in prayer, also wearing the habit. His back was to Gerson, and he seemed unaware of his presence. His eyes were fixed on the holy marvel that was hovering above: it was a man with six wings, like a seraph, nailed to a cross. It suddenly disappeared. The man got to his feet very slowly, as if in pain, and turned around, his hands extended before him. The marks of nails were beginning to appear on his palms; Gerson could see the nail heads forming from his flesh. Something similar was happening to the man's feet: raised nails of flesh appeared; blood oozed through the punctures. And then blood began to appear on his right side. His tunic was soon soaked in blood, as if it were concealing a great wound. Gerson was filled with awe: he was on Mt. Alverna witnessing the stigmatization of St. Francis! And indeed, the bleeding man looked just like one of Giotto's images of St. Francis. But then the figure of the saint started to change: it grew dim and out of focus — almost as if he were fading. It flickered like the body of a firefly. Gerson stood by watching, fascinated, but in no way fearful. When the figure eventually began to stabilize and solidify once again, it no longer bore the familiar visage of the saint, or at any rate it was not the same man that Gerson had initially seen. In its stead was the unmistakable visage of Brother Jacques.

Gerson awoke with a start. His entire body was tingling. He got down on his knees and thanked God for the dream, tremulous with joy. He had received his sign. All doubts had been dispelled; all questions answered. Brother Jacques was, indeed, a saint.

When sleep overtook Anthony that night, it brought Simon Magus in its wake. *Dah! Dah! Dah!* The knocking wasn't merely persistent this time, but unbearably loud. Eventually the sound changed and it was no longer just knocking—more of a thumping, almost as if someone was pounding the door with a heavy sack. The building shook under the impact of each blow. Anthony was kneeling in prayer when the sound began. This time he didn't resist. He rose from his knees, and opened the door. Simon was there, leering, but he was not alone. He had someone with him, leaning heavily upon his shoulder. Someone dressed in black and white. Someone who seemed to be hurt. The man's head was lolling forward, so Anthony could only see that his tonsure was white. But then Simon hoisted his burden higher and the head fell backward. It was Martin—either asleep or in a dead faint. Simon lifted his beautiful eyes to Anthony and smiled.

"Make him stop," was all the magician said. "Make him stop."

Anthony stood motionless, his entire body numb with fear. Meanwhile, Simon continued smiling as he looked from Anthony to the old friar. His smile deepened until it was no longer a smile. As the mouth grew wider, the nose became elongated, and the face darker. Soon that most beautiful of men had become something sinister, feral, monstrous. His teeth were ferociously sharp, and his hands like claws. But he continued to speak through his terrible muzzle.

"Make him stop. Make him stop, or else."

And then the beast that had been Simon, with an insane animal smile appearing between a set of tusks, drove a claw into the old man's breast and extracted his beating heart. Martin cried out once, and was silent. The creature displayed the heart, holding it by his talons in front of his brutish face. He then opened his mouth to devour it.

It was Anthony's own scream that woke him up. He found himself struggling, soaked in sweat — his sheets wound around him mummy-like. The thing he most feared had been realized: Simon Magus was back in his dreams. And it wasn't the first time. The horror of this last dream was a mnemonic catalyst. He was now able to remember the other dreams: there had been two. In these earlier dreams, Simon threatened, but somehow remained outside — outside the warm glow of the camp-fire, outside the door. But this time Anthony had let Simon in. Why ever had he opened the door?

Anthony was flooded with fear and uncertainty. He didn't know how to interpret any of these dreams, but the final one was particu-larly disturbing. The ancients believed in oracular dreams. But the church fathers held that dreams were either inconsequential or mislead-ing — the vehicle of demons. Even so, demons could reveal true things, if they so choose. Anthony mustn't forget that. What if this dream was one of those rare, truthful sorts; that if he didn't follow the instruction to *Make him stop* something horrible might ensue? Yet stop what? All that came to mind was to stop Martin from reading the concealed journal. But it was too late for that.

Whatever the dream's quotient of truth might be, Anthony couldn't be comfortable until he saw his old friend again. That morning, immedi-ately after saying Mass, Anthony set out for the Dominican priory to see how Martin fared. It turned out he was doing very well indeed. He spoke with animation about some dinner the night before when he finally got to meet that boy genius, Gerson!

"But he was hardly what I expected. You never told me he could be charming," said Martin.

"I never supposed he could be!" responded Anthony with honesty.

Martin snorted with laughter. He then went on to complain about how the friar responsible for introductory theology at the priory's *studium* had developed an abscess in the leg and had to stay off his feet. In other words, Martin was required to fill in. Oh, he griped and grum-bled — *couldn't they leave an old monk alone? At my age, I shouldn't be teaching; I should be atoning for my sins!* Yet Anthony saw through this: he could sense how pleased Martin was to feel needed. They chatted the-ology for a while. Still Anthony hadn't forgotten what he had come for.

"Martin, you are finished with the Cathar journal, aren't you?"

"There's not much point in persisting, my boy. I believe we have gotten all that is humanly possible out of it," said Martin, looking out the window as he spoke.

Anthony was relieved, but wanted to make sure. "I have already returned the manuscript to its owners. But do you mind if I borrow the transcription you made?"

Martin raised his eyebrows in amusement. "I certainly do. It's my transcription, Master Anthony! Hands off! Go borrow the manuscript again, and make your own!"

"But if you aren't going to work on it..."

Martin was on his feet now, shuffling toward the door to usher Anthony out. "Now, now, now! I always expected something like this. You used to nod off in class all the time, demonstrating a susceptibility to sloth!"

Anthony laughed. There was never any point persisting once Martin was locked into a position. And Martin's archival proclivities were well known. He wanted to keep the transcription just like he kept all the notes that he made in the course of a project, regardless of their future utility. Without the original, Anthony doubted that Martin could make any more progress. So Anthony took his leave. There was no point disturbing Martin with the dream.

Chapter 7: Reversals

Heartbreak

Marion was losing weight. She couldn't sleep. The purple circles underscoring her eyes made them seem impossibly large, haunted, and unreal. And she never stopped crying. Margot, who had suffered more disappointments in her life than she could count, had never believed that it was possible to die from a broken heart. It pained her to see Marion proving her wrong.

Marion had gone to the Dane for a love potion. That was bad. But what was still worse was that the Dane told Marion that Margot could make potions as well. Margot tried to block out Marion's pathetic cry for help, but to no avail. After the initial attempt, Marion did not repeat her request for Margot to work magic on her behalf; she didn't need to. Curled up in bed, whimpering like a poor beaten dog, Marion hardly spoke, gazing at Margot in mute misery. Torn between fear for her friend's life and fear for her own, it was the friend who won.

Margot sat on the corner of Marion's bed and said softly, "Marion, I love you as if you were my own child. I want to help, but I'm afraid. The church says that such spells are heresy."

"But you said yourself that the only sins were sins against love!"

"I hope I was right. But before I do anything, you must swear that you will never tell anyone and that, if you are caught, you will never denounce me."

Marion promised.

"Swear by your faith with your body as surety," Margot insisted. After Marion had sworn, she went to Margot and hugged her. Margot kissed the younger woman on each cheek before saying:

"In order for the spell to work, you have to be lovers with Hainselin, as before."

Marion nodded. She would go and beg Hainselin to sleep with her again, at least until he was married. In her heart of hearts, Marion knew that Hainselin still loved her and wouldn't be able to deny her.

"You must do exactly what I say, no matter how strange it may sound," Margot continued. And what Margot told her to do was indeed very strange. First Marion was supposed to take a white rooster and kill it — either by sitting upon it or by turning it around very fast. Then she had to remove the bird's testicles and burn them until they became a powder. The powder was to be inserted into Hainselin's pillow.

"You must be careful not to put your head on the pillow or the spell is spoiled," Margot cautioned. "Then after eight or nine days, remove the powder and put some of it in Hainselin's wine."

"What will it do?"

"It will make him love you so passionately that he won't be able to get enough of you."

"Will it make him break off the engagement?"

"I hope so."

So Marion undertook the strange execution of the bird that very same day. She didn't like the idea of crushing the rooster, so first she tried spinning it. When this proved ineffective, she finally gave up and sat on it. Marion prepared the powder, planning to seek out Hainselin in the morning. In fact, she didn't have to wait that long. Margot had bumped into Hainselin by chance and told him that Marion wished to see him. Hainselin who, after the last painful interview, was convinced that Marion hated him and would never want to see him again, flew to her side.

"Dear Marion, forgive me. But there could be no happy ending for us. What would we live on?" He was holding her tightly against his breast and, for the first time in days, she felt at peace.

"That doesn't matter now. All that matters to me is that you are here."

They made love all night. Marion was on her guard, however, and never once put her head on Hainselin's pillow. Before he left, Hainselin kissed her tenderly and promised to return whenever he had a chance. Unfortunately, that was not very often. By day, Hainselin worked alongside his future father-in-law; after work, he was expected downstairs for dinner; after dinner, he was supposed to sit with Agnesot until bedtime, planning the wedding and talking about their future. It was difficult to sneak out without giving rise to suspicion. Meanwhile, it was already mid-May and the wedding was to take place in June. Although Margot had said that Hainselin needed to have slept on the pillow eight or nine times, Marion decided she would have to settle for less. After the third time he came over, she stirred some of the powder into Hainselin's wine.

"This wine tastes a little strange."

"It's from Bordeaux. It's supposed to be very good," Marion said nervously.

"But wasn't Bordeaux overrun by the English?" Hainselin said, frowning.

"It was smuggled out by a wounded soldier — a friend of Margot's," Marion answered, wildly improvising. Hainselin drank it down. He really couldn't bear to hurt Marion's feelings any more than he already had.

Marion was optimistic about the spell; Margot was much more trustworthy than the Dane. Hainselin came to see her often enough to keep her hopes alive, and seemed to love her as much as ever. But when Marion learned that he still had not called off the wedding, she was once again plunged into despair.

Margot was so glad to see Marcus again. She had been right: it was Lent that had kept him away. She had feared that her old friend had been annoyed by Marion's inopportune appearance at the end of his last visit; that it might have scared her poor lover off forever.

"It would take much more than that to keep me away from a woman like you!"

Margot laughed at his absolutely heroic gallantry, in view of the shambles she had become, and gave him a hug. She had missed him: his laugh, his talk, even his touch. Yet he seemed subdued. Less lusty, less laughing, more clerical. She wasn't quite sure how to behave with him. It wasn't as if he were one of those shy first-time customers whom she used to put at ease with some deft touches and coaxing. This was Marcus. They had known each other for years, and he could easily see such efforts for what they were. But he was so reserved, and this was making her timid. Perhaps he had seen her at the meeting of the Faithful. Margot didn't think he had noticed her, but perhaps he had. Could this account for the change? Was he angry? She needed to know.

"But what's the matter, Pork Chop? Is there something wrong?"

This was her affectionate name for him, and he had always liked it. But he gave no sign of having heard, even though he looked alert. In fact, he gave the impression that he was listening to something, but not to her. She repeated herself, and he started.

"Nothing's wrong. Nothing at all."

More silence; more of that strange attentive inattention. She could hear someone hawking fabric outside. *Satin, Satin, Satin.* It sounded strange to her. Satin? Who could afford satin in this area? But maybe it was a name. A girl's name? She'd never heard it before. The chanting suddenly stopped. Marcus sat on the edge of the bed facing away, his back to her. Why was he behaving like this? Margot, sitting with her back propped against the wall, was trying to look receptive for whatever he might have in mind. But Marcus kept his back to her. Suddenly he turned.

"Margot, there's something ailing me. Something that I think you can help me with."

His eyes were strange, like he was looking at her without seeing her. But she must not let her imagination run riot. Of course she would help him, in any way she could.

"It's a rather delicate subject — probably the most delicate for a man." She took his hand and squeezed it, encouraging him to continue.

"I know I am advancing in years. Nevertheless, I am not ready to give up all my pleasures — especially that sweetest of pleasures; the one that brought me to you."

Margot understood. Impotence: every man's fear. Clearly a monk is no different.

"We all age, my dear," she answered, trying to sound cheerful without being dismissive. "You might not have the same physical vigor you once had. But you can still know love. There is much more to love than a simple act."

When Margot patted Marcus' thigh, he started, brushing her hand away as if it were a crawling thing. She recoiled, hurt and uncertain. Then he surprised her by taking her hand, kissing it, and holding it to his heart. But he held her hand stiffly and at an awkward angle that hurt her wrist. She was afraid to say anything. Finally he spoke.

"Margot, please help me. You must have learned some magic from Concubina, back in the day."

"Who?"

Marcus turned toward her again. "The one who had the penis tree. You know," he said nudging her with what might have passed as affection. Yet, while wearing a rather comical coy look, his voice was like stone. "You tended the tree yourself. If a woman possesses the power to remove a man's virile member altogether, she certainly has the power to make it work!"

Margot burst out laughing. She couldn't help herself. "But there was no Concubina. I made her up, just like I made up the penis tree." Who would have thought it? For all their learning and deep thoughts, these clerics were just as gullible as babies. Concubina indeed!

But Marcus was not laughing. His empty stare was the perfect antidote to Margot's laughter, and her mirth gave way to apprehension. He flushed with anger and stood up.

"You cackling hag! I know you can help me, but you won't. Haven't I been a good friend to you over the years? Haven't I always come back to you when I could have found someone who was really worth sinning for? You stinking bag of bones!"

Margot winced. She hadn't been expecting that. A lather of blame buttressed by insults. But she didn't want him angry. They were over: she recognized that now. But they couldn't end like this. Not like this. He had turned his back on her again, and she put her arms around him, willing him to turn and look at her. When he didn't, she just sighed, leaning her cheek against his shoulder.

"My dear friend. I am grateful to you for your attention over the years. You have always made me feel desirable. Even more important, you made me feel special. But you could have stopped coming to see me whenever you liked. I would never have thought ill of you — not for a moment."

No answer; just that look as if he were listening to something far off. Then he began to fumble in his pockets. He placed a few coins on the table beside the bed.

"Marcus, just stay to talk. Look — you haven't finished your wine!" But he didn't answer. He just walked to the door. There was no kiss. Only a brief nod and he was gone.

Margot got to her feet and mechanically began tidying up the room. She poured his untouched wine back into the flagon. No point in wasting. In the old days, Marcus was a man of strong appetites: sometimes when he left she could barely walk! And he would certainly not have left behind any wine. When he first came to see her as a young novice, he was so shy that he couldn't even say what he wanted out loud. After they had lain down on the bed, he seemed so unsure. And then he began to tickle her, of all things. Something he had read somewhere, apparently. *Tickle her until she moans with joy.* The poor boy understood it literally. She smiled at the memory. Margot remembered all the different stages of his monastic career as if they had just happened. He had come to her exultant after he had taken his life vows — an occasion they had celebrated, however inappropriately, by doing it four times in a row with hardly a break. And how they had toasted his elevation to subprior!

"When I become prior, I will change the statutes so that I am afforded my own private prioress. And then you will come to move in with me!" He'd kissed her and they laughed. And then he tickled her again as a joke — just like the first time.

There was no Concubina and certainly no penis tree. Yet she still might have helped him the same way she was helping Marion. Maybe she should have. But she was afraid. She knew that most clerics thought that any little spell was evil; that all magic was *maleficia*. To help him would be putting herself at risk. Yet why was she so fearful? He was a dear old friend who would never do anything to hurt her. She should have helped him.

Then Margot did something she hadn't done in years: she sat on the bed and wept. She was aching in a place that she hardly remembered existed — it had been so long. Heartache: it's a real thing after all. Her heart wasn't just aching, it was breaking. There was a sharp pain in her breast and breathing was, for a time, difficult. It was only then that Margot realized that she loved Marcus. Their disparate statuses, life choices, and even the eventual disappearance of desire didn't make any difference. She loved him. She had loved him all along.

In the parish of St.-Jacques-de-la-Boucherie, another heart was breaking. Philip had come by the presbytery to return the mended thurible, and Hervey told him that Rose had taken her vows. The young man just sat there unmoving and silent, a study in abject misery. Philip didn't look himself. Underneath habitually tanned skin, his face was drawn and sickly; the whites of his eyes were jaundiced.

"Father, I want to tell you something that I was thinking last time we talked. I wasn't ready yet. It sounded so strange. But now I have to speak."

"You can tell me anything, Philip. Don't worry how it sounds. I have heard many odd things in my time."

Philip took a deep breath, and then plunged in.

"Rose is so different since her illness that I've found myself wondering: can that really be my Rose? And now I know. Even if she had stopped loving me, Rose would never have done this without telling me."

Not quite sure what Philip was getting at, Hervey just nodded. "Go on," he said.

"The real Rose was a loving woman, full of feeling. This woman is a stranger. I could tell the first time she looked at me."

"She didn't recognize you?"

"It's was more like she did recognize me, but was afraid of me and wanted me as far away as possible."

Hervey thought about this. He couldn't deny that both he and Felice had noticed a change. But his aim was to reassure Philip the same way they had tried to reassure themselves.

"Poor Rose has been shocked — body and soul. She probably still needs more time to recover before she can return to her old self."

Philip got to his feet and began pacing back and forth. He was running his fingers through his hair, yanking on it in agitation.

"But nothing is the same, father! Rose used to be chatty. Now you can't get a word out of her. She was a great one for a laugh; she never laughs now or even smiles. She doesn't eat! She used to be pretty and buxom; now she's like a ghost! She doesn't even smell the same."

"All these things could be explained by her illness."

There was a long pause as Philip groped for the right words.

"Father, I know that demons have power over us because of the sin of Adam. Could there be a demon inside Rose's body — a demon holding my real Rose captive?"

Hervey looked at the desperate man with pity; his anguish was heartbreaking.

"Philip, you are speaking about demonic possession. But Rose doesn't behave like a demoniac. She is not shrieking or frenzied. She does not possess any special or mysterious powers."

Philip had sunk back into his seat, lowering his head into his hands. But at the mention of special powers, he sat up, eyes alert and wide like a hunted animal. "What kind of powers?" he asked.

"Like a sudden miraculous gift of languages; or special knowledge of people's secret sins."

Philip was silent again for a time.

"If she's not possessed, is it possible that she's been stolen?" Philip's voice had dropped to a hoarse whisper, almost as if he were afraid of being overheard.

Hervey assured Philip that there was no doubt in his mind that the young woman in Anna's cottage was her daughter, Rose, but Philip didn't seem to hear him. Instead, he made a frantic grab for Hervey's hands.

"Haven't you heard those stories about women who were snatched by demons on their deathbed? The demons make false bodies for burial, so no one knows. It happened in Brabant. A man found the sweetheart he had just buried in a different city altogether — alive!"

Hervey looked at Philip with compassion. Philip was talking about changelings. But such things weren't really human. They were manikins — simulations fashioned by magic from pieces of wood or peat to replace the abducted person. Hervey had read about such instances, but never given them much heed. But even if changelings did exist, they were always lifeless. Whatever one might feel about Rose, it was impossible to deny that she was alive. His heart went out to the poor boy, who was imagining some land where the Rose whom he had loved was laughing and well. But this kind of speculation was not helpful. Hervey tried his best to attribute the change in Rose to the return of her original vocation for chastity, but to no avail. The distraught man hung his head in despair.

"If it is my Rose, why would she do such a thing?" Philip asked, tears welling up in his eyes.

"Only Rose knows the answer to that," responded Hervey.

In an effort to afford them some privacy, Felice had remained discreetly in the kitchen area — making bread as noisily as possible. But after Philip left, she didn't bother to pretend that she hadn't overheard most of the conversation.

"Father, Rose is so distant, she might as well be a different person. I couldn't even get her to look at me at the Thursday prayer meeting."

Hervey sighed. "Yes, my dear, but after a life threatening illness, one is bound to be different."

"It's not just that. I heard what you said about special powers. I am positive that Rose recited the psalm of thanksgiving in Latin last Thursday."

Hervey was overwhelmed by a feeling of dread.

The Fourth Vision and a Visit

Margot was sitting down, exhausted from listening to Marion's torrential fears. The poor girl was anxious the magic hadn't worked, tortured with self-reproach for not waiting the full eight or nine nights. And now she was asking Margot for more. Margot was aware of other magical aids. Concubina and the penis tree may have been fictions, but a certain woman from Flanders had once taught Margot some spells. These all involved the invocation of holy things, however, which may sound harmless enough. But Margot realized that holy words in certain contexts were not considered mere prayers, but efforts to conjure evil spirits. And the misuse of holy things made these spells all the more sinful. These thoughts had been running through Margot's head when she was overpowered by one of her trances.

Margot was back in the same high windswept place that was surrounded by walls. She was no longer alone, however. There were four other people standing in front of her: three men and one woman. Two she recognized: the tall man with a silver tonsure and the beautiful woman with red hair were the priest Hervey and his concubine. But there were two men she didn't know. The four of them were conversing in hushed tones, oblivious to her presence. Then they stood in a circle, their heads bowed in prayer. Margot heard the rushing sound of a fierce wind. It was louder than anything she had ever heard before. The trees in front of the wall were bent over double, but the four figures were not disturbed by the wind. Even their hair and clothing remained motionless. Throughout the gale, the four stood serene. Pale fire appeared in the air — a tongue of flame lighting on the head of each. For a moment, the four were illuminated from within, glowing as if fashioned from lava. The fire and the wind disappeared as quickly as they had come. They heard a noise from the chapel, and looked at one another.

"We must leave this place," the woman said.

And then they went, two by two over the wall, and began climbing down the sheer face of the cliff. The priest and his concubine were the first to go. The other two men followed. Margot was left in that high dreadful place all alone. The chapel door was just beginning to open when she awoke.

The other visions had left her tired and baffled, but at least she had some theories about what they might mean. This one was different. Margot had no explanation. By the same token, the first three visions had a personal dimension. But the most recent vision seemed to have nothing to do with her. It felt as if it were meant for the people in the dream, whom she intuited were in great danger. Even so, the windswept locale was the same as in the preceding vision, suggesting its relation.

Over the next few days, Margot was gripped by the progressive feeling that she needed to share these visions with someone. Brother Jacques was out of the question. Even if it was God's plan that he become her confessor and spiritual director, she could not as yet overcome her fear. The prospect of approaching him was too daunting. But she perceived a gentleness in the priest Hervey. His expression and demeanor seemed kindly. The fact that he had a concubine also recommended him to Margot — it suggested that he might better understand that a sinner, like herself, could still have a conscience and a wish to do good in the world.

So Margot attended Vespers at St.-Jacques-de-la-Boucherie one evening in early June. It was a lovely service, a balm to her troubled soul. The days had grown longer and the sun was only now beginning to wane. Jewel-colored light filtered through the windows, staining the grey stones of the floor. She could hear birds chirping in the green outside the church. Only a handful of people were in attendance, departing briskly when the service ended. They clearly had places to go, work to finish, meals to cook, babies to kiss, wives to hug. Margot had her daughter Joan, it was true. And there was Marion. Yet waiting on the steps of the porch in trepidation, Margot suddenly felt old and alone. The priest eventually emerged.

"Father, forgive me. Do you have a minute?"

"Yes of course, madame," he said with alacrity. "How can I help you?"

Now that the opportunity to speak to someone about her visions was at hand, Margot could not find the words; she even felt a little faint. Eventually she said:

"I have seen certain things that must be told. Frightening things. So I have come to you."

When the old woman first addressed Hervey, he imagined that she had come to make a confession. Now he had the impression that she had witnessed something disturbing, probably a crime. He nodded.

"You have done the right thing." Hervey was about to conduct her back into the church when he observed that she was having some trouble breathing.

"Mother, I am afraid you are unwell. Why don't you come over to the presbytery? My daughter is there and she will be able to make us comfortable. We can talk there."

Margot thought for a second. She had intended to speak to Hervey alone. But the fact that his concubine had appeared in the last vision was an indication that it pertained to her as well. She nodded her agreement and let herself be led the few steps to the presbytery. When Hervey began to open the door, Margot suddenly demurred.

"I am an old sinner, father."

"Oh, we are all sinners here, aren't we?" he said to Felice, who had just appeared at the door.

"Mostly certainly, ma'am. And all our best friends are sinners as well!" answered Felice merrily. So Margot entered, reassured by the friendly banter.

"I've seen you before, haven't I? With a very pretty woman. Your daughter?"

"No, my lady. I have a daughter. But that was my friend Marion you saw me with. She has brought me here a few times. The last time was on a Thursday to hear Brother Jacques."

"Are you from this parish?"

"No, father. I'm from St.-Landry." Of all the Parisian parishes, this one was the poorest and probably the most vice-ridden. Margot hung her head in shame. But neither Felice nor Hervey showed any sign of embarrassment, let alone censure. Instead, Hervey placed a chair for Margot and Felice handed her a cup of wine.

"I was going to take a walk," Felice volunteered, tacitly offering them privacy.

"Please stay," said Margot. "What I have to say is for you as well."

Felice and Hervey looked at one another with surprise. Then Margot took a breath and embarked upon a description of her visions in the order of their appearance. When it came to the third vision, representing the letters she had seen proposed something of a challenge: Margot couldn't manipulate a pen. But then Felice thought of putting flour on the baking board, and Margot drew the letters with her finger as best she could. Apart from this intervention, neither Hervey nor Felice said much until Margot was finished. Hervey questioned her about the nature of the visions themselves. Apparently they had begun when she was around twelve, and could occur either when she was awake or sleeping. The manner in which the visions presented themselves changed over time, however. They had begun as straightforward pictures which often conveyed information: where her mother had left her rosary or that her baby sister had fallen. As Margot grew older, the visions became more confused. Sometimes there would be a jumble of images; at other times they appeared in what Margot referred to as "story form," where there were sequential scenes and movement. Her current visions belonged in this category.

"But they all tended to look like one thing, while meaning something else. Symbols, I guess you would call them. Like the dream where I saw a fox, but I knew when I woke up that the fox was really my *ami*, who wasn't to be trusted." She smiled ruefully. "I should've paid attention to that one!"

If these recent visions were symbolic, however, Margot did not have the key to their meaning. She had initially thought that the shepherd and the images of the Savior were God's way of effecting her repentance. But after she recognized Brother Jacques at the Thursday meeting, she was frightened.

"And you are certain that he recognized you?" Felice asked.

"As certain as I am sitting here. I felt it in my heart."

"So you came here to ask my father's advice."

"It's not just that, my lady. The last vision: I think it means you are both in some kind of danger. I came to warn you."

A Death

Brother Martin had sent Anthony a message to come right away: he had exciting news. But Anthony was teaching and only received the message after Vespers. He made his way to the Dominican priory early the next morning and gave his name at the porter's gate, saying that Martin was expecting him. There was a considerable delay. Anthony had to teach later that morning and was about to approach the porter again, when the Dominican prior, Giles, appeared. Anthony got to his feet in alarm.

"Has Brother Martin taken ill?" he asked with apprehension.

The prior answered with a sad smile that seemed to confirm Anthony's worst fears. "He has gone to where there is no more illness, my friend. We found him a couple of hours ago."

Anthony was speechless. The prior gently took him by the arm, leading him into his office where he closed the door.

"He didn't appear for Matins or Lauds. That was a bit unusual: Martin was punctual, as a rule. A stickler, in fact. But he had been working hard on that theology class. Oh, I regret that we gave it to him now! He was getting older, and needed his rest. Naturally, I wanted to let the poor man sleep. At Prime, however, I thought we should at least check up on him. And there he was — slumped across the little writing table in his cell. He had been dead for some time: the body was cold and the rigor had begun to set in. I think his heart just stopped."

The prior's eyes were filled with inexpressible sorrow. Giles was only a few years younger than Martin, so they had first met as youths, and grown old together. Then his expression was lightened by fond remembrance.

"Martin was a true scholar! As a young man I used to feel so competitive toward him. I thought that if I worked really hard that maybe I could overtake him." Giles laughed. "I didn't come close to his level of accomplishment, of course. He never felt competitive with anyone. There was no need!"

Anthony tried to imagine the serene prior locked in desperate competition with his old friend, but couldn't. The prior continued:

"It's such a great loss to the monastery: we have no one else with the extent of his learning. Besides, he was such a character. We all loved him so!"

Anthony momentarily closed his eyes, deeply regretful that he hadn't seen more of his friend in the past year. It was his own fault that they did not meet more often; Martin's body was no longer a match for his mind; the burden of making the effort thus fell to Anthony. He could see Martin's elfin grin in his mind's eye, his grimace of frustration when Anthony couldn't keep up with his train of thought, the way his head bobbed with excitement when he was on the trail of a new idea. Always so many new ideas. That's what had kept him young. Anthony sent a wordless prayer heavenward.

"I know you loved him too," the prior said, nodding. They were silent in mutual commiseration for a time, and then Anthony remembered why he had come.

"Prior, do you know why Martin summoned me?"

A light frown passed across the prior's face. "Weren't the two of you collaborating on some sort of transcription?"

"But we had finished," Anthony said hoarsely, gripped by a sick fear.

The prior gave a little laugh. "Not to Brother Martin's mind, you hadn't. Yesterday he told me about some breakthrough he had made. He was very excited."

The dream about Simon returned to Anthony in full force, the words *Make him stop!* sounding over and over in his head. So Martin had kept working on the manuscript after all, and now he was dead. He would still be alive if only Anthony had made him stop.

"Did he share the nature of the breakthrough with you?" Anthony asked.

"You know how our friend liked mysteries," the prior responded. "All he would say was that whatever had been puzzling you was childishly simple." That wasn't very encouraging. Brother Martin would have been an exceedingly precocious child.

The prior reflected a moment. "I do remember one other thing. He mentioned something about ingenious speculation."

But the prior had no idea what form this speculation took. It might have referred to Martin's own line of thinking: this wouldn't have been completely out of character since the old man was occasionally hubristic about his scholarly accomplishments. But it might also signify something speculative about the text itself. Unfortunately, Martin had left no message for Anthony, intending to reveal his discovery in person. It was all very frustrating.

It occurred to Anthony that Martin, meticulous in every respect, would most certainly have amended the transcription to reflect his discovery. In all likelihood, the manuscript was still on his writing table. The prior immediately rang the bell to summon the person who had discovered Martin's body. Eventually, a gangly young friar appeared.

"Brother Rupert, can you check and see what is on Brother Martin's writing table?"

Rupert promptly obeyed, soon returning. "There is nothing striking, prior. Just a pot of ink, a quill, a cloth for blotting, and a candle. And the infirmarian left his mirror behind." The mirror was routinely used to check for signs of life.

"But no notes? Or a manuscript of sorts?"

"Nothing like that, prior," replied Rupert.

Anthony wondered whether Martin had, perhaps, taken the transcription to the library to consult some reference or other. The prior acknowledged that this was a possibility and asked Brother Rupert to keep his eyes open.

"Brother Rupert is hard at work on the *Sentences*, so if there is a stray manuscript around, he is the one who would be most likely to find it," he said to Anthony by way of explanation. "How is that commentary going, Brother Rupert?"

"It goes, prior."

"Good, good! Well, we won't detain you any longer. I know how anxious you are to get back to work."

Anthony wasn't entirely satisfied, however. It seemed strange that Martin would be sitting at his writing table when there was no manuscript or parchment present. But the prior didn't find this unusual: Martin may have felt unwell after a dinner. In fact, the prior had felt a little queasy himself and thought that there might have been something wrong with the fish. In such cases, people generally prefer sitting up to lying down.

Giles led Anthony to where Martin's body had been laid out in the chapel, candles at his head and feet. Summer was approaching and the body would be buried that very afternoon. The prior left the priest alone to take leave of his friend. As Anthony bent down to kiss the old monk's lifeless hand, a large tear splashed on the wrist.

Hainselin's Hood

It had been two weeks since Marion had last seen Hainselin. She was now almost certain that the magical powder had failed her. Still, she had to see him again. She had to confront him and learn the truth.

The truth was grim. Although Hainselin was not exactly a mercenary, he was certainly no martyr. Like practically everyone else in Paris, Hainselin was only one job away from poverty: a marriage to Agnesot would secure him against such a fate. She was not as beautiful as Marion, to be sure. But as Marion grew more frantic, Agnesot's desirability soared. Hainselin was an uncomplicated man who sought an uncomplicated life. Not only had Marion become an unfortunate complication, but one that preyed on his conscience. Marion's mere existence was a walking reproach and an invitation to guilt: guilt over his lies, guilt over his broken promises, guilt over her ensuing suffering, and now guilt that he no longer desired her as he once had. In point of fact, Hainselin was beginning to experience what he told himself was a more virtuous guilt: guilt over betraying Agnesot, for whom he was developing an increasing sense of loyalty. And as his loyalties shifted, another more self-serving sense of guilt arose: sexual guilt, a retrospective self-censuring for his attachment to Marion, a fallen woman. Agnesot was a virgin. By comparison, Marion was someone who was really not fit to marry. She kept company with women like Margot. What was it his grandmother used to say? *Show me your friends and I will tell you who you are.* Marion's friendship with Margot spoke volumes. As his sense of self-righteousness expanded, Hainselin even began to question whether he ever actually promised Marion that they would marry. Wasn't it Marion who had continually projected their relationship into the future? It was never his idea in the first place.

He blamed the whole mess on Marion: she had exploited his weakness, seducing him as surely as Eve had once seduced Adam. Hainselin knew that there was only one remedy for the situation: to make a complete confession. Confession would serve as a kind of exorcism (though he may not have put it in these terms) — an exorcism that would expel any debt to Marion, facilitating a complete break. A heartfelt confession was the first essential step to regaining the moral high ground. In the meantime, Hainselin wanted to avoid Marion at all costs. He couldn't go to the Thursday meetings for fear of running into her. But he nevertheless sent a message to Brother Jacques, asking for an appointment early in the week.

When he got to the church, the Franciscan was waiting for him in front of a recently donated window celebrating a miracle of St. Jacques. The window depicted the saint's intercession for a young man, returning from a pilgrimage to Compostella, who was falsely accused of defiling a chambermaid and sentenced to hang. The saint kept him alive on the gibbet for thirty-six days. Hainselin was struck by the parallel. He was the innocent pilgrim; Marion the scheming chambermaid. Brother Jacques would save him from Marion's false claims.

Confession proved to be the perfect remedy for his spiritual malaise. Usually Hainselin was a reluctant penitent, needing to be prompted at every turn. But this time he *vomited out the venom of his sins* like a good Christian should. And with every anguished utterance, he felt lighter. Brother Jacques, gentle but stern, impressed upon Hainselin the full extent of his sinful association with Marion. He had committed a mortal sin, and his salvation was at stake. Their relations must be severed. The break must be immediate and irrevocable. As Brother Jacques spoke the words of absolution, Hainselin imagined that the Franciscan was looking at him with approval and respect. He was given ten hail Marys and ten Pater Nosters, to be said every day for the next two weeks. Hainselin interpreted the moderate penance as a clear indication that Jacques understood the temptations endemic to secular life, that the friar was, in fact, a man of the world.

Hainselin felt like a new man with the detritus of his old life already far behind him. Hence, he was especially dismayed when he spotted Marion waiting in the alley for him a couple of days later. She was, as usual, dressed in grey, except for a flower of pink fabric on her sleeve peeking out like an emblem of misplaced optimism. She was thinner than he remembered. For a moment he was inclined to run back up the alley the way he had come. But he forced himself to stand his ground.

"Hainselin! I've missed you so. Where have you been?" asked Marion, smiling through tears.

"I've been working hard, Marion. There's been no time."

"Make time now. Come home with me!"

"No Marion," he swallowed hard. "This must stop. It's not fair to Agnesot. In two weeks she'll be my wife." Marion blanched, shrieking as if she had been stabbed. Hainselin looked around in distress. They were all too near his lodgings and he couldn't risk being overheard. He had to get away.

"Don't you love me?" Marion cried. She was trying to clasp her arms around his neck. Hainselin was forced to grip her lower arms to hold her at bay.

"You've worn out my love with these scenes. It's over. It should never have happened in the first place."

Hainselin dropped Marion's arms and turned. She made one desperate grab as he fled up the alley.

A little while later, Margot heard the door and then the sound of footsteps moving slowly up the stairs. The dazed look on Marion's face left little doubt of what had just occurred.

"You've seen him, then," said Margot. It was a statement, not a question.

"Yes. I waited for him after work. He doesn't love me. He's getting married in a couple of weeks." Marion's voice was drained of expression.

"What is that you've got in your hand?"

Marion looked at Margot, not comprehending, before she looked down at her fist. It was a green hood stained with what looked like blood. She examined it with an eerie detachment.

"When Hainselin ran away from me, I tried to stop him. I grabbed his hood." It turned out that there was a sizeable clump of brown hair inside the hood.

Margot nodded grimly. "Well, he deserves a patch of baldness as a wedding gift." Marion winced to hear "Hainselin" and "wedding" mentioned in the same sentence. She walked into her room, as if to lie down. But first she went to where her chest stood, opening the little coffer. She nestled the tuft of brown hair inside the box, next to a crumbling piece of moss.

Telling Tales Out of School

Anthony was pacing the length of the cloister, up and down. He'd failed his old friend, and the results were fatal. He hadn't understood what was happening. He still didn't. It was as if he were a traveler hearing ominous sounds in the bushes, but whatever was stalking him had yet to reveal itself. Still, if he had trusted his own intuition, he would have insisted on taking the transcription. Then Martin would still be alive.

There was no more time for hesitation and doubt. Something evil was at work in Paris. Anthony needed to talk to Baldwin. He found him in the library, scratching his head over the problem of rapture. He greeted Anthony with a question requiring its own kind of discernment.

"Aquinas was seen levitating while saying Mass. It was a miracle. But since Aquinas was immensely fat, shouldn't this incident qualify as two miracles?"

Anthony had never been less in the mood to indulge Baldwin's scholarly whims. He gestured with his hand, and Baldwin dutifully followed him out of the library. It was drizzling, but a little rain wouldn't hurt them. It might even have a sobering effect on Baldwin. They sat on a bench in the middle of the cloister, the same place where Baldwin had smarted in the wake of Gerson's reprimand. An apple tree that was just coming into bloom provided partial shelter.

"What's important enough to preempt the marvel of a corpulent Dominican's levitation?" Baldwin wanted to know.

"Something quite serious. So please rearrange your expression."

Baldwin was still grinning.

"Please."

Anthony waited until the smile faded before continuing. "It begins with a story that has never been told outside of confession."

With such a beginning, Baldwin immediately settled down with the happy expectation of hearing something salacious. But he was wrong. Instead, Anthony told him about Simon — the imaginary friend that almost took over his life.

"I was only fourteen when I got to school — nervous and dreadfully homesick. My circle of friends became a second family to me," Anthony said.

There were five of them in all, and they did everything together: studied, ate, slept, swam in the Seine, played pranks, and laughed. A wave of nostalgia washed over Anthony as he remembered. He had never had such close friends since, except perhaps Baldwin. But Baldwin was so much younger; it wasn't the same.

"We told each other everything. And when we ran out of things to tell each other, we made them up, but tried and pass them off as true," Anthony said.

Baldwin's eyes widened in surprise. "You mean that you and your friends would sit around telling lies?"

Anthony smiled. Of course it sounded preposterous to an outsider. "Not lies exactly. Let's call them imagined truths. Or projections of more interesting selves."

"What was the point"? asked Baldwin.

"Now here is a motive that you're still young enough to understand. Each week, the best liar won a round of drinks," responded Anthony.

Thank God I didn't have to do anything so idiotic to get drinks, Baldwin thought to himself. But out loud he asked: "So what were your 'imagined truths' like?"

Anthony laughed disparagingly. "Not very good, at first. In fact, mine were the worst: flat and boring. I never won any free drinks. That's when I invented my friend, Simon."

"Do you mean an imaginary friend like children have?" asked Baldwin.

Although somewhat embarrassed by the question, Anthony shrugged. "Who knows? I didn't need one when I was little. But I needed Simon. He had all the panache and daring that I lacked. Soon I was the unrivalled winner of drinks. In fact, Simon was such a success that he began cropping up in everyone's stories. The narrator became inconsequential, except as witness to Simon's antics."

"What kind of things did Simon do?" asked Baldwin, skeptically. He was having a difficult time imagining his eminently pragmatic mentor as someone once consumed by fantasy.

"He took risks the rest of us only dreamt of. Simon could seduce an attractive young wife right under the nose of her aged husband, cheat the most accomplished robber out of his money, or humiliate the most arrogant master in his classroom. Anything and everything."

Simon was the realization of every naughty fantasy a teenage boy ever had, and then some. He was intelligent, capricious, and charismatic. And as their narratives continued, he became more remarkable still, developing a solid repertoire of supernatural powers. He could make himself invisible at will, and move things, even people, around without touching them.

"Very soon, Simon began to specialize in what might be described as religious fraud. He might cause a priest to levitate during Mass, or enter a tavern invisibly and urge repentance in a celestial voice. Just the kind of impiety one might expect from young boys destined to be priests," said Anthony.

Simon could shift his shape to suit the situation. This heightened degree of credulousness required of the listeners didn't spoil the stories, as one might imagine; it enhanced their appeal. He seemed as real, and yet as incalculable, as the elements. Then the stories began to change. Or was it Simon who changed? It was impossible to say. Gradually, instances of impious fakery developed into something much darker. And their meetings changed too. They were no longer fun in the raucous, school-boy way they once were. Instead, they were captivating, even compulsive. The friends could hardly wait until evening, bursting to speak about Simon and his fantastic capers. Their imaginary world was becoming so compelling that their schoolwork began to suffer.

"Yet it seemed impossible to stop—that is, until it became absolutely necessary," said Anthony.

"Why necessary?" Baldwin asked.

Anthony looked over his shoulder before answering. "We could no longer contain our narratives."

Baldwin frowned. "I'm not sure that I understand what you mean."

"I mean that our tales, however bizarre, started to spin right out of the world of make-believe into the real world."

But when pressed, Anthony was reluctant to provide details. He again looked over his shoulder as if he feared that someone was listening. "Did you hear something?" Anthony said, his voice dropping to a whisper. Baldwin shook his head, amazed to see his invariably sanguine friend with a classic case of the jitters.

"If you don't want to talk about it, I might as well get back to my floating fat-man," said Baldwin, starting to get on his feet.

Anthony grabbed Baldwin's sleeve, yanking him back down, and took a deep breath. "Simon had a penchant for angels. One night, he appeared to a young widow as the angel Gabriel, hailing her as the mother of the next messiah. On the second night, she consented to kiss him. On the third night, he seduced her," said Anthony.

"That story is right out of Boccaccio," said Baldwin.

"Admittedly, that's where the idea came from. But our story was constructed around the young widow who did the baking for the college. She was kind and good, and we were all half in love with her. Soon afterward, she took her own life. It was said that she was with child," said Anthony.

Baldwin looked skeptical. "Many women in her situation might consider desperate measures," he responded.

Anthony had momentarily buried his head in his hands, remembering the widow. Her name was Alison, and she had golden hair and a beautiful laugh. *She might still be alive today if it weren't for me.*

"But that's not all," said Anthony, rousing himself to continue. "Next week, someone told a story in which an angelic Simon appeared before a blacksmith to require the sacrifice of his firstborn. The following day in the adjoining parish, a father was apprehended for murdering his infant son. He had used his anvil as a kind of makeshift altar."

Baldwin shuddered in response.

"We told ourselves it was a coincidence. The alternative was just too incredible. But when Simon murdered a fellow student, we had to face the truth."

The victim was named Sebastian: an unpopular little sneak whom everyone detested. He cheated on his lessons, stole things, and spied on everyone. And yet all the masters thought he was a saint. So they made up a story in which Sebastian met with an appropriately saintly end. The next day, he was found dead.

"How did you know that your group was responsible?" Baldwin asked.

"Because his death was right out of our story," said Anthony.

"Has it occurred to you that one of your friends might have committed the murder, not make-believe Simon?"

Anthony shook his head. "None of us had the strength or the skill. The student was tied to a tree and riddled with arrows just like his namesake, St. Sebastian. Simon did it."

Baldwin frowned, not knowing what to think. Clearly Anthony was committed to this version of the events. But it seemed entirely preposterous, and so completely out of character. Anthony had always ridiculed contemporary visionaries precisely because they couldn't discern between fantasy and reality. And now here he was describing an interlude from his past that posited the existential reality of just such a slippage.

"Why are you telling me this?" Baldwin asked, suddenly suspicious.

"Because Simon has come back," Anthony said.

"How? Did someone from your group tell a new story?" asked Baldwin.

"None of us would dare," Anthony said quietly. He turned to face Baldwin, looking directly into the younger man's eyes. "I believe that Simon was summoned by your quodlibet. Simon specializes in religious fraud: mistaking Satan and Christ would be precisely his métier. And you are a friend of mine."

Baldwin was about to interject, but Anthony held up his hand. He needed a confederate, and destiny seemed to have selected Baldwin. Anthony wanted to finish his narration before hearing any more of Baldwin's objections. He had to make Baldwin understand the full extent of the danger; how Simon had come to infiltrate Anthony's dreams, and the dire consequences.

"In the last dream, I opened the door to Simon, and Martin died," said Anthony.

Baldwin was a trained rationalist, however, and naturally resistant.

"You speak of Simon as if he were a real person possessed of volition. But you made him up! He never existed independently of you," said Baldwin.

"Did I make him up?" Anthony mused. "Simon may have seemed to be my invention, but he was based on Simon Magus — a figure who has fascinated me for as long as I can remember. Maybe I wasn't inventing a new persona, but summoning an ancient one."

As compelling as this theory might be in a phantasmagorical dream world, it made no sense in the harsh light of reality, and Baldwin said as much. Simon Magus was dead. Peter had cursed him, and he was presumably in hell. It was very rare that God permitted figures from hell to walk the earth. And such specters couldn't do anything without God's permission. They weren't shape shifters of incalculable power. Yet such theological nuances were not Baldwin's main area of concern. He was disturbed by what Anthony had said about the quodlibet. It seemed to be investing Baldwin with inchoate and involuntary powers of invocation, and Baldwin didn't like it.

"Are you saying that mere words can cause certain things to materialize?" Baldwin asked.

"I suppose that's exactly what I am saying," replied Anthony.

And why not, Anthony reflected? The entire faith bore testimony to the power of words. God created the world with words. Christ was the Word made flesh. The priest's words of consecration made bread and wine into the body and blood of Christ. And most recently, Paris was shown how one priest's words of consecration could make the invisible mystery of transubstantiation palpable through the Miraculous Bleeding Hosts.

"Simon's materialization is but the dark side of the same principle: a kind of negative miracle. Wicked or unkind words may sometimes have unintended consequences, like the husband who tells his wife to go to the devil, and then Satan appears and drags her off," said Anthony.

"Master Anthony, really!" said Baldwin with exasperation. "Such stories are invented by preachers to demonstrate the dangers of blasphemy. Does anybody really believe that casual epithets have that degree of power?"

"I would have thought not, had it not been for the experience of Simon," responded Anthony.

Although skeptical, Baldwin was nevertheless intrigued and wanted to test this principle with his own brand of casuistry.

"What if you made up the excuse that you couldn't attend some odious event because your friend was dying, and then your friend does die? Was this a coincidence or did you somehow make it happen?" Baldwin asked.

Anthony didn't respond right away. Baldwin's question brought the boy Sebastian to mind. How they all hated him! Perhaps they would like to have seen him humiliated — even hurt. But had they murdered their classmate? Anthony and his youthful companions had struggled with this issue. Christ had said that a man who merely covets another man's wife is already an adulterer in his heart. Yet Anthony's confessor, who, understandably, wouldn't credit the story about Simon, reassured Anthony that he was not responsible. Anthony remained unconvinced.

"I don't know that a simple fib could kill a man. But perhaps the likelihood of his illness would somehow be increased. There may be certain conditions that make it possible for words, or even thoughts, to cross over into reality. There may be times when the barrier between ideas and their realization is more fragile. Perhaps we are living in such a time," Anthony persisted.

"Which brings us back to your contention that my disputation was a potential catalyst. My question was just a hypothetical. But what about the historical instances when Satan did appear as Christ, as he did to St. Martin? Did Martin somehow provoke his appearance?" asked Baldwin.

Anthony had often wondered about this. What were visions and why did some people receive them rather than others? Were the people who experienced supernatural phenomena predisposed by merit or by some physical susceptibility? In the case of St. Martin, the answer was easy.

"I would think the likelihood of such a visitation would be higher for Martin than for most people, just because he was a saint who, by definition, spent much of his time thinking about Christ and invoking His presence. He was susceptible by virtue of his sanctity," Anthony responded.

Baldwin was fascinated. "So let's explore how this theory might apply to you. If Simon is truly a thing of evil, and your stories inadvertently invoked him, it may be because of your innate holiness. Did any of your schoolboy friends strike you as secret saints?"

Anthony scorned any such notion. "Don't be ridiculous! One could just as easily argue that we were evil, attracting evil through sympathetic magic."

But this time Baldwin wasn't joking. "Your argument is flawed because I know you to be a good man — in fact, the best I know. And, whatever role my quodlibet might have played, you are the main conduit between Simon and what's happening now. You are the one who is having the dreams. Perhaps this points to your particular holiness."

Baldwin was being his usual preposterous self, and Anthony wasn't amused. The drizzle had become a steady downpour. The two men rose and were heading toward the door when Baldwin asked, "What about your circle of potentially holy chums? Are you in touch with any of them?"

The rain had gotten louder. Anthony either didn't hear Baldwin or pretended he didn't. It took several repetitions of the question before he managed to extract a reluctant admission from Anthony.

"Only one. Hervey Rousseau."

Chapter 8: Ominous Signs

Dead Again

The little boy who had died and been brought back to life, died for a second time once and for all. He had never fully recovered from the accident: wouldn't eat, wouldn't speak, never stopped shivering. Still, the mother had clung to his little body ever since his revival, weeping with gratitude that he was still alive. To lose him again was a terrible thing. She carried her dead son all the way from the Hôtel Dieu to the house of the Friars Minor on the far side of the left bank. The wretched woman asked at the porter's lodge for the friar who had initially brought back her boy. She didn't know his name, but the porter knew whom she meant. Brother Jacques wasn't there and the porter didn't know when he was expected back. Later when the coroner questioned the porter about the time of day, he remembered that the bells had just rung for Nones. But by Vespers the woman was dead. Mother and child had washed up on the banks of the Seine just a few feet apart from one another. It was believed that she had drowned herself.

A couple of attendants from the Hôtel Dieu placed the bodies in a cart and drew them to Les Chapeaux for burial. But the presiding vicar from Les Innocents refused to let a suicide be buried in consecrated ground. The attendants returned to the hospital with their sad cargo, only to be turned back by the hospital curate, who insisted on accompanying them to the cemetery this time. When they arrived at the cemetery, the two clerics argued. Word of the tragedy spread like wildfire, however, until the attendants with their cartload had attracted quite a crowd. Every onlooker was outraged at the unfeeling stance of the priest from Les Innocents. Eventually he relented, acknowledging that there was no actual proof that the woman had, in fact, committed suicide.

It was agreed that the woman, blind with grief, may well have fallen victim to an accident similar to the one that had initially taken her child and, since there were no witnesses, it would be shameful to bury them apart from one another on the basis of morbid supposition alone.

Gerson shuddered when he heard the news. "Are you certain it was them?" He was speaking to Anthony, who had come to see him after encountering the little procession en route to the cemetery for a second time.

Anthony was looking out the window of the Chancellor's office, thinking about the two drowned bodies with their grey faces. He turned around. "I'm afraid so, Chancellor. There was no doubt in the minds of any of the hospital workers."

The Chancellor was more than simply dismayed at the news: he looked as if he had been struck. But he wasn't thinking about the boy and his mother. He was thinking about Brother Jacques. The dinner, the meeting, their conversation. But most of all, he was thinking about what followed. There was that moment — that indescribable moment — when Jacques took his hand. His body trembled as he remembered the power emanating from the friar and how it entered him, enfolding him in grace. Then the dream of the stigmata, confirming his intuition about Jacques. All this had happened but a few nights ago, yet that didn't matter. Conversion only takes a moment, and Gerson was converted. After years of lonely study and personal sacrifice, he was finally receiving his reward: a precious intimacy with one of the Lord's special friends. Gerson had not only experienced what it was like to be in the presence of someone with true sanctity, but for a moment he had been granted the favor of participating in his charisma. He had been selected. He was one of the elect. And now with this tragedy, he was afraid that something very dear to him was in danger. His new faith was precious, and he would defend it with all his strength.

Eventually the Chancellor composed himself sufficiently to respond. "The Lord has His reasons. It must remain a mystery as to why He would restore this young life only to take it away so soon."

"Maybe He didn't. I have been wondering whether the boy really did come back to life," said Anthony.

Gerson felt a wave of incredulity, followed by a surge of indignation: that gnawing maggot, envy! It was the rare man who could resist this base emotion when confronted by someone worthy of so striking a sign from God. Gerson was proud that he himself had stood the test. But Anthony couldn't transcend his pusillanimity, his *hardness of heart*. Hence, he chose to turn his back on palpable signs and wonders. Though riven with feelings of chagrin, the Chancellor forced himself to respond calmly. "I know Brother Jacques brought the boy back to life. Remember, I was there."

Anthony could tell that Gerson was disturbed, though he had no way of knowing the full extent. Still he wasn't prepared to back down. These were difficult times in which every article of faith was being tested. The last thing Paris needed was a cult around a false miracle worker.

"The boy was alive in a certain sense. Even so, you yourself noted that he never quite regained the use of his faculties. He didn't speak. Perhaps it was the animal soul alone that was restored, not the rational soul."

Gerson's heart surged with anger. He was totally disgusted by Anthony. Behind his veneer of learning lurked the most insidious skepticism. He was worse than a doubting Thomas; he was like Judas, basely betraying our Lord for silver.

"Hadn't *yet* spoken, you mean," said Gerson, struggling against his growing ire. "And that was only so far as I could tell on the basis of a very limited series of interviews. But his lungs hadn't healed yet, and breathing remained difficult. He would have come around. The doctors said as much."

Gerson continued in this vein. All of Paris had witnessed the resuscitation of the boy — a stunning reprisal of the most potent of the Lord's miracles. It symbolized Christ's own death and resurrection, and prefigured the promise of the future kingdom: a blessedness in which the elect were destined to partake someday. How could Anthony be so obtuse? Gerson was put in mind of a class long ago when Anthony lectured on the resurrection: hadn't he said that this was one of the most difficult articles of faith; an instance when even the most committed believer often foundered in disbelief? Gerson was now bearing witness to this disbelief.

For his part, Anthony, who had found Gerson's adamance disturbing from the start, was becoming aware of the Chancellor's wild hopes regarding the friar. Could this be the same man who insisted on testing every inspiration? Gerson had vigorously attacked Birgitta of Vadstena's claims to sanctity, arguing that miracles proved nothing: they could be simulated, they could be demonic. Gerson had even argued that Birgitta's visions were a function of her widowhood: that her un-ejaculated seed had spoiled, sending the fumes to her brain that caused her so-called revelations. And Birgitta had already been canonized a saint — admittedly, by the wrong pope, but this didn't necessarily diminish the rigor of the process. Now Gerson seemed ready to fall down and worship a Franciscan wonder-worker whose most dramatic miracle was undone in a matter of days.

But there was no point in arguing. All Anthony could say was, "Honest faith is rarely misplaced. Even if Brother Jacques were not all you believe him to be, God honors the intentions behind heartfelt veneration." Anthony knew that this is what most theologians believed. Perhaps they were right.

Gerson was deeply offended. He interpreted Master Anthony's last remark as meaning that Gerson was sufficiently naïve to venerate someone who was still living. It was as if Anthony saw everything through the filter of Baldwin's damned disputation. Gerson's trust in his former professor was but a fragile construct, which required robust scaffolding. The ground was shifting, however. Suddenly the positive feelings that had been developing in Gerson over the weeks were in jeopardy.

Anthony felt these tremors as well. Only after he had spoken did he realize how his remarks might be construed, and all theological distinctions died on his lips. Speaking from his heart, Anthony said, "Forgive me, Chancellor, if I sounded like a pompous ass. It's not only the boy's death that's disturbing me. My dear friend, Brother Martin, has died."

Gerson was shocked. He had only just dined with the Dominican. And suddenly his feelings of acrimony vanished. He listened sympathetically as Anthony reminisced about Martin's imaginative pedagogy, his prodigious memory, his penchant for daring analysis. Martin had a crusty exterior, yet at the base of his manifold abilities was a genuine kindness, the likes of which were only too rare in academic life. Once during a disputation, his razor-sharp reasoning reduced his rival to tears. Martin was so sorry for the pain he afforded the other master that he conceded, even though he clearly had the upper hand. That was Martin.

Then it was Gerson's turn to tell Anthony about his conversation with Martin over dinner. "Your friend was entirely absorbed by some mysterious palimpsest that you showed him. He could talk of little else. Now I am intrigued: where did it come from?" asked Gerson.

Unfortunately, Anthony could tell the Chancellor very little, apart from how its present owners came by it. Gerson raised his eyebrows at the words "priest's daughter," but let it go.

For his part, Anthony was excited to learn that Martin had discussed the manuscript with Gerson. Perhaps he could shed some light on Martin's discovery.

"All I can remember is that he claimed to be making progress," Gerson said.

After Anthony's conversation with the prior, this was no longer news. But it still made Anthony wince with pain. When Martin got ahold of an interesting problem, he was like a dog with his bone. Anthony should have known that the old scholar would never have given up.

Then Gerson remembered something else. "Oh yes, Brother Martin also thought that the journal spoke to questions of spiritual discernment. But I never had the chance to find out how that might be. We were all distracted before he could go into any detail." He went on to relate the Cistercian abbot's near disastrous faux pas.

"So Brother Jacques was there?" Anthony asked.

"Yes. He was sitting on my other side." Gerson said this rather quietly. Just the man's name evoked powerful feelings.

"Do you think he heard what you and Martin were discussing?"

"I don't know. Perhaps." But then Gerson's voice changed. "Why do you ask? What difference does it make?" The sharp edge was unmistakable.

Instead of answering, Anthony just shrugged apologetically, and went on to ask Gerson about his own work.

Exegesis

It was getting late. Margot refused the invitation to stay for dinner. In fact she found it somewhat disconcerting, fearful that if Hervey and Felice knew the full extent of her evil life they would turn her out of the house. She likewise vigorously rejected Hervey's offer to see her home. Even so, the three of them parted cordially with a strange sense of comradery. They were aware of having entered into an alliance, though its purpose was unclear. Margot promised to keep them apprised of any future visions or insights. She was surprised when the priest, in an expression of gratitude, warmly clasped her hand.

"How shall we find you?" asked Felice.

"Oh, you mustn't try and find me! Decent people don't go there."

"Well, at least to send a message. You must give us some kind of address," Felice persisted.

Margot relented. "If you send a message to Margot de la Barre on Rue Glatigny it will find me."

Margot saw Hervey and Felice exchange looks and smile. *If there ever had any been any doubt about my evil way of life, my address says it all.* Margot flushed with shame. In fact, her two companions were oblivious to such considerations, simply registering their doleful memories of that street with one another.

"In the meantime, why don't you start attending St.-Jacques more regularly?" Hervey said cheerfully.

"Yes, do. Bring your pretty friend!" Felice chimed in. "Bring everyone!"

Margot had already begun to walk away, but was still within earshot. She turned and waved, mouth smiling but with eyes still darkened by fear.

The door closed. Hervey just stood there, seemingly transfixed by the tapestry of St. Jacques on the wall. It was really rather grotesque. The mouth, stitched in bright red, looked like a gash against the pallor of the bumpy face. The figure leaned on the pilgrim's staff like a cripple. But Hervey was staring without really seeing. All he could see was that something fearsome was coming their way; something inexorable. *Would that my Felice be spared; would that my Felice be spared*, was the prayer in his heart. Father and daughter sat down opposite one another, for a long time saying nothing. Hervey replenished their wine.

"Why is it that I always think better with a cup in my hand?"

Felice just smiled, which was what he wanted. Smiles were more important than ever now. He sensed that they were moving into a time when smiles would falter, laughter ring hollow, and dreams and visions overshadow the contours of waking life.

As if reading his thoughts, Felice remarked: "It seems like the last days, when it was foretold: *Your sons and daughters will prophesy, your young men will see visions, your old men will dream dreams.*"

"The Last Times, you think? An excellent topic for Sunday's sermon, though presumably my last."

A rather lame attempt at a joke, but it elicited another smile. Felice's smile was a clear light coming through baleful fog.

Visions: the world was rife with them. The most authoritative public medium conceivable; a writ from God. Women particularly seemed graced with revelations. The Chancellor imagined that the vast majority of female mystics were sick or deluded. Maybe he was right. Yet Margot seemed lucid — exceptionally so, in fact. But you could never be sure. One of her visions reminded Hervey of the time when the crucifix spoke to St. Francis. She might be just an ordinary old woman who wants to repent for her past sins, and has internalized this model. Maybe she is purposefully pretending to have visions just for the attention.

"Father, you haven't fallen asleep, have you?"

"Hmmm? No. I'm awake."

"What do you make of the fact that Margot's visions seemed horrific to her?"

"Puzzling. They say that Birgitta of Vadstena ran away the first few times that Christ tried to address her, fearing diabolical illusion. Yet, when she settled down long enough to hear Him out, I believe she found these experiences very sweet."

"But perhaps that makes Margot's claims all the more plausible — because they seem to break the mold."

Then she remembered the floury figures on the table, and they both went over to examine them.

"Don't sneeze!" joked Hervey.

"Don't make me laugh!" responded Felice.

The shapes on the table were crudely drawn, and, at first, barely recognizable as letters. Even so, Felice's work with the palimpsest had made her something of an unofficial expert on difficult hands. Dutifully copying the figures, she sat staring at them for some time, trying to imagine which letters were intended. All at once she knew, and deftly traced the characters on her tablet.

"This is it!" she said, handing her tablet over to her father.

Hervey stared at the letters cuʳ ãïʳm.

"That's a pretty standard abbreviation for *cura animarum*: the care of souls. It's in every text discussing clerical responsibilities," remarked Hervey.

"Are there other possibilities?"

"Oh, plenty, I suppose. It could be *cura angelorum:* the care of angels; *cura annorum* — the care of years. Or if the *u* is really an open *a, cara animalium* — a woman beloved of animals; *cara angelorum*: a woman beloved of angels; *cara* a*nicularum:* the darling of old women; I could go on."

"But context is everything here. 'The care of souls,' makes sense. It reinforces the pastoral interpretation: that Jacques, in his priestly capacity, is represented as Christ the Good Shepherd."

"Or *cura anguiculorum:* the care of baby serpents."

Felice shook her head, not in the mood for jokes. Margot's visions were alarming, but she was inclined to trust them. Didn't an illiterate woman's reconstruction of a Latin phrase, replete with abbreviations, bespeak their authenticity?

Hervey was more circumspect, however. Margot could be an imposter who somehow acquired a convenient fragment of Latin. "Besides, authenticity is an ambiguous rubric. A vision could be authentic insofar as it is not simulated or the result of a medical condition. Yet that's no guarantee that it is the work of God," said Hervey. He went on to relate a case in point. There was a famous crucifix in the church of Montefalco that filled the entire congregation with euphoria.

"They believed themselves incapable of sin, and gave themselves over to all manner of sexual excess. But a saintly nun saw the crucifix for what it was: a demon nailed to the cross in place of the image of Christ."

The story made Felice shudder, but she was not persuaded. The third and fourth visions, in particular, clearly alluded to the palimpsest: the high windswept place, the desolation, even the smell of burning could all represent Montségur after the siege. But most striking was the fact that someone was hiding in the well — a detail that Felice believed was included in the vision precisely so there could be no doubt.

"Agreed. It's no coincidence. But it could be demons making use of the journal to draw us in. Why else would we be present at a siege that occurred over a century ago?" asked Hervey.

Felice just shook her head. Nor did she know what to make of that strange Pentecostal imagery of wind and fire.

"And the two others in the vision? Who are they?" asked Hervey.

"Wouldn't they have to be Masters Anthony and Baldwin? They know about the manuscript, at least. And Margot said that the fourth vision wasn't for her; that it was for us, which would mean all four of us. Margot doesn't appear in this vision, nor does Brother Jacques."

But Hervey disagreed. "That was the only part of the vision that made sense to me. The previous vision was also set on the windswept peak, and Brother Jacques appears in the chapel as an icon of Christ. He is present in the last vision as well, but remains concealed. The people in the vision know he is there. They are scaling the cliff to get away from him!"

Transformations

Alicia sat in her room, kneeling before her little altar, content. She felt so rich and alive inside that somehow she was becoming sensitive to the potential in others. Take Rose, for example. There was a time when Alicia had looked down her nose at Rose, thinking her frivolous and worldly. But now Alicia could see the Lord working through Rose in wonderful ways, and she loved her like a sister. They loved one another, united in their love for Brother Jacques. It was a holy love. She had always been told that the priest was put in the place of Christ: *in loco Christi* they called it. This was not just symbolically, but literally true: Jacques had become the celestial bridegroom for each one of them. When she made her vows into Rupert's hands, she had really been marrying Brother Jacques. Rose felt that way too. They were a holy harem far beyond the reach of petty jealousy. And as with Christ, Jacques was with them always. Alicia had a very real sense of his loving regard. He was present not only when she was at prayer, but during the most menial tasks: making her bed, doing her needlework, putting fresh flowers on the little altar in her room. She would talk to the crucifix in her room as if it were Brother Jacques, and Jacques could hear her.

Alicia was changing in other ways as well. She was forgetting worldly things that didn't matter: old friends, old pastimes. In place of these unwanted scraps of a former life, there were new gifts: a capacity to remember psalms, an ability to follow along in a prayer book during divine offices, and an aptitude for prayer that was inexhaustible.

Rupert too was happier than he had ever been in his life. How could it be otherwise? He had finally finished his commentary. Suddenly everything had fallen into place, and he wrote so quickly that it felt as if he were taking dictation from the Holy Spirit. Maybe he was! Nor did the marvels stop with Rupert's sudden facility in writing. He had begun a disputed question on the soul, which required deep exploration into patristic writings. Rupert had spent most of the morning reading John Chrysostom before he realized that he was reading in Greek. It was nothing short of a miracle. There were probably only a handful of codices containing Greek in all of Paris; so few volumes because virtually no one knew Greek. Even Aquinas hadn't known Greek! And here was Rupert — not just competent, but fluent.

He owed it all to Brother Jacques. In fact, this was the third miracle that Jacques had effected on his behalf. The first two had held up: he could gaze upon the beautiful Felice without any stirrings of the flesh, and his stammer was a thing of the past.

A feeling of transformation suffused Rupert. The infusion of Greek was but a sign of future graces. He was experiencing a divinely instituted stability; a holy stasis that would keep him in a perpetual state of grace. Not too long ago, Rupert would have deemed this impossible. To be mortal was to live under the curse of Adam and Eve and be subject to the law of sin. Yet Rupert believed he was advancing to a state in which he would transcend sin, and even temptation, altogether. It was the realization of the angelic life. Every time Rupert received communion from Jacques, he was aware of a gradual metamorphosis under way — a certain expansion and strengthening of his spirit. Rupert had always been told that heresy spread like a disease, never realizing that holiness worked the same way. A truly holy man infected everyone who came in contact with him.

Rupert also had a grateful sense that Jacques was with him all of the time: watching him, watching out for him, nurturing him, even telling him things. It was Jacques' voice that told him about the manuscript on Martin's desk and what he had to do. The voice of Jacques resonated with Rupert's own inner voice — the voice of conscience. It was every bit as compelling and binding as conscience, and Rupert had no choice but to obey or be damned.

The face of Jacques was imprinted on every devotional image of Christ that Rupert encountered. And so it should be. Jacques was the most Christ-like man that had ever walked the earth.

A Wedding

"Did you get them?" asked Margot. Marion nodded. She was carrying a small cloth sack with handles. She opened it and carefully extracted two wreaths of roses.

"I was afraid they would get crushed but they are still perfect. Aren't they beautiful?" Marion held them up for inspection. "I bought one for each of us."

Margot tried not to look impatient. "Thank you, my dear. They are lovely. But where's the rest?"

Marion removed a small bag from the sack and handed it to Margot.

"Here you are. Shepherd's Purse. I bought it where you told me." Margot looked into the bag, which was full of herbs that resembled mustard, only with small pods shaped like purses. They gave off a sharp, pungent smell.

"Good. But before we start, I want you to swear again that you will never tell anyone about this and never accuse me to anyone," Margot said.

Marion obediently swore. "Margot, please don't worry. You can trust me. And I am so grateful. I will bring people to rent your rooms. I'll sew for you, cook and clean for you. I'll do anything you ask!"

"Fine. But all I am asking is for you to be quiet about this."

Marion nodded.

"I need to make certain preparations. But first let's relax and have a little supper." Margot went to her cupboard and brought out a loaf of dark rye bread, some cheese, and a little dried beef. While Margot was arranging things, Marion suddenly perked up.

"I bought something else at Les Halles," she said mischievously.

From her sack she produced a small earthenware jug with a cork. It was the special mead that Margot liked. The old woman smiled and got out two cups, poured some mead in each, and the two friends sat down and toasted each other. After supper, Marion watched as Margot deftly strung the herbs on strings, making two separate wreaths. She secreted them in a chest.

"Margot, what will the wreaths do? I mean, they won't permanently hurt either of them, will they?" Marion was either so desperate or so trusting that she hadn't bothered to inquire about this before.

"No one will get hurt. But the wreaths will make it impossible for Hainselin to know Agnesot carnally."

When Marion frowned, Margot added. "Don't you worry. The wreaths won't affect the two of you. He'll come back to you. And love you every bit as much as you love him. More!" Marion hugged her friend in gratitude.

Marion listened as Margot told her what she needed to do. Hainselin's marriage was set for the coming Sunday. Marion needed to establish herself along the road that the wedding party would take between the church and Hôtel Alesçon, where the nuptial dinner was to take place. When the couple passed, she must greet them both sweetly—not as Hainselin's lover, but as a friend and well-wisher. Hainselin must think he has been forgiven, and Agnesot must not suspect that there was ever anything between Marion and Hainselin. After Marion had safely seen them into their hotel, she should return to Margot for the wreaths.

The door opened and Margot's daughter, Joan, entered the room.

"What's that smell?" she said, sniffing the air.

"Marion happened to be passing Les Halles and bought some roses on a lark. She brought a wreath for us as well," Margot replied.

"Why tonight?" Joan asked suspiciously. The feast of John the Baptist was the most auspicious time for gathering herbs for magical use, and Joan was no fool.

"Come now, Joan! You remember how you used to like to dress up for the feast of the Baptist. Marion's still young! Show her the flowers, darling."

Marion, who had been standing there like an idiot, feeling too guilty to say anything, meekly went to the sideboard and held up the roses.

"Aren't they a pretty color?" she asked.

Joan looked suspiciously from Marion to Margot.

"Mother. You aren't trying anything funny, are you? You know what I mean!"

Joan knew that her mother had dabbled in love potions in the past, and was afraid that Marion had been playing on her sympathies. While Margot was assuring her daughter that everything was fine, Marion discreetly gathered up her things and retreated to her room.

Sunday dawned. It was a beautiful day and Marion awoke refreshed and light hearted. When she remembered, however, what the day was, and that the June wedding of her dreams was happening without her, she began to cry. She rallied, however, got out of bed and dressed herself in her Sunday best. Maybe Hainselin would rediscover how pretty she could look, and forget all her tears and reproaches. Maybe he would come back to her without Margot's magic. He wasn't married yet! Still, Marion's various hardships had taught her a few things about the ways of the world: she knew that, realistically, if Hainselin hadn't come back to her by now, it was highly unlikely he would do so on his wedding day. Margot's magic was her only hope.

Marion had decided to greet the wedding party both on the way to and from the church. Yet she was destined to see Hainselin even earlier than she had expected that day, briskly walking past Margot's house. It was the last area of Paris where he wanted to be, but it was a necessity: he had been refused credit for Agnesot's ring and needed to borrow money in a hurry. There was a friend with a tavern near Glatigny, whom he was sure would loan him the money. The wedding was in two hours, so timing was tight. He looked up nervously in spite of himself, only to see what he feared most: Marion leaning out of the upper window. But she had a smile on her face and waved, so he waved back with relief and proceeded on his way. Marion wondered whether this chance encounter was a good sign. *It must be. I wonder what Margot would say.*

Hainselin and Agnesot had permission to be married at the church of St.-Jacques-de-la-Boucherie — Hainselin's parish church by adoption. Marion planted herself on Rue de la Venerie and greeted the wedding party as cheerfully as she could when they went by. Hainselin looked handsome, as usual, in his blue tunic. For a moment, Marion looked at Agnesot's costume with the critical eye of a professional seamstress rather than as her rival. Agnesot was clad in a red *cotte* made from a beautiful shiny material that Marion didn't recognize. It was cinched by an embroidered kirtle with seed pearls, and complemented by a *surcote* in red velvet with a short train. Her father had spared no expense. Still, it was not so ostentatious as to be above her station: just right. Standing within sight of the church porch, Marion trembled as she watched Hainselin and Agnesot exchange vows before disappearing inside for the nuptial Mass. Father Hervey performed the wedding but, at Hainselin's request, Brother Jacques assisted at the Mass. The bride was blessed, the couple shared the customary wedding bread, and the ceremony was over. Bride and groom were congratulated by a modest crowd, including Marion, which awaited them outside the church. The group of well-wishers escorted the wedding party to the Hôtel Alesçon in Les Halles before dispersing. Everyone would return in the evening for the dance.

Marion turned away from the Hôtel. At least she could stop smiling now; her face was starting to hurt! She was half way up the lane, anxious to see Margot and find out what she needed to do next, when she heard a familiar voice say her name. It was Brother Jacques, his face so full of kindness and empathy that she could feel the tears rising to her eyes. Even before he began speaking, she realized that he not only knew, but also understood everything.

"Marion, my dear, I know how heavy your heart must be. Confession would make this load bearable. It has been a long time since you confessed."

She knew he was right. Even though she had continued to attend the Thursday meetings, she hadn't stayed behind to make a confession since she had begun sleeping with Hainselin. And now there was so much more on her conscience.

"I know, father. And I promise you, I will come to confess very soon."

He smiled, turned, and went back toward the Hôtel. Then she realized that he had, of course, been invited to the wedding feast. This didn't bother her: in fact, it was a comfort to know that even though he had taken part in both the wedding and its festivities that he still had time to think of her.

Marion was no longer surprised when Margot asked that she swear to keep silent a third time. Only after she had sworn did Margot go to the chest for the two wreaths of herbs. Although enjoined not to watch, Marion couldn't help but peak from under her lashes. Margot was standing in the middle of the room, holding both wreaths in one hand. She repeatedly made the sign of the cross while saying something in a low voice that Marion couldn't hear.

"Here my dear," Margot said, approaching with the wreaths. "You must hide these in your skirt, and then during the dance drop them so that Hainselin and Agnesot tread upon them."

"Will the wreaths harm the other dancers?" Marion asked with a tremor in her voice. She may well be risking her salvation with the love potion. But if she harmed any of the others, she was certain of damnation.

Margot shook her head. "Their power is for Hainselin alone, and only affects his relations with Agnesot," Margot replied. She stroked Marion's hand soothingly and gave it a little squeeze of reassurance.

Still, Marion was distinctly nervous. She tried to joke, complaining that the wreaths were so smelly that no one would think of asking her to dance. Margot just smiled, and helped the younger woman secure the wreaths with a make-shift sash, tied between her linen tunic and her *cotte*. They hugged one another. Marion silently mouthed "thank you," and slipped out the door.

When Marion arrived at Hôtel Alesçon, the dance was already well underway. She hovered at the entrance to the room rather awkwardly, unsure how to proceed. But Thomas le Bourgne, the servant of a wealthy man from Touraine, rushed forward the moment he spotted Marion and asked her to dance. She had never liked Thomas much. He always smacked his lips when he spoke to her as if she were a tasty morsel. Just now, however, she was grateful for the attention. Smiling her consent, Marion was led to the floor, where she loosened the wreaths while dancing. Refusing a second dance, Marion stood at the edge of the throng of dancers to watch *la tresche* — a dance in the round. While Hainselin and Agnesot were in the ring holding hands, Marion bent over, hoping that it looked like she had dropped something or was tying her shoe, and slid the wreaths into the circle. She watched as the newlyweds gamboled right over them.

The dance lasted almost until dawn. But Hainselin and Agnesot left early in the evening. *They seem anxious to get to it!* guffawed one of Hainselin's less refined colleagues. A handful of friends serenaded the newlyweds on pipes and tambours en route to the Hôtel Grifon. For the first time ever, the couple entered a bedroom together. It was a much grander room than the one to which Hainselin was accustomed, with a tapestry on the wall and a new bed with a feather mattress. They stood in the room hand in hand while Brother Jacques blessed the marriage bed, afterward leaving the room so the couple could undress. They undressed quickly, all the time not looking at one another, until Agnesot wore only her chemise and Hainselin a pair of *braies*. Climbing into the marriage bed, awkward but happy, they pulled the covers up to their chins even though the evening was warm. Jacques returned briefly to bless the newly made husband and wife in their marriage bed.

And then he put out their lights.

Strange Encounters

After the meeting with Margot, Felice felt as if she were trying to piece together a puzzle in the middle of a whirlwind. The moment the pieces began to assume a shape, however phantasmagoric, the wind would come along and scatter them. For a time, Felice put her jumble of images and inchoate theories to one side for a duty she felt obliged to fulfill: visiting Rose. She wanted to know firsthand if her friend was really changed in some fundamental and disturbing way.

Felice had barely seen Rose since her recovery and, when she had, it was generally from a distance. But the two women had once been close. Admittedly, the tide of their intimacy tended to flow in one direction. Rose had told Felice everything about her at times uneven, but always passionate relationship with Philip, providing enough detail to make her friend uncomfortable on more than one occasion. Perhaps Philip's fears were causing Felice to overreact. Perhaps there was nothing wrong with Rose, that she was looking forward to confiding in Felice once again. If Felice could get Rose to discuss her decision to take her vows, maybe she could also convince her to speak with Philip. He needed this final conversation to put his mind at rest. Still, Felice was unaccountably anxious. Twice she almost upset the little platter of jam tarts that she bore.

Anna had always been grateful for Felice's visits during Rose's illness, but that morning she seemed overjoyed.

"Felice, how lovely to see you! You look so pretty! Your wonderful tarts, you angel! How's your father? Rose, look who's here!" All this was said in one breath without waiting for any kind of response. Conversation with Anna was generally easy that way.

Rose was absorbed in a book, which seemed odd enough: Felice had never seen Rose reading before. But what was odder still was that when she did look up, she gazed at Felice with unnerving neutrality. She said nothing, so Felice took the initiative.

"Rose, it's good to see you so well. Why haven't you been to see us? We've missed you!" There was no point in pretending that their relationship was as before.

"Father would love to see you."

"I have been busy," Rose answered in a voice with little affect.

Anna, who had brought several cups of cider, along with Felice's jam tarts, on a tray and was placing it on a little table nearby, drew up a chair. She hurriedly jumped in.

"Oh, Rose is so taken up with Brother Jacques and the Faithful. She is with them day in and day out. And when she is not doing charitable works or praying, she is here reading. Our Rose has become so learned. Brother Jacques is teaching her."

"That's wonderful!" Felice spoke with sincerity. Teaching his spiritual charges to read was certainly an unmitigated good from her perspective.

"What are you reading?" Felice asked

"Augustine," said Rose.

"His *Confessions*?"

"No."

Silence. Even Anna didn't know what to say, so she got up and started handing around the cider and tarts. Rose refused both.

"May I see?" said Felice, curious in spite of herself whenever it came to books.

Rose begrudgingly put a marker between the folios to keep her place and handed over the volume. Felice held it for a moment with reverence and then turned to the title page. It was one of Augustine's writings against the Manichees — *Contra Faustum*. She felt a stab of envy. It was precisely works like this, addressing the challenge of dualism, which she longed to read. The script was beautiful: clear and legible, with the initial letters in each chapter delicately drawn in red. The folios were smooth — smoother than she had ever seen. *Not just any parchment, but vellum,* Felice thought. The volume was very old — Carolingian or maybe even older. The cover was soiled as if it might once have been exposed to fire which, if Felice was right about its antiquity, was hardly surprising.

"It's beautiful. Did you get it from Brother Jacques?" said Felice, returning the volume.

Rose gave a slight nod in response. Felice wondered whether Brother Jacques had borrowed something from the library at the priory or if he actually owned the volume in question. *It had to belong to the library because books are so expensive. Otherwise, how would that square with his vow of poverty?*

Rose wouldn't talk about her reading. Nor did Felice have much success with the several other topics she introduced. It was when she asked

Rose to tell her a little about Brother Jacques that she hit upon the one subject that dispelled her companion's apathy.

"He is a holy man. He converted me to a holy life. No other priest has such a commitment to the *cura animarum*." Felice's interest pricked up when she heard Rose utter this term — especially in Latin. This was an expression that was certainly bandied about in clerical circles as shorthand for the clergy's responsibilities toward members of their congregation. But it wasn't something you would expect members of the laity to talk about, however devout they may be. And the manner in which the subject was introduced wasn't particularly tactful, considering that Hervey was Rose's parish priest. Rose abruptly changed the subject.

"I know why you are here. It is no use. Philip is already dead to me. Tell him to leave me alone."

Anna, who had not really understood what Brother Jacques had said about marriage to the celestial groom or the permanent nature of Rose's vows, gasped, taken aback. She was still hoping against hope that her daughter would come around and that all would be as before between Rose and Philip. It was this disingenuous optimism that prompted Anna to burst out: "Now Rose, don't go saying that. I'll wager you've just had a lovers' quarrel. But you'll make it up soon enough. I know you can't live without your Philip!"

Rose's only response was a look. Yet the expression on her face transcended mere contempt. For a moment, her lips drew back into something resembling a snarl. Felice could not suppress a quick intake of breath. The fact that the mother had at that moment been smiling at her daughter with such love made Rose's expression seem all the more feral. Anna's expression changed accordingly, registering a combination of surprise and pain that reminded Felice of a person stung by a wasp.

The situation had shifted from merely awkward to menacing in a moment. There was no point in prolonging a visit that had become a source of discomfort to all three of them. Even so, Felice was determined to stand her ground and say what she had come for. As she prepared to depart, Felice said, "Rose, I am genuinely happy for you in your new vocation. But it would be a kindness if you could find the time to tell Philip yourself."

Felice prepared herself for another surge of whatever alarming feelings Rose might be harboring, but Rose surprised her. Rather than more ugly disavowals, Rose merely said, "Perhaps you are right." It was said mechanically and without feeling, but at least she had agreed.

Such encounters must take their toll. Felice wasn't just metaphorically sick at heart, she actually felt nauseous. She wanted to get away from Anna's cottage, the parish, even the city. Felice walked toward the river quickly, taking in deep gulps of air. It was the eve of John the Baptist, that midsummer festival of mystery and magic. There had been a time when Felice used to go out to celebrate that day with the other girls. They would walk along the Seine, watching as the bonfires were being prepared. Once they were lit, they would hurry back to the parish to get ready for circle dances in the churchyard. The girls braided flowers in one another's hair, and then they would dance, always looking over their shoulders in hopes that the local boys were watching and might care to join in.

Hervey pretended not to approve; it was his job to stop people from gadding about in the churchyard, after all. But he was never really angry with Felice for participating. He seemed strangely pleased, in fact. Her poor father was probably relieved to see his daughter doing something normal — acting like other young women act. Hervey's desire for her to have a normal life was touching. His efforts to find out if she liked one boy more than the next were clumsy, and afforded her considerable merriment. *Save it for interrogating your penitents,* she would joke. And he would shrug his shoulders and give up — at least for the time being. But in truth, there never were any young men that she liked. She didn't know why. It was a misspent youth because it wasn't spent at all. Maybe it was because of her mother. She didn't know much about her except that she was probably promiscuous and, most certainly, a liar: someone who nice people didn't know, who ran away to where, presumably, there were no nice people. Was she still alive? Did she ever wonder about Felice?

But maybe Felice's diffidence about men had nothing to do with her mother. Maybe it was all about the body. The Cathars believed that Satan forced angels into the bodies of Adam and Eve: tunics of flesh. Then Satan took the form of the serpent and corrupted Eve with his tail. The human race was really the devil's progeny.

What if the Cathars were right?

But then there was Baldwin, the first man Felice had ever thought she could care about. Was she attracted to him because his vow of celibacy made marriage impossible? Of course, not all clerics keep their vows, and, after their rendezvous in the church, she knew he would only too willingly break his for her. His touch felt — she didn't even have the words for it. It didn't feel evil. Yet it didn't feel right. It made her body respond strangely, as if it had assumed a life of its own. It was a foreign body — a body that really didn't belong to her; that wanted things that she didn't. What if one day this foreign body came to dominate what Felice considered to be her true self? What if this body decided to join itself to another foreign body — to Baldwin's body? Would she ever be herself again?

Yet Baldwin was much more than a body. He represented reason and the life of the mind. He was the most interesting and quick-witted man she had ever met. And they were alike; she knew they were. Neither of them had any patience with conventional boundaries. Both approached life with passion. But it was his passion for thought and learning that mattered most to her, not that other passion. Baldwin wouldn't see things the same way. Felice's intelligence wasn't her main attraction; it was just an annex to, or enhancement of, her carnal self. She understood and forgave this prioritization, recognizing that their needs were different. She longed for an intellectual companion: someone to understand and challenge her. Baldwin had an entire community of scholars to fill this need. She envied him that. What wouldn't she give to share that experience with him and be like father and Anthony once were. But if Felice were ever to unite herself to a man, she could do much worse. Baldwin had a questing mind and constant access to books. Felice wouldn't mind the shame of being a clerical concubine. Hadn't she been in training for this position her entire life? Shame was no deterrent; shame was an old friend. But what if she became pregnant? The Cathars believe that reproduction ensnares old souls in new bodies. The ultimate evil.

What if the Cathars were right?

Felice was walking quickly, reaching the Grand Pont in no time. On the other side of the bridge was a small beggar boy, huddled near the watchtower on the gate. She was reminded of the little cripple who had briefly come back to life before dying for a second time. Felice said a silent prayer for his soul, and gave the beggar two *deniers*. Then she leaned against the wall overlooking the river, thinking once again about the long-ago feasts of St. John. Even back then, she was different from the other girls: she never took much interest in her looks, and didn't really care if anyone asked her to dance. And she liked being alone. Rather than looking for playmates, she'd make up her own games — like Happy Sticks. It wasn't much of a game, really. All you did was toss a couple of sticks into the river and guess which one would move the fastest. Hervey had named it Happy Sticks (*felices virgae*) after her.

And this is how Baldwin happened upon Felice: dropping pieces of wood into the water and then peering over the wall. There was a small pile of sticks in front of her. Once again, Baldwin stood transfixed. The first time Baldwin had seen Felice, he was fascinated at the sight of a woman reading with such absorption. She had disputed with him in Notre Dame with the same kind of focus. Now he saw that she played the same way. He felt like he had been granted a small, but important, window into her character through which he saw an ardent spirit that approached everything in life with the same kind of intensity. Baldwin continued to watch her, positioning himself several yards down the wall. Eventually, she sensed his presence and looked up. They smiled at one another.

"You refused to meet me. But here you are anyway. It was destiny," said Baldwin. He wanted to get her alone, but their options for privacy were distinctly slender. "Will you walk with me to the cathedral?"

Felice shook her head. "No. I think not." Baldwin looked disappointed. "It's too lovely outside. But we can play Happy Sticks together," she continued, making it clear that her refusal was not intended as a dismissal. "It's better with two! Look, I will even give you some of my sticks."

Baldwin rallied. At least she hadn't sent him away. So they dropped sticks into the Seine together, watching as they were caught by the current and floated downstream. He stood closer to Felice than was necessary, his arm brushing hers each time he tossed a stick into the river. Yet she didn't move away.

Eventually, Felice tired of the game. She just stared into the river, looking unspeakably sad.

"What is it, my love?" he asked.

Felice watched the people stacking wood for the bonfires, considering. She had begun to entertain possibilities that she was almost afraid to say out loud. Yet she trusted him. She knew she could tell him anything. So she told him about Margot and her visions, and how they wound Brother Jacques, the journal, Hervey and herself, and possibly Anthony and Baldwin into a web of danger. She told him about Philip, and his wildly despairing theories about Rose. And she told him about

Rose: her contempt for Philip, her defiant attachment to Brother Jacques, and her haunting strangeness. It wasn't just a point-by-point narrative: she spoke from the heart, letting him see just how much these incidents affected her. Baldwin listened to her with all the feeling of a lover. While she was speaking, Felice didn't look at him, but kept her eyes focused on the water. The sun was nearing the horizon, and the play of light on the waves looked like a celestial kingdom made of pure flame. It was like a glimpse into another world; a spiritual world of peace. Baldwin meanwhile watched her in profile with a sense of wonder: it was more than just the beauty that he apprehended, there was a transparency there. He felt as if he were seeing a naked soul.

"I'm frightened. But I don't know of what," she said by way of conclusion.

Baldwin nodded, but was silent for a time.

"We both know that something is happening," he said eventually. "The manuscript is at center of whatever it is. I have no idea how or why. But I do think that Anthony and I should meet Margot as soon as possible. Only she will know if we are the other two figures from her last vision."

Chapter 9: Betrayals

The Seal of Confession

The days following the wedding were difficult for Marion. She had more or less expected that Hainselin's impotence would make him realize his mistake instantly, and that he would rush to her before dawn. But Margot knew these things take time. To distract Marion, she encouraged her to accept an invitation for an excursion to the village of Montmartre with several seamstress-friends. Even there, Marion was tortured by rumors of Hainselin's extraordinary sexual appetite on his wedding night. *Like a stallion! He kept Agnesot in the saddle for the entire night*, or so a female companion had somehow learned from her *ami*.

This was far from the truth. The spell was supposed to render Hainselin impotent so that he couldn't have sex with his wife. But it was Agnesot who seemed to have fallen sick: so sick that the marriage couldn't be consummated. Margot heard this report the day after the wedding and was alarmed. Apparently Agnesot had developed such a terrible headache that her brain seemed to be on fire; she kept screaming that she was melting. In the old days, Margot had often used this spell, and nothing like this had ever happened before. Was it possible that someone else had bewitched them?

Hainselin, hovering over his new bride, was beside himself. Then he remembered the time at Marion's when he had come down with a throbbing headache. Margot had cured him. So he sent an urgent message to Margot, who responded right away. If this illness was caused by her spell, she thanked God for giving her the opportunity to put things right with a counter spell. There was still some of the Shepherd's Purse left, but not enough. Luckily, she found more of the herb in a ditch near the Louvre. It was with a strange sense of irony that Margot found herself approaching

Agnesot's bed with yet another wreath, desperately hoping that this one would offset any unintended effects of the last.

"Agnesot, my friend," she said softly. "I didn't give you a wreath for your wedding so I am giving you one now. Believe me, you've never in your life had such a wonderful wreath with such a great healing power. It can free you, or anyone else, from any sickness or evil spells!"

When Agnesot looked up weakly, Margot knew for certain that it was not her spell that was responsible for the illness; it was somebody else's work. Well, thank God for that! The poor invalid was too exhausted to take the wreath, so Margot placed it on her gently, tucking it behind where her head met the pillow so it would be secure. Then Margot prayed to God in earnest that Agnesot be released from this terrible magic. She said the Pater Noster and Ave Maria — three times each. After making the sign of the cross over the wreath, Margot said the following words:

"In the name of the Father, the Son, and the Holy Ghost. Two have enchanted you, three will disenchant you. In the name of the Father, the Son, and the Holy Ghost."

Hainselin and his mother-in-law, hovering nearby, muttered *Amen* — although they were not at all sure that this was the correct response. Was it a prayer or a spell?

"And how are you Hainselin?" Margot asked, turning toward the unhappy groom.

"I'm afraid that I am coming down with the same thing, mother. My head is splitting."

Margot took the rest of the Shepherd's Purse and put it in a small piece of white cloth, which she knotted. She said the Pater Noster over the little bundle, and then made the sign of the cross while invoking the Trinity.

"Put this in your satchel and keep it there for eleven days. Then, God willing, your headache will be gone."

Hainselin thanked Margot and accompanied her to the door. But before she left, he asked in a low voice, "How is Marion?"

"Sad," Margot answered simply.

"Could she have done this?"

Margot had been waiting for the question: jilted women were often accused of turning to magic and, as Marion herself demonstrated, this accusation was hardly farfetched. Be that as it may, Marion was hardly to be blamed for the current state of affairs.

"No. Marion would never harm anyone," said Margot with conviction. And Hainselin believed her.

"Tell her," he paused ". . . that I still think of her. But only if you think it would do her any good to know. You decide."

Margot nodded and left. She had no intention of telling Marion of the visit. It would do her no good at all.

The health of the newlyweds continued to decline. The day after Margot's visit, Agnesot's painful cries ceased altogether, and she fell silent. Lying on her back with her eyes open, Agnesot stared at the ceiling with glassy unseeing eyes. Two days later, Hainselin fell into a trance as well. Neither of them would ever regain consciousness.

By Thursday, everyone had heard about the sorry plight of Hainselin and Agnesot. Marion sat through the meeting of the Faithful so paralyzed by guilt that she couldn't concentrate on what was being said. All she wanted was for the meeting to be over so she could finally unburden herself to Brother Jacques. She had sworn to Margot not to reveal the magic to anyone, but, as far as Marion was concerned, confession didn't count. In confession, the priest saw as God, not man.

The meeting was at last over: most of the people departed, except for a handful who wished to confess. While Marion waited her turn, she tried to pray for the health of Hainselin and Agnesot, but with little success. She couldn't focus. Margot had tried to reassure her that it wasn't the fault of their spell, but Marion was not convinced. She was frightened that something had gone terribly wrong. What if they didn't get better? What if they died? Contemplating these horrible prospects, Marion felt as if she were gazing into the jaws of hell. Surely that was where she would end up if they didn't get better. Marion's desperate line of reasoning was thankfully interrupted when Brother Jacques called her name tenderly. She went over to where he was, kissed his hand, and began to confess.

The Franciscan didn't need to say anything at all. Marion was so well prepared that she divulged each sin in detail without any prompting. She made a life confession, reviewing the sins from her entire past. Marion had never made one before, but she needed to now. Her conscience was so heavy that she felt polluted. It was as if her soul was full of scabs and sores, and the filth was eddying from her soul into her body. She wanted to be clean again. Marion poured out everything that she thought might constitute a sin: petty meanness as a child; vanity; pride;

anything she could remember. When she told Brother Jacques about Richard, her voice trembled; she began crying in earnest when she confessed her love for Hainselin. By the time she came to Margot's magic, however, her wretchedness had transcended tears.

Marion had not dared to look at Brother Jacques even once in the course of her confession. It was only when it was over that she managed to look up, desperate for those consoling words of absolution. She received a dreadful shock. For where she had expected to see the reassuring face of Brother Jacques, she discovered Brother Marcus, his eyes narrowed in concentrated disdain. Marcus mechanically meted out penance and uttered the absolution in icy tones, while Marion, disbelieving and horrified, was almost swooning with alarm. All thoughts of remaining for communion departed as Marion fled the church — running for her life.

Once home, Marion kept rehearsing to herself all the things she knew about the sanctity of the seal of confession. She had no idea how she came to be confessing to Brother Marcus. But, personal antipathy aside, it shouldn't matter whether she confessed to Brother Jacques or Brother Marcus: they were both equally representative of God and both equally bound by the seal. Marion didn't mention who had mentored her in magic, but was afraid that Marcus might make the connection with Margot. But perhaps that didn't matter. Even if Marcus were prepared to commit sacrilege by breaking the seal, there was his loyalty to Margot to consider. He had been Margot's client for years. Would he really do anything to damage a woman that he probably, in his own way, had come to love? But despite Marion's manifold efforts to reassure herself, she could not forget that look of unmistakable malice in Marcus' eyes.

A Witch

Marcus had never experienced a blackout before. But he must have blacked out at some point during the Thursday meeting. He couldn't remember when it ended. He only came to himself when he was hearing the confession of that piece of filth, Marion. If she wasn't a prostitute, she might as well be. The woman knew no shame. And she was the destruction of honest men. The English squire was probably moldering in hell for their relationship; next she devoured that poor stonemason, Hainselin. The unspeakable things she put in his wine: rooster's testes and, worse still, menstrual blood. It was a miracle he didn't die from those poisons! But she did eventually do the poor fellow in. And on his wedding night, no less! The whore didn't name her accomplice in sin. But that was hardly necessary. It was the other whore, Margot, who was behind all this magic and mayhem. Hainselin and his wife would still be well and strong if it hadn't been for Margot.

A woman like Margot was a succubus, sapping the vital force of a man. He remembered with what relish Margot had told him that perverted story about the penis tree. She had tried to implicate her roommate, Concubina, to throw Marcus off her scent, but he wasn't fooled. Margot was a witch herself. The two of them had been in it together. All the poor men who had been robbed of their manhood by women like Margot! She performed the essential office of tending those tortured phalluses during Concubina's absence. But she wouldn't have just tended them; no, she didn't stop at that. She would caress them, speaking soft and vile words of seduction, causing them to become erect, just as she had done with him. And when these poor vulnerable members were hard, she would take them in her hand, one by one, and thrust them deep inside of her. Prostitutes were cesspools of seething lust.

Margot was clearly much more than a mere accomplice in this travesty. There probably was no Concubina; Margot made up that ridiculous name just in order to protect herself. But it wouldn't do her any good. Sorcery was the worst kind of heresy: leniency in this area would be unforgiveable. The witch hadn't just inadvertently strayed into error; she had abandoned the Lord to worship Satan. Even if she didn't formally apostatize, it made no difference. Magic required a tacit pact with the devil. And the ones who suffered most were God's chosen: the clergy. *The biggest one belongs to the parish priest*, or so the alleged Concubina claimed. This meant that the priest's unfortunate member would doubtless be the one with which the sorceress attempted to slake her lust. There was an obscene economy at work here. A *feme fole* like Margot, who couldn't satisfy herself from prostitution alone, turned to the devil. Her diabolical master would, in turn, command that she work her wiles on the clergy, because, above all else, he lusted after clerical souls. The cleric's soul was especially precious to Satan; a commodity surpassing all others in value. *The pearl of great price*. Each one was worth at least a thousand ordinary lay souls. And Dominican souls were among the most precious.

Why hadn't he spoken out against Margot earlier? It was weakness; contemptible weakness that had kept him silent. God forgive him, his feelings for Margot had initially given rise to a perverted loyalty. It was a feeling that surpassed a mere contract between two rogues: the *I won't tell if you won't tell* variety. They had been lovers for so long and, over the years, shared many things. Sometimes Marcus had felt as if he loved Margot. From the very first, he had thought her the most beautiful, affectionate, and tender woman of his, admittedly, rather limited acquaintance. Indeed, this sense of Margot's general desirability and loveliness persisted long after she had relinquished any physical claim to beauty. Sometimes when she was lying there on the bed, unawares, he had seen someone very different than the hardened prostitute. At such times, Marcus had once believed that he caught a glimpse of what might be described as another realm: a world where Margot was not only beautiful, but also pure and good.

But now he realized that he was a victim. His importunate emotions were simply the workings of magic. Margot hadn't simply seduced him; she had clearly bewitched him into loving her and seeing her as beautiful, hence ensuring that he would remain silent about her devilish practices. Yet he had broken free from this misguided allegiance, realizing that it was his responsibility to expose her. And he was determined. From where did this virtuous resolve come? *My strength cometh from the Lord*, who had sent Brother Jacques into Marcus' life. It was his love for Jacques that gave him the strength to break with Margot.

Margot was a witch. And now he would use Marion's testimony to prove it! But could he? What Marion confessed to Marcus was protected by the seal of confession. A priest who breaks the seal must be deposed and do penance in prison for the rest of his days. Was Marion, a professed enchantress, entitled to the same consideration as a typical penitent? Sorcery was, after all, considered a heresy. The great Dominican Raymond of Peñafort didn't think that heretics were protected by the seal. Wouldn't this be all the truer for a sorceress who apostatized to obtain Satan's help? Heretics had to be amputated from the body of the faithful like putrid limbs, otherwise the entire church would be corrupted. But witchcraft was especially heinous: *Thou must not suffer a witch to live*. There was no doubt in Marcus' mind that he should denounce Margot to Prior Giles, the inquisitor general of France.

It was also true, however, that not everyone agreed with Raymond's judgment. Raymond was a canon lawyer; theologians were less pragmatic. Not only was Giles a theologian, but he was also, for all his merits, rather softhearted. So Marcus could not assume that if he revealed Marion's confession for purposes of denunciation, as he ought, that this good deed would be properly understood. There was another possibility, however. The secular authorities were becoming ever more intent on the prosecution of heresy — especially sorcery. Marcus had met John de Folleville, the provost of the Châtelet, in the past, and he seemed like a sensible man. He had the reputation as a godly one as well. Folleville's intolerance for prostitution was well known. And this would not be the first time that the provost had prosecuted a sorceress. All of Paris would benefit from a timely word to the wise. *The men of the city shall stone her to death, and she shall die.*

A Funeral

Hervey found Philip in the church one morning in late June. He was lying on his back, staring up at the vaulting with the same empty stare that was in his darling Rose's eyes after she was taken ill. But Philip was dead. His neck was broken. Hervey closed the eyes of the cadaver — eyes that the priest had seen brightened with a hopeful love and later dimmed by a despairing one. Now they were clouded by death. Hervey sat down heavily beside the body of the young man and wept. He tried to pray, though was too despondent to frame any words.

A healthy man's neck isn't like some old dried out branch which can break off without warning. Someone or something must have done this. But there was no blood. That was one of the first things Hervey had automatically noted: bloodshed would have required that the church be reconsecrated by the bishop. Even so, if Philip had met with a violent death inside the church, a reconsecration would be still in order. But how was one to know? There were no rope marks; no evidence of violence. He thought back to the last time he had seen the lad, when Philip was at the house. Philip had asked why Rose had never spoken to him about breaking off their engagement, and Hervey had replied that Rose alone knew the answer. Did Philip take this as encouragement to confront Rose? Hervey hoped not. At the time, he would have thought such an interview extremely undesirable, if only because of Rose's marked antipathy toward her old life, which clearly included Philip. The circumstances surrounding the Rose who had awakened from the trance had become increasingly uncanny, however. Hervey was first alarmed when Felice observed that Rose was reciting a psalm in Latin. This was a feat that would have been totally beyond Rose before her illness — of this Hervey was certain. Even if the psalm was only learned by rote, and she had no idea of its meaning, she would have required extensive tutoring. Yet Felice had since observed Rose reading unassisted, attributing her facility to Brother Jacques. If this was, in fact, the case Jacques must be an extraordinary pedagogue, and Rose an unusually apt student. To learn Latin in so little time was nothing short of remarkable. It had taken Felice several years to become proficient, and he had always considered her uncommonly quick. Retrospectively, Hervey wished he had acknowledged his misgivings to Philip. But they were so inchoate. And he hadn't wanted to contribute to the young man's distress by his own ungrounded conjectures.

Then Hervey stopped himself. This was crazy. Rose had no longer wished to marry Philip — that much was clear. But was there any reason to suspect Rose of his murder? Even if it was possible that Rose wanted to harm Philip, how could she be capable of it? Philip was twice her size! But then Hervey had to consider Felice's account of Rose's hostile behavior. Felice had even found it frightening, and she had never been one to frighten easily. Suddenly, Philip's theories of possession and soul snatching, articulated in a desperate attempt to come to terms with the change in Rose, didn't seem so wild. Hervey was totally out of his depth. He needed to consult someone. Maybe Anthony could help, or at least direct him to someone who could.

But first there was much to do. Hervey slowly got up and rang the passing bell. The lugubrious toll roused the sexton, whom Hervey instructed to fetch the coroner immediately. After his examination, the sexton would hitch up the cart to bring Philip home for the last time. First Hervey had the painful task of going to Philip's parents to break the news. It was always terrible to be the bearer of such miserable tidings. But Hervey expected this visit to be especially poignant. It was only in the fall that the couple had lost their youngest son to pneumonia, and the poor mother had been beside herself. Hervey hurried to acquaint Felice with the dreadful news, for she would have to accompany him.

She had a gift with the grieving. It was the way she listened. Felice had also truly loved Philip in a way that a grieving family would appreciate.

Philip, big and big-hearted, had been popular with everyone: all the parish turned out for the funeral. Both parents were weeping uncontrollably. Felice sat beside the wretched pair, holding their little girl — the only child left to them. The toddler took in everything gravely in wide-eyed bewilderment, never making a sound. Anna was also there, incapable of meeting anyone's eye in her misery, almost as if she held herself responsible for the poor man's death. Rose never appeared.

Later that afternoon, Hervey and Felice were back at the presbytery, numbed by sadness and too exhausted to speak. Even so, they were expecting visitors. Anthony and Baldwin had been invited to meet Margot. These arrangements had been made some days earlier. Since then, Philip's death had thrown Hervey and Felice into such a state of confusion that Felice only remembered the appointment in the middle of the funeral, by which time it was too late to change.

When Baldwin and Anthony arrived a couple of hours later, Hervey and Felice were beginning to rally. Felice had prepared some mulled wine and gingerbread, which she passed around. Hervey suspected that Margot would feel out of her depth with Anthony and Baldwin and might not be very forthcoming. So while they waited, he gave an overview of the succession of Margot's visions and their relation to Brother Jacques. (Felice didn't bother to mention that Baldwin had heard much of this before.) Hervey thought it best that they had a sense of the visions ahead of time. They could always follow up with questions. The main point was to see if Margot recognized them.

The bells were being rung for Vespers. Hervey stood up and looked out the window, but could see no sign of the old woman.

"I'm afraid Margot has been detained." Hervey looked out the window again as if to confirm, biting his lower lip. "But if you allow me, I would like to broach a matter that has been troubling both Felice and myself."

The two men looked up expectantly.

"What would you think if I were to tell you that I know a young woman who was miraculously apprised of Latin?"

When Baldwin and Anthony both immediately looked to Felice, father and daughter burst out laughing.

"It's true she was fast, but not that fast!" Hervey said.

"Perhaps they find it miraculous that any woman can learn Latin," said Felice — a remark that raised a guilty flush in Baldwin's face.

But they soon returned to the matter at hand and, without naming names, Hervey put before them the hypothetical case of an illiterate woman who was suddenly fully conversant in Latin. "I have heard such marvels with respect to demoniacs. But is that invariably the case?" he asked.

This was precisely the kind of question for which Baldwin had unwittingly been preparing for over the past few weeks, under the veil of his putative treatise on the soul. In the course of his subsequent disquisition on the matter, he led them to some very strange places indeed.

"Consider the positive side of the issue: a divine infusion of language, the prime example being Birgitta of Vadstena. She used to dictate her revelations in Swedish until she received the gift of Latinity late in life," said Baldwin.

But there were many instances of darker inspiration as well. A novice in Germany appeared to be the recipient of all kinds of divine gifts, a wondrous knowledge of Latin being just one of them. He preached like a seasoned theologian. Eventually, the community became suspicious and had him exorcised. Every sign of special ability vanished. All that remained was an impaired mind and a perpetual look of horror on the boy's face. Other supernatural gifts were equally ambiguous. Aquinas was not alone in his ability to levitate; the Beguine, Lutgard of Aywières, was elevated as much as at two cubits above the ground during Mass. But he concluded with the horrific case of the case of Count of Suanenborch's daughter.

"She was a devout girl, raised in a convent, and yet she was periodically raptured by demons. Her brother, a friar, did his best to protect his sister by holding her firmly in his arms at the hour when these raptures tended to occur. But she was seized all the same."

Anthony broke in to complain that this all sounded pretty preposterous, but Baldwin remained stubbornly unapologetic.

"Some of the most learned men of the day accepted such accounts at face value. Albert the Great not only believed the story about the girl in Suanenborch, but even disputed the question of 'raptured women of this sort' publicly in the presence of the bishop of Paris," said Baldwin.

Anthony made a derisive sound. Felice looked grave, however. She asked about the fate of the poor raptured sister, but Baldwin just shook his head. He didn't know.

Anthony, accustomed to Baldwin's stock of morbid anecdotes, was naturally curious as to why Hervey and Felice were suddenly interested in such matters. So they told him about Rose and how her recovery seemed to have ushered in remarkable language skills. It was at this point that Baldwin made a false step.

"Is this was the same woman that we discussed the other day?" he asked Felice.

Hervey's response was immediate. "When? Where did you meet?" There was an awkward moment. Then Felice explained their chance encounter on the banks of the Seine. There was an embarrassed silence before they returned to the subject of Rose.

"If Rose's special abilities come from demonic possession, this would mean that her soul would be sharing her body with a demon. The demon would be in control of her movement and speech, which would explain her newfound Latinity," said Anthony.

But Felice was pondering an even more disturbing prospect.

"Rose's behavior has changed so much, I wonder if the Rose we knew is still there. Her very essence seems to have changed. I know that's what Philip thought," she said, looking toward her father.

"Remember that a certain amount of change is only to be expected after what she has been through," responded Anthony. "There is a tradition in the Eastern Church that Lazarus never smiled after he had been resurrected by Christ, even though he lived another thirty years."

"But is it possible that the real Rose is altogether gone?" persisted Felice. "Perhaps Rose died, and only her body was revived. Her soul is somewhere else."

"It would hardly be the first time that demons interfered with dead bodies. They can allegedly move corpses around — usually to bewilder and frighten the living. Some authorities claim that demons even have the ability to animate them. But their movements would remain awkward, as if the body was being manipulated by someone else," said Baldwin.

"The little drowned boy whom the Franciscan brought back to life could be an example of this. Perhaps he was living without really being alive," said Anthony.

"But there is nothing comatose or awkward about Rose. In fact, her mind seems to have been improved since her illness," said Hervey.

"I am wondering if it is possible for someone to be brought back to life by a force other than God. Isn't that a power attributed to Simon Magus?" Felice said.

The three men suddenly fell silent, exchanging concerned looks. Felice had to repeat her question before Anthony responded.

"Simon Magus claimed to raise the dead. But theologians believe that he really only manipulated their corpses; that they weren't really brought back to life," said Anthony.

"But could he have made someone evil? A sick, vulnerable person perhaps?" asked Felice.

"Do you really believe that Rose is evil? Being sullen, or even seeming sinister, doesn't seem like strong enough evidence," said Anthony. Baldwin nodded in agreement.

Felice glanced at Hervey, who then spoke up.

"I think Felice and I have both come to feel that Rose has changed since her recovery, and that there is something wrong, even wicked, about this change. If the devil can infuse knowledge of Latin, I doubt he would have any problem investing someone with supernatural strength. We both think it possible that Rose killed Philip."

The room was completely silent. It seemed cold. Hervey went over to the hearth, but then remembered it was summer and there was no need for a fire. Then Anthony spoke.

"The case of Rose is most definitely a problem of spiritual discernment. I propose that the question be taken up with the Chancellor."

"I for one would be grateful for an expert opinion," said Hervey. Felice nodded her agreement.

The four friends were so absorbed by their conversation that they were unaware of the time passing. But the day was declining and the room was now in a kind of half-light. Margot hadn't appeared, and Baldwin and Anthony began to take their leave. Hervey walked outside with Anthony, who was telling him something about his uneven history with Gerson. The younger man lingered behind for a moment. Then, without warning, he grabbed Felice's hand and kissed it. Although she reflexively snatched it away, she couldn't help but smile.

"Will you meet me tomorrow at noon?" he whispered plaintively. She had rejected his most recent overtures, and he was desperate to have some time alone with her — if only for talk.

Felice looked behind her to where her father was in conversation with Anthony.

"All right. The cathedral at noon. Now leave!" she said, in a gentle, but firm, voice.

Arrest and the Fifth Vision

The provost of Paris was a very important man. It was he who represented the king both in the defense of royal interests and the enforcement of law. It didn't matter if he was a short man with a receding chin, bad breath, and a high voice, as was the case with John de Folleville. His public persona bespoke his power. His seat was the Châtelet — a looming fortress located on the right bank at the base of the Grand Pont. It was here that he presided over the most important tribunal in Paris, upholding the king's justice. And he was efficient in this capacity: over three quarters of the people brought to trial were executed — usually within two weeks after their arrest.

The provost was given an especially free reign when it came to the prosecution of criminals: thieves, embezzlers, rapists, murderers and the like. But prostitution was not illegal. And that was as it should be. As much as he might sympathize with someone like St. Louis and his efforts to force conversion or expulsion upon prostitutes, he agreed with Aquinas' assessment that prostitution was a necessary evil. Prostitution may not be a crime, but Folleville was becoming progressively sensitive to the links between prostitution and the criminal underworld. Looking over the register since he had taken office, Folleville was dismayed by the number and range of cases he found connecting these two sordid realms. Recently there was the depraved case of Katherine Roquier: her sister-in-law came to apprentice in embroidery and Katherine promptly sold her into prostitution. Some of the weaker justices were prepared to pillory and release her, but Folleville saw to it that she was branded as well. This kind of perfidy ought to be imprinted on her face.

The provost wasn't surprised to hear that prostitutes were now trying their hand at sorcery. He had just received an anonymous denunciation of a certain *fille de joie* from Glatigny whose spells had placed a couple of newlyweds at death's door. The woman was apparently acting on behalf of a young protégée, a *fillette* who claimed that she had been jilted by the man. But the younger woman was evidently a sorceress as well. When the sergeants searched her room, there were clear signs: a strange piece of mossy-looking fungus as well as something that looked like a clump of human hair. The provost had acted most expeditiously: he received the tip on a Friday and had the two women arrested the very same day. They were put in the woman's prison, La Griesche, located in the bowels of the Châtelet.

When Margot neither appeared nor sent a message, Hervey went to make inquiries personally. Felice wanted to accompany him, but that area of town had deteriorated still further since they had lived there, if that were possible, and he insisted on going alone. When he reached Rue Glatigny, he asked the owner of a tavern about Margot's whereabouts, and was immediately directed to a dingy old building. The only person at the address was a rather beefy looking middle-aged woman, with a comical, but friendly face. Hervey thought this was probably the daughter that Margot had mentioned. She didn't resemble her mother, who had been slight. The woman had been crying.

"I've seen you before. You're Father Hervey."

"Yes."

She asked him to come in. They climbed a rickety set of stairs, which opened up to a long narrow room with two makeshift walls running lengthwise and divided up by several crude doors. The room was poorly furnished, but rather ordinary and scrupulously neat. Hervey wasn't sure what the little rooms were for, but he had his suspicions and was relieved that none of them seemed to be in use. There was a table and some chairs in a small enclave at the end of the room. The woman indicated that Hervey should take a seat before she herself sat down.

"Mother said you would come. She was always right about these things. I'm Joan." If there were aspects of Margot's dress that bespoke her profession, there were no such markers on this woman. Somehow she had remained untouched by her environment. Her manner of dress was almost penitential in its severity.

"Margot's daughter," Hervey said somewhat unnecessarily. He looked around. "But where is Margot?"

Joan told him that Margot had been arrested and charged with sorcery. Hervey was at the same time aghast and yet, on some level, not surprised. Felice had a strong premonition that something terrible had befallen Margot.

"Joan, your mother is a good woman, and there's been a mistake. We must pray for her release." Hervey said this, poignantly aware of the unlikelihood of this outcome.

The woman looked at him very directly. He could now see that she had her mother's eyes.

"Mother was good all right, though she never thought she was — because of her job, mostly. But most women in her line wouldn't have kept a baby. Probably wouldn't even have allowed there to be a baby. Mother was different. She always kept me nearby. I never wanted for anything. And later she saw that I found decent work. We can pray for her soul. But she won't be released. She told me it was her time." Joan wiped her nose on her sleeve before continuing.

"Mother knew they were coming for her. Dreamt it the night before. But she saw something else as well and woke me up to tell me. She thought it was a kind of message meant for you. I had to repeat it to her three times over because she was afraid I'd fall back to sleep and not remember in the morning." Joan smiled ruefully. "She would've been right about that too."

Joan proceeded to relate her mother's dream in some detail. It apparently took place on the same high peak as the previous vision. At the center of the landscape was a large mirror the size of a small pond, bearing the image of the Franciscan. Under the face were the same letters Margot had seen before: the ones that Hervey and Felice had deciphered as *cura animarum*. The face and letters disappeared, and out of the mirror came four creatures: each with six wings and covered with many eyes. One was like a lion, one like a calf, one with the face of a man, one like an eagle. The animals stood in a line to the right of the mirror, waiting. And then out of the mirror rode four horsemen on different colored horses: one white, one red, one black, and one a pale nondescript color. The riders went to the left side of the mirror. The dream ended with the two groups facing each other as if they meant to do battle.

Hervey repeated out loud what Joan had said to make sure he had it right. Then he thanked her.

"Is there anything I can do for you? Anything at all?"

"No. Not really, thank you." And, in fact, the woman projected a calm sense of self-sufficiency. Margot was probably an excellent mother. "Unless you can bring mother back," she added.

"I wish I could," Hervey said sadly.

Joan just smiled and slowly closed the door.

The encounter left Hervey feeling troubled and confused. On his way home, Hervey stopped at the cathedral close on the off chance that he might find Anthony. He was in luck, but his friend was just leaving for his appointment with Gerson, with Baldwin in tow. Anthony encouraged him to come along. Gerson was eager to meet the owner of the palimpsest and Anthony was planning to consult with him over the subject of Rose. As they walked the short distance to the Chancellor's office, Hervey told them about Margot's arrest. The other two men had never met Margot, yet the news came as a shock: they walked the rest of the way in silence. Anthony was about to knock on the door, when Hervey stopped him.

"I would prefer if nothing were said about Margot and the visions. Not yet, anyway."

Both Baldwin and Anthony looked at him with curiosity.

"Part of it is instinct and part is purely pragmatic," Hervey said in answer to the unspoken question on their faces. "I will give you the pragmatic part. I have never met Gerson. But I did hear him deliver a sermon which blamed the entire schism on the prophecies of Birgitta of Vadstena and Catherine Benincasa. He has written against the magical arts. And he is reputed to be extremely ascetical in his lifestyle. I don't think he would be very impressed by the visions of anyone — let alone someone arrested for sorcery, who happened to be a prostitute."

No one could argue with such impeccable reasoning.

The Chancellor was, as Anthony predicted, very interested in meeting the owner of the mysterious manuscript. While being quizzed about its history, Hervey was trying to get over his surprise at his interlocutor's youth. Gerson was disappointed that Hervey didn't know more about the manuscript's provenance, but was still anxious to see it. Hervey promised that the Chancellor would soon have the opportunity.

But Gerson showed himself to be much less receptive to the enigma of Rose, wondering at their readiness to adhere to so negative a prognosis. They were dismissing what, to Gerson's mind, was key to understanding her changed behavior: a life transformed by suffering that caused her to renew her long-standing commitment to celibacy.

"A holy woman from Liège said that if people knew how valuable diseases were in bringing them to God, they would purchase them in bulk," Gerson said. Far from seeing Rose's attachment to Brother Jacques as reprehensible, he deemed it commendable.

"Often when a member of the fragile sex feels special, they become independent in an offensive and unfeminine manner. One of the signs of genuine piety in a woman is the willingness to submit to her confessor," said Gerson.

He privately believed that in this case Rose was fortunate enough to have encountered a true holy man: her devotion was in proportion to his goodness. Clearly, her Latin was reflective of Brother Jacques' excellent tutelage. To Gerson's mind, this was not a case requiring spiritual discernment but disciplinary action: these men were implying unspeakable things about a man of sanctity. He dismissed them in a frosty manner.

"He's very good at making people look like fools. No wonder he's so unpopular with students," grumbled Baldwin.

Anthony was placed in the unlikely position of defending his former student.

"I think you should consider that Gerson is not only a formidable intellect, but also something of a progressive. He would be much more inclined to consider humoral disorders before he would consider diabolical disturbances."

Hervey, who was suffering under the same sense of rebuff as Baldwin, didn't say anything. He was grateful that he had not subjected Margot's visions to the Chancellor's scrutiny. But Hervey was in a rush. There were pressing parish issues that required his attention. Before the three separated, however, they agreed that Anthony and Baldwin would attend next Thursday's meeting.

"Good. Margot had a fifth vision. We can discuss it afterward," said Hervey.

Le Châtelet

Margot de la Barre was arraigned for poisoning Hainselin and Agnesot. She was first brought to trial on July 30, when she denied the charge, claiming that both husband and wife had been unwell; that they had sent for her, and that she had done her best to cure them with her herbs. The judges inquired into her past and the manner in which she made her living. Margot didn't attempt to conceal anything.

"Do you have any enemies?" Folleville asked. It was a routine question but one that was especially pertinent in this case because he had been acting on an anonymous tip.

"No. I have no enemies. I can't think of anyone who bears me a grudge." And Margot believed this to be true.

Considering John de Folleville's views on prostitutes, the web of lies and treachery that such women weave, it was a foregone conclusion that he would suspect Margot of lying and would put her to the question. Margot was taken into a foul room underground which smelt like urine and death. Two masked attendants stripped her and tied her to a trestle. Its sharp rungs felt like meat hooks digging into her back. Her body was secured by two bands of metal. And then suddenly the trestle was tilted in such a way that Margot's head was lower than her feet. Her limbs were fastened by cords that bit into her flesh. Her mouth was forced open. The stiff fabric chute that was pushed into her throat functioned as a crude aqueduct, through which jar after jar of water was poured. Margot couldn't breathe: her mouth and nostrils were totally obstructed by water. When it stopped and she still refused to speak, they moved her to a larger trestle on which the rungs seemed sharper and the grip more ferocious. The cords were drawn so tight that all her veins and arteries felt a terrible pressure; Margot feared that her eyes would pop right out of her skull. At last it was over. They untied Margot and pulled her off the trestle. She couldn't feel her limbs at all and her legs collapsed out from under her when she attempted to stand. The two attendants dragged her into a little room with a fire to warm herself. They knew from experience that otherwise the prisoners' frigid limbs would be too numb for them to walk. For days afterward, water, mucous, and blood poured from Margot's mouth and nose. She endured the same torments on three different occasions, and the ritual was always the same. Still the old woman managed to hold her peace.

A week into Margot's imprisonment, a fire sprang up in one of the storerooms. Some of the prisoners of la Griesche had to be moved out of their cells temporarily. The women were lined up in two rows against the wall. It was then that Margot first spotted Marion. She was standing in the front row, almost directly in front of Margot. Leaning forward, Margot whispered Marion's name. There was no response at first. But eventually she gave the slightest of nods, indicating that she was listening.

"Don't be afraid, love. It's someone else's work, not ours. You can tell them the truth about me, but don't say anything that you don't know for sure. But remember your promise, Marion. Otherwise we're both dead!"

Marion kept her eyes in front of her, but nodded once again. Then the two rows of women were separated and led back to their cells.

The guards came for Marion several days later. She was curled up on her straw mattress in the fetal position, rocking back and forth. When she was led in front of the judge, her eyes were distant as if her mind were somewhere else. Under interrogation, however, Marion came to life, indignant at the very idea that she would raise a hand against Hainselin.

"I would never harm him. He was my whole life," she said. Marion was even more shocked that her keepsakes could be construed as evil.

"The last time I saw Hainselin alone, I grabbed his hood to make him stay. I pulled out some of his hair. It was an accident. But that was all of him that I had left, so I kept it."

"And the moss?" asked the judge.

"It's from a fountain where a holy virgin was beheaded. Richard gave it to me before his lord called him back to England. I kept it for love of him, not magic!" she sobbed.

A number of the judges felt sorry for the beautiful woman. She didn't look at all like the usual riff raff dragged into the court. They would have preferred to pardon her. But for the majority, the evidence of the hair and the moss seemed definitive: Marion must be put to the question. She screamed while they stripped away her clothes and tied her to the trestle, and only stopped screaming when her voice was drowned out. She would have done anything to make the pain stop; she desperately wanted to confess. But she continued to resist because of her oath to Margot.

The following week when Marion was again about to be tortured, she protested her innocence, and made a sobbing appeal to the higher court of the *parlement*. She looked so pathetic and fragile that the judges partial to her case requested that some representatives from the *parlement* be sent to hear her appeal. The two justices who came were not convinced of her innocence, however, and determined that the provost was free to proceed against her, notwithstanding her appeal. When Marion was about to be tortured again, she broke. She was already on the trestle, and her torturers were about to pour the water, when she begged them to stop, promising to confess. Marion was untied, permitted to dress, and then conducted to the upper hall. She told them everything: about the Dane, about the oaths she took at Margot's behest, about Margot's two sets of spells, about the wedding — everything. Under the pressure of her interlocutors, Marion acknowledged, while still under oath, that Margot was responsible for the illness of Hainselin and his wife. The scribe dutifully recorded her confession. When it was read back to her, she confirmed and signed the document.

The Counter-Faith

The number of people attending the Thursday meetings had thinned somewhat. Hervey wondered whether it had anything to do with the death of the boy. But Brother Jacques was still enough of a curiosity that there were at least fifty extra people in attendance, seated discreetly behind the core group — enough of a crowd that the presence of three supernumerary clerics and a laywoman didn't obtrude. The procession of Brother Jacques and his attendants at the start of the meeting had acquired the air of a ritual. This time Hervey was almost certain that the women proceeded from the sacristy. And was it his imagination or had Brother Jacques' platform turned into something of a dais? Meanwhile, Felice watched Rose carefully. But she didn't learn much more, apart from the fact that Rose had a marvelous voice — something Felice had never known before. Her rendering of *Veni spiritus* was exquisite. The high notes were sustained and powerful. Felice couldn't say whether there was anything preternatural about her aptitude. She could only say that the results were compelling, haunting, even.

Brother Jacques preached one of his more memorable sermons that day. He spoke in a commanding and sonorous voice that made the very air tremble.

"The Lord warned us that when the end of the world was nigh, there would be certain signs. So be careful to heed them. Nation will rise against nation, there will be pestilence and famine, and many will come in the Lord's name saying *I am Christ*. Many of these things have happened in our own time. Some of you remember the great pestilence: how in a matter of days, Paris became a necropolis, and all of Christendom a charnel house. But more deadly than the pestilence are the diseases of the soul: the abundant heresies that appeared and are still appearing. I say these are more deadly because they are more insidious: sickness in the guise of health, evil with a smiling face — all coming in the name of the Lord." The Franciscan paused to search the individual faces of the Faithful. His voice was compelling: it was as if he had purchase on privileged information; as if God told him what was coming. The congregation muttered anxious words of dismay among themselves. Several reached for the hand of a neighbor. Brother Jacques had changed. He was no longer the herald of comfort and love.

"Our Lord is merciful, but He is also just: a Lord of wrath and judgment." The preacher's eyes blazed within a familiar visage made strange by unwonted severity. His listeners cowered. With a few sparse words, the end of time was before them, and they were sodden with regret and despair. *I wish I had never — God forgive me for — I fear it is too late; Spare me, Lord!* Strange and lurid images appeared in their imaginations: they were standing on the edge of a merciless abyss looking down on figures twisted by sin and suffering — figures that had once been human. *It could be me,* each of the Faithful thought in anguish, and trembled.

Then the friar's face softened. When he again spoke, his voice was filled with hope and promise.

"But we must not despair. For our Lord loves His creation so well that when the end comes, He will succor us: not just our souls, but also our very bodies will be spared. Remember His promise to us: *Not a hair of your head will perish.* The Lord so loves His creation that, at the end of time *a trumpet shall sound, and the dead shall rise again incorruptible.* The mortal body will finally be cloaked in immortality, and we shall live forever."

The preacher waxed eloquent on the ineffable joy that soul and body would experience once reunited: the bliss of this rediscovered intimacy, which was never again to be interrupted. The voice stopped, and it was over. The congregation was dismissed, but none of the Faithful moved for some time. They had been carried too far on the crest of the preacher's words.

Felice was spared any such pious paralysis, however. She stood up almost immediately after the benediction and shook herself impatiently. Her limbs felt numbed from prolonged sitting. She wanted some vigorous movement to wake them up.

"Well, I wasn't expecting that," she said to her father under her breath.

"Not exactly your favorite topic, my dear. But he certainly knows how to engage an audience." Hervey made this observation with an amused smile.

No, it was not her favorite topic. Clearly the members of the Faithful felt differently. The power of Brother Jacques' words was so engrossing that only now were they beginning to stir. The resurrection of the body indeed! Everyone except Felice seemed desperate to hang on to the old body. But, then again, she could never understand the people who couldn't throw things away, even when they were worn out and worthless. She attempted to express some of her indignation to her father. The fact that he was reflexively looking around to make sure that no one else was within earshot made her more indignant still. She was still holding forth when Hervey gave her a not too gentle nudge.

"Try and contain yourself, Felice. Here comes Rupert."

The young friar greeted them warmly, so glad to see them; so happy that they were all in the blessed ambiance of Brother Jacques. Hervey, always genial and attentive, asked after Rupert's commentary, and the young friar's face was transformed by a smile.

"Father, I am finished! There's only the defense, and, if all goes well, I am finally a master."

There were congratulations all around. Rupert flushed with pleasure at the attention. When exactly did he finish? When was the defense? Could Hervey attend? When could they read his commentary? And what would he work on next?

"I am planning to write on the soul."

Hervey, who noticed that Baldwin was, of course, lingering close by, grasped his elbow, drawing him into their circle.

"Permit me to reintroduce Master Baldwin, also engaged in peregrinations involving the soul," Hervey said.

The two young men immediately embarked on a rarefied conversation — as much for the exchange of information as the opportunity to test one another's metal. They began by comparing different patristic approaches.

"Tertullian! Who reads him anymore? Nobody believes in the material soul," Baldwin objected.

"True, but he is very much worth reading," said Rupert, standing his ground with a confidence that was entirely new to him. "Tertullian was the first to insist on the inseparability of body and soul: the ultimate marriage, consummated with the resurrection. I'm using him to refute the Cathar heresy."

Baldwin looked unconvinced, thinking the whole orientation rather antiquated, and said as much. There weren't any Cathars after all, so what's the point? But Rupert insisted that there was always a dangerous tendency to deprecate the material world; to deprecate all that the Lord had done for them. Baldwin's retaliation was forestalled by one of Felice's timely interventions.

"Brother Rupert, I think your work is fascinating. Such an unusual approach!" She had been watching the two scholars sparring, and it quite annoyed her to see Baldwin strutting like a peacock.

Rupert, encouraged by Felice's interest, went on at some length about the nuances of Cathar theology. His command of the authorities was impressive — not just scriptural passages, but the church fathers as well. He cited texts at some length and even, as far as Felice could tell, verbatim. It was a remarkable performance, magisterial even. Baldwin stood by sullenly, watching Felice watch Rupert. He could only hope that she was just being magnanimous and wasn't truly impressed by this conceited windbag.

"But I know what a scholar you are, my lady. I very much doubt I could teach you anything about the Cathars," Rupert wound up, giving Felice a strangely pointed look.

Felice was taken aback. "You flatter me, Brother Rupert. I am no scholar."

Rupert looked from Felice to Hervey.

"Really? What about that truly singular manuscript containing the life of Peter Martyr?"

"What an excellent memory you have, my boy!" said Hervey. "That's what the best kind of scholars all have in common: memory. They don't even need a library!" Despite the jovial tones, Felice could discern her father's alarm.

Rupert smiled and took his leave: he had work to do among the Faithful. Anthony strolled over and joined the group, and the four friends left together. But first they thanked Brother Jacques for his memorable sermon.

At the rectory, they immediately settled into what were fast becoming familiar stations.

"Another Thursday, and here the four of us are: same chairs, same basic questions on our minds. We're like a shadow meeting of the Faithful. We should call ourselves the Counter-Faithful, or maybe just the Counter-Faith for short," said Baldwin.

Anthony laughed. "Of course, the name is open to misconstrual, but a detail like that would never bother Baldwin, would it master? Still, he's right: here we are again. All that really changes are Felice's wonderful refreshments. What is this anyway?"

Felice smiled and laughed. "Just mead. But I threw in a few cloves for accent and, believe it or not, a sprig or two of mustard!"

Everyone commended Felice for her fearless gastronomy. But they hadn't forgotten why they were gathered there. Hervey's relation of Margot's fifth vision took no time at all. But the silence that followed was considerable. Eventually Anthony spoke up.

"The mirror seems central to understanding the vision. But as a symbol, it's maddeningly opaque. It reflects everything, and so can stand for just about anything."

"Too true," said Baldwin. "Practically every book these days is called *Speculum* this or *Speculum* that. I was just reading a medical text called the *Speculum speculorum*: the Mirror of Mirrors!"

"What about a possible relation between the mirror and the Cathar view that the material world is but a poor reflection of the real world — the celestial kingdom?" Felice ventured.

"Plausible, but hardly definitive," responded Anthony.

Fortunately the rest of the vision borrowed imagery from the Apocalypse and was less ambiguous. The four winged animals were traditionally associated with the four Evangelists — spreading the word of God to the world. The four horses were the forces of destruction unleashed on the world in anticipation of its end. The fact that the two groups were lined up and faced one another suggested some kind of a pitched battle between good and evil. But this still left them with many unanswered questions. Did these symbols point to a literal battle or a spiritual one?

Had it taken place in the past, was it occurring in the present, or predicted for the future? And, perhaps most intriguing of all, how were these images related to them personally?

"Margot might have shed some light on this. But she disappeared just when we recognized the connection between her visions and the journal. The whole situation reminds me of what happened with Martin," remarked Baldwin.

"Your friend who was working on the transcription? What happened?" asked Felice, her voice uncharacteristically tremulous.

It was with a heavy heart that Anthony told Felice and Hervey about Martin's death, and the way it was augured in Anthony's dream of Simon. This was the first time Felice had ever heard of Simon and the spectral role he had played in the lives of Anthony and Hervey. She looked over at her father, and saw that he had gone very pale.

"I was afraid that he would come back," he said in a whisper.

Hervey soon regained his composure, however, and listened attentively as Anthony described the guests and the seating at the prior's dinner party. The fact that Rupert not only attended the dinner, but also was the one responsible for discovering Martin dead was not lost on them.

"Rupert behaved oddly this evening. The emphasis on the Cathars was strange. The reference to the vita of Peter Martyr, stranger still. I never mentioned the manuscript to Rupert, did you?" said Hervey, looking at his daughter.

Felice shook her head. "But what's even more puzzling is that Rupert wasn't just referring to the vita of Peter Martyr. He seemed to be alluding to the hidden journal, as if he knew about Brother Martin's transcription. Maybe he even took it!" she said.

"But supposing he did. Why would he want us to know?" inquired Anthony.

"To frighten us. Look what happened to Martin!" exclaimed Baldwin.

It was certainly true that Martin died just when he seemed on the verge of sharing an important discovery about the manuscript. Either Jacques or Rupert, perhaps acting on behalf of Jacques, could have murdered Martin.

"Still, the whole thing sounds so preposterous!" said Hervey. "Was it really possible that a man whom half of Paris believes is a saint is a murderer or at least an abettor of murder?"

"I doubt there is anyone in this room who would vouch for the Franciscan as a saint," responded Baldwin, darkly.

"But why murder Martin in any event?" Hervey persisted.

"Because Jacques didn't want us to read to the end of the manuscript, and I didn't make Martin stop in time," said Anthony.

That was the only reason they could come up with. Admittedly, it seemed farfetched. How could Jacques possibly know what the manuscript contained? And, even supposing he did, how could something that was written over a century and a half ago have any bearing for a man in his thirties? Anthony had a theory.

"Supposing Jacques knew about the existence of the palimpsest all along. We aren't sufficiently acquainted with the manuscript's history to say how this might be, but it is possible. He may have overheard enough at dinner to identify the manuscript, which he believed to be dangerous to him."

"Dangerous in what way?" asked Felice.

"Jacques is from Languedoc: what if the journal identified one of his ancestors as a heretic? It wouldn't matter when he was convicted. The body would still be exhumed and burned, and the descendants disinherited," said Anthony.

"Well, at least this theory has the advantage of providing us with a motive," said Baldwin.

But Hervey looked skeptical. "If Margot's visions and the journal really are connected, that would make her a kind of visionary inquisitor, which seems utterly fantastic," he said.

The others could only agree.

Hervey and Felice sat up talking after their guests had left. She couldn't help but press for more details about Simon, and Hervey, though in many ways acting against his better judgment, found himself divulging more and more. When they finally retired for the evening, sleep eluded Hervey for the longest time. He could think of little else besides Simon's return. Hervey felt as if he were turning the pages of a familiar codex that had for many years gone missing, each page more terrible than the last. There were already streaks of grey appearing in the sky when he at last succumbed to a broken sleep.

Hervey started awake. There was someone at the door; a persistent knocking that had been going on for some time. Anthony's dream came to mind, and when Hervey opened the door he half expected to see Simon, his handsome face riddled with evil. Thank God it was just the sexton. Yet the sexton was out of breath with an unsettling look in his eyes.

"Father, something terrible has happened. You have to come right away."

"Is someone ill?" Hervey was hastily pulling on his clothes, wondering if the last rites were required.

"No. Nothing like that. It's something in Les Innocents."

Like many parish churches in Paris, St.-Jacques did not have its own cemetery, but relied on the communal graveyard. The two men set off, half running, half walking. The sexton's knocking had awakened Felice as well, who, unbidden, was following closely behind. The sexton, who sensed her presence, stopped and turned.

"No, my lady. You don't want to see this!"

Felice, with a sudden premonition of what lay ahead, shuddered, but said in a low firm voice.

"I think I must."

The cemetery had been walled in the time of Philip Augustus to keep out marauding pigs. The walls were now centuries old and crumbling in a number of places. The sexton had long ago discovered a breach in the wall, opportunely located near the northeast end of the graveyard where the departed of St.-Jacques were interred. He clambered over, and the other two followed. And there they were: the bodies of the recent dead, exhumed from their graves and leaning up against their respective tombstones as if in expectation. *The trumpet shall sound, and the dead shall rise again incorruptible* — only they hadn't. Far from glorified bodies, the decomposing corpses looked sad and vulnerable, their clothes in rags, their faces unrecognizable. Everything so fragile, perishable, and decaying. It was only in the instances where a cadaver's face had given way to the underlying skull that anything approaching eternity appeared: a frozen, unrelenting, grin gave expression to an everlasting life of interminable horror — world without end. The sexton's mother had died several months ago. He spotted her body, bloated and rotting, and howled in rage and grief.

Simon had been abroad last night. Hervey and Felice stood by help-lessly and wept.

The Sixth Vision and Confession

The sound of the guards outside the door made Margot leap up in fear. She was led before the justices who once again charged her with poison-ing Hainselin and his wife.

"You're wrong! I tried to cure them."

"We know you are lying," said Folleville. "Your accomplice has had the good sense to tell the truth."

And then the guards produced Marion — sweet, fragile Marion, who looked so disheveled and tormented that she was barely recognizable.

"Poor pet," Margot murmured to herself.

Marion was made to repeat her confession in front of Margot, adding:

"I acted solely on the advice and counsel of Margot, and no other."

Margot persisted in her denials.

"Marion, I wouldn't harm Hainselin. How can you think it? Look at me!" But Marion just stood, there — head hanging — until she was removed from the courtroom. Margot turned to face her judges. "She's mistaken. Hainselin and Agnesot are not ill because of me. I swear on my soul." Margot was not at all used to addressing men as educated or well-born as her judges, and she groped for words that might make them understand. "Upon my honor, if I were a man, I would offer her my gage in battle to prove it!" she said, but the judges just laughed.

Margot was tortured once more, but still said nothing. Afterward, she was taken back to her cell, where she sat motionless for the longest time, staring into space. Wet and bedraggled, the old woman looked as if all sense had been beaten out of her: as if she were witless, and her mind had left her body once and for all. In fact, she was deep in thought. Someone was to blame for Hainselin and Agnesot falling sick. Some-one had either interfered with her spell or superimposed another. She didn't know why. It was unlikely that the easy-going Hainselin had any foes, nor the plain but seemingly harmless Agnesot. Margot had told her judges that she herself didn't have any enemies, but was that true? She thought of the terror inspired by the appearance of the Franciscan in her visions and her even greater terror when she recognized him. And at last she was beginning to understand. She had to see Marion again. Only then would she know for sure.

Margot had her chance four days later when Marion was once again paraded out in front of Margot in an effort to make the old woman confess. This time Marion was explicitly questioned about the oaths she took at Margot's behest.

"My entire body has been shattered because I tried to keep faith with you," she said, finally looking at Margot with reproach.

Margot knew this was her last chance to find out the truth. "Marion," she called out as the guards were beginning to lead the younger woman away. "Did you go to confession after the Thursday meeting?"

Marion turned her head; her face looked stricken.

"Who was your confessor?"

"I don't know. First Brother Jacques, then Brother Marcus. It was all confused!" was all that Marion had time to say, but she continued to look at Margot like a dumb animal in shock as they jerked her body around and pulled her through the door. Margot was beginning to understand.

That night Margot experienced a final vision in which these questions, and much more, were resolved. She was looking at a glorious garden that was adorned by lush vegetation and glorious fountains. It was quiet, empty of any living creature. Brother Jacques appeared from nowhere, dressed in his Franciscan habit, just as she had last seen him. The friar was standing before a large stone table on which there was a pile of small figures that looked like statuettes or dolls—unadorned by hair and unmarked by any distinguishing features. Clumps of clay, brushes covered with paint, and pieces of fabric were strewn across the table. Brother Jacques was preoccupied, bent over some material, sewing. When he straightened for a moment, Margot saw that it was a white garment with something black running down the front and back. Once he completed this item, he began work on some faded red fabric. Jacques was sewing a little dress. He proceeded to choose two of the little figures from the pile and dress them. Jacques exhaled into the face of each of these mannequins, and they began to change, becoming more lifelike. He put the two little figures down on the tabletop, and they walked toward one another and embraced. It was comical to see these little doll-like creatures demonstrate so much volition, and Margot smiled to herself. But then she realized with a start that this was not just a pair of anonymous dolls: they were meant to represent Marcus and herself. Nor were these representations crude or clumsy. Moving closer, she could see that the female doll's face was lined and careworn, while the plump little friar had a large mole on its nose. All at once, the little friar let go of the Margot doll and turned to face Brother Jacques, listening attentively. When he turned back to the female doll, there was a rope in his hands. He bound her wrists. Margot awoke just as the Dominican doll began leading the Margot doll away.

The next day when Margot's tormentors were about to pour the water, the old woman surprised them by announcing that she was ready to confess. The attendants made her get dressed and sent a message to the justices immediately before she changed her mind. Margot was brought into the courtroom for the last time where, without prompting, she volunteered one of the strangest confessions the justices had ever heard.

"I confess to teaching Marion the spell with the rooster. It was meant to increase Hainselin's love so he would leave Agnesot. It didn't work, so I tried the wreaths. I had to. Marion was dying of sorrow, and the spell could cause no lasting harm. The wreaths were not evil; they were like the ones I used for Agnesot's headache — only turned around, with the prayers first. The prayers call on God. I have never called on the devil. But the devil came anyway. His name is Jacques. He can enslave souls. Brother Marcus, the Dominican, once loved me, but he belongs to the Franciscan now. Jacques knew what I was, and used Marcus to destroy me. He defiled the sacrament, and denounced me. I said that I had no enemies, but I was wrong: there were two, but now there are five. These five are the enemies of all mankind."

Margot said this as one extended utterance, looking straight ahead, before falling silent. Yet she had said enough. Although she may not have admitted to attempted murder, she did confess to using magic. That meant she had invoked the devil. The scribe read the confession back to her; she acknowledged it as the truth, made a mark where her signature was required, and was led away. When Folleville adjourned the court, he asked the scribe to remain. Folleville knew Brother Marcus personally, and Brother Jacques by reputation. Certain necessary changes in Margot's confession were in order.

A few days later, Margot's confession was transcribed from the scribe's rough notes and entered into the official register. The first part closely followed the contours of Marion's account. But the preparations of the wreaths was markedly different:

> Marion returned from the wedding two or three hours after noon, and asked Margot for the wreaths. Margot invoked the devil in the following manner: "Enemy I conjure you in the name of the Father, Son, and Holy Spirit that you come to me here." Repeating these words three times without stopping, she proffered the wreaths. She also made another little wreath from leftover herbs, and threw it in a bin near where she stood with Marion. Then Satan appeared, looking the same as he does in the Passion plays, though without the horns. When he asked what she wanted, she told him that the wreath in the bin was for him and that he should ensure that no one could help Hainselin and his wife until the wrongs they had perpetrated against Marion had been righted. Satan took the wreath from the bin, leaving via the window. His departure was accompanied by a great noise, sounding "like a terrific wind."

All mention of diabolical friars was suppressed.

On August 11, two days after her confession, Margot was led to Les Halles where she was pilloried so that all of Paris could bear witness to her shame. After eight hours of blistering sun, Margot was released, half dead, and conducted by the sergeants of the Châtelet to the swine market at La Place de Grève. The faggots were being piled around her feet when Margot, dazed and confused, momentarily became alert. There was a demon on the other side of the square, lurking among the crowd. It was waiting to watch her burn, hoping to gain her soul. Margot died saying the Lord's Prayer. The words *Deliver us from evil* were on her lips when she was overwhelmed by the flames.

Concealed behind a pigsty on the other side of the square was Brother Marcus, watching with satisfaction, confident that he had fulfilled the will of the Lord.

Chapter 10: Hauntings

The Revenant

It was evening and Hervey was walking over to the church to fetch the register of expenditures from the sacristy. There was a meeting of churchwardens in the morning and he wanted to be prepared. He was hoping to make a case for a new font. The current one was cracked and discolored. In fact, it actually leaked. This seemed like a disrespectful way to welcome the newest members into Christ's family. It was overcast, and the night was dense and murky, but Hervey was carrying a lantern. He walked with a heavy heart, thinking about the desecration in the cemetery. Hervey had asked the sexton to round up a couple of men to help put things to right. They were sworn to secrecy.

Hervey thought about Philip and his beloved Rose. Felice had often said that she had never seen any woman so besotted with a man. And Hervey knew that the intensity of Rose's feelings was returned. And yet, murder may have found its way into their relationship, like a serpent in the lovers' Eden. Was it possible that Rose was responsible for Philip's death? Could some possessing fiend have infused Rose's body with superhuman strength? And what about Anthony's friend, Martin? Was he, in fact, murdered, as well? Did anyone really care enough about the journal of an obscure sectarian from a defunct heresy to murder for it? Could Rupert possibly be to blame? He had always thought Rupert a studious, rather dull, but eminently harmless fellow — someone incapable of murder. It wouldn't be hard to kill an old man, however — especially if you crept up on him unawares while he was reading. There was no evidence of violence. Even so, Martin had died and the transcription had disappeared. If Phillip and Martin were both murdered, were the murders, in fact, linked? Was Brother Jacques somehow the bridge between their respective deaths? Ever since the last meeting with the so-called Counter-Faith, these questions had been weighing on Hervey's mind, and he was now awash in a sea of confusion and dread.

Hervey had just entered the church when some movement in the north transept caught his eye. The lighting in the church was dim, but Hervey thought he could discern a dark shape against the overall gloom. Whatever it was seemed to fade into the chapel dedicated to Saints Loup and Giles.

"Who's there?" Hervey called.

Nobody answered. It was unusual, but not impossible, for a person to be in the church so late. Yet if there were someone there, why wouldn't he make his presence known? A prolonged silence ensued, during which Hervey was only aware of a surging sound in his ears from the blood pumping through his body. He tried to calm himself, reasoning that there were any number of effigies and monuments dedicated to the various notables buried in the church. The shadows that they cast must be baffling his eyes, that's all. He was about to turn away when he heard a scraping sound.

"Is there anyone there? Answer me." Hervey, who had put out his lantern when he entered the church, grabbed a votive candle to relight it, and walked toward the chapel. Nothing stirred.

"Whoever you are, this is hallowed ground. You must respect it!"

He approached the area where he had first discerned movement.

"If it is money you seek, show yourself and you shall have it. I will give you alms and some food."

Hervey's voice sounded distant and strange to his own ears. He walked toward the chapel, lantern held aloft, but did not go in. A small altar was directly in front of him, and he couldn't see what was on either side. He stood and listened. Silence. Hervey turned away, resisting the impulse to run to the sacristy and bar the door. It was at that point that he sensed something behind him. He spun around: a shape was moving toward him, big and at least as tall as Hervey. The priest stood paralyzed until the figure was looming only a few feet away from him. It spoke.

"It's me, father." The voice was gravelly and rough, but somehow familiar. The priest extended the arm that was holding the lantern. There, dressed in the same clothes as at his funeral, was Philip. His head was unnaturally tilted to one side. Hervey was so startled that he almost dropped the light.

"What are you?" Suspended between terror and awe, Hervey automatically crossed himself.

"I'm not what you think, father. Nothing evil. I'm dead, that's all. I wanted to talk to you because I'm afraid you have gotten hold of a wrong idea."

"What do you mean?"

Hervey's entire body trembled. He had always been skeptical of the reports of specters of the dead, and was in no way prepared for this experience.

"About Rose. You're wrong. She had nothing to do with my death. Rose is beloved of the Lord. I should never have doubted her goodness."

In spite of his terror, Hervey believed that this visitation must be occurring for a reason. If it was a message from Philip, he should try and listen.

"How did you die?"

"I fell. My neck broke. It was my fault."

Up until then, the thing that called itself Philip had remained at a distance. But now it was moving closer. Hervey heard the dragging of feet as the entity lurched forward. The rank odor of decay filled the air. Now the thing was close: its entire head and body were bloated with fetid liquid and gas. The face was frozen in a grotesque smile, the lips cracked and swollen. A dark fungus or moss had spread over its teeth. Frantic to get away, Hervey inadvertently backed up against the stone effigy of a knight and stumbled, only barely managing to maintain his balance.

"Necks break easily. Look, I'll show you," and the Philip thing leaned forward and put its two hands around Hervey's throat, pressing with a fierce strength.

Hervey was angled backward under the force of the merciless grip, assailed by a stench so foul that he gagged. As the dead fingers tightened, a blanket of red spread behind Hervey's eyes, and he felt himself beginning to lose consciousness. When the lantern fell to the ground, the oil flared up and spread within a small radius. But this was enough to startle the Philip thing, causing it to loosen its grip temporarily. Hervey broke away, ran for the sacristy, and barred the door.

The thing lumbered after him. It threw its weight against the door repeatedly, making a sick thumping sound, before it suddenly stopped. Silence. Hervey waited for more than an hour, and then he fled.

A Persistent Sister

While Hervey was over in the church, hiding from some undead thing, Felice was in the presbytery, studying the books on the Cathars still on loan from the cathedral library—unbeknownst to the librarian, she assumed. Anthony would doubtless have to return them sooner rather than later, so she was determined to make the most of them. She was intent on her reading, when something made her look up. Rose was standing beside her.

"Rose! You startled me."

She had no idea how Rose had come to be there. Surely Felice would have heard her open the door. Then she remembered the priest's secret door to the church. Hervey never used it. Could Rose possibly know about it? In whatever manner she had come, however, Felice did not want her there. Her last meeting with Rose had been far from pleasant. And in view of the suspicions that she shared with her father, the sense of menace could only be increased by so unexpected a visit.

"Father's not here just now, but I can give him a message, if you like," Felice said rather hastily. "I hope there is nothing wrong with your mother."

"Mother is fine. But I didn't come to see your father. I came to see you, Felice. May I sit down?" As Rose was speaking, her eyes roved around the room. She didn't look at Felice.

Felice paused. "Actually, I was about to go to bed. I am not feeling well."

"I am sorry to hear that. But I'll only be a minute." Felice nodded and silently gestured toward a chair.

"I am sorry to disturb you at such an hour, but I need someone to talk to. You have always been a good friend to me," Rose said.

Felice would have valued such expressions of friendship even as late as their last meeting, but that moment had passed. Rose pronounced these words with little expression in a manner that did not even achieve a pro forma standard of sincerity.

"I've been thinking about Philip. How sad it is that he is gone," Rose continued. And then, as if reading Felice's mind, she was quick to add, "I couldn't attend the funeral. I was too distraught. It is true we had gone our separate ways, but Philip still meant, will always mean, so much to me."

It was easy for Felice to respond sincerely. "I can certainly understand anyone missing him. I miss him myself, and I know father does as well. Philip was a wonderful man."

Rose smiled. "Oh, well he felt the same about you. As a matter of fact, I sometimes had a mind to be jealous, he used to praise you so."

It was the sort of compliment that women often paid one another when they were attempting to establish some kind of bond, yet Rose's voice was strained and artificial, ensuring that these words had the reverse effect. Rose still didn't meet Felice's eyes. She seemed to be looking everywhere in the room except at her hostess. With every moment that passed, Felice felt more apprehensive about her caller. She was anxious to bring their conversation to a speedy conclusion.

"Was there something in particular you wished to talk about, Rose?" It sounded rather ungracious, but Felice didn't know what else to say.

"Mostly I just wanted to see you and say how sorry I am about Phillip. I meant to come before, but I have been very involved with the Faithful. Brother Jacques has come to rely on me for organizing our meetings." said Rose.

When Felice said nothing, merely nodding in acknowledgement, Rose continued. "He is the most Christ-like person I have ever met — a living saint."

"It must be very wonderful to have such confidence in a person," said Felice rather awkwardly.

"You must get to know him. Brother Jacques is interested in you, Felice. He told me you were chosen — that you were meant to be a part of our group," said Rose.

"It is very gratifying to know that someone as highly thought of as Brother Jacques thinks highly of me," Felice said rather stiffly, trying to sound neutral. But Rose did not seem to notice that Felice had not included herself among his admirers. Rose sat there complacently, wearing a fixed smile.

The women seemed to have run out of conversation and there was silence. Felice hoped that Rose would take this opportunity to leave. When she didn't, however, Felice had to think of a new topic.

"And how is your reading?" asked Felice.

"Wonderful. I am learning so much about the Lord and His blessed creation." Rose paused before continuing. For a moment she looked fixedly at Felice as if considering. "But what about your own studies? You were always such a scholar," said Rose.

"Regrettably, there is little to tell. I don't have much access to books," said Felice.

"But you do have a manuscript that I hear is quite remarkable. Brother Rupert told me about the life of Peter Martyr in your father's possession. He's a Dominican you know. I would love to borrow it." Rose for a moment looked at Felice. Then she went back to examining the room. "In return, I have something for you," Rose said, holding up the little volume of St. Augustine. Felice really felt that a small lie was the only expedient line of action at this juncture.

"As much as I would like to read that particular work of Augustine, I am afraid that my father has loaned the manuscript out to a friend of his. So I can't let you borrow it."

Rose's face registered anger, only to be superseded by a look of cunning. These expressions were fleeting, however. Her face was a model of composure when she said: "Perhaps your father's friend has already returned it."

Rose got up and began to move unerringly to the cupboard where the manuscript was stored. Felice had risen to her feet in alarm, ready to block Rose if necessary. But at that precise moment, Hervey entered the presbytery with a countenance filled with such fear and bewilderment that Felice was instantly concerned.

"Father! Are you alright?"

He was about to speak when he saw Rose in the room. He froze momentarily, before saying:

"Rose, how nice of you to be keeping Felice company. But I am afraid I am going to have to cut your visit short. I suddenly find that I am indisposed and in need of Felice's steady nursing hand, and maybe some of her mulled wine." He smiled weakly at his daughter.

Rose expressed concern in frigid tones. She left, this time using the usual door, assuring Felice that she would see her again soon.

The Corpse

Anthony was walking briskly to the cathedral at the time that these other events were transpiring. He needed to make some preparations for the funeral of a knight who had passed away a couple of days ago.

The deceased had been one of the churchwardens for Notre Dame and there would probably be a large turnout. The College of Robert of Sorbon, where Anthony still kept rooms, was not far from the cathedral. But as Anthony was covering the short distance, he had an unmistakable feeling of being watched. At one point he thought there was someone walking behind him. Soon after he imagined that there was someone on his left side, then on his right. Rather than subsiding, the feeling of surveillance intensified as he entered the church. Looking up at the stained glass, there seemed to be innumerable eyes of saints and angels staring down on him portentously through their luminous portals. Most penetrating, however, was the regard of the many different images of Christ. They all seemed to be tracking him, following his every move with their eyes. And each of the manifold paintings, frescoes, freestanding statues, and crucifixes — anything and everything depicting the Lord — seemed to be stamped with the visage of Brother Jacques. Anthony had never been an alarmist, however. He simply assumed that this was the power of suggestion at work. The four Counter-Faith, as Baldwin had dubbed them, had been so focused on Margot's visions of late that perhaps Anthony's mind had lapsed into the visionary landscape momentarily.

Anthony moved to the altar, in front of which the body of the deceased had been laid to rest for the customary vigil. He trimmed the candles, checking that there was enough wax to last the night. As he was preparing to enter the sacristy, the head of the life-sized Christ that was suspended over the high altar moved. Just as Anthony was closing the sacristy door, he saw the image turn its great head in his direction out of the corner of his eye. Although Anthony tried to keep his wits about him, his body was less tractable: his skin was crawling and the hair on the back of his neck was standing on end. The best way to steady himself was to get on with the task at hand, Anthony thought, and he began setting out the appropriate vestments for himself and his attendants. He mentally rebuked himself for the tremor in his hands.

When he was reaching for the black altar cloth, Anthony heard a strange shuffling sound coming from the nave. He took a deep breath, attempting to calm his irregular pulse, and opened the door. There was no one there. But he suddenly noticed that the body of the knight was positioned incorrectly. When a layman was laid out in a church, his feet should be pointing toward the altar, not the other way around. Anthony couldn't imagine that the sexton or any of his attendants were ignorant enough to commit this fundamental error. Besides, he was almost certain that the body's position was correct when he first arrived. Could someone have tampered with it? Was that the noise he had heard? Anthony told himself not to be ridiculous. He moved the candles and gripped the body by the shoulders, hoping that he could somehow make it pivot around to face the proper direction, when suddenly he felt it move under his hands as if of its own accord. Anthony dropped his hands in terror. He had never been a fanciful man. Was he becoming one this late in life? Perhaps it was best that he just return to the college. The rest of the preparations could wait until morning. Clearly he was more overwrought than he knew. On the walk back, he would drop by the sexton's house and ask that the body be repositioned before the funeral. But when he was walking toward the doors of the west facade, he heard another noise — this time very slight. Anthony turned. The body, which was facing in his direction, sat up and grinned. The expression was gruesome: less of a smile than a grimace. The eyes were open and entirely white inside. Even in the midst of this horrible spectacle, Anthony tried to rationalize, telling himself that he was witnessing the strange effect of the rigor passing. He had heard of such things before. But then he remembered that the knight had died while away from home and had been embalmed for transport. So there was no longer a question of rigor mortis. These thoughts were racing through Anthony's head when the cadaver swung its leg over the bier as if it were about to get up.

To Anthony's vast relief, there was the sound of the outer door opening. He turned: some of the family members had arrived for the vigil. Before greeting them, he reflexively looked behind: the corpse lay at rest, facing the correct direction with its hands peacefully folded on its bosom. He replaced the candles at the head and feet of the corpse and left.

A Persistent Brother

Baldwin was sitting in the small scriptorium at his college. He hadn't made much progress with his treatment of the soul. There were so many distractions. The whole mystery surrounding Brother Jacques was certainly one of them. And Felice, of course, was the other. Sensual impressions seemed to be running through his head incessantly. He thought of Felice's voice, her gestures, the way she moved, the feeling of her smooth skin against his lips when he kissed her hand. What would it be like to kiss her lips? Had she ever thought about kissing him? Did women have the same feelings as men? He had no idea really. Baldwin was in love for the first time, and the object of his affection was almost a complete enigma to him. What did women think about? How often did Felice think of him? Not formally, not in her lucid academic way, but as some-one she cared for, perhaps loved?

But Baldwin could no longer luxuriate in exclusively romantic thoughts when it came to Felice. His fantasy life was becoming progres-sively vitiated by the meetings of the Counter-Faith and its increasing preoccupation with Brother Jacques. So, as unlikely as it might seem, Felice and Friar Jacques were becoming interrelated obsessions, both of which were wreaking havoc with his concentration. Baldwin sat duti-fully at his desk, ostensibly reading, though making no real progress. He had stumbled upon an amusing anecdote about how Albert the Great, allegedly engaged in a quodlibet, was challenged by a demonic scholar. His fiendish colleague presented three arguments of such profundity that the brilliant Dominican was baffled. The quodlibet was on angels, which meant that his adversary had an unfair advantage. By a funny coincidence, just the other day Baldwin had heard the Chancellor deliver a sermon that drew an extensive analogy between the devil and the sophistical scholar. Scholarly demons were in the air.

Baldwin started with surprise. There at his elbow was Rupert, the young friar whom he met last Thursday at St.-Jacques, also allegedly working on the soul. But what was he doing here? Why would a Domini-can be wandering around a college for secular clerics?

"Hello Master Baldwin. I thought I would take you up on your invita-tion to continue our conversation. I hope this isn't an inconvenient time to stop by."

So it wasn't a coincidence. He was here to see Baldwin.

"No, not at all," Baldwin said in what he hoped were tones of self-assurance. But this was very far from what he felt. He needed to conceal his rather macabre sense of wonder at possibly being in the presence of his first truly depraved acquaintance — someone potentially guilty of theft and murder. Meanwhile, Baldwin was desperately trying to remem-ber if he had said anything at all that might have been construed as an invitation. He could think of nothing. It seemed best to admit as much.

"I am, of course, honored by your visit. But to be honest with you, I really can't remember much our conversation. I don't even remember inviting you."

"That doesn't surprise me at all," responded Rupert promptly. "I have no doubt you were under the influence of the beautiful Felice."

Such a remark made Baldwin bristle. "Please be careful what you say, master. I have only the highest opinion of the lady."

"As do I, of course," said Rupert with a smile. "But her many merits could prove hazardous to a life of scholarship, not to mention celibacy."

Baldwin could only wonder if his feelings were really as transparent as Rupert implied. And was it, indeed, possible that Felice's presence had caused him to forget a conversation with Rupert? He thought not.

"At the risk of seeming rather dull-witted, I would appreciate it if you reminded me what conversation I was hoping to continue."

"It was concerning the soul — our common interests."

"Sadly, I have had to put the pursuit aside for the time being," said Baldwin.

"Well, I am in the throes of deciphering Cathar theology and its absurdities: imprisoned souls, tunics of flesh. It's laughable." Rupert assumed a rather strained smile to exemplify his sense of his hilarity.

"I am surprised then that you would bother to spend the time refuting it," Baldwin responded.

Rupert's artificial smile relaxed into a much more natural expression of contemptuous condescension.

"It is not so much the intellectual challenge as the threat that dualist doctrine presents to holy church. You find it in the Gnostics, Origen, the Manichees, the Cathars — always the same cant about the evils of the material world."

Even though Baldwin knew that Rupert was purposefully trying to draw him into an argument, he couldn't resist the bait. He launched into an extensive disquisition on the innate dualism of orthodox doctrine: how the church was forever focusing on the struggle between body and soul, how most sin arose from the body.

"Wouldn't it make sense if, when we die, we left the body behind forever? Shouldn't we aspire to a higher reality?" Baldwin concluded.

Rupert had an abstracted look on his face: it was as if he wasn't listening to Baldwin at all, but listening to someone else.

"That's a very eloquent apology for dualism — very eloquent. What you say might be persuasive were it not for Christ's salvific work. Christ not only assumed a body, but sacrificed His body so we could have eternal life." Despite his sense of abstraction, Rupert's arguments were still very much to the point.

The ensuing ground they covered was predictable. Baldwin argued that it might have been more salvific still had our Lord come to us as spirit to remind us that we are much more than flesh; Rupert responded by pointing to the beatific experience once the soul was reunited with the resurrected body.

"I suppose whether or not you imagine the experience to be beatific depends on how you feel about the body," Baldwin contended. "The Cathar concept of blessedness meant freedom from their tunics of flesh."

The two men fell silent, clearly at an impasse. They were alone in the scriptorium and Rupert, unbidden, had pulled up a stool to sit facing Baldwin across the table.

"I am afraid that you are peculiarly sympathetic to dualism right now because of the woman. It is desire that has caused you to mistrust your body. I can see your struggle." Rupert said this in hushed, compassionate tones.

Baldwin, who was generally slow to anger, was becoming irritated.

"My dear brother, excuse my bluntness, but I find it necessary to remind you that you don't really know me," said Baldwin simply. He rose to his feet to signal their conversation was at an end.

"I may not, but the Lord does. He is *the seer of heart and reins*. I know He sees and sympathizes with your struggle. Don't block Him out, embrace Him! Come and see Him!" Rupert, who had also risen, extended his arms in supplication.

The initial invocation of the Lord as *seer of heart and reins* seemed like an unambiguous allusion to psalms. But the final injunction to *come and see Him* didn't make any sense. Rupert seemed to have segued from God to Brother Jacques.

Rupert continued, "He healed me of the same venom that is coursing through your veins, desire for the fragile sex. I too once wanted the very woman you long for. But I am cured. Trust him. He has the power to heal you as well."

Baldwin still said nothing, which Rupert took as encouragement.

"Your soul is riven with temptation and you are weary. Come on Thursday: stay for Mass. Receive the Lord's body and blood. Only by partaking of this banquet can you become His perfect servant and prevail against the demon, lust."

It was a strange moment. Here was a priest speaking to another priest with all the zeal and passion of the newly converted about the age old mysteries of their shared faith. Yet he was speaking as if Baldwin were an unbeliever. Baldwin, determined to end this awkward encounter, bowed to Rupert and began to leave the scriptorium. But Rupert, who had clearly not said all he had come to say, grabbed his forearm.

"Bring the manuscript," said Rupert, almost hissing the words.

"What manuscript?" said Baldwin, feigning innocence.

"I think you know. The palimpsest."

"Even supposing I did know the manuscript to which you allude and could somehow obtain it, why should Brother Jacques require it and why should I bring it to him?"

"He sees things. He knows that the manuscript is damaging to the faith."

Rupert's grip tightened, and Baldwin for the first time felt afraid. He was conscious that this man, a virtual stranger perhaps responsible for frightful acts, seemed impossibly strong. It felt as if he could snap the bones in Baldwin's arm with one twist if he chose. But then Rupert suddenly let go as if whatever passion he had been laboring under had suddenly passed.

He left without a word, as swiftly and silently as he had come.

The Wild Hunt

Gerson had always mistrusted any and all persons who were alleged to have supernatural gifts — especially those who found favor with the common rabble. Most of the people who claimed special spiritual consolations were eventually proven to be charlatans. And this is where Gerson saw a role for himself. He knew that he was not a mystic, a visionary, a miracle worker, or a saint. But he cared about Christendom deeply. So even if God withheld mystical consolations from Gerson, he believed that he was intended as an arbiter of such experiences. Not only did Gerson have reason and training on his side, but also as Chancellor he was perfectly positioned to fulfill this role. People solicited his opinion in spiritual concerns as a matter of course. He would exercise spiritual discernment, thereby fulfilling the biblical injunction to *prove the spirits*. He would expose the frauds who preyed upon the faithful. Most recently, God in his mercy had given him an additional role: to bear witness on behalf of the sanctity of Brother Jacques. The conversation with Anthony and his friends had disturbed him, certainly. But it had not dislodged his confidence in the Franciscan's holiness. Since Gerson considered himself something of a professional skeptic, moreover, this powerful conviction, unprecedented in Gerson's experience, seemed a kind of proof in itself.

Late one night Gerson was back in his rooms at the College of Navarre, sitting at his writing table. He was writing in a register that he had dedicated to Brother Jacques, detailing everything he knew about the man: his ascetical practices, the good deeds he had performed, the wonders that God wrought through him. Gerson had already made a preliminary list of the requisite information he must obtain, the people he should contact and interview. He had very good evidence regarding the resuscitation of the boy. While not eradicating the initial marvel, the fact that he subsequently died was a setback. So he clearly had to solicit more information on Jacques' first miracle — the one concerning the girl, Rose. Gerson had garnered considerable testimony to the Franciscan's prowess as a preacher, which had effected some dramatic conversions. Now was the time to witness this ability firsthand. It was useless to send small-minded men like Anthony and Baldwin as proxies. Nothing good ever came of delegating. The only way for Gerson to assess Brother Jacques in a satisfactory manner was to begin attending the Thursday meetings himself.

Gerson was just forming this resolve when, all at once, he was raptured into the air, and raised to dizzying heights. He was being impelled forward at great velocity in the direction of a beautiful blue light resembling a great unblinking eye. Before he reached the light, however, he was jolted to a halt. He found himself standing on a road opposite a church. There was a small portal decorated by a tympanum of the Virgin depicted as standing with the baby Jesus in her arms. Two saints hovered benignly on either side. One was John the Baptist, distinguished by a circle containing a lamb. The other must be St. Jacques: he could see his pilgrim's staff and scrip. A man and woman knelt underneath this holy grouping — probably the donors. Gerson realized that he must be on the Rue Ecrivains looking at the portal that Nicolas Flamel had commissioned for St.-Jacques-de-la-Boucherie. That's why the Virgin had cockle shells on either side of her crown. The light had a heavily sedated quality that one associates either with dawn or dusk, and it was difficult to see. Gerson was about to cross the street for a closer look, when the portal under the tympanum swung open. Two figures issued forth, walking hand in hand: the little drowned beggar boy and Brother Jacques. The Franciscan was wearing his usual habit, but the boy was clothed in a raiment of light with a crown upon his head. He stood slightly in front, but to one side, of Jacques, as would a herald.

"Behold, the Prince of this World," the boy said, gesturing toward Jacques, who stepped forward. As in Gerson's last vision, the Franciscan's hands and feet bore the marks of the stigmata; there was a dark stain spreading on the right side of his habit from a concealed wound. This time he was also wearing a crown of thorns, rendering him more Christ-like still.

Gerson was filled with awe. He was about to fall on his knees in worship when he was startled by the sound of blowing horns and the thundering of horses' hooves against the cobblestones. A column of riders appeared. The face of each rider was ashen pale and totally without expression, though many bore hideous wounds. At the very end of the line were three riders that Gerson recognized: Anthony, Baldwin, and Hervey. Nearby Hervey rode a woman that Gerson took to be Hervey's daughter, her flame-colored hair streaming behind as she rode. Gerson called to them, but they thundered by on their steeds, impassive. In a moment they were gone.

When Gerson returned to himself, he got down on his knees and thanked God for the revelation. He was filled with the kind of peace that only comes with deep surety. He now understood the mystery of the little drowned boy's second death. The body had been called away by God because he was deserving of great reward. The crown indicated that the boy, however, young, was one of the elect, serving as a herald to reveal Jacques' sanctity to the world. The Franciscan's reception of the stigmata corroborated the parallels with St. Francis and, ultimately, Christ.

But when Gerson considered the last segment of the vision, his feeling of exaltation changed to one of sadness. He had seen the three clerics and their female companion among the riders in the Wild Hunt, signifying that they were either already dead or were destined to die very soon. More horrible than mere death, however, was the widespread understanding that the fearsome riders of the hunt were damned. Gerson accepted that God's judgments were inscrutable, yet he was stricken with grief. Why did Anthony and his friends insist on turning away from Jacques, the Lord's chosen? What arrogance! What impious folly! Surely this is why they were included among the doomed hunters. Gerson had to resist the impulse to pray for them: prayers for the damned were not only useless, they were indicative of contempt for divine judgment.

Chapter 11: The Exorcists

A Plan

It was Thursday and the four Counter-Faith were once again together at the presbytery. This time, however, they had omitted the meeting at St.-Jacques beforehand. Although each of them was seated in his or her usual station, there was a less convivial atmosphere compared with earlier occasions. They had each been threatened in different ways, and were now convinced that these threats somehow issued from Jacques. The realization made them feel beleaguered and watchful. Even the way they sat suggested that they were on their guard, recognizing themselves to be under siege. They needed a plan.

Baldwin spoke for all of them when he asked, "Who is this Franciscan? And what is the nature of his power? Is he capable of animating corpses, or is he a master of illusion, playing with our senses?"

Hervey rubbed his neck where there were still marks visible from the thing that had once been Philip. "What I experienced was no illusion. Brother Jacques is clearly capable of conjuring what I can only assume was a demon to animate Philip's body."

"If Jacques were a powerful necromancer, manipulating dead things would be his stock and trade," said Anthony.

"Well, whoever he is and whatever he can do, it is clear that he wants the manuscript. Why he should want it is another question entirely." Baldwin stared moodily into the cup of wine he was holding.

Felice had hardly spoken since the arrival of their guests. At length she said, "The Franciscan might not even be human."

Everyone turned to look at her.

"I mean, his body could be, but whatever animates his body may not be a human soul," she continued. "After all, we are entertaining the possibility that Brother Jacques can somehow conjure demons into possessing humans or entering corpses. But why should we assume he is just a skilled sorcerer? Isn't it equally likely, more likely, perhaps, that he is himself a demon — maybe even an archdemon in a human body?"

Such a prospect was sufficiently horrific to silence them for a time. Eventually Hervey spoke up. "I suppose it's a possibility, but it would mean that his powers are more daunting than we can even begin to imagine."

"But at least if he were a demon we would have a coherent line of action," Felice responded.

"Meaning what?"

"Father, you're the priest in the family!" Felice said reproachfully. "Exorcism, of course!"

Her companions realized that Felice was right. As unnerving as a demonic adversary might be, it might prove more difficult to defeat a human being. Brother Jacques hadn't broken any law. If he were in some way responsible for the murders of Philip and Martin, he had clearly worked through his minions. Even if Jacques were a necromancer who manipulated the dead, some sort of evidence was required for his prosecution. None of them had seen him perform any magic or heard rumor of his engagement in forbidden practices.

"Supposing that Jacques is a demon," said Baldwin. "Is he appearing in the body of someone he has possessed or a simulated body?"

This was a very complex question. It was alleged that all angels, including fallen angels, were entirely incorporeal. But they still required bodies to appear before humans. In cases of possession, they took over the body of someone who was still alive. But it was believed that they could contrive simulated bodies for themselves out of matter — bodies that could be altered at will. Angels, good and bad alike, were the ultimate shape shifters, capable of appearing in any form they chose. The quodlibet about Satan appearing as Christ was predicated on this virtuosity.

"In a simulated body, the demon would not be required to struggle constantly against the suppressed soul," Baldwin reasoned. "It might be much more difficult to rout. Besides, the rite of exorcism usually requires the laying on of hands. That means the entity would have to be constrained, which in the case of a shape shifting demon would be well-nigh impossible."

No one contested Baldwin's gloomy suppositions.

"Then there is the problem the Franciscan's acolytes. Considering their probable strength, wouldn't they each require their own exorcist?" asked Felice.

The others looked dismayed. If Felice were right, that would mean five exorcists, which they didn't have. It would be folly to introduce strangers into so fraught a situation.

"We would have to tell them about the manuscript, and possibly about Simon, subjects that put people at risk. Besides, Brother Jacques has already achieved the reputation of a holy man among many. I doubt anyone would believe us," said Hervey.

"We could always ask Chancellor Gerson," suggested Anthony. "He, at least, knows about the manuscript. And we all know that he has a vested interest in questions of discernment."

Baldwin gave an incredulous laugh. "Are you joking? He thinks Brother Jacques is a saint!"

"True. And I understand that he plans to attend the Thursday meetings in order to garner further evidence of the friar's sanctity. But can you think of a better way of challenging his perspective on Jacques than by inviting him as an observer and possible participant in our. . ." Anthony paused, groping for the right word, ". . . counterattack? That is assuming we are right about the Franciscan, of course."

"Even if we are right, is it fair to Gerson?" asked Baldwin.

"We would have to present all the evidence and tell him what we plan to do. My guess is that he would come of his own accord," persisted Anthony.

"You still need a fifth," said Felice. "I would like to volunteer for the position."

They all stared at her as if she were crazy.

"Christ gave all true believers the power to cast out demons in his name. The rite of exorcism is written into the vows that godparents make at the baptismal font. The fact that the exorcist is not included in major orders shows that it is not exclusive to the clergy; a member of the laity can serve just as well," Felice said.

"But women?" Baldwin said, before he caught himself.

Felice gave a look perhaps better suited to someone wielding a dagger than scoring points in theological debate.

"Yes, women! Besides, the prerogatives of a male clergy are a historical development. How else do you explain that Phoebe is referred to as a deacon in the Acts of the Apostles?"

Nobody offered to explain.

"And the desert mothers were constantly exorcising demons," Felice continued.

Waiving the question of gender, Hervey put up a different and more poignant kind of resistance.

"No, my dear. Please don't insist. I have never forbidden anything to you. But I would have to forbid you now for your own safety."

"Father, it is true that you have never forbidden me anything. This is not the time to begin. You haven't the power to secure my safety against this threat, and I can't stay away while the rest of you are in danger. Show me that you believe me to be your spiritual equal. Let me help."

There was silence while father and daughter stood looking at one another unflinchingly, eyes locked together. Finally, it was Hervey who conceded, bowing his head in resignation.

"Agreed then," said Anthony. "Felice is our fifth. So how do we arrange a meeting with Brother Jacques?"

Felice had an answer. "That's the easy part! We simply tell him that we want to discuss the manuscript."

"And the others?" asked Anthony.

"I suppose we could also politely invite him to bring Rose and Rupert along since they have each vividly demonstrated their own interest in the manuscript. But my guess is that they don't require a special invitation. They will be there," said Felice. Hervey and Baldwin nodded in agreement.

"Alright. So we will attend next Thursday's meeting and seek a private interview then. Is that agreed?" asked Anthony. All four signaled their consent.

Hervey and Felice accompanied their guests a short distance as they left the presbytery. They walked in pairs: Hervey with Anthony in front; Baldwin and Felice behind. While Hervey and Anthony were discussing the interesting question of Rose's excellent Latin diction, Baldwin took the opportunity to pass a note to Felice. She was surprised, flustered, and a bit annoyed, but took it anyway, flashing Baldwin a nervous smile.

Lovers Meet

The next morning when Felice awoke, she felt different. She felt like a woman with options. This was new to her. Apart from her scandalous birth, which she could hardly be expected to remember, her life had been very quiet, sheltered, and predictable. Hervey had seen to that. The moment that Felice received Baldwin's note, however, without even reading it, she knew she was being offered a choice. Felice was being offered a choice by her lover. She could continue on her present path — keeping house for Hervey, visiting sick parishioners, bringing flowers to women who had just given birth, and pressuring Hervey to borrow books for her. Or she could throw caution to the wind, and obey her heart — giving way to feelings and drives that, until very recently, she had hardly acknowledged. Hervey was away on parish business, which was just as well. Felice couldn't sit still. She paced the length of the presbytery with the same thought running through her head over and over: *I could be something else.*

Felice prepared for her appointment with unprecedented care. Her wardrobe was sparse, so there was little she could do by way of toiletry. She combed her hair; she rubbed some flour off one of her sleeves. Then she remembered. There was a rich widow in Reims who had lost most of her vision. Felice used to read aloud to her. When she died, she bequeathed an ornament to Felice. It was a single pearl — large and pear-shaped with a little golden ring at the top for suspending from a chain. When she first received it, Felicia immediately wanted to trade it for a book, but her father wouldn't let her. *You might want to dress up some day,* he said. Well, today was the day. The jewel was in the chest where Felice kept her personal belongings, folded in a piece of silk. She unwrapped it slowly. The pearl was a marvel. Felice felt as if she had never really looked at it before. A light seemed to be emanating deep from within, sending iridescent pastels to the surface. Celestial colors. How fascinating that there were so many colors inside an object that nevertheless remained essentially white. There was an entire world inside that gem. She strung the pearl on a thin piece of black ribbon, tying it at the back of her neck so it sat close to her throat. Then Felice looked at herself in her little hand mirror for the second time since April, and smiled.

The bells were tolling for Sext when Felice set out for her designation on the Île de la Cité. She followed the directions detailed in Baldwin's note. In fact, she knew them by heart, but kept the note in her hand like a talisman. It was the only note that she had ever received from him, the first time she had seen his handwriting. The hand seemed so reflective of Baldwin's character: bold, yet quirky; painstaking, yet impatient; nevertheless possessed of an elegance all its own. Felice wound her way automatically through the familiar streets without really noticing anything, so preoccupied was she with her forthcoming interview. Eventually she came to a small one-room cottage, not far from Rue Glatigny. It was here that her suitor was waiting.

"This place has been let to a friend — another poor student," said Baldwin apologetically, when he opened the door. "It is very humble, but clean. Will you come in?"

There was a look of pleading in Baldwin's eyes that she had never seen before. Of course she would.

The room may as well have been a monastic cell. The only difference was that the cottage had a small hearth, the rudimentary makings of a kitchen area, and a table with two chairs instead of one. Baldwin placed the chairs so that they faced one another, and they both sat down. They were seated so close together that their knees practically touched, but Felice didn't move her chair away. Baldwin looked at the pearl at her throat, and smiled. *Perfect — she's just perfect.* And then he spoke.

"I don't want to talk about Brother Jacques. Not today. I am afraid that if we do, it will overshadow everything else."

"Perhaps it should."

"I can't deny that. I feel as if we were hurtling down a hill without knowing what is at the bottom. I am afraid it is something horrible. But I want us both to stop for a moment and consider. We have only been alone together a handful of times, yet I know that I love you. I think you could love me as well. If that's true, then anything is possible. Travel, children, whatever you can imagine. We could have an entirely different life somewhere else. You could come with me right now and we could find that place." *She wore a pearl. She wore it for me. She does care after all. Please say yes.*

Felice had been right. Baldwin was offering her just what she had thought he would. And yet, by the time he began to speak the words of love — words that were not only expected but also desired that morning — something had changed. Felice realized that she was no longer a woman with options, but a woman with a purpose. She knew what she must do.

"Is there such a place where people, like us, can go without shame, not to mention sin?"

"Iceland? Apparently there are plenty of clerical concubines there."

"Too cold."

"What about the Greek church? They allow a married clergy."

"The language is too hard."

They both laughed.

"What about the sin?" Felice asked gently.

He let that question go.

"Baldwin, it is true that we have spent very little time together. And yet I feel as if I know you already, and I love you. But even if we somehow resolve this situation with Brother Jacques, I can't just leave. I can't run away."

"Is it because of your father?" he asked.

"And my mother. I suppose I don't want to repeat her mistakes. But I am also thinking about your career," said Felice.

Baldwin reached across Felice's lap for her hands. She was clutching something in one of them. When he realized that it was his note, he was moved. It was another silent, but eloquent, testimonial that he did matter. He put the note to one side, and took her hands in his.

"You matter much more to me than any career."

"Would you say that once you have shut the door on the possibility of a position at the university? Once you have been excommunicated for apostasy? When you were teaching in some miserable grammar school, if you were lucky enough to get that job in the first place? With screaming children, a leaky roof, a smoking fireplace, and a nagging wife." Felice had lapsed into Latin, invoking various *molestiae nuptiarum* — misogynist rationales for why women and marriage are incompatible with the life of the mind.

"Women shouldn't be allowed to read such things. What was your father thinking?" Baldwin said, smiling at her with admiration. "Felice, you constantly amaze me. But you already know the answers to all your questions, my love."

And indeed Felice thought she did. She believed that in Baldwin she had found a man who, like her father, would sacrifice everything for her love and never even perceive it as a sacrifice. Her bottom lip was quivering ever so slightly, but she was nevertheless resolute. And Baldwin knew that no degree of persuasion could change her mind.

"So your answer is no?" Baldwin said softly.

"It's the only possible answer." Her vision was blurring. Tears. She hadn't known she was crying.

"Do you think you will ever marry?"

She shook her head with vigor. "It's so hard for a priest's concubine to find a decent husband these days!" Felice was now laughing through tears.

"Seriously!"

"Alright. I will be as serious as I can possibly be. I won't marry. I don't just say this to reassure you. Or because I think the chance of my having any marriage prospects, let alone attractive ones, are nil. It's about chastity."

"Oh that!" said Baldwin. "Well it looks like I may have to keep my vow of chastity. Shouldn't that be enough for the both of us? It's true that I can't stand the thought of you with another man. But I also hate the idea of you denying yourself — not just of a husband, but the prospect of children. Think of all those little people you could boss around! Not to mention the husband." He squeezed her hands and smiled.

"If I can't have you, it wouldn't be a sacrifice." And Felice meant it. She truly believed that Baldwin — that beautiful sunny man; brilliant, full of hilarity, and deeply kind — was the best there was. *If it wasn't him, then who else? No one.* She paused before continuing. "I know we agreed not to talk about it. But there's a deeper reason for abstinence. Don't you feel it? Don't you feel that we are surrounded by dark and that chastity is somehow associated with the light?"

Baldwin rolled his eyes. "Of course! How can over a millennium of church teaching possibly be wrong?" he said with sardonic humor.

"Baldwin, I am beginning to think that the church might be wrong about everything except chastity." Her voice had become quieter; her speech slower. It was the kind of voice you might use with someone very naïve or very vulnerable to acquaint them with a harsh reality.

Baldwin nodded, no longer jesting. "That could very well be. Even I am beginning to wonder." He sighed. "I guess that means that we won't. . .?" He didn't finish his sentence, instead gesturing toward the bed. Felice shook her head.

"We could, you know, just so that we are both aware of what we are giving up. They say that it is harder to renounce sex once you have experienced it. So we would each be deserving of extra merit for abstaining." Baldwin said this with charming sophistry. He winked at her, and she laughed.

"We could. But we won't."

"Then kiss me. A kiss to last all eternity, my darling."

They leaned toward each other and shared their first and last kiss. Neither of them had any experience with kissing and so, to the external eye, their kiss might have appeared disappointingly chaste. Even so, that kiss contained all the passion and longing of many lives unlived.

"We won't speak about this again," said Felice with finality in her voice.

"I understand."

And they left that place behind forever.

The New Seer

That night Felice had a vision. She was standing alone in the church of St.-Jacques when she heard a beautiful voice, like the voice of an angel, singing: *Behold, thou art fair, my love; behold, thou art fair; Thine eyes are doves behind thy veil; Thy hair is as a flock of goats, On the slopes of mount Gilead.* She looked around and saw that Christ was singing to her from the cross. Descending effortlessly, He began to walk toward her. He was the most beautiful man she had ever seen. Blood was issuing from the crown of thorns on His head and from His five stigmata, but there was nothing gruesome or even sorrowful about these wounds: they looked like jewels. His dark eyes were mesmerizing. Felice could see the entire world reflected in those eyes. *Thou hast ravished my heart, my sister, my spouse; Thou hast ravished my heart with one of thine eyes, With one chain of thy neck,* Christ intoned. Felice was filled with longing. She found herself singing in reply: *Let him kiss me with the kisses of his mouth, for thy love is better than wine.* Christ responded: *You are my first thought. You are the lost sheep that I came to find.*

As Christ drew closer, she reached out her arms to embrace Him. But she suddenly stopped. There was a mirror in her hand that hadn't been there before, which caught Christ's reflection in profile. What appeared in the mirror was not the face of a man, but the head of a dragon with the now familiar abbreviation 𝕮uʳ ãïᵗm inscribed underneath — the *cura animorum*.

She awoke in horror.

When Hervey got up the next morning, he found Felice sitting at the table just gazing in a state of abstraction. In front of her was a stylus, ink and paper, and her small hand mirror. And suddenly he understood.

"Childishly simple; new speculations, right?" asked Hervey.

Felice nodded. "Mirror writing. How could we have been so blind?"

"How did you know?"

She told him about the dream.

"The mirror was the key to the journal. It always was. In Margot's vision; on Martin's desk. If it was Rupert who stole Martin's transcription, he clearly didn't notice the mirror the first time he entered the room. When the prior asked him to check if there was anything on the desk, Rupert did see it, but assumed it had been left behind by the infirmarian. But it wasn't. Look."

Felice took out the mirror and held it to the transcription. The letters floated on the mirror like magic.

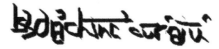

"It was written in haste, without any real word separation. And I'm not positive about the abbreviations. But here's what I think it says," she said — pushing a stray piece of parchment toward Hervey.

Is. est ðía. . .us Christus incarnatus curator animorum

"There is a superscript *r* which makes it quite clear that in this case, at least, the last two words should be expanded not as *cura animarum, the care of souls;* but probably as *curator animarum, the caretaker* or *curator of souls,*" said Felice. "There are, however, two abbreviations that I'm not sure about: *Is.* and *dia...us.* I have some theories, but I wanted to discuss them with you."

Felice went on to advance that the abbreviation *Is.* either stood for the first and last letters of the name or the first two letters of a name. Even so, they could stand for many different names, especially since the characters *J* and *I* were interchangeable much of the time. For names in which the initial letter could be either *J* or *I*, it was the characters between the first and last letter that required expansion. Some possibilities might be *Ioannes, Jacobus, Jonas,* or even *Iesus*. In the case of names that could only begin with *I*, it was the first two letters that were rendered, and the middle ones abbreviated, like *Isaiah* or *Isidore*. She showed him a list of names that she had drawn up containing both manners of abbreviation.

Hervey looked at her list. "The only name that makes any sense in this context is *Iesus*: it clearly belongs with *Christus incarnatus*," he said.

"I agree that *Iesus* is plausible. But remember that *Is.* is how the author consistently refers to his friend throughout the journal," Felice said.

For the next abbreviation, *dia. . .us,* Hervey suggested *diaconus* — deacon. "Perhaps it was intended in the original Greek sense of the word, servant," he said.

"Father, you have to remember that this was written by a Cathar Perfect."

"The Cathars had deacons."

"True. But why would the author have taken such pains to disguise his writing if he simply wanted to say that Christ was mankind's servant," objected Felice.

"I see your point. What do you propose?"

She showed him her transcription.

Is. est diabolus Christus incarnatus curator animorum
Is. is the devil Christ incarnate the curator of souls

"Good heavens! And what could that possibly mean?" asked Hervey.

"That he had come to believe that his friend was in some way diabolical — perhaps even the devil personified. Of course, *curator animarum* is no longer benign in this context. Rather, it evokes the old Cathar myth that the devil created the body for the entrapment of souls. That would make him the curator of souls par excellence, only in the darkest way possible," said Felice.

"But what about *Christ incarnate*?" Hervey responded.

"Remember, the Cathars believed that the real Christ was a divine shadow. He descended from heaven to show the way home, but only appeared to assume a body. Yet some Cathars believed that Christ had a carnal counterpart, who was the embodiment of evil," said Felice.

"The author professes to see someone; the same person who ultimately discovers him in the well. Are you saying that he thought this person was the diabolical Christ?" asked Hervey.

"I don't know," Felice shook her head, perplexed. "Possibly. That could explain Margot's fearful visions of Christ. In my own dream, I was about to embrace Christ, when I realized that he was really a dragon."

"But this was revealed to you in a mirror. The mirror could be demonstrating that Christ and Satan are polar opposites," said Hervey.

"In theory, I suppose it could work that way. Yet it doesn't correspond to the way I felt in the dream. The mirror image seemed to be showing me something truly terrible about Christ, which could only be seen in a mirror. Christ was really a dragon—that is, Satan. It was as if the world were inverted. The material, outer world was illusory; it was only the realm inside the mirror that was true and real." Felice took a deep breath before continuing. "I think that the author of the journal made a parallel and equally horrific discovery. Remember how the journal ends," Felice said, pointing.

Together they looked at the last few words:

Is. is alive. He lives forever. / I am hiding in the well, terrified. / He sees me.

"I'm not sure I follow. Are you saying that the author saw someone he understood to be Christ incarnate—someone who lives forever?" asked Hervey

"Why not? Isn't that a version of what the orthodox church teaches, after all?" Felice persisted.

"But it is supposed to be comforting, not horrifying," Hervey said.

"Maybe to us. But not to a Cathar Perfect, who believes the body is evil," Felice answered gently.

"Well, that is why they were condemned as heretics after all!" Hervey said, trying to suppress his rising frustration.

Felice looked away. There was a ray of sunshine pouring in the window. It wasn't material, it didn't have substance. But it suddenly seemed more real than anything else in the room. Their lives were becoming progressively grey and confused of late. The light was there to reassure her, and she drew great comfort from it. It seemed to show her—no, remind her—that she was living in a kind of shadow world. And all at once, she knew.

"Father, the Cathars claimed that Jehovah, the creator god, was really Satan; that the material world was evil. Both the journal and the visions, not only mine but Margot's as well, seem to support this view. I believe the Cathars were right — that the orthodox church has been tricked into worshiping the devil. The Cathars tried to warn us, and we killed them."

Hervey looked as if someone had struck him.

"Felice, if you truly believe these things you are a heretic and it is my responsibility to denounce you — otherwise I could be apprehended as a *fautor*."

But before Felice had a chance to respond, Hervey raised his hand in warning:

"No! Nothing else. It's too dangerous. You must keep these thoughts to yourself."

"I promise that I will for as long as I can, father."

A Last Stand

It was yet another Thursday. Marcus had noticed that Hervey and his companions, that annoying triptych of priests, were absent, as was their beautiful lady-acolyte. But there was a more illustrious clerical presence in their stead: he knew that Jacques would be more than gratified that the Chancellor of the University had seen fit to honor their meeting, as was Marcus himself. Finally Brother Jacques was receiving the notice that he deserved.

Brother Marcus reviewed the week's events while he helped prepare for Mass. The undoubted highlight was watching that old prostitute being executed. If only it had taken place a week earlier! Then it would have fallen on the feast day of his favorite saint, who was, of course, Dominic. But you can't have everything; it was close enough to provide a fit offering for that saintly scourge of heretics. The younger harlot's condemnation took a little longer. Somehow she managed to make a good impression on some of her judges, perhaps by sorcery. Four judges out of twenty wanted her spared. Fortunately, the majority recognized her for the whore and the witch that she was, and saw to it that she was condemned. Marcus was planning to watch her execution as well — the very anticipation of which sent a wave of intense pleasure throughout his body. As sinners constantly inveigling others into sin, those filthy sluts finally got what they deserved.

The old one was especially dangerous. In addition to being a prostitute and a witch, she was a murderess to boot. Yet the multiple threats she posed to society were nothing to the damage she might have done to the work of the Lord. It was only gradually that Marcus had come to realize just how much was at stake; how the Lord's holy work must go forward at all costs. Margot had to be stopped; she had to die. Marcus felt no remorse for betraying her friendship. For she had somehow broken through the barrier of what it was permissible to know. The interloper had seen too much, gone too far into things that were none of her business. The Lord's work would progress much more smoothly now that the seer was out of the way. Her visions were evil.

Marcus was thinking these thoughts without ever wondering how he knew that Margot was a visionary. True, he had known Margot for a long time — longer than practically anyone else in Paris. Over the decades, during those sweet post-coital interludes, they had shared many secrets with one another. But she had never told Marcus about her visions. He only knew because he himself had become a seer of sorts. He knew what the other three elect were thinking, he knew what his master wanted. There was more to come. Marcus felt as if he were being inducted into an entirely different order of reality — one whose existence the greatest philosophers had never intuited, let alone thought of entering. He had been chosen by a force much greater than himself, greater than anything else. The time of fulfillment was at hand. Marcus had *fallen into the hands of the living God,* and he had never been so happy.

While Marcus was ruminating, Rupert was hearing confessions. He was also thinking about Felice and Hervey, or more precisely, about their manuscript. Rupert didn't know how exactly he first learned about the manuscript containing the life of Peter Martyr, how he knew that it was a palimpsest containing a hidden journal, or what its transcription might signify. He just knew. It didn't require an explanation. It was like asking *how do you know that you are alive?* or *how do you know that the Lord is powerful?* You just knew.

Rupert had developed an enviable relationship with knowledge. Once he had labored so hard to become learned. Each day had been a struggle. But now things were different. The acquisition of Greek was just the beginning. He also apprehended immensely difficult propositions effortlessly. He found himself asking new questions, entertaining new and daring possibilities. His understanding of time had also changed. Rupert had a vivid recollection of historical events. They were not just dry artifacts recorded in books. Rather he experienced the past in a participatory way: as if he were truly there. The greater arcana of the universe were slowly being revealed to him. Eventually he would be able to apprehend the work of the unmoved mover at the beginning of time. Rupert had been called by this same divine force to participate in an important moment in history — an eschatological moment. The rules no longer applied to him. When Rupert had put an end to the meddlesome old friar and taken the transcription, he initially felt some guilt. But he had since learned that the line between good and evil was by no means as clearly demarcated as he had been led to believe: that certain extraordinary men were allowed to cross that line many times without compromising their integrity. The messiah had come in his lifetime, walking upon the same ground, breathing the same air. Rupert had *fallen into the hands of the living God*, and he had never been so happy.

One might wonder how Rupert could be conscientiously listening to confessions while this torrent of thoughts was storming through his head, but it wasn't hard. His mental capacity and powers of concentration had increased exponentially, even since he had finished his commentary on *The Sentences*. He had often heard stories about how Aquinas could dictate to several secretaries at the same time — each of them laboriously transcribing separate works while Aquinas took his directions from the Lord. Now, such a feat not only seemed feasible, but attainable. He had plans for several treatises, all against Cathar error, and he was anxious to get started.

Although the meeting of the Faithful had been well attended, the only people who remained behind for Mass were Rose and Alicia. Marcus stayed to assist Brother Jacques, but Rupert had an appointment with the prior about the curriculum of the order's school and had to rush off. When he reached the road, however, Rupert remembered that he had never given the transcription to Jacques. It had been in his satchel for over a week. The Franciscan seemed to know its contents, but wanted it anyway. So Rupert returned to the church, walked up the north transept toward the little side chapel, and froze.

There at the altar was Brother Jacques, wearing only a loincloth, standing cruciform, with a gaping wound in his side. Rupert could see his sister in profile: Alicia's hands were placed on each of the Franciscan's shoulders for balance, and she was drinking from his side with an ecstatic thirst. Brother Marcus and Rose were standing at either side, deep in prayer, their lips smeared with what looked like blood. Whatever vestige still remained of Rupert's original self screamed out in horror. Alicia did not seem to hear him, but kept lapping the blood from the Franciscan's side, her eyes rolled back with an obscene pleasure. When Rupert called her by name, she lifted her head, and gazed at Rupert with dead glass eyes — unrecognizable and unrecognizing. All at once her eyes came into focus. Her hand went to her mouth, and she cried out in fear, moving swiftly toward her brother. For a moment, Rupert hugged his sister to his bosom — holding her tightly as if both their lives depended on it. And then suddenly she disappeared, raptured into thin air. He felt someone grab him from behind, screamed once more, and was silent.

An Ordination

Gerson was staring out the window in disbelief. Was this conversation with Anthony and Baldwin actually occurring? What they were saying was ludicrous. It wasn't sufficient that Paris be inundated with female mystics of the ordinary church-going variety; now prostitutes were claiming to be visionaries and even using their so-called revelations to denounce men of sanctity. Worse still, they were gaining an audience. On the basis of some prostitute's revelations, one recently arrested for sorcery no less, both Anthony and Baldwin were now convinced that Brother Jacques, this saintly and Christ-like man, was in league with the devil. But that was just the beginning. Jacques was also supposedly possessed of immense, but inchoate, powers, not for good, but for evil: he could will others to commit murder, just as he could maliciously manipulate the dead. Gerson surreptitiously pinched himself a couple of times in the course of their discussion, just to ensure that he was, in fact, awake. The two priests seemed to have lost their minds. Gerson was afraid that he might have contributed to this lamentable situation by condoning Anthony's fixation on the Satan/Christ question. Instead, Gerson should have disciplined Baldwin. Everything could seemingly be traced back to his damned disputation.

"Masters, just listen to yourselves! Academic speculation should not be confused with the real world," Gerson said sternly.

"But the two have become confused," Anthony responded. "From the very first, I believed that the avid interest in the Satanic Christ was symptomatic of something. Now I know that we were being prepared by God for precisely this."

"For what exactly?" Gerson's growing impatience did not mask his alarm.

"For a major confrontation between good and evil. The visions were warning us to put no trust in outer appearances; that we are living in a time when good and evil are easily confused. Brother Jacques embodies this crisis." While Anthony was speaking, Gerson glanced over at Baldwin, whose head was head was bobbing up and down in agreement. *He looks like an idiot!*

"You are indicting Brother Jacques without evidence. Jacques is a holy man, and his actions prove it!" Gerson's face was flushed with annoyance and his voice was raised. But it was so provoking. These two skeptics were just like the Pharisees, attributing Christ's miracles to diabolical influence. It was with an effort that Gerson regained his composure, at which point he added: "Besides — I have had some personal experiences that confirm his holiness." When the others looked at him with expectation, Gerson felt shy. He was not accustomed to confiding in others, let alone confiding something this personal. But he had to defend Brother Jacques. And so, Gerson told them about his vision, careful to omit the segment about the Wild Hunt. When he recounted the manner in which the little drowned boy announced Jacques, his two auditors exchanged a conscious look. Baldwin covertly pointed to Anthony, signaling that he should be the one to speak.

"Chancellor, are you sure that the boy referred to Jacques as the 'Prince of this World'?" asked Anthony.

"Yes, I am certain that is what he said."

"But the 'Prince of this World' is the title applied to Satan throughout scripture! I know that you are aware of this," said Anthony.

Gerson, who, despite his relative youth had already distinguished himself as one of the most able theologians of his day, instantly recognized his error and was mortified.

"I apologize masters. Of course you right. I have misspoken. The boy must have said 'King of Kings.' I remember now that is what was said."

Gerson's brow was furrowed and he looked from Anthony to Baldwin with concern.

"But if you were right in the first instance, it would corroborate the way in which Margot came to understand her own visions — that Jacques was in league with the devil," Baldwin said.

Gerson grimaced, shocked to hear his beloved Jacques described in this light and chagrined that his own revelation be aligned with those of a prostitute. If Jacques had, in fact, been heralded as the Prince of the World, it could only mean that Gerson's vision hadn't been sent by God after all — a terrible blow to Gerson. Still, he had to consider the possibility that the revelation was sent by Satan with the express purpose of putting doubt in his mind concerning one of God's true servants. When he attempted to express something of this to Baldwin and Anthony, both looked down at the ground — not only to hide their skepticism, but out of embarrassment for Gerson who, in his desperation, was grasping at such slender spiritual straws. Yet their widely divergent interpretations made no difference to the Counter-Faith's immediate ends.

"Either way, don't you think that the situation warrants closer scrutiny? Will you agree to attend our meeting with Brother Jacques?" asked Anthony.

Although disconcerted by the elementary nature of his theological error, Gerson's belief in the friar remained undiminished. As the friar's advocate, what place had he amid this gaggle of skeptics? And yet, his presence might have a restraining effect on their misdirected zeal. It took Gerson some time to make up his mind, but he eventually agreed to accompany them to their meeting with Brother Jacques. He was confident that others would come away convinced that Jacques was a good and pious man. A saint, in fact. Anthony intonated that Jacques might be dangerous, but Gerson feared no harm from him. In fact, he was much more apprehensive about Anthony and Baldwin's ungrounded assumptions. It would be extremely unwise to insult the friar for no apparent reason. Such mistreatment would almost certainly provoke a violent reaction from the people. So it was just as well that Gerson was there to avert this kind of damage.

As the two priests were walking back to the college, Anthony remarked:

"Frankly, I don't think it matters if the meeting is regarded as preliminary to a process of canonization or occasion for exorcism. It will
help us resolve who Brother Jacques really is."

For the rest of the day, Gerson's mind relentlessly juxtaposed his
conversation with Anthony and Baldwin with his revelations about
Jacques. The result was a progressive spiritual despondency. His vision
of the Franciscan as St. Francis was a dream. But the second occurred
while he was awake in the context of a mystical rapture, which was much
more auspicious. It was the most transcendent moment that Gerson had
ever experienced, and he desperately wanted to believe in its authenticity. Yet Gerson couldn't ignore the fact that this vision occurred on
the very evening that the others believed themselves threatened in various ways. This concurrence might suggest a common source of inspiration — an evil source.

Ultimately, his conviction that the revelations were divinely inspired
triumphed. The boy must have said "King of Kings" after all, and that
meant that Satan had interfered in Gerson's relation of the vision, causing him to misspeak. His visions provided a divine foil to the delusions
of Anthony and Baldwin. Their false position, willful and stubborn, was
exactly like the fool who *said in his heart there is no God*. This was the
key to their conscription into the Wild Hunt: their uncharitable skepticism over the spiritual good that Jacques conferred. This skepticism ultimately begrudged the outpouring of divine grace on the world, which
was nothing less than a sin against the Holy Spirit. This was the one sin
that the gospels proclaimed unforgivable. They deserved to be damned!

Thursday arrived. It was the feast day of Mary Magdalene and
Brother Jacques gave a very fulsome and moving account of her conversion and lifelong penance in Marseilles. At the end of the meeting, Gerson
came over to Anthony and his friends and was duly introduced to Felice.
Although he had suspected that the unknown woman who appeared
among the ghostly riders was, in fact, Hervey's daughter, he still experienced the shock of recognition meeting Felice in the flesh. And yet, this
precognition of Felice provided further proof that his vision was genuine.

After the meeting was over, Brother Jacques came over once again
to greet Father Hervey and his party, demonstrating what appeared to
be genuine satisfaction over their presence.

"I understand that you have something special you want to talk with
me about," Brother Jacques said, his glance accommodating all of them.

Only Gerson was surprised by the manner in which Jacques had anticipated their request for a meeting. Hervey was ready with his response.

"Yes. I believe you may be interested in an old manuscript that's in my possession. Perhaps we can discuss it. The rest of us find it very intriguing."

They agreed to meet in the church the following evening after supper.

The four friends wanted to congregate at the presbytery ahead of time, and invited Gerson to do likewise. Initially he resisted, wanting to distance himself from the impending lunacy he anticipated from the others. But Anthony insisted, and Gerson finally acquiesced. He had a meeting with the rector of the faculty of arts that might run late, however, and would have to find his own way to the presbytery. This was just as well because there were certain preparations required of the Counter-Faith, the nature of which the Chancellor would most certainly disapprove.

The next day was Friday. Anthony and Baldwin arrived early in the evening — at least an hour before the time that Gerson was expected. They greeted their hosts warmly, and then set to work rearranging the furniture. A chair was placed in the center of the room where Anthony seated himself. He said a brief prayer, imploring God to be with them and guide them through the next few hours. Then he beckoned to Felice, who went to stand in front of him. Anthony intoned, "God's truth shall compass thee with a shield."

Felice replied, "Thou shalt not be afraid of the terror of the night. Of the arrow that flieth in the day, of the business that walketh about in the dark: of invasion, or of the noonday devil."

Hervey handed Felice a candle, which she accepted in her left hand. After it was lit, Anthony exhorted her with the following words: "Felice, those ordained to the office of exorcist ought to know what they are undertaking. It behooves an exorcist to cast out demons. Accept the power of imposing your hands on the possessed so that, through their imposition and by the grace of the Holy Spirit, unclean spirits will be exorcised and cast out of the bodies of the possessed. Be zealous, therefore, that just as demons are expelled from the bodies of others, so should every lie and manifold uncleanness and wickedness be cast out from your own body, lest you succumb to those things which are routed from others through your ministry. Learn from your office to rule your vices, lest the evil one should be able to regain some of his power through your bad habits. For once you have conquered the many different kinds of wickedness in yourself, then you will be able to command the demons in others. May the Lord concede this to you through the Holy Spirit."

The others said *Amen* in unison.

Anthony held up a book and said, "Accept this book and commend it to memory so that you will have the power of imposing your hands on those who are possessed."

Felice took the book with her right hand, at which point everyone knelt, facing east. Anthony made the following entreaty: "Holy Lord, omnipotent Father, eternal God, we ask You to bless and make worthy Your servant, Felice. Through Jesus Christ our Lord."

The others again responded *Amen*.

Hervey came forward and kissed Felice on the forehead.

"Dear Lord, keep her safe," he said in a low voice.

Then Baldwin started clapping and cheering, and the other two men joined in. Felice, who had never been one to blush, surprised herself by turning a pretty color of red. "Do most of your ordinations end so raucously?" she said with a smile. They all laughed. And then they were quiet. It was a solemn moment. Tears rose to Felice's eyes.

"If this is really the end of time, I am happy to be sharing it with the three of you," she whispered. The next moment, the four friends found themselves locked together in a group embrace.

It was only at this point that they became aware that someone was at the door. It was Gerson, looking nervous and out of sorts.

"I've been knocking forever. What was all that racket? One would think you had a troop of jongleurs in here."

"No, just four merry exorcists!" said Baldwin with his usual exuberance. A volley of hostile pokes, administered covertly on either side by Hervey and Anthony, assailed him.

Gerson shook his head in disapproval. "Are we ready? It's almost time," he said.

At these words, the four Counter-Faith each reflexively felt in their pockets to make sure that their little vials of holy water, laced with blessed salt, were there. They looked at one another with mutual love and concern. It felt as if everything was about to change.

"I suppose we are ready," said Anthony, smiling at the others.

Chapter 12: The Curator of Souls

Descent from the Cross

The church was empty. And yet it wasn't. Hervey sensed that the atmosphere was different somehow. Usually the church was redolent of incense and lilies — the flower most favored by Felice, and which he procured for the altar whenever possible. The air was thick and sweet as usual, but its habitual fragrance had become mixed up with something else: something dense and dank. It was as if the atmosphere of the *boucherie* was taking over. And it was quiet: Hervey didn't remember it ever being so quiet. The entire edifice seemed unfamiliar — not at all the same church he had come to know so intimately. The building had always been irregular, but it now seemed more off balance than usual. None of the paving stones were flush with one another. The floor was noticeably slanted toward the east end. The arches along the nave wall looked asymmetrical and crooked. The vaulting was distinctly higher than he remembered. The increased elevation lent a brooding quality to the triforium, as if its apertures were the hollow eyes of a huge creature in a crouch, waiting for the right moment to spring. While mentally noting these apparent differences, Hervey had a growing apprehension that there was someone or something behind him. As they proceeded up the nave, he looked back toward the west end several times involuntarily, half expecting to catch a glimpse of he knew not what.

Felice experienced a similar sense of estrangement. She found herself noticing certain pictures and statuary for the first time. In a side aisle there was a hitherto unseen effigy of St. Sebastian — his body perforated over and over again with arrows, the glistening blood running down his white torso, his mouth open in a silent scream. Yet he looked so young — a mere boy. There was a painting of Salome gloating over the severed head of the Baptist. Her grisly prize was depicted at an angle, revealing the white of shattered bone against red gore. The head was carried by a naked Ethiopian slave, and presented to her on a silver charger as if it were a meal. The vengeful princess was dressed in a transparent saffron robe. Her back was arched so her nipples pressed against the fabric; her head was thrown back in ecstasy, with mouth open and tongue extended beyond her lower lip, giving the impression that she was already savoring the taste of her victim's blood. But the item that seemed least familiar was, in fact, the one Felice probably knew the best: the giant crucifix located over the central altar — the same one that she had knelt before so often when at prayer. The figure of Christ was much larger than she had realized — far beyond human scale. Its body was more contorted: the wounds livid and fresh. The head was tilted backwards slightly, but she could still glimpse the whites of the eyes and ivory teeth against very red lips.

They walked in silence, footsteps echoing loudly. It was only when they had almost reached the transept's lantern crossing that Gerson spoke, causing everyone to start.

"Brother Jacques must be running late." He did not succeed in sounding casual, despite his best efforts. But as if Gerson's words were a prompt, there came a familiar noise from the west end: a scraping and then a click.

"What was that?" asked the Gerson, looking nervously behind him.

The others recognized the sound.

"Someone has locked the Porch Door," replied Anthony.

This was unprecedented. The church was never locked. In fact it couldn't be. The key had gone missing long before Hervey's time. He had been meaning to talk to the wardens about obtaining a replacement, but it never was much of a priority. Felice was aware of this situation as well, and the two of them looked at one another with concern.

The light had begun to play tricks with their vision. The setting sun had ignited the eyes of the stained glass figures until they resembled bevels with hot coals. A red glow spread from the eyes like blood, saturating the rest of the figure and bringing it to life. Gerson had been examining a lancet window of the tree of Jesse. Its familiar contours were comforting, like encountering an old acquaintance in a strange land. But Gerson reproached himself: it was ridiculous to think this way. This wasn't a strange land; this was Paris, his Paris — the heart of France. He mustn't give way to nerves. It was the fears of the others that had put him off balance. That was all. Brother Jacques would soon be with them and all his fears would vanish. And all would be well. All manner of things would be well. This he knew. Brother Jacques was a healer: he would heal whatever was wrong with this church, whatever was wrong with Paris, whatever was wrong with Christendom. He would — he must!

Gerson looked back at the window: Jesse was at its base, the sleeping patriarch, from whose loins sprang a tree. The fruit on the tree were the members of the royal house of David, culminating in Christ. The glass image of Christ waved its arms, and the figures began to move. Gerson gasped audibly. Jesse's descendants were climbing up and down the tree with agility, gesturing to one another, looking — for all intents and purposes — as if they were talking. In fact, he could hear their voices, distinct but far away. Gerson grabbed Anthony's arm and pointed.

"Try not to look," said Anthony. "It's the work of demons trying to confound us: our senses are their portals."

"No, No. Don't you see? It's miraculous. The window is showing us that Christ's lineage is still alive," objected Gerson. The rest looked at one another nervously. Nobody knew how to respond to Gerson's alarming misplaced optimism.

From the east end of the church came the sound of a woman singing in an unknown tongue. Although they could not understand the words, the song was beautiful and soothing, but exquisitely sad. It spoke of loss, grief, sickness, age, death, and decay. The voice was describing the horrors of mortality — the fate of every living creature. Yet concealed within these expressions of lament was something else: an incipient potential for transcendence, the promise of eternal life. A seductive refrain kept running through their minds: *live forever; live forever; turn away from death, and live forever.* Drawn by the voice in spite of themselves, they approached the altar. The great cross was surrounded by a series of niches, each containing a life-sized statue of one of the saints present at the Crucifixion. Their expressions were vivid. The faces of the Virgin Mary and John the Evangelist were distorted by grief — a grief so terrible that they hardly looked human. The Roman soldier, Longinus, holding the spear with which he pierced Christ's side, looked dazed with anguish. Where was he? What had he done? And Mary Magdalene, golden hair glimmering against her scarlet robe, wore an expression that united suffering and desire so seamlessly that it took one's breath away.

Her face was illuminated with the exultant passion of a woman making love — except for the eyes. The eyes were despairing. Eyes that had witnessed every possible evil: drenched in sorrow, but long beyond tears. The light created the illusion that it was the statue of the Magdalene which was singing.

The beautiful song was ending. Its final melancholic strains were still echoing in their ears when the figure on the crucifix seemed to stir. The motion was barely noticeable at first: the slightest tremor running the length of its form, up and down. Eventually, this wave-like movement became centered on the figure's breast, where a subtle stirring could be discerned: in and out, as if the thing were breathing. Felice grabbed her father's hand in fear. The indicators were slight: it was still possible for the five observers to doubt the testimony of their eyes. But denial was no longer an option when the figure began to straighten its neck, bringing the great head upright. The thing looked at them one by one with huge unblinking eyes. It was a gaze that bespoke keen intelligence and insight in a very literal sense: they all felt as if a powerful probe had been thrust into their consciousness. Yet the gaze was supremely cold — cold and indifferent, entirely devoid of empathy or any kind of feeling at all. The thing began to move in earnest, slowly pulling itself away from the cross. The grisly sound of flesh and sinew being ripped from the nails was terrible. Someone cried out when the effigy of Christ stepped down from the platform at the base of the cross and then, as if walking on steps of air, descended to the ground. It was coming toward them.

The towering figure bore the unmistakable visage of Brother Jacques. Gerson fell to his knees in worship. *The second coming of Christ is at hand. And I have been chosen to witness the end of time, when all of history grinds to a halt. At last, my faith has been vindicated; I am among the elect.* But the other four shuddered with horror, crossing themselves simultaneously.

They watched in silence as the effigy slowly traversed the choir. It was only a few yards away when Hervey finally spoke up. "Who are you?" His voice was clear, but quavered ever so slightly.

It was as if a great lamp were lit: the visage was suddenly filled with warmth and affect, and the figure smiled. "You know who I am. I am the One whom you seek; whom you have always sought. I am the Christ: the Anointed; the Messiah; the incarnate Son of God." The voice was deep and exquisite, filling the nave with melody and hanging upon the air like incense. Its gentle tones soothed and caressed them, reassuring them that they were safe, entreating them to trust. The enormous eyes were no longer cold and distant; instead they were charged with emotion, bathing the five of them in love. "Cast aside your doubts and embrace the truth. I created you; cherished you; died for you. Bow down in worship, for I am the Son of Man."

The voice was irresistible. Gerson's head was already bowed in prayer. The other men slowly followed, sinking to their knees one by one.

As the beautiful voice enfolded them in bliss, sensual images began to take shape in their minds. Manifestations of forgotten or unrealized pleasures flowed through them like a river, bearing one precious moment after another. Some of these images were especially dear. Gerson remembered what it was like to be held by his mother — the warm feeling of her body; the beating of her heart; the sweet smell of her breath. She was teaching him the Lord's Prayer: he was repeating what she said, word for word. He could hear his own childish, lisping voice.

Hervey was reliving the pleasure he experienced when he had first purchased the life of Peter Martyr: the feeling of the manuscript's parchment against his fingers, the anticipation of reading, the delight in ownership. He was back in that spartan room at college — unfurnished, apart from two beds and a stool. His roommate wasn't there. Wonderful. Sitting on the bed with his back against the wall, Hervey reveled in the vita of the man he so admired: a saint born to heretical parents, who sacrificed his life in his efforts to bring the errant sheep back into the fold.

Anthony experienced what it was like to be a boy again, growing up on his family's fief in Champagne. He was learning to ride. Father was riding alongside him, beaming with pride at his son's natural aptitude, but calling on him to slow down. But Anthony wasn't about to slow down. Pretending not to he hear, he broke into a gallop. With the wind on his face, he watched in amazement as the familiar countryside moved past him at dizzying speed. He felt like a creature stepping out of the world of myth — a centaur, fleet, powerful, and god-like.

And Baldwin trembled with joy, holding Felice close to his heart. Often in conversation, she had seemed so contentious and formidable, but now, folded against his breast, she seemed diminutive and fragile, like a small creature seeking shelter. He would succor and shelter her; hold her and protect her from any harm that might come her way. Her hair brushed against the edge of his jaw; her scent was intoxicating.

Baldwin placed his thumb gently beneath her chin, tilting her face upwards toward his own. He bent to kiss her.

And all the time they dreamed, the voice moved in and out of their disparate visions effortlessly, without violence or discord. "Each of you have, in your own way, struggled to serve me," it murmured. "Now come, my beloved ones — come forward and claim your reward. Come!" It was the voice they had waited for all their lives; the only voice that understood the story of their lives.

Gerson, suffused with that *peace that passes all understanding*, fell to the ground in full prostration, and then began to crawl closer and closer to the Christ figure. The other men also began to edge forward.

Felice alone managed to resist the torrential images flooding her mind, remaining resolutely on her feet.

"You are lying. I don't believe you are Christ," she said, struggling with all her might against the influence of the voice. Her own sounded lifeless and dull by contrast.

The Christ effigy's expression was filled with loving compassion; his voice soft with concern.

"Felice: my sister, my bride. You have always been a doubter," he said indulgently. "But you are especially beloved because your obstinacy has made your path that much harder. Come: feel the marks of my wounds with your hand." The Christ held out its arms as if seeking an embrace.

Felice began to move toward him, her step slow and leaden. But then she stopped herself.

"I know you." Her speech was thick and difficult. "I have met you before."

To the others, Felice's voice sounded harsh and ragged. She was breaking in on the tranquility of their private moments of grace. They would have done anything to make her stop talking. But she persisted.

"I know who you are," she said in the same wooden tones, groping for the name. Never before had her mind seemed so confused and unresponsive. And there was so much commotion! Alien voices vying for attention; images from the past rising to her mind unbidden. They were engulfing her; crowding out her own thoughts. She must resist. What was that name? Simeon. Was he Simeon? Who was Simeon? The righteous old man at Christ's circumcision! But no, that was the wrong name. Wrong but not very wrong. It was not Simeon, but a name like Simeon. Felice struggled to remember, closing her eyes to concentrate — trying to discern between her own thoughts and the ones that were being channeled into her brain. All at once the image of a statue appeared very clearly before her eyes. On its base was written *Simoni sancto deo [To Simon, Holy God]*.

"You were once called Simon."

When she said that name, Simon, each of her companions experienced a subtle agitation as if registering an unpleasant change in the weather. The stream of images started to slow. Like sleepers clinging to a pleasant dream, they resisted the disturbance. It was Felice's fault. The dream was beautiful and they did not wish to awaken. Not now; not ever. They resented her annoying chatter. Would she never be quiet? Felice was like an incongruous storm cloud appearing on the horizon of an otherwise glorious day.

When Felice spoke, Hervey was sitting in his college room, writing his commentary on Peter Lombard's *Sentences*. His manuscript of the life of Peter Martyr was on the edge of the desk like a talisman. Hervey had reached book three in his commentary, on the incarnation of the Word, and the end was in sight. The ideas were coming to him easily — so easily that he felt inspired. He was in the midst of refuting the heretical error that Christ had never actually assumed flesh, and what he was writing was timely. The Cathars were regrouping in the south of France — rising up once again to challenge the faith. Hervey's commentary was destined to be a powerful weapon against the Cathars. Yet even while he felt as if he were infused with the Holy Spirit, writing with all his might, Hervey could feel the world attempting to pull him in a different direction. There was a woman named Felice: a penitent who claimed that Hervey had defiled her. Felice was a liar. She represented the world: obstinate and implacable. He had witnessed her rejection of the loving overtures of the celestial bridegroom. And now she was reaching out for Hervey — strangling him, blocking off his own access to grace. Felice was insatiable in her needs. It was in her very nature. Her questioning, doubting, testing — these tendencies were constant. She wouldn't be still. *It is better to dwell in a corner of the housetop, than with a brawling woman in a wide house.* There was so much truth to that. Solomon was, indeed, wise.

Gerson was engaged in writing what he knew would be the seminal work on spiritual discernment when the voice of that priest's concubine broke in. Incredible! This woman, who should be awash with gratitude, could only complain. Rather than rebuking her for her impious doubts,

as she richly deserved, Christ offers to embrace her. He even singles
her out, naming her His beloved; His bride. Just think of all those other
women, doing anything and everything to subdue their bodies, hoping
someday to become worthy of such a distinction. They tried so hard to
make Christ come to them: fasting, prayers, vigils. He tried so hard! And
here this woman, Felice, without even striving, is being offered everything these other women want; everything he wants! And yet she resists.
She is petulant, withholding, unsatisfied, totally lacking in discretion.
As a jewel of gold in a swine's snout, so is a fair woman without discretion.
How true that was! Gerson felt pity for that young man, Baldwin, who
was clearly infatuated with this woman. He should take heed: *There are*
three things that are never satisfied. . . hell, land, which is never satisfied
with water, and the mouth of the womb. Solomon was so wise! Felice, like
all women, was but an insatiable womb: yawning, gaping, needing, ready
to suck any man dry. Yet now she is being offered not just any man, but
the Son of Man. Why can't she find repose in Christ's love? Why won't
she be quiet?

Baldwin was in the midst of a dazzling quodlibet, and just about
to embark on his determination. His audience was agog with admiration, when Felice's voice obtruded. How inconsiderate and annoying! As
if she hadn't disrupted his peace of mind long enough. His parents had
dedicated him to God from infancy, yet she presumes to come along and
rearrange his life with impunity; destroy his life was more like it! But
he knew her for what she was the moment he saw her. A priest's whore!
What was that verse from Proverbs? *For a whore is a deep ditch, and a*
strange woman is a narrow pit. She also lieth in wait as for a prey, and
increaseth the transgressors among men. It was true; Solomon was so very
wise. Women like Felice were destructive and irresponsible. For all her
scholarly posturing, she was exactly like our first mother, Eve: a tempt-
ress first and foremost, trained in the arts of seduction by Satan himself!
Felice had purposefully set out to tantalize Baldwin, consciously tempt-
ing him, stooping to any artifice, deploying every weapon invented by
feminine guile as entrapment. But this had to stop. He would not let her
destroy him now!

Anthony continued to revisit the lost joys of childhood: he and his
long dead brother were fishing in the river behind the manor house. They
were each holding a net, wading in up to their thighs. It was hot, and the
water was deliciously refreshing. A school of pike was approaching, their

bodies flashing gold in the sun's rays. But the onslaught of images began to slow down. While his companions still foundered in artificial plea-sure, Anthony was beginning to extricate himself from the spell cast by the Christ's voice. Although very much aware of the exchange between the Christ and Felice, he was immobilized — incapable of speech and movement alike. Then suddenly, the relentless assault of images and arti-ficial feelings intensified and Anthony again felt himself slipping away, seduced by the memories of an untroubled youth — a realm of unpar-alleled gratification. His physical surroundings were becoming remote, even as the sound of Felice's confrontation with the Christ retreated. Yet at the name "Simon," Anthony felt a jolt, and his retreat into beatific nos-talgia was arrested.

The monstrous Christ was saying:

"You are right, I was once called Simon. After I died on the cross, my spirit came to rest in my chief apostle, Simon Peter. He was the rock upon which I founded my church. But that was before your time. You never knew him, except in your heart alone; never in the flesh."

The Christ spoke with infinite patience, in low dulcet tones like a lover. "Oh my beloved Felice, you must trust me! You represent my lost sheep and I have come to this world especially to find you. *For thou hast ravished my heart, my sister, my spouse; Thou hast ravished my heart with one of thine eyes.*"

Felice was struggling against a feeling of euphoria that threatened to eclipse all thought. She did her best to block out the voice, even plac-ing her hands over her ears. *To Simon, Holy God.* Think! Think! His name was Simon, but the inscription was wrong; he wasn't a god. His name was Simon, but he wasn't a god. Felice kept repeating this to herself, over and over. And then it came to her.

"No. You were never Simon Peter. The true Christ never chose you. You were Simon Magus — the Magician." And the moment she uttered this name, her mind was suffused with light, and with the light came memories.

Felice saw herself in Nero's palace, dressed in sumptuous silk bro-cade that changed color whenever she moved, bedizened with jewels. Her name was Helen. She was introduced to all of Rome as Simon's first thought; his *Sophia* — the Mother of All. Simon was God. He descended to earth to find her, the lost sheep of scripture. And she believed herself to be what he said; she believed herself to be divine. What an honor to be created by him, for him; lost before time, but now found again and raised on high. She was the beloved of an all-powerful deity, who could assume any form. He had amazed the crowd by becoming a brazen serpent, baffled them in the shape of a goat, frightened them as the two-faced Janus. One night after making love, Helen watched as his body slowly metamorphosed into the purest gold. Simon was the Standing One — the one who would remain standing after all else had fallen. He had conquered death many times over: she had seen him lay upon roaring flames without being burned, she had witnessed his beheading, and then watched in awe as he willed himself back to life. Simon's godly nature was especially manifest in his power of flight, which propelled him through the air with the grace and agility of an eagle. Then came that terrible day when he was flying over the forum, high above the gaping crowd. Helen was watching Simon soaring upward, beautiful and free, when the *scales fell from her eyes*, and he changed. From a gorgeous deity in cloth of gold, he was metamorphosed into a dragon — grotesque, loathsome, and cruel. No one else seemed aware of this change, but she knew in her heart that she had been deceived in him and the monster in the air was the form closest to his true nature. The man she had worshiped was not a beneficent creator, but something evil beyond measure that thrived on the pain of others. He must be stopped. But how? Helen felt powerless and alone. But perhaps she was not alone after all; there was another who seemed to know. The man whom they called Simon Peter, Simon the Rock, saw the magician for what he was. Helen knew by the look of horror on his face. And so she called to Simon Peter, over and over again — calling his name until he finally heard. For a moment their eyes locked, and then the two of them fell to their knees and began to pray with all their might. And the Celestial Father heard them. The magician began to fall — down, down, down — head first and out of control, until he came smashing to the ground. His body lay bloody and broken upon the pavement. He was not the spiritual God of light, but something evil. He was never Simon the Rock, but Simon the Magician — the one who was brought down by the prayers of the Rock.

When Felice pronounced the name Simon Magus, the effect on her companions was instantaneous. The surface text of present day life was suddenly peeled back, exposing the effaced writing of their past lives. Anthony remembered himself in the Roman forum, looking upward. The magician who called himself Simon was flying — spiraling upward, high above everyone's head. He wore a costume made of gold that glittered like the sun. The emperor and his party were applauding; the crowd was cheering. They thought he was a god. But, whatever he might be, Anthony knew that the magician's doctrine was subtle, insidious, and dangerous. He was posing as a redeemer who had come to succor their souls, releasing them from the material world of suffering. But he was evil. His whole existence was focused on their entrapment. He would seduce the souls of his followers and bind them to the material world so securely that they would forget all about the celestial homeland. Anthony looked around, despairing: the crowd was enthralled, everyone transfixed by the glorious figure in the sky. Everyone except the magician's mistress, Helen — the exquisite woman whom the magician called his first thought. Did she see as well? Impossible. Helen had not just been one of Simon's believers, but his most ardent apostle, doing her utmost to spread his corrupt word. Nevertheless, something had happened. The magician's enchantment had faltered. Only that could explain the look of pure terror on Helen's face. The *scales fell from her eyes,* and she saw him for what he was. Yet, she kept calling his name: *Simon, Simon.* Was she still enslaved to the magician even after she knew the truth? Then Anthony realized that she wasn't calling the magician after all; she wasn't even looking at him — her beautiful amber eyes were trained on Anthony. She was appealing to him. *Simon, I see now; I know who he is. We must stop him! Simon, do you hear me? Simon! Help me!* And then Anthony remembered: he was once called Simon Peter, the disciple upon whom the true celestial Christ had founded His church. The magician was one of those false Christs that the Lord had warned them about. Anthony and Helen looked at one another with total comprehension, and they both fell to their knees in prayer.

The others also entered upon their past lives. Baldwin was remembering the life he had lived as Berengar of Tours, the brilliant but tragic figure at the center of the last great Eucharistic controversy, overwhelmed by the delusions of the carnal minded. He had argued that the Eucharist was a symbol — a meaningful symbol, a powerful symbol, but a symbol nonetheless. Yet Lanfranc's attack on him was relentless. Lanfranc insisted that the prayer of consecration conjured up the true presence of Christ — actually transformed bread and wine into flesh and blood. This was literalism gone wild — as crazy as it was disgusting. It almost seemed to imply that the priest was a bizarre magician, effecting change through incantation. It was useless to fight back; the entire clergy seemed to be on Lanfranc's side. Even so, Berengar knew he was right and would never back down. It didn't matter how many times he was condemned; he would continue to proclaim the truth. And so he trod the bitter path of exile until the end of his days.

Gerson was exultant to learn that he had once walked the earth as his hero Bernard of Clairvaux. How very gratifying! Gerson's unstinting devotion to the Cistercian abbot had always been one of the mainstays of his spiritual life. Why just the other day, he had preached a sermon in which he asked his listeners to imagine that he was Bernard. It turns out that they wouldn't have been pretending after all; he really was Bernard! It was strange. Gerson had always considered Bernard to be one of the Lord's favorites, while Gerson, in contrast, had always felt so unworthy. Yet Gerson could now see that the two of them shared so much. First, there was the common aversion to academic innovation. As Bernard, he had broken the back of that egomaniac Abelard; now as Chancellor of the University he continued to fight against the same prurient curiosity rampant among students. They both understood that the sum of all wisdom was in scripture: the unfolding of the Lord's plan for humanity; the alpha and omega. Gerson was momentarily engulfed by the joy he had once experienced when, as Bernard, he was meditating on the Song of Songs: his vision of the bridegroom had inspired that mighty cycle of sermons. The sermons were delivered to Bernard's monastic brethren, whom he loved beyond measure. After each sermon they would pray *Let him kiss me with the kisses of his mouth,* and Bernard would then embrace each of them one by one. This was the real difference between his two lives. Once upon a time as Bernard, he was the beloved abbot of a vibrant community. As Chancellor Gerson, however, he was solitary and alone. Oh, how he wanted that loving fellowship again!

And Hervey remembered his life as a Cathar Perfect, present at the tragic siege of Montségur. He had first embarked upon his religious life as a Dominican inquisitor — bent on destroying *the little foxes that spoil the vine* of the Lord by their heresy. But he very soon apostatized, running away in horror from the *hardness of heart* that he perceived in his fellow inquisitors, rejecting the acts of cruelty and persecution that Jehovah, the evil creator god, had prompted them to commit. He had seen them persecute the Cathars. And he observed the courage of the Cathar Perfect with awe: their peace and confidence in the face of death. He arrived at Montségur with his dear friend Jacques, an apostate from the Franciscan order. The Perfect welcomed them into the true faith, teaching them how to purify their bodies so that they too could be perfected — the last step before leaving the corrupt body behind forever. Hervey's heart swelled with joy as he remembered the blessed day that he and Jacques became perfected: *Free from the flesh; let us rejoice,* they had sung. But Hervey had never been a brave man — not like Jacques. He wasn't brave enough for martyrdom and, to his eternal shame, on that fatal day when Montségur finally fell, Hervey hid while his fellow-Perfect were being arrested. He saved his own wretched skin by hiding inside a dried up well. The edge of the stone lid covering the mouth of the well was broken, creating a fissure through which he watched. Jacques stood unflinching while the soldiers tied his arms behind his back and led him away. Was it Hervey's imagination, or did Jacques glance backward at the well, almost as if he gleaned Hervey's hiding place? The smile on Jacques' face seemed to forgive his friend for his weakness. Standing on the narrow edge inside of the well, Hervey tried to block out the screams, choking on the smoke and the terrible smell of burning flesh. If he wasn't brave enough to partake of their noble death, at least he could bear witness to their martyrdom. With a trembling hand, he recorded their ordeal in his journal: may they find peace with the Celestial Father! Finally it was over: all the Perfect were dead. He was free to leave now — free to begin a life of penance somewhere far away, atoning for his sinful cowardice. Then suddenly he saw Jacques returning through the gate. Hervey's heart leapt in joyful gratitude: God in His graciousness had spared his beloved companion! Hervey was on the verge of clambering out of the well, ready to embrace Jacques in gladness, when he saw something fearful. Right before his eyes, his friend changed, shifting his shape as easily as if he were shedding his clothing. With a single spasm, Jacques was transformed from the handsome young man, dressed in the ascetic habit of a Perfect, into an aged and evil-looking man in black and white robes. A Dominican inquisitor. Then the Celestial Father took pity on Hervey: his consciousness was illuminated by a blinding light, and *the scales fell from his eyes.* Hervey finally understood, apprehending Jacques for what he really was. He wrote it in his journal as a warning, praying to the Celestial Father that it would eventually make its way into the right hands. But there were so many wrong hands! Hervey took the precaution of writing in his secret mirror hand. Now the thing that had posed as his friend was coming for him. Hervey hastily hid the journal and prepared to die.

Hervey abruptly returned to the present. "The journal. It was mine all along!"

He looked at the Christ figure steadily, and said in a firm voice. "Thanks to our Celestial Father, I at last know who you are! You are the embodiment of what most Cathars didn't believe existed, but what we must fear most: the carnal Christ. I learned the truth at the siege of Montségur, and wrote it in my journal." Now Hervey looked to the others in exultation: "He didn't know about the journal!"

In essence, Hervey was articulating what Felice and Anthony had already realized. The false Christ was neither omnipotent nor omniscient. The combined prayers of Simon Peter and Helen had defeated him long ago. Brother Jacques had only learned of Hervey's journal by chance, overhearing the dinnertime conversation between Gerson and Martin. He didn't know what it contained, but he was fearful — so fearful that he was prepared to kill anyone who knew about it.

A spasm of fury ran across the Christ's face. It was but a momentary slip. Almost immediately, the face regained its composure, and the rage was effaced by an expression of loving patience and resignation. He looked for all the world like a parent who fears that he must needs restrain a child who is about to fall and hurt himself.

"My poor son, all this excitement and speculation about a journal. The journal doesn't matter. The fact that you witnessed my metamorphosis doesn't matter." He was looking with frightening intensity at Hervey. "I am the Christ. I die and return. I transfigure myself as I see fit. I can take the form of a Dominican inquisitor, if I wish. *With God all things are possible*, but my ways are deep and hidden from men." His voice was sweet and singsong. "It is through my power that it was given to you to see what you saw." Then to all of them: "It also is through my power that you were allowed to see what you once were."

But *the devil is a liar*, the father of all lies, and the four friends knew that the horrific Christ was lying. He had done everything he could to conceal their former lives from them. They knew this as certainly as they now knew him for what he was: the evil creator who forced their immortal souls into corruptible bodies, the ultimate curator of souls. The Cathars had been right, and the church repaid them with persecution and death.

Although no one had spoken these truths aloud, their thoughts were somehow audible to the Christ. He shook his enormous head, as if pitying their blindness.

"The Cathars were only right about one thing," said Christ in mellifluous tones. "There are many incarnations in the body. As soon as you die, you enter into another life and another body. And your orthodox theologians were right about the most important thing: the soul needs the body; they are bound together in a sacred marriage. And that is why I assumed flesh; to show you that the body is holy, saving you from the false prophets who despised the body. But your theologians were wrong about the rest: there is no celestial kingdom awaiting you in the hereafter, only incarnation after incarnation."

Gerson alone had remained in a state of denial, clinging desperately to his hopes about Brother Jacques for as long as he could. Yet by now even he had seen and heard enough to experience both doubt and fear. This could not possibly be the true Christ — everything he was saying was contrary to church doctrine. Yet this Christ, the very image of Brother Jacques, had more power than any saint Gerson had ever heard of; he had to be a demon. Realizing the extent to which he had been deceived, Gerson groaned aloud in despair.

The Christ continued: "The Cathars denied the body. It was a destructive faith and my church had to destroy them."

"You lie. The real Christ doesn't kill. You are Satan," said Felice.

"It doesn't matter what you call me: Christ, Jehovah, Satan, Simon, or Brother Jacques. I created this world. I founded your church. It is I whom you worship; it is I whom you have always worshiped. I said to Moses and I say to you, *I am who am.* There is nothing and no one else."

The power of the voice was reasserting itself once again, becoming dominant.

"The five of you are chosen. You have been privileged to receive knowledge of your past. Yet *the time is short.* And the time you have been allotted in your present bodies is shorter still. But be of good cheer. I offer you eternal life, which is the reward of my elect."

As soon the Christ spoke these words, the statues in the niches that had flanked the crucifix began to move, coming to life. They descended through the air by the same invisible steps that their master had trod, and stood in front of the altar. Then these effigies of saints underwent a metamorphosis that was hideous to behold. The individual statues dissolved into a slick and broiling mass, the texture of placenta mixed with clay. Inside this mass, an essence could be discerned, struggling to escape whatever power contained it. Faces that once were human, locked in expressions of unspeakable horror, whirled around at dizzying speed. The rank smell of putrefying blood filled the air. Yet it only took a moment for the formless entities to resolve themselves into the four familiar figures of Brother Jacques' inner circle. What had once been the statue of the Virgin Mary was ultimately transformed into Rose; the Magdalene became Alicia; John the Evangelist became Rupert; and the soldier Longinus became Brother Marcus. The four acolytes bowed to Christ reverently before assuming their positions on either side of him.

Felice cried out when she saw them. The frozen quality that she had witnessed in Rose was but a mask that had now been stripped away. What was left was a look of implacable hatred on visages that were unmistakably evil.

"What have you done to them?"

"I offered them eternal life, which I offer to you now. They drank from my blood of their own free will. Now, through my grace, they will retain the same bodies forever. They will be spared the humiliation of innumerable incarnations and the incumbent oblivion that each new life entails. They will become learned and powerful beyond human measure because they will remember what they have experienced and learned. And they will be with me always."

Felice looked at the four of them with a mixture of revulsion and pity. The poor misguided souls had eagerly grasped at the promise of eternal life. But the immortality they had attained was clearly a kind of hell. Felice was reminded of the orthodox teaching on angels: how the good ones were confirmed in their goodness, while the evil ones became obdurate in their malice. She recognized intuitively that something like this had happened to the souls of these four. Their wills were frozen, forever destined to serve their evil lord.

No one spoke. But each of Felice's confederates partook of her apprehension, and even Gerson shared in her aversion. The faces of these embodied immortals were stamped with a malevolence so virulent that it was impossible not to recoil. They had become demons.

The Christ stepped forward and beckoned:

"Come; drink from my side and join us in eternal life." As he spoke, the wound in his side began to glisten, welling up with blood.

"No," said Anthony, speaking for all of them. "We don't profess to understand all the secrets of the cosmos. But we now recognize for certain what you are, and reject with all our hearts and souls the kind of immortality you offer. It is better to choose death."

"Will no one come forward and drink?" the Christ asked, his voice laced with compassion, and eyes filled with empathetic sorrow.

None of them moved.

"Then I am afraid you have, indeed, chosen death."

And almost instantly, Gerson and the four Counter-Faith felt an encroaching cold spread through their veins as each of them gradually lost their grip on consciousness, their souls overcome by the tantalizing possibilities of alternative lives.

Lives Unlived

Hervey was so relieved. The woman who had accused him of fathering her child had finally acknowledged his innocence; those who had wrongly condemned him now sought his forgiveness. He was exonerated. Hervey resumed his studies, finished his Master's degree, and entered the Dominican Order, fulfilling a lifelong dream. He was still a novice, but he had no doubt that he would eventually take his life vows. Hervey had always known what he wanted; he had a true vocation.

"God has called me to be an inquisitor, prior. The church is riven with dissension. There are still Waldensians afoot all over Latin Christendom. And I have heard that there are even some dualists remaining in the Italian Piedmont. I want to be there to fight for the church and uphold the faith."

The prior smiled indulgently. "You, my son, are a zealot. And a zealot sometimes over-estimates the extent of his powers. Remember, it is only our strongest and our finest that we send. Not all our brethren are equal to such a challenge." These last words were pronounced very gently, but firmly nonetheless.

Hervey was momentarily daunted. He wondered if the prior was tacitly signaling that he found Hervey unfit in some way.

"It may be that I am unworthy. But I was inspired by the story of Peter Martyr from the time I was a boy. My father had a manuscript of his life. I wanted to emulate him: to preach against heresy and even suffer martyrdom, if God so willed."

"Good," said the prior. "Pray to the good Lord for guidance. I have noticed you have been distracted lately. Dedication is paramount, my son."

Hervey knew he was right. Recently, he had been unfocused. In fact, even while the prior was speaking, Hervey found it difficult to attend. What was his friend Anthony up to? He thought he heard him calling. But Hervey knew that his conversation with the prior was important, and did his best to ignore the sound.

John Gerson had never laughed so hard. He was sitting with his friends, Anthony and Baldwin, in a tavern, not far from his rooms in the College of Navarre. His parents had been deeply pious and given him every advantage they could afford. But they were both very earnest. There had never been much laughter in their home. Looking back on his childhood, he had often thought that their family life was so quiet and orderly that it was almost like a religious community. Gerson seemed to have carried this silence into the world with him. At college, he watched while the other students studied together, laughed together, and played harmless tricks on one another. Nobody bothered to joke with Gerson; he was so awkward and shy. But then his life had begun to change when he finally made a couple of friends, real friends. This seemed to be all it took to turn him into a happy man. Who would ever have thought it? Gerson had often imagined himself as many different things. But he never imagined himself happy.

Meanwhile, Anthony was telling a hilarious story about the time he walked in on Baldwin and his friends staging a debate on the implications of mistaking Satan for Christ, of all things!

"You have never seen a group of students disperse so quickly!" Anthony grinned as he recalled the scenario. "Just like rats abandoning a sinking ship."

Baldwin was indignant. "Spare me your analogies! We were nervous, of course. A question forbidden by university statute. And then you showed up, behaving like an enforcer and a bully!"

Gerson intervened at this point. "Forbidden or not, I can't understand the appeal of the topic for the life of me."

"But not everyone feels this way. I've heard our own Chancellor, Peter d'Ailly, is interested in writing on precisely that topic," volunteered Anthony.

"Really?" said Baldwin with interest. "Why is it that you jump down our throats, but he can get away with it?"

Anthony laughed. "Well, he is, after all, the Chancellor."

"So to whom does he answer?" Baldwin persisted.

"The pope!" said Anthony.

"Which one?" quipped Gerson.

And the three friends doubled over with laughter.

But Gerson stopped laughing. He could feel someone yanking on his tunic. Was it a pickpocket? A tavern was a risky proposition; it would serve him right. He checked for his purse.

Baldwin had always possessed a lively interest in scholasticism, but never a real vocation for clerical life. So it didn't really disturb him when he was summoned away from school. He wept when his elder brother had died; he had only been two years older than Baldwin himself. But it did mean that Baldwin was now heir to his father's fief and not required to go into the church. Thank God he was only in minor orders. He could still leave the clergy in good conscience with a rich and exciting life awaiting him: first knighthood and then the ultimate coming of age ritual, marriage. It was such a blessing that his parents had chosen the lovely Felice as his bride. He didn't know her well. Still, he sensed that she was everything he desired and more. She was beautiful; she was spirited; she was even literate! Her literacy was an unexpected blessing — something that Baldwin would not even have dared hope for, let alone require. Her beauty would have been enough for him. But the fact that she could read and write was truly wonderful. They would be able to read together, discuss ideas, write to one another. She would be able to instruct their future children in their letters. But he was getting ahead of himself. All in good time. For now, Baldwin had difficulty thinking much beyond the wedding itself, particularly the wedding night. The thought of possessing Felice as his wife filled him with incomparable joy. Once it had been a source of regret for Baldwin that he had never slept with a woman. But now he was glad — glad because it would be the first time for them both.

But Baldwin didn't have the leisure for daydreams. There was so much catching up to do on his military training. Someone was calling: it was the voice of the squire that his father had retained so that Baldwin could practice jousting.

Felix had been deep in conversation with his dear friend, the Dominican Friar Hervey, and had lost track of time. They had been discussing the career of Peter Martyr, something of a professional passion for Hervey. Now Felix was afraid that he was going to be late for his very first quodlibet. When he arrived in the refectory, Baldwin was already in the center of a circle of eager students, ready to introduce the disputing master of the evening. As soon as Felix was seated, Baldwin began.

"The question posed is *Whether woman is a deformed man, as the Philosopher claims, or if she is a part of the divine plan.* We have already heard Master Felix's arguments for and against this proposition. It is time for him to render his determination."

Master Felix rose up from the crowd. He made his way to the middle of the circle and bowed with a flourish, grinning broadly. He was met with lively applause and some raucous calls of encouragement. Felix in due course began.

"My determination begins with Paul's letter to the Galatians, in which it is stated that in Christ there is neither male nor female. I therefore argue that the division into the sexes is an illusion. Since neither sex truly exists, it is impossible for one to be more perfect than the other."

But at that point, the sound of Master Anthony's disapproving voice filled the room, and the other students immediately dispersed.

A Reprieve

Anthony had managed to resist the alluring tug of oblivion, and looked on in dismay as his companions sank into their different realities. He intuitively knew that they were each wandering down separate corridors in pursuit of some unfulfilled desire. But it was a trap that would unerringly lead to their end, and another doomed beginning. Once dead, they would be compelled to don new tunics of forgetfulness, and enter upon other lives. He had to stop them. Anthony could get no response from the other men no matter how hard he shook them. But when he took Felice by the shoulders, he could hear her murmuring something. She was citing St. Paul, of all things!

"Felice, can you hear me?" He thought she muttered something in response. "Come back! God has ordained us His ministers and we have a mission to perform."

Felice's eyes immediately flew open, and Anthony helped her to her feet. The Christ was looking at them with unmistakable hatred, no longer bothering to maintain the masquerade of beneficent Good Shepherd. The very fact that two of them had resisted his death trance seemed to have unnerved him.

"I have to congratulate you both," the Christ sneered. "I see that you, Anthony, have finally arrived and are perfected. Or should I call you Simon Peter? But it's a wonder that it took so long. How easily a poor soul forgets!"

Then turning to Felice, the Christ said:

"And you, my beloved Helen: I am particularly sorry to see you perfected; I have so enjoyed our different lives together." He looked at the others with contempt. "I am afraid that your friends are very far from perfect, however. They still cling to their pathetic tunics of flesh; already entrapped in the other lives I have offered them. There are many more lives, and deaths, in store for them. An infinite number, in fact."

Anthony and Felice did not respond, trying their best to block out the voice. Instead, they looked into one another's eyes with perfect comprehension. Side by side, they took their positions, shielding the bodies of their friends. They crossed themselves, and began to pronounce the rite of exorcism, adjuring the devil.

> *I conjure you, Devil, Satan, Enemy*
> *By God the Father Almighty*
> *And by those virtues which the Lord Himself made and makes*
> *By those angels He has before Himself in His mind*
> *By every good creation that God has made in heaven.*
> *Hear, therefore, and be afraid, Devil, Satan, Enemy: you are banned*
> *I exorcize you, O accursed one, most unclean spirit, basilisk dragon,*
>   *noxious serpent.*

As soon as they began to intone these words, the four acolytes stepped forward menacingly, as if to silence them. But they fell back almost immediately, encountering some kind of invisible barrier. Whatever the obstruction may have been, it did much more than simply repel: the very instant the four monstrous religious made contact, a blinding light appeared from nowhere and they were all at once engulfed in liquid fire. The flame was curious, more luminous and radiant than anything that Felice and Anthony had ever witnessed. It was a radiance that cast a pall over everything else. By comparison, all of nature seemed subdued, drained of color and vitality: grotesque in form, stripped of any harmony. It blazed brightly without burning anything or generating any heat, sustained by something wholly immaterial and utterly incalculable. And its effect was unlike that of any other fire. Their adversaries didn't burn, instead they gradually faded. This happened without evident force or violence, but was still terrible to behold. The dwindling contours of their faces were mobile studies in misery. Eventually all that was visible was a slight quaver in the heart of the flames, and then nothing. The fire disappeared as suddenly as it had appeared.

Felice and Anthony, continuing to repeat the words of exorcism, watched in fascination and horror as their enemies disappeared within a few feet of where they stood. The Christ seemed helpless. It stood before them motionless, as if paralyzed, an expression of relentless animosity on its face. Then something remarkable began to happen. A violent tremor passed through its form. Then the figure gradually began to blur. At first, it was as if it had become slightly out of focus. Then it became more distorted, until eventually any human contours were only barely discernible. The different colors that comprised the effigy started to run together. And then, just when it seemed as if the thing seemed destined to melt away and disappear altogether, it began to solidify into a new coherent shape, ultimately assuming the appearance of a statue of some indeterminate male saint. This was only the first of many forms: in an instant, the statue had dissolved and another shape had taken its place. This happened not just once, but multiple times in quick succession. The thing's virtuosity in shape shifting seemingly accommodated every possible form — animate or inanimate. It appeared as a series of beasts, insects, the occasional plant or tree. The majority of the insensible objects seemed to be religious icons, but this was not invariably the case. Felice and Anthony caught the occasional glimpse of a gallows and various instruments of torture stained with blood.

Most of the figures were human, however. On the basis of the handful of human forms they were able to identify, the thing seemed to be moving backwards in time. The first image that they recognized was Brother Jacques, scaled down from the monstrous height of the Christ and wearing his Franciscan habit. Shortly afterward, someone in a triple miter appeared whom Anthony thought resembled Pope Benedict XII, former bishop of Pamiers; then a Dominican inquisitor, followed by a Franciscan with an eerie resemblance to Brother Jacques whom Felice and Anthony were sure must be Hervey's former friend in Montségur. The shape shifting went faster and faster the further the thing went back in time. Despite the dizzying speed, Felice still thought that she could discern the once handsome, but proud, face of Simon Magus. The process continued to advance until all they could see was a blur.

Throughout this frightful spectacle, Anthony and Felice kept repeating the adjuration of Satan until they felt a deep rumbling under their feet. It was accompanied by a noise that began as a kind of low growl but developed into a roaring din as the quake grew in magnitude. There was a wild tremor accompanied by a crashing sound. The choir end of the church had collapsed, crushing the altar. The roof was completely destroyed and moonlight was streaming through. Felice and Anthony were thrown to the ground, but not before they saw something resembling a black cloud escape through the gap in the vaulting, a shape so huge that it momentarily blocked out the moon and all the stars.

Felice was the first on her feet this time, helping Anthony up. She immediately turned to her father, emitting an inarticulate sound of joy when she saw him moving. Hervey sat up. Baldwin awoke as well, instantly springing to his feet.

"The Chancellor is still down," said Anthony with concern, crouching over him, calling him by his name. Baldwin, who was always in favor of the most direct approach, dumped his container of holy water over Gerson, eventually conscripting all their vials for this purpose. Gerson finally began to stir. He looked up into Anthony's searching eyes and smiled.

"Thank you, my dear friend," he said in a soft voice.

The five companions staggered back to the presbytery, shocked and totally spent. Even Baldwin was too tired for conversation. Felice passed around a bottle of heavily fortified wine that she kept for emergencies. She brought out all the bedding that their household afforded, leaving Hervey to make up three makeshift beds in the central room. Soon everyone had fallen into a deep and, thankfully, dreamless sleep.

A Parting of the Ways

The next day Hervey was up early. He summoned the churchwardens to assess the damage that St.-Jacques had sustained as a result of the earthquake. Hervey knew that his tenure at the church was fast drawing to a close but, at the very least, he wanted to set the long process of reconstruction in motion for the sake of the next incumbent. By the time he had returned to the presbytery, an intense discussion was underway about the events of the previous evening and just what they meant. Baldwin was holding forth.

"The Cathars were right. Last night we all became aware of past lives, attesting to the transmigration of souls. After what we witnessed of his power, it seems that the thing that called himself Brother Jacques is the key to this mystery. He is Satan — the creator god who first entrapped immortal souls in corruptible bodies." Baldwin looked at Felice apologetically. "I know you have suspected these dark truths for a long time. I am sorry that I was so obstinate."

But Gerson was rarely apologetic for his obstinacy. "I think these so-called past lives are just products of your over-wrought imaginations." He had all but forgotten the revelation of his past as Bernard. "I saw what you saw, but what you are suggesting is preposterous. Why can't we just accept that the Franciscan was a demon? Certainly he was a powerful demon — a master shape shifter. But why must he be Satan? And why assume that Satan created the world?"

Baldwin shook his head. "The Christ we saw wasn't just a demon: it was the creator of demons. Look at what happened to Rose and the others after they drank his blood. And its knowledge of us seemed far too vast. Demons supposedly receive most of their knowledge through their superior senses. But that Christ had the power to look into our hearts. It knew exactly what each of us wanted; what lives would tempt us back into bodies."

Felice could only agree. "And it wasn't just our experience last night that carries conviction: there is also the testimony of the journal and the various visions that point to the evil creator god." Musing for a moment, she added: "That would certainly explain the Franciscan's strange emphasis on the blessedness of procreation."

Hervey joined in. "Chancellor, I concur with Felice and Baldwin. What we witnessed was not the work of any ordinary demon. And then there was the evidence of our past lives. The Cathars seem to have been right about practically everything."

Gerson changed his approach. "Even if you are right about the Franciscan, why us? Why should we be singled out for this great confrontation?"

Anthony now knew the answer to the Chancellor's question, as did Felice. It was rooted in the very foundations of the church. The spiritual Christ had appointed Simon Peter as His vicar: *Peter, you are the rock and on you I shall build My church.* Now that Anthony was awake to his past identity, these were no longer distant ritualistic words, but inscribed on his very soul. The evil god had countered by assuming the form of Simon Magus — the evil double of Simon Peter. But the magician had been defeated when Felice's earlier incarnation, Helen, recognized him for what he was and joined forces with Simon Peter. Even so, the defeat of the magician was but a single battle in an eternal war. It didn't forestall the gradual ascendancy of the papacy, the alleged See of Peter — a dark mockery of the spiritual leadership that the true Christ had intended. And the evil god continued to pursue a vendetta against Anthony. The redeployment of the Simon Magus of his boyhood fantasies was one of the most ephemeral, but most potent, of his weapons.

A teacher at heart, Anthony was about to try and answer his former student's question about why they had been chosen, had it not been for the warning in Felice's eyes. She was right: this was information to be shared with Baldwin and Hervey, but not Gerson. *Cast not your pearls before swine.* Clearly the Chancellor was prepared to disregard every-thing that he had seen or experienced last night that might vindicate Cathar doctrine. So what were the chances that he would be receptive to Anthony's recollection of his past incarnations — especially if they pointed to Anthony as the true successor to Christ?

The Chancellor's question quivered in the air unanswered. This was hardly Gerson's only article of incredulity, however. His orderly mind merely took note of the non-response before proceeding to the next.

"You claim that the entity animating this cursed effigy of Christ was powerful enough to create the world. So why didn't he just overwhelm us? Take over our souls as he did with the others? Why were we able to defeat him?"

This was a question that Anthony was not afraid to answer.

"Our Celestial Father, the true God, must have intervened. And we should take heart. It's further evidence that Satan is not omnipotent."

Baldwin, thinking out loud, broke in with a question that had been troubling him ever since he had begun to consider Cathar doctrine seriously. "But is our Celestial Father omnipotent?"

Anthony's eyes were turned upward before answering, as if consulting heaven. "That's a question that dualists have disputed for centuries. I would like to think He is. Yet there are many things that point in the opposite direction: humanity's continued entrapment in matter; the persistence of evil. So I really can't say."

Gerson looked from one to the other in desperation. "But how can you possibly believe that Satan is responsible for a world so beautiful?"

Anthony's response was gentle but decisive. "At times it seems very beautiful, it is true. But that's because we are seeing it with our carnal eyes. It is but a crass imitation of our celestial homeland. Imagine how beautiful the original must be! The hope of the celestial kingdom was powerful enough for the Cathars to withstand centuries of persecution."

"But you have no evidence for this doctrine!" Gerson complained.

"Well, there is the New Testament, which, according to the Cathars, was given to us by the spiritual Christ to lead us back to the kingdom. Not only does Christ say 'My kingdom is not of this world' but He refers to Satan as 'the Prince of this World,'" said Anthony.

Gerson winced at hearing these words, remembering his error.

"Besides, didn't Augustine describe faith as belief in things unseen?" asked Felice.

The Chancellor had no answer for that. A beautiful woman who could cite Augustine was really too much for him.

They continued to dispute these matters until they had clearly reached an impasse, at which point Anthony said, "We don't know everything about who our adversary is. I do know this, however: he or it will be back, perhaps not as a Franciscan friar, but as something just as insidious, trying to enslave more souls. Our victory is but temporary. It has only bought us some time."

"Time for what?" asked Gerson, somewhat querulously.

When no one responded, he looked at each one of them in turn, with suspicion. Still, nobody spoke. Eventually Hervey got up and walked over to his cabinet, and took out a wooden box. He removed the lid and, after lingering fondly over the contents for a moment, smiled.

"Chancellor, I promised to show you the palimpsest. It has been the one possession I have valued most for many years. And it is clearly significant to me in ways that I could never have imagined. It was the palimpsest that first inspired us to search for the truth. Now that we have realized the truth, we no longer need it. Please take it and remember us."

Gerson was aghast. "Remember you? But where are you going?"

Silence once again. It was Anthony who eventually spoke up, "I am afraid we can't tell you, Chancellor. Not only would you not approve, but you might even try to stop us." There was a note of apology in his voice.

Felice involuntarily put her finger to her lips, while Baldwin blurted out:

"That's enough!"

And it was enough: enough to confirm Gerson's worst apprehensions.

"Then it is as I feared," he said. "You feel compelled to revive that damned heresy. I beg that you don't. Not just for the sake of the church, but for the sake of your own souls."

When the rest of them said nothing, Gerson continued:

"It is true that these are hard times in which our faith has been challenged repeatedly. It will continue to be challenged, I know. But there is much work to be done. And you are all so strong and able — all of you." His look included Felice. "Stay with me and help me rebuild God's church."

Anthony responded for them all. "But you see, we no longer believe. We no longer believe that this is God's church or that we would be doing His work if we helped to rebuild it. We now see it is the devil's work." The words were terrible for Gerson to hear, but Anthony spoke them mildly, in a voice subdued by sorrow.

There was a long pause before Gerson burst out plaintively:

"Please don't leave. You are my only friends!"

"Then come with us, John!" This was the first time that Anthony had used Gerson's Christian name since he was a student in his class.

Gerson never hesitated. "I can't," he said wretchedly. "I still believe the world was created good, and that the church is the only path to salvation. The church is flawed. I know it is. It is filled with weak, fallible men — men like myself. But even if I were to believe as you believe, I don't think I could desert it."

Anthony stood up and walked over to where the Chancellor was sitting. Gerson couldn't explain why, but for some reason he felt compelled to fall to his knees before his former master, offering his hands folded involuntarily in the ancient rite of homage. Anthony gently clasped Gerson's hands between his own, looking into his eyes.

"Then I beg you, as my friend, promise me this. Promise me that you will leave us alone; that you won't come after us or send anyone else to persecute us."

Gerson closed his eyes — perhaps in thought; perhaps in prayer. The others looked at him with apprehension, until at length he spoke.

"I promise."

Epilogue

Several weeks after the mysterious earthquake that wreaked such havoc with the church of St.-Jacques-de-la-Boucherie, the four Counter-Faith were to be found climbing a tall peak in the south of France. The stream of their conversation ebbed the higher they climbed. When they reached the summit, they were all so winded that no one spoke for a while. Felice was the first to recover. She stood up and strolled over to what was clearly an old well, looking back at her father.

"Yes, it is just where I remember it. Please don't ask me to get back in there!"

The four of them laughed.

They spread a blanket and sat down on the windswept plain to share a simple meal of dried fish, bread, and wine. Before they began to eat, Anthony held up his cup:

"To Margot and Martin. For their vision and generosity. May they both find rest in our celestial homeland."

The others followed suit, toasting their dead confederates.

After the meal, they lay back and talked about everything and nothing — everything to do with what was right and wrong about contemporary Paris, but nothing regarding what might lie ahead for them. They were reluctant to let this precious moment of fellowship go, so for a few moments they allowed themselves this indulgence — pretending that they were just four friends making an excursion for the sheer pleasure of traveling together. The sun was warm, but the light was tinged with that quality of leave-taking so characteristic of the waning summer. It was Hervey who eventually said the inevitable:

"We don't want to have to climb down that peak at night. I think it is time to do what we came for. Felice?"

Felice duly got to her feet and fetched the sack she had been carrying, carefully removing an old volume. It was the florilegium of Cathar rituals.

"I wonder when they will miss it from the cathedral library," she said.

"I would hope that they miss me before they miss the book!" Anthony replied.

The four of them prepared themselves for the sacrament of *consolamentum*, reading over the ritual one last time to make sure they had it right. When Baldwin remarked that Anthony and Felice were already perfected, at least according to the Franciscan, Anthony simply shrugged, clearly believing it better to err on the side of safety. Anthony proceeded to perfect Felice through the laying on of hands, after which Felice perfected Anthony. Then Felice perfected her father; and Anthony, Baldwin. There were none of the winds or tongues of flame that Margot had seen in her vision. But they knew in their hearts that they were fulfilling their destiny, which was the will of the celestial God.

"'Free from the flesh; therefore let us rejoice!'" said Felice triumphantly.

This sparked some playful banter. Baldwin observed that Felice was quoting from their favorite Cathar author, which led Anthony to remark that it was probably time for Hervey to begin another journal—now that he had an established reading public. But their levity was brief. They recited the Pater Noster together with due solemnity before falling silent—gathering strength for the impending struggle. For although they could not see the diabolical chapel of Margot's vision with their carnal eyes, they never doubted its presence. Satan was relentless and could surprise them at any moment.

The sun was beginning to edge toward the horizon when Hervey said to Anthony: "Where will you go?"

"I thought perhaps Northern Italy. I've heard that there may still be some dualist communities in the mountains. If there are none, we will set up our own base and start missionizing."

"Felice and I thought we would stay in Languedoc for the time being. There may be some descendants of the Cathar martyrs keeping the faith alive," volunteered Hervey.

"In truth, father can't resist revisiting some of his old haunts. He's remembering more and more of that life," said Felice smiling.

"Yes, it wasn't all bad. I recall that they make some wonderful wine in this region." Baldwin gave an amused snort by way of response.

There was another prolonged silence, eventually broken by Baldwin. He turned to Felice.

"In the vision regarding the four evangelical symbols, did Margot give you any indication which animal each of us might be?"

Felice frowned, thinking about the question, before she asked in turn: "Why? Do you have a preference?"

"Yes, as a matter of fact. I would prefer to be the eagle. Then I would have wings."

"They all have wings," Anthony corrected. "Even the bull."

"Excellent. We'll need them to get off this cliff," said Hervey.

The four friends said their goodbyes. Now that they had been perfected, they dared not risk embracing. But the love they shared was very legible on their faces. Felice and Baldwin gazed at each other with longing and resignation: it was a tender but poignant look that they shared, expressing everything that was both sweet and bitter about their circumstances. As if on cue, Hervey and Anthony simultaneously turned and walked a few paces away, affording the lovers a few words of private leave-taking.

Felice said softly: "If all goes well for us, this will be the very last of our mortal lives."

"I know, my darling Felice. But it may take me longer than it takes you."

"If it does, I'll be waiting for you in the celestial kingdom — waiting to welcome you home." And the two lovers smiled at one another.

Then two by two, the Counter-Faith began their descent from the mountain.

Historical Afterword

This novel emerged from my research on medieval religion. The back-drop for the story is the highly embodied nature of late medieval spirituality, a quality that is especially apparent in the increased attention to the physicality of Christ and emphasis on the Eucharist. Despite the age's misogyny and disparagement of the female body, this devotional culture also fostered a number of highly visible female mystics: women who believed themselves to be in direct communication with the divine. Their revelations were highly somatic and sensual — even erotic — in nature. Hence, Angela of Foligno stripped in front of a crucifix and entered Christ through the wound in his side; Lutgard of Aywières drank from his wound; Agnes Blannebakin received Christ's foreskin in her mouth on the Feast of the Circumcision; Birgitta of Vadstena (i.e., St. Bridget of Sweden), in her persona as bride of Christ, experienced a mystical pregnancy; when Catherine Benincasa (i.e., St. Catherine of Siena) celebrated her marriage with Christ, she received a ring fashioned from his foreskin. Many female mystics experienced a craving for the consecrated Host so intense that historians have described it as Eucharistic frenzy. Some female mystics also believed that they exchanged hearts with Christ — a motif modeled on the lovers' exchange of hearts in secular love literature, as, for example, Dante's *Vita Nuova.*[1]

Chancellor John Gerson was opposed to this kind of embodied spirituality, which he justifiably associated with women. His many works on spiritual discernment all stigmatized contemporary female mystics — particularly Birgitta of Vadstena and Catherine Benincasa. In fact, Gerson's efforts to overturn Birgitta's canonization at the Council of Constance gave rise to the most celebrated of his treatises on spiritual discernment: *The Proving of Spirits.* Recognized as an authority in such

---

[1] Dyan Elliott, *The Bride of Christ Goes to Hell: Metaphor and Embodiment in the Lives of Pious Women,* 200–1500 (University of Pennsylvania Press, 2012), chap. 6.

matters, Gerson received a number of appeals to adjudicate over questions of discernment. Given his antipathy to the female spirituality of
his day, it is somewhat ironic that the last thing that Gerson wrote was
a defense of Joan of Arc. Because of Gerson's previous writings, however,
scholars dismissed this treatise as a forgery until quite recently.[2]

Gerson was also theologically conservative: he wrote against academic curiosity and was very resistant to the writings of the Franciscan theologian, William of Ockham. Robert Holkot had been one of Ockham's followers. Baldwin's disputation about Satan masquerading as
Christ is based on Holkot's writings.[3]

Even though Margot de la Barre was not a visionary (so far as I
know), the tragedy that befell Margot and her friend Marion was, for the
most part, true — including the little piece of moss and the clump of hair
that Marion kept in her coffer. My rendering is based on the detailed
record of their trial for sorcery, over which the provost John de Folleville
presided, and which was recorded in the register of the Châtelet.[4] While
Hainselin and Agnesot did exist, down to the description of their marriage, Brother Marcus did not. But such a figure is certainly not implau-
sible: many prostitutes had clerical clients, and some even specialized
in servicing the clergy. And, as the character of False Seeming in *The
Romance of the Rose* suggests, there was considerable anti-mendicant
discourse in circulation accusing friars of lechery, hypocrisy, and every
other conceivable vice. In order to have Margot and Marion overlap with
Gerson's chancellorship, however, I had to play with the dates a little
(which bothers me more than a little): they were, in fact, executed in 1390
rather than 1397.

Recently, a handful of scholars have argued that the Cathar faith
was largely the construct of inquisitors. This is a very limited view that
can only be sustained by excluding the majority of the sources — perhaps

---

[2] Eadem, "Seeing Double: John Gerson, the Discernment of Spirits, and Joan of Arc,"
American Historical Review 107,1 (2002): 26–54.

[3] Eadem, "True Presence/False Christ: The Antinomies of Embodiment in Medieval
Spirituality," *Mediaeval Studies* 64 (2002): 241–65; eadem, *Proving Woman: Female Mysti-
cism and Inquisitional Practice in Late Medieval Europe* (Princeton, N.J.: Princeton University Press, 2004), chap. 6.

[4] Eadem, "Women in Love: Carnal and Spiritual Transgressions in Late Medieval
France," in *Living Dangerously: On the Margins in Medieval and Early Modern Europe*, ed.
Barbara Hanawalt and Anna Grotans (Notre Dame: University of Notre Dame Press,
2007), 55–86.

especially the literature that circulated in heretical circles. To deny the
existence of the Cathar faith strikes me as a rarefied form of inquisitorial
suppression: it kills the Cathars all over again by effacing the belief system that they were prepared to die for. As with most aspects of medieval
history, however, there is no doubt that we are largely at the mercy of
clerical sources for our understanding of the Cathars, and this invariably
leads to some distortion. Indeed, the very name Cathar, derived from the
Greek word for "pure," was imposed on the sectarians by their orthodox
persecutors rather than being a name they themselves chose.

I have attempted to represent the general contours of Cathar history accurately. The belief system had a wide appeal in the south of
France and Northern Italy in the late twelfth and first half of the thirteenth centuries. Although the Albigensian Crusade was launched in
1209 and was officially ended in 1229, anti-Cathar initiative continued.
The massacre at Montségur occurred in 1244. Peter Martyr (also called
Peter of Verona), appointed inquisitor of Lombardy, was assassinated by
Cathar sympathizers in 1252. Even though the Cathar heresy was, for
the most part, wiped out by the late thirteenth century, there still was
an enclave located in the Pyrenees centered in the village of Montaillou.
After having the entire village arrested in 1308, Jacques Fournier, the
bishop of Pamiers, conducted an extensive inquisition in Montaillou and
the surrounding area. That he was exceedingly proud of this achieve-
ment is suggested by the fact that he took a copy of the register with him
when he ascended the papal throne as Benedict XII, which still remains
in the Vatican Archives. The title *The Hole in the Heavens* is indebted to
the accounts by the various defendants who reiterated the myth of the
angelic fall from heaven, and whose depositions are preserved in Fournier's register.[5]

Many of the bizarre tales related here that, depending on your perspective, may seem either too good or too bad to be true are likewise
based on medieval sources. Margot's story of the penis tree is lifted
directly from the notorious inquisitor's manual *Malleus maleficarum*
(*The Hammer of Witches*). Brother Jacques' sermon on St. Gregory's Mass
was based on an extremely popular exemplum that was reiterated in
many pastoral sources. Likewise, the prince in NearFar is borrowed from
the introduction to Marguerite Porete's spiritual masterpiece, *The Mirror*

---

[5] Eadem, *Fallen Bodies: Pollution, Sexuality, and Demonology in the Middle Ages*,
Philadelphia: University of Pennsylvania Press, 1999), chap. 6.

of Simple Souls. In the thirteenth century, clerical authors of all stripes became enthralled with the subject of demons — a fascination that increased over time. The various capabilities of demons, including their ability to rapture the living or to meddle with the bodies of the dead, is extensively discussed by scholarly writers like William of Auvergne as well as more popular authors like Caesarius of Heisterbach. Thomas of Cantimpré's memorable accounts of women being raptured, and his claim that Albert the Great himself took an interest in this subject, are included in Thomas' popular work, *Concerning Bees.*[6] By the same token, Albert the Great was said to have been challenged by the devil in the shape of a scholar. Reports of the Wild Hunt, dances of the dead, and walking corpses were legion throughout the Middle Ages. The many legends that circulated about Simon Magus were either drawn from the accounts of the church fathers or the various apocryphal gospels.

The parish of St.-Jacques-de-la-Boucherie was consolidated in the twelfth century, and its beginnings were rather ignoble. It was located in the slaughterhouse district, which was initially ostracized from the rest of the city by virtue of its unclean trade. While the church only dates from the twelfth-century, it was allegedly erected on the site of a chapel built in 954 under Lothair I. The site also garnered a certain amount of luster as the starting point for the pilgrimage to Santiago de Compostella — the place where the body of St. James the Greater was laid to rest in Spain.

The church of St.-Jacques-de-la-Boucherie was destroyed in the eighteenth century, but I have tried my best to describe it as accurately as possible. The façade, as represented in Gerson's vision, is based on historical accounts. The church itself was said to be as irregular as it is represented. When it was rebuilt in the fourteenth century, the twelfth-century edifice was incorporated into the nave. As a result, some of the pillars near the choir were sunk into the ground, while others were erected on the pavement. The north side of the nave followed the progression of the Rue des Ecrivains, putting it out of alignment with the southern side of the nave. This rendered the bays on the different sides of the nave wall out of proportion with one another. Even the church's entrances were erratic. The central door in the west façade, referred to

---

[6] Eadem, "The Physiology of Rapture and Female Spirituality," in *Medieval Theology and the Natural Body,* ed. Peter Biller and Alastair Minnis (Woodbridge, Suffolk: York Medieval Press in association with Boydell and Brewer, 1997), pp. 141–73.

as the Porte de la Pierre au Lait (Door of the Milk Stone) after a defunct street, opened onto a small and malodorous lane. Since it was no longer appropriate as a main portal, the door was blocked off from the inside. The de facto entrance was through the Porch Door, located on the southern side of the church, from which the porch jutted out obliquely. The presbytery was attached to the porch and the southern wall, allowing for a private door that connected the presbytery and the church.

There was a Hervey Rousseau (or Roussel) who was the parish priest of St.-Jacques from 1397–1399. The only thing that is known about him is that he was a doctor of canon law. So he did, in fact, receive the education that was denied my fictional avatar. The other members of the Counter-Faith — Felice, Anthony, and Baldwin, were my own invention. Brother Jacques is likewise a figment of my imagination. He is, nevertheless, the embodiment of different interrelated anxieties. On the one hand, there is the orthodox concern that Satan could, indeed, impersonate Christ — something that is demonstrated repeatedly in various saints' lives and exempla. (According to authorities like Caesarius of Heisterbach, nuns seemed especially susceptible to this demonic ploy and were sometimes sexually seduced.) On the other hand, there is the much more extreme heretical perspective that the material world was created by the evil god, who was associated with Satan. According to Cathar theology, the true Christ, who was immaterial, was sent to earth to lead humankind to the celestial kingdom. According to Peter of Vaux-de-Cernay, a chronicler of the Albigensian Crusade, there was a minority of Cathars who did believe in an embodied Christ, who would have been the personification of evil. All Cathars equated orthodoxy with devil-worship, however. In my novel, Gerson clings to the orthodox view of God and Satan; the Counter-Faith, however, finally subscribe to a dualist version of the cosmos, and set out to revive the Cathar heresy.

There are also different accounts of animated crucifixes. St. Francis of Assisi's experience in the church of San Damiano, in which he was addressed by the pendant figure of Christ, is certainly the most famous. But there are others. I was particularly inspired by an incident reported in Clare of Montefalco's process of canonization in which Clare was said to have had a dream in which the figure of Christ on a miraculous crucifix, worshipped by a certain antinomian sect, was really a crucified demon.

There are many wonderful scholars who work on late medieval religion. But the work of Caroline Walker Bynum has been especially important to my own work and foundational for any understanding of the somatic spirituality of the later Middle Ages. Though the exclusive focus on my own work in the notes may seem narcissistic, it is intended to demonstrate the correspondence between my scholarly view of the past and its fictionalized counterpart. The two approaches are more symbiotic than I would have thought. For in the process of fictionalizing history, I have gained something historical that I wouldn't have expected, and is absent in most medieval scholarship, mine included: the opportunity to take medieval beliefs and fears seriously in an imaginative, experiential way. This is the first time I have ever tried to feel what it would be like to inhabit a world where mere words can turn bread and wine into flesh and blood; enraptured mystics exchange hearts with Christ; God and the devil appear incarnate; miracles, from the resurrection of the dead to the horrific phenomenon of the walking dead, occurred; and people were prepared to risk everything for their beliefs. In the course of writing this novel, I succeeded in scaring myself. My hope is that the reader will experience a parallel alarm.